KV-057-466

To Graham & Lisa
With all best wishes
Hilda x

THE LAST CONCERTO

HILDA PETRIE-COUTTS

Copyright © 2007 . All Rights Reserved.
No part of this book may be reproduced, stored in a retrieval system, or transmitted by any means without the written permission of the author.

ISBN 13: 978-1-59664-005-4

Printed in the United States of America
This book is printed on acid-free paper.

TABLE OF CONTENTS

PREFACE

It was May 2004 and the grounds of Garnford Manor were looking at their loveliest. A frothing sea of white blossom stirred in the orchard, rhododendrons and azaleas framed beds of spring flowers, massed glowing colours forming jewelled casket about the house, while across vista of spacious lawns, the lake shimmered in muted silver.

Above all, Garnford's soaring walls of faded red brick, surmounted by tall, slender chimneys, silhouetted imposingly against the sky, looking slightly at odds, with the modern research building, small hospital and bungalows that spread behind its bulk. None approaching from the main road, along gracious, half mile avenue of oak and beech, swaying in fresh green leaf, would have suspected that the old manor house was in actual fact an AIDS centre.

The spring sunshine was unusually hot and Tristam Bagshaw jerked his paint smeared shirt open to the waist, before stepping back to stare appraisingly at his canvas.

'Not bad——not bad at all,' he muttered. 'Hermione should like it. At least I hope so! Seems to have captured the mystery of her favourite grotto.'

He turned away, wiping his hands on a turpentine rag, stretched and yawned contentedly, before sinking down onto a stone seat, beside the small Italian fountain. What a relief! It was finished. Would need time to dry of course, but could be shown at tomorrow's family gathering.

It was so peaceful here! He stared about him reflectively. Bees droned urgently between the profusion of banked gold and purple Alpine flowers, nestling between rocks, where a small stream gurgled, their fragrance blending with the smell of his oil paint.

'I can see why Hermione loves this place——and mother too,'

he murmured. 'But I wonder what Garnford really looked like, before my family decided to turn the house and grounds into the combination of hospice—bungalows for AIDS sufferers, and research centre. Wish I could remember!'

'Talking to yourself now, Tristam?' The voice sounded lightly amused and Tristam looked up in surprise and slight annoyance——then smiled.

'Uri! What are you doing here?'

'Well——there's a warm greeting! You might sound a bit more welcoming———-!' The newcomer's protest was cut off, as Tristam leapt to his feet and caught his younger brother in a bear hug.

'Forgive me———-pure astonishment old fellow! Thought you were still in Vienna!'

'Flew in this morning. Took a taxi down——pure extravagance I suppose, but I couldn't wait to get here!'

The two young men slapped each other on the back, obviously delighting in each other's company.

'How did the concert go?'

'You should have been there! Well, the 'Rose Concerto' was a challenge———I had never played the duet with Madeleine Beck before. But she's awesome——-not as good as mother of course, but———-!' Uri's eyes were shining. Tristam thought he had never seen his half brother look so animated.

'Yes———I remember her at that Mahler concert in the Usher Hall last Christmas. She's a powerful musician already, as well as an extremely attractive girl. How old is she———-about eighteen?' Tristam's thoughts explored the memory of the fiery Israeli girl who had taken Edinburgh by storm, as she was now doing in the rest of Europe. Tawny gold eyes and thick, waist length, black hair——and a magnetic personality! He suspected that his brother was smitten.

'She's a marvellous person, Tristam.'

'Then I'm surprised you were able to tear yourself away from

Vienna so soon!' Tristam smiled tolerantly.

'Oh——well————I wanted to get back here for the family reunion tomorrow. And in any case, Madeleine took a flight to Tel Aviv this morning. But we'll be meeting again soon!' Uri glanced towards the easel set up a few yards away and walked across to look at Tristam's canvas.

'That's wonderful, Trist! Your canvasses always challenge the senses. In this one, you can almost feel the spray from the fountain————and that amazing light! How do you do it?' Uri swung back to face him and then gave a short chuckle.

'Well————what's so funny, Uri?'

'Why——the two of us! I mean, just think! Your father, Sir Peter Bagshaw, was a world famous composer and violinist. Certainly I'll never be able to match his genius! How I wish I could have met him! Yet you, his son, have become not a violinist, but a pianist——as well as having this amazing gift for art.' Uri stabbed a finger in the direction of the canvas.

'I know what you mean, Uri. For your father is a wonderful pianist. Who has not heard of the famous Leopold Heine. Yet here you are, not a pianist but a violinist————and with a bit more application, should become a reasonably good one—in time!'

His blue eyes crinkled at the corners as he teased his brother.

Uri scowled in mock annoyance and within minutes, the two of them were pummelling each other in mock fight, struggling, laughing, rolling over on the grassy pathway.

'Boys! What are you doing————up——up!'

At the unexpected sound of their mother's voice, they sprang to their feet, sheepishly dusting their clothes down, as Rosamund Heine, who had once been Lady Rosamund Bagshaw, tried to look stern, as she ran her eyes fondly over her two tall sons. She glanced at Tristam, who was the image of his late father but whom he only dimly remembered. Here again were Peter's penetrating grey eyes and waving hair——his eagle nose. Then she looked at Leopold's son, Uri, who had his father's dark good looks and intense manner.

'How long were you standing there, Mother,' asked Tristam as he embraced her, trying to keep paint smudged hands away from her cream suit. He glanced at her admiringly as he allowed his brother Uri, to take, kiss and fold her in his arms in turn. She was in her early forties, but could easily pass for at least ten years younger.

Uri let her go and looked around. 'Where's father then? Is grandmother here too———and Rodrigo,' he asked?

'One question at a time boys. First of all, I want to have a look at that canvas.' Rosamund advanced towards Tristam's easel and stared long and hard at the painting, it's glowing colours still wet.

'You have captured this little grotto so perfectly, Tristam! And oh, how your work reminds me of my mothers own. She was a wonderful painter———and I think you have inherited her gift. In fact, there is no doubt about it!' Her jade green eyes were soft, as memories of Sylvia Lake came flooding back.

'Mother. Anyone seeing that extraordinary painting in Garnford's chapel, could see what tremendous talent Sylvia Lake had. I will never be able to match it,' said Tristam quietly.

'My son———you will one day. But perhaps all of us have to learn certain lessons from life before we can express a little of well, something beyond ourselves.' She pointed to the stone bench and sat down with one of them on either side of her.

?What is it that we have to learn,' asked Uri lightly.

Rosamund glanced at him thoughtfully, before replying in a low voice. 'I believe a certain mystical quality is released through great joy or———sorrow! Perhaps no life untouched by such emotion can produce a painting such as you referred to———or music comparable with the 'Last Concerto! Nor to the 'Rose of Sharon,' she added glancing at Uri, whose father had composed this last.

Tristam nodded. 'You still haven't told us how much you overheard just now?'

'Only that you were discussing the fact that although you are both musicians, neither one of you has followed his own father, in the choice of his instrument. Leopold and I have often wondered at this. But in any case, what does it matter.'

'But it is strange,' said Tristam and Uri nodded. Sylvia smiled.

'You know Tristam, your fathers closest friend, the wonderful old pianist, Maestro Ernst Morgenstern, was overjoyed when you chose the piano————and Leopold is more than delighted with your progress.'

'But what about me. I sometimes think that father is disappointed, that I'm a violinist—-not a fine pianist like him!' Uri jerked the words out words that had been worrying away deep inside him for many years.

'Never think that, Uri! Leopold takes as much joy in your playing as much as he does in Tristam's————and after all, I have spent some small time as a violinist myself!' There was a hint of mischief in her eyes.

'Now listen both of you. Leopold, Hermione and Rodrigo are already at the house, or at least, in that part of Garnford that remains private to the family. We flew in from Malaga on an early flight!'

'Uri has only just arrived here too,' said Tristam.

'How did the concert go, Uri darling?' Rosamund asked the question with a slight quiver about her mouth. She knew that Uri had performed the 'Rose Concerto', the amazingly poignant concerto her first husband had composed, with it's beautiful slow movement, that they had played together on so many occasions, violins soaring around the concert halls of the world before spellbound audiences. 'I should have been there,' she added regretfully.

'You can't drop everything to follow me around Europe,' smiled Uri. 'But it was good, mother. And she was wonderful!'

'She————?'

'Uri's lost his heart to the beautiful Madeleine,' teased Tristam.

Uri hardly noticed his brother's words. Rosamund glanced at him curiously.

'Madeleine? Oh————-Madeleine Beck? The young violinist I have heard so much about? Is she really so good, Uri?'

'Yes,' he replied huskily. 'She is a superb violinist mother. But more than that————she is————-well————I am going to ask her to marry me one day!'

'But you have only met her a few times, haven't you,' replied Rosamund.

'Father told me, that he fell in love with you, the very first time he met you————and asked you to marry him that same night!' Uri slipped an arm around her waist.

'Well————-she didn't marry him then, did she,' put in Tristam firmly. 'She married my father————-Peter Bagshaw.'

'But he married her as soon as he was able to————after Peter's death, Tristam. He knew from the first that he loved her————-and always would. I feel the same way about Madeleine.'

Rosamund looked at his serious face. He meant it that was obvious. And yes, he was his father's son!

'You must bring Madeleine to meet me————to meet all of us, darling. When we return to Spain. Now————let's get back to the house, for the others will be waiting for us.'

'You go on with Uri ————-I have to pack up my paints.' Tristam lifted the canvas carefully from the easel, as Uri and his mother walked slowly back towards the house, along the pathway where sweetly perfumed creepers intertwined and met overhead.

A soft buzz of conversation could be heard through the half open door, as now looking considerably cleaner, Tristam finally walked in. His eyes swept around the music room, where his family had congregated and he stared at them all with affection.

His stepfather, Leopold, was seated at the piano, playing something Tristam had never heard before. The notes were rich————an oriental flavour, he thought. His mother, Rosamund, stood at his side, while Uri bent forward studying the hand written sheet before his father. He lifted his bow.

Then Tristam's gaze turned on the elderly couple, relaxing on the green sofa, beside the copper urns of delicate ferns, which banked the windows. Hermione's silver head was as always, elegantly coifed, her blue eyes seeming wistful, as she stared not at the figure before the piano———-but at that amazing painting that dominated the room.

Her husband, Rodrigo Mendes, once world famous conductor, was following her gaze, with understanding, and reached his fingers out to touch her own.

For that painting portrayed two very special violinists——— Rosamund, whom Hermione had brought up———and her late son, Peter Bagshaw. When they had married, she had been filled with joy. This painting had as Tristam knew, been painted by Sylvia Lake, Rosamund's true mother, who had for whatever reason, stepped out of her daughter's life for many years.

Questions which Tristam and Uri had often put to their parents and grand parents, as to what had really occurred all those years ago, had always been put aside without any complete answer. Tristam looked up at that painting of his father, Peter Bagshaw with Rosamund at his side, their violins bowing in unison, their eyes shining with love———and he wondered at Sylvia's genius. So vividly had she portrayed, their artistry———so that the sound of the 'Rose Concerto' almost came floating around the room.

'Ah———there you are Tristam,' called Hermione, seeing him first. 'Come over here and kiss me!' She reached out her arms and he walked swiftly across, and bent over her, his lips brushing her tenderly on the cheek.   Then he grasped her husband's outstretched hand.

He glanced back to the piano, where his stepfather continued to play, seemingly not having noticed his entrance, so absorbed was he in his music, until Rosamund touched his shoulder lightly. He swung around and beamed a smile at Tristam.

'Tristam! Good to see you again, son! What do you think of my new composition?' Leopold's dark eyes returned to the keyboard of the concert grand, as his fingers once more swept across it, producing more of that warmly exotic oriental theme.

'It's pretty spectacular stuff——-very dramatic, Leopold.' He never called his stepfather dad or father——always Leopold.

'Film music, Tristam.'

'You are writing a film score?'

'Yes. For a new American movie——'Twilight Zone'——set in the Middle East.'

'Congratulations! A film score—-that is something different I must say!' Tristam's eyes sparked with interest. He looked curiously over Leopold's shoulder, staring at the manuscript.

There was a discrete knock at the door. A rosy cheeked, fair haired, middle aged woman in a navy dress and white apron looked towards Rosamund.

'Dinner is ready to be served, Lady Rosamund.'

'Thank you, Mrs Chalmers. Come along everyone. I for one am starving.' Chattering easily together, the little party made their way to the dining room, where arrangements of spring flowers and crystal, fine china and silver reflected in the polished surface of the long, mahogany table, set for six. They seated themselves, observed from the walls, by many portraits of Garnford ancestors. A young maid and a solemn faced waiter, whom Rosamund had never seen before, bore in the dishes and the wine. Mrs Chalmers had engaged agency staff for this rare visit by members of the family.

The meal was delicious. Prawn cocktails, then roast wild duck delicately flavoured with orange, followed by a fresh fruit salad and cream, the wine deliciously cool and invigorating. Rosamund nodded her thanks to Mrs Chalmers.

'That was marvellous, Mrs Chalmers.'

'Thank you, my Lady.'

'Yes. It was really very good,' agreed Hermione with a smile, adding——'Perhaps we could take coffee in the study.'

There was a hint of sadness in the eyes of both women, as they entered the study sacred to the memory, of the son of one and the late husband of the other. A momentary flash of emotion, as they exchanged glances, before seating themselves on the worn leather couches.

'Perhaps we can go back to the music room later,' said Leopold, who never felt completely at ease, in this room, which still seemed to bear the imprint of his predecessor.

Much as he had admired Peter, he was glad that he and Rosamund had never made Garnford their home. Partly of course, it was because most of the building was now involved with the care of AIDS patients, only a few rooms of the great house being kept for the family's infrequent visits. But apart from that, Garnford would always undoubtedly be associated in their minds, with that amazingly courageous and talented musician, who had grown up here and whose memory would forever linger on within its ancient walls.

Rosamund had seated herself at Peter's desk. She spread her hands out, stroking the wood in absentminded gesture, as she stared at the family she loved so dearly. Who would have thought, that after the pain she had endured, all those years ago, life would again bring so much happiness. Not the same intense joy she had experienced with Peter perhaps. But a deep content, a feeling of being surrounded by love. Now too, she could look backwards as well as forwards, seeing her life in context.

'Tomorrow, we will meet with the doctors and scientists who are constantly striving so hard to find a cure for this horror that is AIDS,' she said quietly. 'We will also visit all of the patients and tomorrow night, I think if you are all agreeable, we will give a concert, for all those well enough to come up to the hall. A concert in memory of Peter!' Her eyes were damp as she said this, but the glance she shot towards her husband Leopold, was one of deep affection, reassuring him of her love.

'Of course, Rosamund darling. We will all play our hearts out,' he said and meant it.

Tristam, who had been sitting on the arm of one of the leather couches, suddenly jumped to his feet. He stared at his mother interrogatively. 'It's time, don't you think? Time to tell Uri and myself, the whole truth about what happened here at Garnford all those many years ago. I think you owe it to us, to drop the veil of secrecy that has always hidden past events.' He stared at Rosamund. His mother's eyes had widened in surprise.

'Why——Tristam. You already know a great deal of what happened, before I married Leopold. But——yes. I suppose perhaps, I should attempt to tell you everything.' She looked across at Hermione. 'If you will help me, that is, Hermione. To fill in the gaps. Tell the boys. Do you agree, Leopold?'

Her eyes locked with the dark gaze of her husband. He shrugged, feeling slightly uneasy. Why had Tristam found it necessary to demand explanations of things long past. But the truth would perhaps at last, lay a lot of memories to rest.

''We will all try to tell you the story. A story that you have the right to hear——a wonderful story!' It was Rodrigo Mendes who spoke.

'Go on then,' said Uri, who was him self intensely curious.

?Tell us about Garnford, as it used to be. The complete recent history of the family.'

'And of how the 'Last Concerto' came to be written,' said Tristam in a low voice.

'Very well then,' replied Rosamund. 'But I think your grandmother should start the tale, which began long before I came into the life of Peter Bagshaw.' She glanced across at Hermione again, who nodded, and stared down into her coffee cup. Where to start? Where to start? With Natasha, of course! That trip to Austria, Peter had made with his first wife—a trip that had ended in tragedy.

CHAPTER ONE

Lady Natasha Bagshaw lay drowsily against the embroidered pillows, wealth of mahogany dark hair covering the hollow her husband's head had just pressed. She had been falling asleep in his arms, exhausted after their tempestuous lovemaking, when Peter had stirred restlessly, risen and stolen downstairs. Now the notes of his violin rose almost eerily, to blend with the soughing of the night wind, whose singing gusts poured down between the mountain peaks, shaking the pine trees and rattling the shutters of their Austrian chalet.

He was playing one of his own compositions. Natasha listened, as she had done, during the three years of their marriage, admiring his amazing talent—-the sheer beauty of the music that enchanted the night—-but also experiencing resentment, that his career as both world famous violinist and composer, occupied almost every waking moment of his life. It was not that he did not love her—for she knew that he did, cherishing her for good looks and elegance, combined with that charisma surrounding her, as a minor member of the late Russian royal family.

'I am only one of his possessions,' she murmured into her pillow——-'Like his treasured Stradivarius violins and Garnford.' She fell asleep, thinking of their home in the rolling Hampshire countryside, the centuries old manor house that had been in his family for generations. Who would eventually inherit it, she wondered, since she could not give him the son, she knew he secretly yearned for?

'Gute morgen, Gnädige Frau! Your breakfast is here!'

The bustling Austrian housekeeper who kept the chalet in constant readiness for their periodic visits, set down the tray and pulled the curtains, letting the sunlight flood in.

Natasha sat up and stretched. 'Thank you, Ilse. Where is Sir

Peter?'

'He has been up for three hours already—-indeed, I wonder if he ever sleeps, for I heard him playing, long into the night!' The woman smiled kindly, thinking that there might be problems in being married to a musician, even such a romantic figure as Sir Peter Bagshaw. But Natasha wanted no sympathy and the slightly cold exterior she presented to the world at large, prevented the housekeeper from making further comment.

'You slept well, darling?' Sir Peter smiled approvingly, as she appeared before him, elegant in her cream slacks and matching pearl sewn, mohair sweater, hair worn high, in preparation for the winter sports they would soon indulge in—-and the style reminded him of the girl he had first met at Vienna. She had been sitting alone in a box then, hair swept high as it was now, surmounted by a shimmering tiara and wearing black, in deference to the death of her great aunt, who had been her last living relative. For once, he had not been performing himself at the Opera House, but had come to enjoy the wonderful playing of his dearest friend, the old pianist, Ernst Morgenstern, whose genius always commanded packed audiences.

He thought back to his urgent interrogation of all in the reception foyer, trying to discover the identity of the regal woman with the slightly remote look. Who was she? It was dear old Ernst who had enlightened him. Natasha Golanskya came from a background of sadness and mystery. She was a music lover and it would seem, wealthy in her own right, but lived a quiet lifestyle.

He kissed her now and led her to the table in front of the windows. 'Sit, darling. Ilse has just brought fresh coffee.' He poured a fragrant cupful for her and sat opposite as she sipped it. She raised her face towards the glorious view framed by the green shutters. The sun was streaming in through the glass. How very beautiful it all looked. She stared down into the valley, where a little village nestled, then her eyes sped upwards to the jagged mountains above, the sun striking gold into their towering peaks.

It looked a perfect day for skiing.

She put her cup down. 'I'm going to get my suit on. We may as well make an early start, for the weather couldn't look better." She smiled at him, wondering why he looked slightly uneasy. 'What's wrong, Peter?'

'Well——you may as well know. I had a telephone call this morning from London. They want me to appear at the Albert Hall tomorrow night. Yehudi is ill and————-.'

'No! It's just not fair, Peter!' Two spots of colour glowed in the cream of her face. 'We are almost at the end of 1980 and this is the first real break we have had this year——and you promised me, that we would have a full two weeks! We have only been here for four days!' Natasha glared at him indignantly, determined that for once his work should not intrude into a rare moment of peace.

'You look adorable when you are angry,' he teased, reflecting how rarely she did show annoyance. His black brows drew together over his slate grey eyes consideringly, as he ran a hand absently through his hair. 'I might be able to return in a few days time,' he placated her.

'You know that is not possible—-you are fully booked for months ahead!' All the faint resentment carefully suppressed over the last few years, suddenly surfaced, as Natasha faced him. Then she stretched her hands out helplessly. He was musician first and husband afterwards. So it was and so it always would—and there was no use in trying to fight the situation.

'Well—-we may as well make the best of today,' she sighed and saw her reward in the look of tenderness he directed at her.

He tucked the fur wrap over their knees, as the horse drawn sleigh drew them swiftly over the snow, bells jingling merrily. The horse snorted, its breath steaming upwards in the crisp air. It didn't take long to reach the point at which the ski tow whirred. They climbed out of the sleigh, arranging a time with the driver, for their return. As they made their way towards the high tension, coiled wire, that was to bear them upwards, they glanced about

them. A young family walked ahead, mother, father and two tod-
dlers. They had noticed them on the previous day and Peter
waved a cheery hand. One of the children saw that wave and started out towards him on his tiny skis, almost reached him, then lost
his balance and shot into a bank of loose snow. The toddler set up
a protesting wail.

As Natasha watched, Peter swished forward, to bend over the
little boy. He scooped him up and held him to his chest protectively, until the young mother hurried back to retrieve her youngster, with a word of thanks. As the musician handed over his
protesting burden, he was amazed at the sudden feeling of longing that surged through him. How utterly irrational—-children
meant nothing to him—never had done.

Perhaps it was resentment born of her earlier disappointment
that caused Natasha to behave as she did next. She had watched
the little interlude with the child crossly.

'You are disappointed in me, aren't you,' cried Natasha angrily,
not caring that she was being totally unfair. 'You know that I cannot give you children! Would it be fair, to risk bringing a
haemophiliac into the world? Of course not! So why do you stand
staring after that boy!' Her dark eyes were flashing fire and Peter
stared at her in amazement. She was usually so serene—-never
raising her voice. With her graceful manners, impeccable dress
sense enhancing her dramatic beauty, passionate response in their
most private moments, she was all that Peter Bagshaw had ever
dreamed of in a wife. So why this sudden outburst? Perhaps she
was unwell?

'Natasha—-my dearest.' He tried to slip an arm about her. 'It
doesn't bother me in the slightest, that we cannot have children.
Why should it——-when I have all possible joy in life—-with you
whom I love—and my music!'

'I saw your eyes just now—-the way you looked at the boy—the
way you held him!'

'Natasha—-you are not making any sense——-wait——

where are you going? We must wait for the guide!' Peter snatched at her arm, but she shrugged him off. Her voice was low as she replied-

'I'm sorry, Peter! I don't know what came over me—suppressed maternal longings, I suppose. Exercise is what I need. What do we need a guide for? I know the mountains—love them! Come on——you'll be safe with me!' Tears shimmered on her eyelids, as she forced a smile to her lips. He noticed inconsequentially how the glossy peach lipstick, matched the trim on her close fitting cap. Then her lithe figure soared away from him, as she shouted that he should follow.

The ski tow had deposited them high above the village. Below them, other couples who had come up on the lift with them were already starting their swoop downwards. But Natasha insisted on climbing further up, towards the summit. She stood staring speculatively on the downward slope, on the far side of the mountain.

'That way——I'm going that way!' She had rounded the shoulder, giving way to the giddy drop below them.

'No, Natasha——I forbid it! It's incredibly steep——dangerous!' His voice held authority, but she shrugged.

'That is what life is for——to live dangerously!' Her intention was plain. She raised one of her sticks in challenge.

'Come on, Peter!' She was crouching, swooping down the slope like a bird, zigzagging between snow covered rocky outcrops. Peter watched her in horror——then drawing a deep breath, followed. He didn't hear the shout behind him, from the man who was making wild gestures.

'Wait——you fools! There are avalanche warnings on that route!' Faster and faster Natasha flew, with Peter some hundred yards behind her. There was a rumbling above their heads, that became thunderous in its roar, as the massive weight of dislodged snow, came swooshing down at the speed of an express train. It carried rocks and trees in its path striking the slope just in front of Peter——sweeping the woman he loved, to her death! He screamed out in horror—then a rock caught him on the temple, rendering him unconscious.

'Peter——Peter my friend————it's Ernst Morgenstern!'

'He can't hear you sir. He's now been like this for three days, deeply unconscious. X-rays show no fractures——-so we think that perhaps it is psychological shock!' The young nurse shook her head sympathetically.

'His hands are undamaged?' The elderly visitor bent over the bed, examining his friend's hands, from anxious eyes.

?These fingers have swept countless audiences to joy and tears,' he said softly. 'You do know of course, that your patient is the world famous violinist and composer, Sir Peter Bagshaw!'

'What's that? He is the famous violinist, you say, sir, ' asked a questioning voice. The uniformed police officer bowed courteously to Ernst Morgenstern, before transferring his gaze to the injured man. 'If he has not yet regained consciousness, then I suppose he does not yet know that his wife is dead. What a tragedy!' The officer stared down sadly at the still figure, glancing at the dressing that covered the deep gash above the left eyebrow. It was an arrogant face, even in the repose of unconsciousness, he thought. Those thick brows, the haughty eagle nose, the lines of impatience about the parted lips, spoke their own message to one used to making judgements of his fellow man——then he noticed a slight tremor pass across the patient's features.

'Nurse——come here. I think he is rousing himself. He is regaining consciousness!'

Sir Peter Bagshaw returned to a world that was full of pain. Not the mere pounding, throbbing ache in his temples, which would desist, leaving residue only of occasional headache. Infinitely worse, was the deep soul anguish, of knowing that the wife he had adored, who had filled his whole world for the last three years— inspiration for his music, charming companion and passionate lover—-was now dead, her life snuffed out by that crushing weight of snow! He would never be able to play again——for what could his music now offer, but the same anguish which assaulted his every waking moment and denied him the solace of dreamless sleep. For nightmares afflicted Peter, for months afterwards, only gradually decreasing, as time slipped by on leaden wings.

But life goes on. Sir Peter Bagshaw gradually picked up the threads of his former life, even finding that the pain, that had shot emotional splinters into his mind, had perhaps sharpened his sensitivity when interpreting some of the great works of classical composers. It was almost four years, before he was again a hugely acclaimed figure on the concert platform. The Maestro, the notes of whose violin, stole like moonbeams upon the air—-or poured sobbing crescendo of melody into the ears of a silent audience, who sat spellbound by his talent——rising at the conclusion of the work, to shout and clap their tribute to an incomparable artist.

But it meant nothing! Now that Natasha had gone, all was mere emptiness. The flowers thrown ecstatically at his feet served only to remind him of the red roses he had used to introduce himself to her. Nevertheless, he went through the motions of correct behaviour, bowing gracefully and granting the customary encore.

Many women made passes at the man with dark hair touched with silver peaks at the temples and those brooding, slate grey eyes. They dreamed of touching the scar above his left eyebrow, caused by the rock that had caught him on the mountain, where his Russian wife had died, leaving him almost without the will to live, for so many years.

He was a romantic figure, so they thought, but thinking him less so, when their advances were brusquely ignored. But his music——ah——-none could ignore the majesty of his playing! And so he went from the capitals of Europe, to America, Australia———Japan, retiring every so often to his Hampshire home, Garnford, to rest——and to start composing again. At last, within new composition, he found release from all the pent up longings that bruised his heart. The pain of Natasha's death lessened and he found himself dwelling only on their happy moments.

'Will you walk in the gardens with me, Peter? The spring flowers are a glory.' The woman with beautifully coifed blond hair, walked to greet him with outstretched hands.

'Mother——when did you arrive?'

'Early last night. I heard you playing and told the servants not to disturb you. How long are you at Garnford for?' She stared at him questioningly. He drew her to him and placed a light kiss on her brow.

'Perhaps for a few weeks. I'm not sure. But its wonderful to see you!'

'London is quiet at the moment. I was bored with bridge parties and polite conversation——heard that you were here and had Roberts drive me up. I have also come for a specific purpose.'

'You have?' He looked at her, startled. 'What is it?'

'Come with me, Peter.' She beckoned to him imperiously, and with a slight smile of amusement, he followed. She led him out of the pleasant blue drawing room, in which they had been talking, into the hall, with its minstrel gallery and great screen. Many portraits in ornate frames, stared down on them from its soaring walls, of Bagshaw ancestors, reaching back to Tudor times. She led him around the hall, on an unspoken mission, directing his attention initially to the Holbein, which portrayed a man with familiar dark eyes and eagle nose, wearing slashed doublet. Next she paused before a cavalier with a lovely wife at his side, painted by Lily. Again she pointed with slender finger, to the man's face, the thick, black brows, fierce nose, firm lips outlined by beard and moustaches. The dress was different—close fitted coat, worked in gold, lace ruffles at throat. They walked on, pausing before one portrait after another——then up the great staircase, where further portraits stared down at them, showing the same characteristics. At last, Lady Hermione Bagshaw stood still. She was looking at the portrait of his father, who had died in a motor crash, when Peter was only five.

'Well, Peter?'

'Ah——I have it! You want me to have my portrait painted? Really mother——I do not know that I can spare the time!' He placed an arm carelessly around her shoulders.

'Have you so little perception, that you think that is all I want?' She looked at him incredulously.

'But I don't understand,' he said. But he did——and flinched from what he feared was to follow——and knowing her son well, feeling the rebellion welling up inside him, she merely smiled.

'Let us go into the garden,' she said.

It was surprisingly hot for May. The magnolias were in bloom, great, pale, waxen cups, uplifted to the sunshine. Tulips and daffodils made a bright splash of colour in the well kept beds, that bordered the gracious H shaped house, its cherry brick, mellowed by time, sweeping solidly up to the sky, surmounted by its many slender chimneys. Lady Hermione stared along the beech lined avenue, that led to the keeper's lodge and the road beyond, then turned, to walk round to the back of the house. As they passed the orchard to the right, a froth of apple blossom drifted across their feet.

'Shall we walk to the lake,' asked lady Hermione?

'You will damage those dainty shoes, Mother,' he said restrainedly.

'Never mind my shoes, Peter.' She pointed to the gracious sweep of lawns in front of them, and the blue waters of the lake, glittering in the sunshine. 'Is it not all supremely beautiful?'

'I do not want to walk to the lake,' he said heavily. He was thinking of the boat, now beached on the shore, where Natasha had sat with him in the past, when he had sweated as he rowed them across the mile long stretch of water.

'Then we will take the path of the fountains,' she said patiently. They entered a leafy pathway, where carefully trained creepers,
met overhead. The air was sweet with orange blossom, as they
stopped in the magic of a small grotto, where a fountain played
and water gurgled between rocks. Bright patches of gold and purple alpine flowers, glowed jewel bright at their feet.

'Is it not lovely, Peter,' she said softly. 'The house———these
gardens, lovingly tended over the centuries, each generation
adding to the heritage———your heritage, Peter!' Her blue eyes
were trained upon his face as she faced him squarely, raising determined chin. 'Who will inherit all this, when you die, Peter? What
will happen to Garnford?'

'I don't know———and although I suppose it sounds like heresy
to you, who have always been taken up so much with these
affairs———I do not really care!' The words hung like a challenge
on the air.

?But I do, Peter! It is your duty, as the last remaining male
descendant of the house of Garnford, to produce an heir!'

His face darkened with anger, but he chose his words carefully. 'Natasha is dead, mother! Even when she was alive, there was
no possibility of a child———and you know the reason why—her
fears!'

'Fears that were not fully justified. The chances of your having a child with haemophilia were slim. I loved Natasha too,
Peter. She was all I could possibly have wanted in a daughter-in-
law—-except for the fact, that she did not give you an heir.' He
turned to her furiously, then stared to walk back the way they had
come. 'Wait———Peter!' She ran after him, placing a firm hand on
his arm. 'She is dead. I know how you have suffered—-and I have
suffered with you. But Peter———you are alive and with you, your
duty to father an heir for Garnford!'

'In order to do that, Mother, I would have to take another
wife———and that I will never do. Let us talk no more on this subject!' She looked at his angry face and wisely desisted. The seed

was sown. True that seed would have to be watered and nurtured, to come to fruition. But Hermione possessed an iron will and an unquenchable spirit. It had given her the strength, to get over her husband's death all those years ago and to pour all her love into the rearing of a five year old son; placing his first miniature violin in his hands, when she discovered his love of music. She had fostered his growing talent as teenager—and when at last, he had carried off the prize at Leningrad, for musician of the year, she had known that he was on his way—-she could step back.

All her happiness had been in him—his achievements—his gift for composition. When he had taken the concert halls of Europe by storm, she had at first been present at each opening night. Then he had met Natasha—-and after their surprise marriage in Austria, she had drawn aside, delighted that Peter had chosen so well—a girl of breeding and charm. Natasha had been ever supportive of Peter in his music and under her influence, he had produced his finest work——the 'Hope for the Nations' concerto. So Hermione had retired from Garnford, to take up residence in her Knightsbridge house. Garnford was maintained by a full compliment of servants, during those times when Peter was abroad. The butler, Harrington, was that treasure all owners of great houses dream of. Under his guidance, the house was run smoothly, the grounds beautifully kept. He had watched Peter grow up, from tiny baby, to distinguished musician. Yes, they had indeed been fortunate in having such a loyal dedicated servant and friend.

They re-entered the house. Peter already felt slightly ashamed of his bad temper. Not that he regretted the decision he had given her in the slightest——but perhaps he could have tempered his words more diplomatically. He knew what a debt he owed to Hermione, had a very deep affection for his mother, although he rarely showed it. Now he attempted to make small show of reconciliation, for their quarrel.

'Come into the music room, mother. I want you to hear the theme I have been working on.' She accepted the olive branch, and entered the gracious room that had been refurbished by her late daughter-in-law. All was in tones of cream, from the long velvet curtains, to oyster silk couches and deep piled carpet. The walnut table reflected in its shining wood, the one splash of colour in the room, a bowl of crimson roses that Sir Peter had ordered should be constantly renewed.

On the window seat, lay one of his violins——sheets of hand written manuscript thrown on the floor beside it. But it was to the portrait above the Steinway grand, that Hermione's eyes flew. It was a painting of Natasha, wearing a low cut gown, in white silk, worked in gold and seed pearls. Her hair was piled high on her head. Pearls gleamed at ears and throat—-the Garnford pearls—-and in her hand, she held a single red rose. Peter had insisted on having her painted, just after their honeymoon. It seemed to dominate the room. Natasha's lips were parted in a slight smile, as though she were about to speak.

Hermione had the feeling that Natasha was still alive, dominating her son's life, as her portrait did this room. Framed photographs of her, stood on the several small tables. Hermione frowned. He had to learn to let go. This room was a shrine to Natasha—and she knew that this was not healthy.

'Now—-listen to this phrase——-and tell me what you think,' he said. He swept the bow across the strings of the lovely old instrument and Hermione listened—all thoughts of Natasha gone. For this plaintive melody, exploring the emotions, touching the heart, suddenly exploded into joy. When he put aside his bow, he looked at her, almost apprehensively.

'Well——your impressions?'

'Oh, Peter! My son——this will live on, long after you and I are dead. This has immortality in its every note. Its beautiful!' For answer, he caught her to him, in quick embrace.

'I am going to call it, the Rose Concerto,' he said softly. Her heart sank. It was still of Natasha that he thought—but at least, he was composing again——and this truly was better than anything he had ever written before.

'I cannot wait to hear the finished work, Peter,' she gave him a sudden smile. 'When I stopped at the village, on my way here, I met the headmistress of the local high school. She had heard that you were at the house——and asked me if you would render the school a great favour?'

'What is it, then?'

'To be present at their school concert, tomorrow night. It seems there is a girl called Rosamund, who plays the violin. Mrs Parkhurst would like your opinion on the child's ability and of course, it would be a real joy for the pupils and staff, to have you present. Will you go?'

He looked as though he would refuse, but her eyes pleaded. It would be a small thing to do, to heal this morning's breach.

'Very well. Tell Harrington to give the school a ring. When does it start?'

'Eight o'clock.' She gave him a smile of pleasure. 'Thank you, Peter!'

The following evening, two visitors arrived from London. One was Rodrigo Mendes, the conductor, the other Sir Adrian Moulting, the famous cellist, whose rendering of Dvorack's Concerto in B, had brought the audience to their feet, a month ago.

'Peter—my dear fellow! How good it is to see you again,' cried Rodrigo. 'We spoke to your mother on the phone last night—and she whispered that you were working on something new? The sun was shining—we were curious——and here we are!'

'She had no right to tell you,' growled Peter unsociably. Then a grin spread across his face. But since you are both here—well, welcome. After we have had lunch, I will get you to listen.'

'We will have a wonderful evening,' cried Sir Adrian, shaking Peter's hand. 'We thought we might stay the night?'

'Of course—-there is only one problem though. I have promised to attend a local school concert. I suppose I could cancel it, but—-'

'Why—we will all go. After all, each one of us, started his musical carer in a school concert,' smiled Adrian, with a wry grimace. 'It will be a small price to pay, to hear your new work!'

She was small, the child he had come to see. Thin face, wispy fair hair, bony arms and knees—-but when she started to play, Peter sat forward in his seat, eyes snapping with interest. His colleagues also were giving their full attention to the twelve year old girl, who was playing a theme of Albinoni. They ignored the harshness in the quality of sound produced by the cheap violin—but each man recognised the inherent mastery the child had of her instrument, that indefinable something that sets the true musician apart.

The other children were quite good—-one fifteen year old boy playing his horn with obvious talent—-but it was to the child Rosamund, that Peter made his way at the conclusion of the concert, when staff, children and guests, drank cups of tea and helped themselves to sandwiches and cakes.

'Your name is Rosamund? I heard you playing—-would like to speak to you.' She looked up at his six foot height, from serious pale green eyes, her appraisal calm. He sank down onto the nearest chair, taking her hands and pulling her gently towards him. He did not immediately release those hands, but lifted them up, noticing their slightly roughened texture and the chewed finger nails.

'You must take care of these fingers,' he said. 'Tell me about yourself, Rosamund? Where do you live?' She pulled back from him, small face taut with youthful dignity.

'I do not choose to speak with strangers,' she said. He looked at her, dumfounded, then burst into a peal of hearty laughter.

'Stranger! Do you not know who I am, child?'

'You live in the big House——and your name is Sir Peter Bagshaw. But to me, you are a stranger! What interest do you show in our village, even though most of your work people come from here? You are always away from the place!'

There is something else, which I am sure you know about me, Rosamund. I also play the violin.' He saw from the flash in her eyes, that she was well aware of this. 'It was in my capacity as musician, that your head mistress asked me to be present tonight—and in particular, to listen to your playing.'

'And? I suppose you want to tell me that I am no good!'

She thrust her hands into the pockets of her regulation navy skirt, head thrown back. 'One day I will be a famous musician too. In the meanwhile, I can manage without either help or criticism from people like you, who rely on your wealth for your prestige!' The words slapped into the air, and Sir Peter rose to his feet.

'Rosamund——there are two points I will pick up, from what you have just said. Firstly, every musician worth their salt, has to be able to accept criticism, for from it we learn and grow—-secondly, we have to treat members of our audience with courtesy— for they are doing us the greater courtesy, of coming to listen to us!' Her pale face flushed with embarrassment and he knew he had struck home. A bustling figure pushed towards them. The head mistress face was wreathed in smiles. It had made this school concert the most memorable ever, to have the company of Sir Peter Bagshaw, together with the additional bonus of Rodrigo Mendes, the famous conductor and Sir Adrian Moulting the brilliant cellist.

'Sir Peter! So you have met our little Rosamund.' Mrs Parkhurst glanced inquiringly at the silent child and tall musician. 'Dare I ask your opinion on her?'

'She has much to learn—-in many ways.' He said slowly. But if you are asking if she will make a violinist—-then the answer is yes. I would like to meet her tutor later on.' He watched as the head Mistress dismissed Rosamund, who walked away without a backward glance.

'Tell me about the child, Mrs Parkhurst. What is her background?'

They seated themselves in a quiet corner, the teacher arranging the folds of the purple evening caftan, which concealed her portly form. She drew her brows together in thought.

'Well—her father was one of your workers, until last year—when he died in that tractor accident.' She paused tactfully, wishing to continue, but not wanting to appear to criticise her guest.

'No-one told me of any accident! What was the father's name?'

'Tristam——Tristam Lake. I felt sure that you must know about what happened. Mr Lake had been driving his tractor, when he struck a puppy hidden in the long grass. It was on a steep slope—-the rough ground half way up Benson's Hill. It would appear that the man climbed down from his tractor, to examine the dog—-but he had forgotten to put on his brakes—the tractor rolled—went over him. They say he didn't really have a chance.

'Did he die instantly?'

'No. But he suffered a ruptured spleen and died in hospital. It was in hospital, that he was well enough to answer a few questions—and admitted the fault was his——that he had forgotten to put on his brakes.' The woman's face was sad.

'What difference did the matter of the brakes make?'

?The estate said his family was not in a position to claim compensation for his death—-and as they had been living in a tied cottage, the mother was told to move. Mrs Lake now lives in the Bull Hotel, where she works as a barmaid. The child lives there too—and helps to wash glasses and also does some cleaning work—unofficially, that is. Rosamund is not allowed to practice her violin there—so we let her stay on here at night, for an hour or two. I usually work late myself, you know.' She watched his face. 'I love music, Sir Peter—-but am not myself a musician—yet once, I had a very dear friend, Edward Grierson. We have some of his original manuscript here in the school, which we treasure highly.' A slight film of tears dampened her eyes—and Peter wondered what secret romance had brightened the youth of this middle-aged woman.

'Mrs Parkhurst—-I must admit that I feel very disturbed by all you have revealed to me, regarding Rosamund's background. Changes must be made, that is obvious. What is the mother like?'

'Sylvia Lake drinks too much,' said the teacher bluntly. 'I do not think that such was always the case—-but since her husband's death!' and she shrugged, 'Well, things have not been easy for her.'

'Nor I should think for Rosamund.' He paused in thought. 'Tristam—-Rosamund,' he said musingly. 'Perhaps not the most usual names to find in a farming family.'

'Rosamund's grandfather lives in America. He was once a well known actor, and his wife was much in demand in New York—as a violinist.'

'Not—-Melissa Lake?'

'Yes—-did you ever meet her?' she looked at him curiously.

He shook his head. 'Alas, no. I believe she died some years ago. But I have certainly heard of her.' He seemed deep in thought. 'Why did Sylvia Lake not contact her father-in-law for help,' he asked?

?It would seem that there had been a family quarrel, the old gentleman washing his hands of his son, when he married against his wishes. I only know all this, because Mrs Lake told me when I visited The Bull, when I was trying to help. Rosamund is a sweet child, Sir Peter!'

His dark brows were caught together, an unfathomable expression in his dark grey eyes.

'Do you suppose musical talent runs in families.' He asked?

?Is is an inherited factor?' He looked interrogatively at the teacher.

'I believe that this is possible,' she said slowly. 'But how much is due to a musical parent fostering latent talent in a child—-and how much to direct transmission of talent in the genes, is something only a scientist could tell you.' Their conversation was brought to an end as Sir Peter's two friends joined them, making jovial remarks about the general excellence of the children's recent performance.

'Please, will you have Rosamund's tutor call on me tomorrow, at the house,' said Peter lightly———'and tell her to bring the child with her.'

The fire was burning brightly in the huge fireplace, sending showers of sparks up the ancient chimney. The men sat back in their leather armchairs, sipping their brandy. They had just partaken of a superb meal and had retired to Peter's den, a mixture of library and private sitting room. Strangely it was the one room, which bore no traces of Natasha—for she had rarely penetrated here——-so it bore Peter's stamp alone, had been room used by him as a boy, when he wished to be alone, to study or compose.

'Peter———when you have completed your new concerto, I would esteem it an honour, to be able to conduct it for you,' said Rodrigo, eyes smiling at the prospect.' How long do you think it will take?'

'Perhaps—another two months——-if I remain here, and work on it!' Peter's lips pursed. As he thought. 'Rodrigo———I will be more than delighted if you will undertake his work, for I can think of no-one better qualified than you, to conduct—'The Rose Concerto'.

'The Rose Concerto———-that is what you are calling it?' Adrian looked at him musingly. 'You do not think that name is perhaps——-well, too light, for such a work?' The cellist shook his head, stroking his small grey beard. 'When you think of roses—you think of scented gardens, and———-.'

'And of love,' said Peter softly. 'This work is my bequest to Natasha's memory.' His grey eyes darkened with memories.

'Who cares what it is called———-for in any case, you may wish to revise the title, when the work is finished.' Rodrigo's Spanish accent became more pronounced, as he continued, with open expression. 'Dear friend———this music you have created, is full of tenderness and passion. A great work, glorious in its concept, a glowing palette of all that is fine in man's soul! If indeed it were to be your last concerto, you could contribute nothing finer to the posterity of mankind.' He spread his hands expansively. 'I can say no more!'

Peter drew his breath I slowly, and rose to his feet.

'You—think that——about it? You truly mean that?' His eyes filled with tears, which he hastily blinked away, and rose to his feet. Rodrigo also rose.

'Peter—-when you were younger, your compositions were full of fire——dramatic in the extreme. 'Hope for the Nations' stirs the breast with the fineness of its theme, its power. But this new work encompasses not only the heights of joy—but pain. Only one who has experienced the full gamut of life's emotions, can even begin to produce music of this sort. My friend—- to have listened to it earlier, even in its unfinished state, was to realise the beauty, the tremendous appeal it possesses.' He clapped Peter in his arms.

'I concur with everything that Rodrigo has said,' added Adrian. 'I insist that you include me in the production—if you wish, that is?'

'I do wish. Thank you, Adrian.' The men spoke long into the night, as the light Spring wind blew playfully down Garnford's chimneys, in booming gusts. Hermione sat before her dressing table mirror, brushing her blond hair, a slight smile curving her lips. As she slipped into bed, she heard the strings of his violin vibrating through the house. Was it her imagination—-or were the chords full of—hope?

CHAPTER TWO

Peter stepped back, as the limousine slid effortlessly down the drive, bearing Rodrigo Mendes and Sir Adrian Moulting, back on their way to London. Their genuine delight in his new concerto, had provided fresh impetus to complete the work as soon as possible——but finding the time to do so, might prove difficult, as an important series of concert engagements across America, loomed ahead in two months times——-still!

He was about to re-enter the house, when he paused. Three figures were advancing along the drive, on foot. He frowned impatiently. Now, who————? As they drew nearer, he recognised the child Rosamund. Of course——-he had invited her to come here today. His butler, Charles Harrington stood at his side, surveying the two women and the young girl, with surprise.

'I will see what these people want, Sir Peter.'

'It's all right, Harrington——-I know. The child is Rosamund Lake. She plays the violin rather well. One of her companions, is doubtless her tutor.'

Harrington nodded. 'The other lady, is Mrs Lake, sir,' he said.

'Show them into the blue drawing room, when they arrive. I am going in—there's something I wish to look for.' He could hear the slight murmuring of female voices, borne towards him on the light breeze, as he made to disappear—as a strident young voice pronounced-

'I want nothing to do with that man——and you can't make me!'

He chuckled slightly in wry amusement, as he mounted the stairs. He opened a tall walnut cabinet, which occupied the far corner of his library. In it, reposing on shelves lay violins of varying sizes. He lifted one up and held it curiously. He had been a similar age to Rosamund, when he had played this particular instrument—-remembered hours of patient scales and arpeggios, until his ear became attuned to every slightest nuance in those selected compositions, his old tutor allowed him to attempt. He tuned the violin, then turned his attention to the ivory tipped bow. It had been re-haired before being put aside, when Peter had needed the next size in instrument. He reached for a bloc of rosin and started to rub it on the horsehair, with sure movement.

Now he faced the two women, who had risen from their chairs at his entrance. Rosamund was already standing. She was staring out of the window, rebellion in every inch of her thin frame. He advanced into the room.

'Sir Peter Bagshaw,' said Harrington. He was about to introduce the women, but Peter forestalled him, with a request for coffee and Harrington withdrew.

'Now ladies—-may I know your names?'

''I am Sylvia Lake, Sir Peter.' The speaker, a fair-haired woman in her late thirties, was wearing an orange and brown striped cotton dress and worn brown sandals. Her face had once been very beautiful, Peter judged, but now bore the ravages of pain and dissipation.

'Mrs Lake——I only heard of your husband's terrible accident and tragic death last night. I am more sorry than I can say. Obviously there are matters to be put aright——and I promise you that this will be done and soon. I know myself the distress in losing a partner. You must allow me to make amends for the unfeeling attitude of my solicitors. In the meanwhile, I will merely state, that the cottage you used to occupy with your husband, is to be repainted—and will be ready for you to move back into, next week.'

'Why—-Sir Peter—-I don't know what to say!' Sylvia Lake's hazel eyes filled with tears, as she looked at him almost uncomprehendingly. 'But I don't know if I will be able to afford the rent,' she blurted!

'There will be no rent. Indeed, I will have a pension paid to you from the estate, which should have been done at the time of Tristam's death. No———-don't be distressed. Life will be much easier from now on—and you will be able to devote more time to your daughter. She has musical talent, you know.'

A sharp exclamation of anger punctured the silence of the room, as Sylvia Lake fumbled for words of gratitude. She had downed several glasses of cheap wine this morning, before braving the visit to Garnford. The shout came from Rosamund, who had turned small furious face upon Peter.

'Money! It is all people like you think the world's about! Well——we don't need you—-or your money! Mother—you are not to accept anything from him!' Rosamund's eyes were full of furious tears.

'Rosamund! You just apologise to Sir Peter at once.' The mother's face looked almost comical in her dismay. For answer, Rosamund burst into a flood of tears and rushed out of the room. Peter looked after her, wondering whether to follow. He decided to complete his business with the two women first.

'Please, do not worry over your daughter's outburst. I have the feeling that she loved her father very dearly and in her hurt, is blaming me in some way for his death.'

Peter's face was sad, as he said this. The woman nodded.

'Yes. She fairly worshipped Tristam——-and he thought the world of her. He taught her to play the violin———then Miss De Vere realised the girl could play and started to coach her at school.'

'I see. So you are Miss De Vere———Rosamund's tutor?' Peter smiled encouragingly at the dark haired girl, who had so far remained silent. She took his proffered hand with a firm clasp.

'Yes, Sir Peter. The girl has unusual talent, hasn't she!' She didn't ask, but stated and Peter nodded agreement.

'How long have you been teaching her, Miss De Vere?'

'For almost three years, Sir Peter. During that time, she has made amazing progress——-nor do I take credit for this. Rosamund possesses a natural talent—and sensitivity far beyond her years. By nature——and I hope that Mrs Lake will forgive me for being so blunt, she is inclined to be rebellious. She is also very reserved and does not mix easily with her fellow pupils. Yet place a violin in her hands and she is another creature.' She watched his face, gauging his reaction to her words. Would a man as wonderfully gifted as Sir Peter Bagshaw and so heavily committed in the music world, really be prepared to help the awkward, ungracious child, who had just stormed out of the room?

Peter's face was thoughtful, as he turned back to the child's mother.

'I understand that there have been difficulties over practice times—that Rosamund has been advised that she may not play her violin in your home at the hotel. I also know that the headmistress has encouraged Rosamund to stay on at school at night, to practice there. I hope that it will be open to your daughter to practice as much as she needs to, once you are back in your cottage?' His words, gently spoken were a command nevertheless and Mrs Lake nodded her head in agreement.

'Yes——of course she will be able to play all night, if she wants to. Obviously a room above a public bar, hasn't been the easiest place for her to practice her violin. All those scales——well, there were complaints you know. I need my job.' She spoke listlessly and Peter realised just what a traumatic time both mother and young daughter had been through. There was a discreet knock at the door, cutting through his thoughts, as a young maid brought in a tray and set it before them.

They sat sipping their tea, while Peter continued to ply the two women with questions, building up a fuller picture of his protégé——for he had now determined that he would help the girl———when he stiffened in shocked surprise. For the notes of a violin were borne hauntingly towards them——the music, a fragment of his new composition———the Rose Concerto!

'Excuse me.' He rose hurriedly to his feet and left the room precipitately. He paused just long enough in the corridor to estab-

lish from which direction the sound was coming—but knowing
that it had to be from the music room.

Rosamund had placed his manuscript on the music stand, which
she had positioned just below the portrait of Natasha. She was
using his own favourite Stradivarius, although the instrument was
too large for her, but it wasn't the sight of that priceless ancient
wood, tucked beneath her determined small chin, that held him
enrapt——but the melody that soared upwards to the beautiful
woman above. For Rosamund was playing with a mastery that
held him motionless. Not only was she interpreting each note cor-
rectly, but capturing all the deepest poignancy of this tribute to
his dead wife.

She had not seen him enter. Peter walked over to the table,
where two other of his violins lay. He picked one up, tuned it and
stepping across the thick piled cream carpet towards her, on quiet
feet, positioned himself behind her. Now his violin picked up the
theme, a magnificent cascade of grace notes embellishing the
melody, full of wild emotion. She did not even turn, but continued to follow the manuscript, her notes blending with his. Only
when they had reached the end of the passage, did she lower the
violin and swing round to face him——and he saw that her eyes
were full of tears.

'It's beautiful,' she said softly. 'It is your own composition?'

'Yes, Rosamund. I call it the Rose Concerto. I am glad you like
it.'

'You wrote it for her——the lady in the picture?' She raised her
bow to Natasha, glancing at the single red rose, the painted fingers held.

'Yes, child,' he replied huskily. 'That lady was my beloved
wife, who died four years ago——and I miss her, just as you
miss your father.'

For a few minutes, there was complete silence in the room.
Then Rosamund fixed compelling green eyes on him and asked
with the directness of childhood—'How did she die? She looks

very young?' For reply, Peter gave a deep sigh, as he glanced once more up at the portrait.

'There was a skiing accident. She died in an avalanche—-but I lived, although sometimes I wish————!' He bit off the end of the sentence, suddenly realising that he was speaking to a child, for so attuned had they been in this exchange, that all thought of her identity had escaped him.

'But she will always live——in your music,' said Rosamund. She walked over to the table and put the violin lovingly down. 'It is a wonderful instrument,' she said wistfully.

'But far too large for you, at this stage! But you certainly cannot be allowed to continue with that monstrosity you were using at the school!'

'My father bought that for me,' she cried spiritedly!'

'Oh, I'm sorry. But Rosamund——I am sure that the father who gave you that violin, would also approve that now you have started to master the early stages of our craft, that you should now have a more appropriate instrument.' He turned to the door. 'Come with me.' She followed him to the west wing, into his study, where the violin he had selected for her, lay on his desk.

This was mine, when I was about your age. Pick it up——I want to be sure that the size is right. It might be fractionally large.' He watched as she tuned it and lifted the bow. She played a few remembered chords from his concerto, and he nodded, satisfied. 'It is yours now, Rosamund. Use it well. Now come—— we had better find your mother and your tutor.' He took the violin from her and put in a case, before returning it. He saw that she was chewing on one of her nails, face embarrassed.

'I was very rude to you, wasn't I! The fact that you are a wonderful musician and a nice man doesn't make me change my mind about rich people though. I still hate people who think they can get all they want in this world because they are wealthy.' She lowered her eyes, before she continued awkwardly, 'But I apologise for being rude to you—and I accept this violin, for the sake of the lady in the picture.'

It struck neither of them, that this was perhaps a very illogical statement, for to them, it wasn't.

The door opened and they both swung about. Lady Hermione stood smiling in surprise, to see their young visitor. Rosamund stiffened, at the sight of this elegantly dressed woman, with perfectly waved hair.

'Mother——allow me to introduce Rosamund Lake——the young lady you asked me to listen to, at the school concert.

Rosamund——this is my mother, Lady Hermione. If it were not for her, we would not have met!'

'How do you do,' said the child, extending a thin arm to Hermione. Lady Hermione took the hand, with its chewed nails and roughened palm, into her own.

'How do you do, Rosamund.' She glanced up at her son. 'Who was playing with you in the music room? I was in the garden below. I thought Adrian Moulting had gone?'

'Rodrigo and Adrian left about an hour ago. It was Rosamund that you heard. She had wandered into the music room on her own, found my manuscript——and you may judge of the result!' He exchanged glances with his mother, who was now surveying Rosamund with curiosity. Then her eyes fell on the violin case and she recognised it.

'Peter has given you one of his early violins,' she said softly. 'Rosamund dear——you lost your father a year ago and I know that this must have saddened you. Peter's own father died, when he was a little boy of five. Music has a way of expressing all the feelings that well up deep inside us—and helps to bring healing, to the sad ones. Having heard you play, I know that you will put that violin to good use.'

Rosamund turned green eyes back to Peter's face. So he also had lost his father when young——and Lady Hermione had gone through the same grief as her mother. Perhaps wealth didn't really make as much difference in people's lives as she had thought.

'Come—-let us find lemonade and cakes for you,' said Hermione in brisker tones—'Or better still, you must stay for lunch!'

'My mother and Miss De Vere are here too,' said Rosamund.

'Then please take me to them,' said Hermione.

Later that night, Peter sat talking with his mother. Their subject was the twelve years old girl, who had dominated his thoughts since the morning.

'Did you know that her grandmother was Melissa Lake, the American violinist, who died a few years ago?'

Hermione shook her head at this question. She knew nothing of the Lake family, nor indeed had taken much recent interest in any of the people involved as workers on the estate, never mind their relatives. She had a vague recollection of a good looking man in a tractor—-why yes, he had on one occasion, mended a puncture to her car, a friendly man with a good-humoured smile—red hair and beard. His name had been Tristam Lake———Rosamund's father! She suddenly felt very guilty that she had not taken any steps to investigate the circumstances of his death, when Harrington had spoken to her of it, on one of her intermittent visits to Garnford. From what Peter now told her, the widow Sylvia, had been very shabbily treated. She resolved to do all she could in the future, to help the child Rosamund.

'She is a very unusual child—remarkably talented for one who has had to endure such difficult circumstances.

Mrs Parkhurst was telling me, Rosamund remains at the school for several hours in the evening, when others have gone home— and after that, has had to help her mother washing glasses at the hotel and finally trying to find time to do her homework. I am sure she has not been eating properly, for she looks very thin.' There was concern in Hermione's voice as she spoke.

Peter sipped his whisky reflectively.

'No-one could call her an attractive child, could they! With that

wispy hair, bony arms and knees and slightly aggressive manner—
-well!' He smiled as he stared into the fire.

'She has lovely eyes, Peter. Haven't you noticed them—-the
colour of jade! As for her hair—it only needs cutting and groom-
ing. Thin limbs will fill out one day and as for her withdrawn—
almost suspicious attitude, this is only a defensive reaction to all
she has been through.' Hermione spoke with rare perception. She
was delighted that Peter was showing some interest in another
human being—even if this was merely a child. At least his
thoughts were being directed outwards, instead of to the
unhealed hurt within.

'Tell me mother—-do you suppose that musical talent runs in
families——-that if two talented musicians should marry, they
would produce a child similarly gifted?' It was the same question
that he had directed to Mrs Parkhurst. His mother looked at him
shrewdly. Had her words regarding his duty to provide an heir for
Garnford, been working subconsciously, she wondered? If he
should ever marry again, then her deepest wish was for his happiness and fulfilment. Certainly nothing but disaster would follow
upon a marriage entered into for the wrong reasons——and
selecting a wife merely for her musical aptitude, although providing a blending of interests, would be inadequate motive, should
love be missing. She shook her head.

'Peter—-I do not know the answer to your question. Indeed I
do not think any human being could give you an assurance that
even the most wonderfully gifted female musician, could give you
a child in the same mould.'

'Don't look so serious,' he said teasingly. 'It was only a hypo-
thetical question. As for myself, I shall never marry again.
However, I intend to help young Rosamund all that I can.
Perhaps you will watch over her progress from time to time, when
my work takes me abroad?' Then they spoke of other matters,
until at last, he arose restlessly and with word of apology, made his
way to the music room. Ten minutes later, his violin stroked

throbbing beauty into the night, as he worked on the next movement of his Rose Concerto.

It was several months later. Christmas was only a week away and
Peter had just returned from a triumphant tour of America. His
intention was to spend Christmas at Garnford, where he would be
able to rest and continue work on his Rose Concerto, which had
been put aside in August, when he had left for the States. Now
feeling drained after a gruelling few months, he longed for the
quiet of the Hampshire countryside. He arrived at his mother's
Knightsbridge home, to receive an ecstatic welcome from
Hermione.

'Peter, dearest! Oh——how marvellous that you are back,' and
she kissed him!

'Mother——how are you? You are looking wonderful, as
usual!' The words echoed truth, for Hermione was glowing with
happiness at having her son back.

'Come—sit down! Have you eaten——-I'll have Agnes prepare
something'

'I ate on the plane——and all I want right now, is to sleep. But
first, I have a gift for you.' He felt inside his jacket pocket and
removed a flat package. 'For you darling——-for being such a
wonderful friend, as well as mother,' he said softly. 'Go on——
open it!' His slate grey eyes were tender, as she flushed in pleas-
urable surprise.

'Should I not wait until Christmas,' she said dutifully, but her
fingers were already undoing the leather case. She gasped in
delight, as she saw the shimmering sapphires, revealed on their
white velvet cushion.

?Why——oh, Peter—-how absolutely beautiful! They must
have cost a fortune!' She ran to the heavy Venetian mirror above
the marble fireplace and stood looking at her reflection, as she fastened, first the sapphire collar about slender neck, adding the pendant earrings to dainty ears. The deep blue stones surrounded by
tiny diamonds, the whole set in intricate golf filigree, glittered

with rainbow light. Hermione understood jewellery and knew the magnificence of her son's gift.

'They suit you,' he said simply and laughed tiredly, as she gave him a grateful kiss. 'I have brought a small thing for young Rosamund,' he said. 'Tell me if you think it is suitable.' They sat together on the sofa, as he produced another smaller box and handed it to her. Hermione opened it, and looked with interest at the small jade pendant, set in antique gold, that lay revealed. She fingered it gently.

?What an unusual piece, Peter. It's lovely——and just the colour of the child's eyes. It looks very old. Is it?'

He nodded, explaining the purchase had been a careless gesture, when in an antique shop. 'I saw the pendant amongst some other pieces of jade——-remembered your having said that Rosamund's eyes were that shade! I asked the elderly proprietor if he knew the history of the pendant. He said it was supposed to be a tear, which a Chinese princess had once ordered carved in memory of her dead lover——-whom the king, her father, had had executed! But I am sure it was only a story invented for a curious tourist.'

'What a sad tale. It is certainly shaped like a teardrop. Why—— there is something carved into it——-and lined in gold.'

'That is the name of her dead lover.'

'Oh——-I see.' Hermione's eyes were troubled. 'Well, I suppose it's all right to give her. You don't think it could bring bad luck?'

'Mother! I don't believe this. You are the least superstitious of all people——of course it cannot bring bad luck!' His lips curved into a reassuring smile. 'How is our young protégé getting on? Have you seen her recently?'

Hermione hesitated. She looked vaguely uncomfortable.

?Well Peter——I do not usually listen to gossip. However, Harrington mentioned it is being spoken of in the servant's hall, that Sylvia Lake has been drinking heavily——and she has a man friend, who is constantly at the cottage. Mrs Parkhurst, whom I went to see, is worried about Rosamund. Seemingly the games mistress reported noticing heavy bruising on the girl's body——but Rosamund always explains such marks in satisfactory manner. For instance, a fall from her bicycle or slipping in the woodshed! But you know Peter, I just feel uneasy——a sort of sixth sense that something is wrong.'

Peter's lips tightened. He had barely given a thought to little Rosamund since he had been away—but thinking of her now, he realised that he felt a sense of responsibility for her—a vague tenderness.

'Well Mother——when we motor down tomorrow, we will make time to call on Sylvia Lake and see just what is going on. But now——if you do not mind, I am feeling exhausted. Would you think me very rude, if I were to go to bed!' Her eyes swept over his face and saw the lines of strain and tiredness. For answer, she led him to the bedroom, which was always kept in readiness for him. He kissed her goodnight and too tired even to take a bath, fell into bed.

The next morning was bright with sunshine. Peter dressed and breakfasted and excused himself to Hermione, whilst he went on a shopping spree to nearby Harrods. The famous store was decked out for Christmas and although early in the day, was a throng with shoppers. He managed to make those purchases he needed and waited while they were elegantly gift- wrapped.

'It cannot be! Peter! Peter Bagshaw!'

He swung around as he heard the voice——and gave an exclamation of utmost amazement. For standing by the counter was his old friend Ernst Morgenstern. The famous old pianist and the violinist clasped each other in emotional greeting.

'Ernst! What are you doing here——away from your beloved Austria?'

'A Mozart Concert at the Albert Hall last night. I was in Paris last week—in Berlin the week before that. I must admit that I am

feeling more than a little weary. But you, dear friend—I hear wonderful things of your American tour—that you are being spoken
of as the world's finest violinist!' The old man's eyes misted with
emotion as he surveyed the younger musician, whose career was
once almost over, when the wife he had adored was killed. Time
could indeed heal all things, it would seem, for Peter's eyes had
lost the haunted look that had attended his tragic loss.

'Yes—-I suppose things went well enough in the States. People
were wonderfully responsive—and appreciative to the degree that
I felt quite humble. Still—I'm glad to be home for a while. I want
to get back to the new composition I was working on before the
tour.' He turned his attention to the smiling assistant, who was
indicating that his purchases were now ready—-their distinctive
dark green and gold wrappings enhanced by lustrous bunches of
ribbons.

'Let me take some of those for you,' exclaimed Ernst. 'I will
help carry them to your car.' The two men worked their way
patiently between the festive crowds, until at last, the green suit-
ed doorman bowed them out.

Peter stowed his purchases carefully in one side of the Roll's
capacious boot—and sighed in relief that his shopping was finished—-except of course, that he should now purchase a gift for
dear old Ernst.

'Where are you staying, Ernst?'

'At the Dorchester. I came here by cab—-it didn't seem worth
hiring a car for three days. I return to Austria tomorrow.'

'Don't go!' Peter's dark eyes were bent impetuously on the old
pianist. 'You don't have to, do you? I mean—you have no concerts arranged this close to Christmas?'

He knew he was extremely reluctant to part with this dear
friend of his. In a way, Ernst Morgenstern had taken the place in
his life, of the father he was too young to remember. And for his
part, Ernst had become very attached to the young English boy
whom he had first met when he had to judge a competition in

Vienna of aspiring young musicians drawn from all around Europe. That had been almost twenty years ago—the serious faced youth, whose singing bow had carried off the bow in that early competition, now thirty-five year old virtuoso. Ernst smiled.

'So—-you would kidnap me, eh! Why not! I would be enchanted to see Garnford again—-such a marvellous old house. But more importantly—I want to know more of this work you are composing. To hear it, I am more than delighted to cancel my flight home.' His reward was the warm smile that touched Peter's lips—lips that rarely parted to real smile.

'Well——let's go. But first, I have to make another purchase. You sit in the car——I won't be a minute.' Peter hurried back into the store, making for the jewellery department. Cuff links would make the ideal present he mused. Ernst had a wonderful collection of them, his only failing! But before reaching the jewellery department, he paused before a stand, displaying a collection of semi precious stones. His eye was drawn to a geode—-whose dull, rough exterior would have given no indication of the loveliness within, until the spherical stone had been split in half—the half displayed here, showing the hollowed out heart of glittering crystal. An incomparable artist had wrought a tiny violin and bow, which were suspended in the geode's jewelled heart by a soldering of fine gold springs, which caused the violin and bow to quiver when the geode was handled. The violin would remind Ernst of him, he thought.

'I will take that,' he told the assistant, nor inquired the price, merely tendering a card.

Hermione was delighted to meet Ernst again, who kissed her hand with old world courtliness.

'Dear lady—-you have captured the secret of eternal youth,' he said and smiled to see her blush. He thought now of the courage of this middle-aged woman, who had thrust away her own heartache when bereaved, to encourage and support the talent she had noticed early in her young son. Peter Bagshaw who would

not be where he was today, had it not been for the efforts of
Hermione. She had never remarried or made any other attach-
ments following her husband's early death, all her love being centred on Peter——and his heritage, Garnford Manor. He knew that
she had withdrawn during Peter's happy marriage to Natasha,
picking up the threads of her individual life again——but that she
had been of the utmost supportiveness, during the last few years
when he had mourned the tragedy of a life bereft of his beloved
Natasha.

'I am so very happy that you are coming to Garnford with us
for Christmas. Do you have to collect your luggage——or have
you already done so?'

'It is in the boot——which is where I am going to stow our
things now,' said Peter.

'Charles will take them down, Peter. But perhaps you could
take these packages and place them on the back seat—they should
not take up too much space. They are just a few purchases I have
made for little Rosamund.'

Soon they were on their way, leaving the bustling heart of
London far behind. Now the Rolls purred effortlessly through
sleepy villages. It was intensely cold. The thick crusting of hoarfrost on bushes and grass, not yielding to the thin sunshine——but
gleaming like an ice gallery from some incandescent dream. But
inside the car it was warm and comfortable as the feeling of shared
content between the three travellers, as they chattered lightly,
enjoying each other's companionship. They stopped at an old inn,
near Petersfield, and sat beneath its dark oaken beams near a
crackling log fire, as the waiter served an excellent meal. They sat
talking afterwards—Ernst and Hermione sipping their Grand
Marnier, Peter making do with iced tonic water.

'Who is this Rosamund, you have been mentioning,' asked
Ernst curiously?'

'Who indeed! An ungracious, strong willed twelve year old,
with a fierce dislike of wealthy landowners——and who was quite

scathing in her remarks to me, when we first met. Her father died a year ago——an unfortunate accident on my estate, the whole affair handled disastrously by the estate manager and lawyers. The child and her mother were forced to leave the tied cottage that had been their home——and to move into a pub, where Mrs Lake has been working as a barmaid, to support herself and her child. But Ernst, this is the important point. Rosamund has an amazing talent as a violinist! She truly is quite extraordinary!'

'So——a farm worker's child——-and a genius!' Ernst leaned forward, interest sparking in his old eyes.

'Her grandmother was Melissa Lake,' put in Hermione.

'But I knew her slightly. We met professionally. This child's father must have been the son she mentioned, Tristam. I am more than sorry to hear that he is dead.' He shook his head sadly. 'Does Melissa's widower, the actor Dryman Lake, know that his son is dead——and his daughter-in-law in straightened circumstances?'

'I understand that he cut all connection between himself and his son, when Tristam married Sylvia against his wishes. Presumably Mrs Lake would have informed her father-in-law of her husband's death. But I know little of the family, beyond the fact that this prickly small girl, picked up a page of my manuscript—of the Rose Concerto——took my violin and proceeded to play that page as though she herself had composed the music! Need I say more? The child has an almost frightening natural talent.'

'Why, I cannot wait to meet this little prodigy,' cried Ernst. 'Will we see her today?' He slipped her mink around Hermione's shoulders, as they left the inn and clambered back into the Rolls.

It was already dark when the car entered the estate and the lights from the huge bulk of Garnford Manor blazed a welcome ahead. But Peter diverted along a narrow lane, which led to several small cottages, one of which was surrounded by a holly hedge, the scarlet berries gleaming in the car lights.

'Wait here—I will just make sure they are in,' said Peter, as he

got out. Through drawn curtains, light glowed. He knocked at
the door, drawing his brows together as he heard angry shouting—the sound of something heavy being hurled against the window, the crash of splintering glass, as the window shattered, frag-
ments falling out onto the dim shapes of last summer's flowers in
the bed below.

'Don't tell me what I can or can't do with your mother—-you
little slut!' the voice was thick with anger, slurred with drink.
Peter heard a well remembered high young voice reply—-

'You have no right here in our home. Now just you get out. If
you lay another finger on my mother—-I will call the police!'

'Be quiet, Rosamund! He'll kill you———-leave her alone, damn
you! Run Rosamund————-run!' Sylvia Lake's voice was
wild with fear. Peter didn't wait for more. He pushed the door
open and rushed in. He was just in time to snatch Rosamund back
from the beetle-browed, roughneck towering over her. The man's
face was contorted with rage, his eyes glazed from the effects of
the alcohol he had been consuming steadily since early afternoon.
One arm was poised in mid air, as he stared stupidly at Peter, suddenly thwarted in his attempt to hit the child, fearlessly con-
fronting him.

Sylvia gave a gasp of relief. She was holding onto the table, one
hand raised to her bleeding mouth.

'Sir Peter,' she whispered.

'Who is this then, woman———-one of your fancy men?' The
man squared up threateningly to Peter. 'Give me that child—-and
get out of here, whoever you are, if you don't want my fist in your
face!'

'Rosamund,' said Peter quietly——-'I want you to go outside
and get into the car with Lady Hermione.' For once, Rosamund
did not protest. She knew instinctively, her mother would be safe
now—that the tall man with the steady, grey eyes would deal with
this situation, could be trusted. With a backward glance at her
mother, who nodded approval, she slipped out of the door.

'Now——you! What's your name?' The authority in Peter's voice penetrated the alcoholic fumes that befuddled the man's brain.

'Bert Hampton. What's it to you? What the hell do you mean by coming in here?' The man adopted a threatening stance, bunching one of his fists belligerently.

'Well, Bert Hampton, you will leave this cottage——and if I see you back on my estate, I will have you arrested for trespass!' Peter's voice took on a quiet menace of it's own.

'What do you mean——leave the cottage. I live here——with her. She's my woman!' Sylvia looked down sullenly, at his words, her shamed look mute confirmation of what he said. 'This is her home,' the man continued. 'She can tell me to leave——you can't. Want to tell me to leave, Sylvia?' The intimidating look he cast on Sylvia caused her to shrink back trembling.

'She is asking you to leave—immediately!' Peter glanced towards Sylvia. 'That is so, is it not?' She flinched beneath his dis-passionate gaze and slowly nodded her head.

'Yes——please go, Bert. I want you to stay away from me. I've had enough.' Her husky voice gained in confidence, as she blurt-ed the words out.

'Why——you——-!' He let out a string of oaths. It was some of the foulest language Peter had ever heard. Then before Peter realised his intention, the man sprang at him, a great blow send-ing the musician sprawling on the floor. But Peter was instantly on his feet, although his head was ringing from the blow he had just received. The man rushed him again, but this time Peter was ready for him. Those hands able to coax the most exquisite sounds from his violin had also gained him a black belt in judo. The affair was soon over——the man lurching painfully out of the door.

'I'll be back, Sylvia——,' he muttered malevolently, staring at the frightened face framed in the doorway. 'Yes——you may well look scared—because when I return, you will wish you had never been born——and as for the kid———-!'

'Threatening violence, eh lad? Are you all right, Sir Peter. We got here as soon as we could!' The uniformed officer placed a restraining hand on Bert Hampton as he spoke. Then seeing Peter's look of amazement, he grinned. 'Your mother spoke to the station on your car phone. We will take over now. This lad is an old client of ours.' The officer glanced at Sylvia's cut lip and swollen face. 'Did he do that, Mrs Lake?'

'Yes——but I don't want him charged. Just make him keep away from the cottage.' Her voice broke on a sob. 'I've been all kinds of a fool.'

'Don't upset yourself, madam. As for this man, he will be safely locked in the cells tonight. When he has sobered up in the morning, we will discuss the matter further.' He turned back to Peter. 'Are you all right, sir?'

'Yes———-and I hope he is,' replied Peter with a slight grin. 'I learned a few useful tricks on self defence, when I was in Japan.'

'Really——-maybe we should come to you for a few lessons some time. Come on Hampton——-into the car!' Two other officers manhandled the protesting man into the police car, which had drawn up just behind the Rolls. 'I will call on both you and Mrs Lake, in the morning,' said the officer. The police car reversed in a neighbouring drive and sped off into the night.

'Well Mrs Lake——Sylvia,' said Peter gently. 'I expect you would like to clean yourself up and get some rest. May I suggest that your young daughter stays at Garnford tonight——and that you call there tomorrow.' He looked at her compassionately for she was sobbing uncontrollably now.

?I will send a woman round, to help you sort this place out,' he added, looking at the mess of damaged furniture, empty beer cans and wine stained carpet. 'I will have the window mended in the morning. Oh——-do you have Rosamund's violin?'

Sylvia Lake nodded and he heard her feet going heavily upstairs. He opened the kitchen door, looked at the sink piled with unwashed greasy plates, at the table littered with more lager cans and stale food. The unpleasant smell made him draw back in distaste. What had been happening here? He heard her coming downstairs again. She held out his old violin case and a carrier bag.

'Here are a few things for Rosamund—-her nightdress and a change of clothes for the morning.'

His face as he walked away down the drive, was grim. That poor child! She must have endured so much, during the months of his absence. Well—it would be different now. His feet crunched on the gravelled path, as he returned to his car.

Rosamund was sitting white faced, between Ernst and his mother on the back seat. He got in, placing her violin on the front seat next to him together with the pitiful torn carrier bag, containing her possessions.

'Your mother is safe, Rosamund. That fellow will never be coming back, that I promise you. But for tonight, your mother needs to be by herself—and therefore, I want you to be our guest at Garnford. He didn't hurt you, did he,' he asked, turning his head to look at her?

'Not this time,' she whispered. 'Oh——you found my violin! Mother hid it, because he wanted to burn it. He——he couldn't stand the sound of it, you see.' Peter swallowed an oath, and the car swept forward, turning into another lane that led back to Garnford.

Hermione flung a handful of perfumed bath salts into the pale green bath and placed a fleecy towel on the velvet topped stool beside it.

'Now, have a lovely, relaxing bath, dear Rosamund. I have brought you one of my robes—-it is a shortie, but it will be the right size for you—and a nightdress that should do.

Rosamund glanced at the delicate lace trimmed, pink lawn— and the soft rose, mohair dressing gown and raised her eyes in mute gratitude to Hermione. How could she ever have thought that this woman was hard and conceited? Tears welled up into her eyes—-she was so tired, so hurt emotionally.

'Have your bath—-and get into bed. I will come and see you later. Cheer up, my dear. Life will be good in the future—you will see!' Hermione closed the bathroom door and glanced around the connecting bedroom. She had placed Rosamund's violin against the cushioned armchair. The old four poster bed, with its cream hangings, had the covers pulled back ready for the child and Hermione had placed an old doll, from her own long distant childhood, on the pillows. She touched its china face and long lashes whimsically, stroking the blond hair and thinking back to another bedroom, where she had slept as a girl—-until she met and married Peter's father—those few magic years together, before he died in the car crash. But at least, he had left her his son—her beloved Peter. Now another child had entered her life.

True to her promise, she returned later, with a cup of hot chocolate. She knocked and hearing no answer came quietly in. Rosamund was on her knees by the bed. She was praying and Hermione stood stock still, as she heard the child's impassioned prayer.

'Please Father—-take care of Mummy—-and look after my Daddy, who is with you. Oh, I do miss him so, Lord. And please—-will you help me to be a good violinist.' Hermione coughed. Rosamund straightened up, rose from her knees and sat on the end o the bed.

'Daddy taught me to pray,' she said. Hermione swallowed. Then she put down the cup, went to the bed and put her arms about Rosamund.

CHAPTER THREE

The following morning dawned crisp and bright. Rosamund woke and stared about her unfamiliar surroundings in perplexity—then memory flooded back, and with it, the trauma of last night's happenings. She slipped out of bed and drew the heavy rose curtains. The scene that greeted her eyes made her gasp. It had been snowing in the night and now the sun sprayed dazzling crystal onto the bare branched trees, turning the lawns into shining carpet of white. In the distance, the lake shimmered under this early sunshine, as a stiff breeze spanked its waters into gold tipped waves.

'Oh—-how beautiful,' she murmured. Then slipping into the cosy dressing gown, she went through to the bathroom. When she came back, she looked around for her clothes—but there was no trace of them. She returned in chagrin to the four poster bed. She wanted to get back to the cottage, to check that her mother was all right.

'Good morning, Miss! Here is your breakfast,' said a cheerful voice, as a young maid knocked and entered. An appetising smell rose from the silver tray, which the girl placed on the bedside table. 'My name is Elsie, Miss. Lady Hermione has asked me to look after you, whilst you are here.' Rosamund stared at her bemused. It seemed strange that anyone should be required to look after her—after all, she was not a baby. But the maid, in her burgundy dress and white frilled apron looked kind—and not too much older than Rosamund herself.

'Thank you, Elsie. Do you know where my clothes are?'

'Lady Hermione said to tell you, she would be bringing your clothes, once you had breakfasted.' The maid bobbed her head and went out. Rosamund lifted the tray onto her lap. There was bacon, sausages and eggs and tomatoes—and crispy fresh rolls and a jug of coffee. She suddenly realised how hungry she was. There had been no regular meals during the last few days of the school holidays—-just a few hastily prepared snacks—and the ever present smell of alcohol. She had eaten school dinners during term time and on return from school, had been absorbed in her homework and music practice. She had not at first realised her mother's growing dependency on alcohol—it became part of a pattern, which later came to include another person coming to live in their cottage——and worse, to share the bedroom, where her father had slept with her mother.

A cold hatred for Bert Hampton had filled her young heart, tempered with extreme contempt. Although only twelve, she realised that this man was merely preying on her mother's weakness and grief, gradually dominating her, until Sylvia's will crumpled beneath his over powering personality. Bert had a strong physique and forceful swagger, which made women surrender to him with amazing ease. When sober, he had a rough charm of manner—but when drunk, which was almost every night, he became a very dangerous person. Rosamund had watched in horror, as he would assault her mother, his anger arising from a drink damaged brain, on any slight pretext. She had always managed to conceal her own fear of him, desperately trying to intervene every time he had battered Sylvia's helpless body. Frequently she had gone to school, hoping that the staff would not notice her own bruises.

She gave a small sigh, as she put her tray down. The breakfast had tasted wonderful. How good it must be to live in surroundings like this all the time, where everything was clean—where no one ever shouted or swore—where there was no cause for fear! But she must get back to the cottage soon. She remembered Sir Peter giving her an assurance, that Bert Hampton would not be returning there. If only she could believe this.

Hermione smiled in pleasure, as she surveyed Rosamund. One would have been hard put to recognise the dishevelled youngster of yesterday, in the attractive young girl who smiled shyly back at her. Hermione had brought a hairdresser up from the village, with a commission to do something about the girl's wispy fair hair. Now it was cut into a short, shining cap. The wine and green, Italian styled dress, it's softness disguising her bony arms, and the ruched leather, wine coloured boots, which thankfully fitted, completed the transformation.

Rosamund had already stared in amazement, at her reflection in the long, gilt framed mirror.

'That cannot really be me,' she said in awe. Then a feeling of guilt stole over her. Here she was, bothering over her appearance, when her mother must be terribly miserable on her own, at the cottage.

'Lady Hermione——you have been really kind—and I thank you. But please understand, I must go home to Mummy now.' She glanced down at her new clothes. 'I think perhaps——I should take these things off——and keep them for best! I will spoil the boots in the snow,' she explained, 'and I expect I will have some clearing up to do in the cottage.'

'You will not have to walk child. We will go over in the car,' said Hermione. 'And as for cleaning the cottage, Sir Peter sent a woman over last night, to help your mother sort things out. Now, come downstairs with me. Ernst and my son are waiting for you——oh, and when you go out later, there is this cape to wear. The sales woman in Harrods assured me that they are very fashionable with the young, this season.' She watched as Rosamund tried it on, its dark green wool looking just right with the boots, the strings at it's neck, trimmed with tiny gold bells, which Rosamund twirled excitedly.

'Lady Hermione——its——its, oh!' and she spread her hands, words evading her.

'Forget the 'Lady' Hermione——just call me Hermione, child. Now come!'

Rosamund slipped the cape off her shoulders and folded it

across her arm, before following Hermione downstairs, to the drawing room. A huge Christmas tree dominated the room, its branches glittering with delicate glass baubles, the winking fairy lights bringing flickering glow to the thick ropes of tinsel, which festooned it in shining loops. She had never seen such a tree—and Rosamund's eyes shone with delight. The two men stared at her in bewilderment. Surely this wasn't the same child—but it was—and seeing this so very normal, tremulous joy of childhood, in one who had already experienced so much of pain————how to tell her now, of this fresh disaster, that had come into her life. Sir Peter composed the stern lines of his face into a smile.

'Why, Rosamund—-you are beautiful,' he said and meant it.

'Indeed, a very charming young lady,' added Ernst Morgenstern. The old man walked over and whimsically lifted her hand to his lips. As the blushing child and the old pianist started to talk together, Peter drew his mother over to the window.

'Read this,' he said! He handed he a badly scrawled letter, the words smudged.

"Dear Sir Peter Bagshaw,

I do not know what you can think of me, after last night—-but I do know what I think about myself. There are no excuses. Drink and loneliness can make a person behave in the most appalling way. You also have suffered bereavement, Sir Peter, and rose wonderfully above it. Perhaps if I had been gifted in some way— music, writing or art—I might have channelled my grief in this way. But I am just an ordinary woman, not terribly well educated—no accomplishments. All I ever had, was my wonderful husband, and he is dead.

Yes—I know I have a lovely young daughter, who is the image of her father, she even has his mannerisms. To look at her, is to ache after Tristam. So I tried to replace him, with that creature you threw out of my cottage last night. I think I have come back to my senses—am sober at least, this morning. I didn't sleep last night. After helping that kind woman you sent over, to clean up the place, I sat up in my room thinking.

I am going away. I am going to try to make a new life for myself. It does not include Rosamund—and this is for her own sweet sake, for I do not know what lies ahead. But one fact is plain. I am not at this time, a suitable person to look after my little girl—-nor do I want a lot of inquisitive social workers poking their noses in my affairs. So you see, I am throwing myself on your mercy, Sir Peter—for I am leaving Rosamund in your care. I know you have told me, that she has much musical talent, and so I am asking you to take her into your household and help her in her future life. Please tell her not to feel too badly about this. It truly is for her own good. I will always love her—always, always love her. Ask her to forgive me.

Sincerely,

Sylvia Lake."

After reading the letter, Hermione gave it back to Peter, eyes shining with tears, her mouth quivering. That poor woman, she thought.

'Oh—-Peter! What do we do now? Try to find Sylvia and bring her back?'

'I don't think so. She obviously wishes time to sort her life out. It cannot have been an easy decision to take——to give Rosamund up, for I know how much she loves her daughter. What might look to the world as a selfish act, is indeed the opposite. She wants the best for Rosamund and I am touched that she has placed such faith in me. Will you help me to look after the child, mother?' Peter's slate grey eyes, held Hermione's gaze questioningly.

'I will treat her like the daughter I never had,' replied Hermione softly. 'But how are we to tell her, Peter——how to explain, that having lost her father, her mother has now disappeared from her life!" Hermione shook he head sadly. Then she straightened her shoulders resolutely. Life had presented her with a new challenge and she picked up the gauntlet.

'Rosamund——come here my dear.' The girl had been chatting animatedly with Ernst Morgenstern. She looked up happily at Hermione.

'It's time for us to go?' She walked over to the older woman, then paused, as she glimpsed the sadness in Hermione's eyes. 'What's wrong,' she asked? 'Has Bert Hampton come back—— has he hurt my mother again?' Her face was taut, as she waited for Hermione's reply.

'No——that man will not return. Never fear that. But Rosamund dear, your mother has gone away for a little while. She has been feeling very upset you know. She is still grieving for Tristam——only allowed that man to come into your lives because she was very vulnerable after losing your father. She made a mistake. It is easy for this to happen at such times. But now she wants to be by herself for a time, while she heals up. She knows that however much she loves you, and she does love you very much indeed——that it is in your best interest at this present time, to grow up in an atmosphere of stability. Rosamund——your mother has asked Peter and myself, to look after you. Will you let us do that, my dear?' Hermione bent down and slipped her arms about the bewildered child.

'It's not true————it can't be,' cried Rosamund brokenly. 'Mother would never go away without me. I know she wouldn't!' Tears had gathered in her eyes. She dashed them away with impatient hand. 'I have to go to the cottage,' she said and before Hermione could stop her, had fled the room. The three adults stared after her——then Peter dashed in pursuit. By the time he had raced to the bottom of the stairs, he came face to face with Harrington. The butler stepped aside, as he called out that Rosamund had run out of the main door.

'She wouldn't stop, sir! She is wearing no coat—and it's snowing!'

'Where's Roberts?'

'Polishing the Rolls, sir!'

'Tell him to bring the car the car, Harrington. Quick man——quick, while I get the keys to the cottage!' Harrington rushed out to the garage, his shoes sinking in the snow, calling to the chauffeur. Roberts looked up in surprise, as the butler hastily explained the situation. Roberts swung the car out onto the driveway, as his employer threw himself in beside him The Rolls purred forward, its tires crunching the snow. They saw the little figure running through the snow, some fifty yards ahead, then as she heard the car behind her, she turned suddenly off the driveway, cutting off in a tangent, in the general direction of the cottage.

'She is going to take the path through the fields, sir!' The chauffeur looked after the child in concern, seeing the dress fluttering about her in the wind. Although it was not snowing too heavily, it was bitterly cold.

'You drive the car round to the cottage and wait for me there. I'm going after her on foot—jut in case she should get into difficulties!' Peter's feet sank into the deep snow, as he panted after her fleeing figure. Across the fields they ran, over a style, and then along a narrow pathway where bushes almost met overhead. She slipped, scrambled to her feet and set off again.

'Rosamund——wait!' He had been calling after her all the while and was almost breathless from this mile long run through the snow. He could hear her panting breaths now and ever so often the words, 'Mother——mother,' as still she ran. At last the pathway led into the lane where Holly cottage stood.

Rosamund rubbed the snow out of her eyes, as she tried to open the door. It was locked. She looked round desperately, as Sir Peter at last caught up with her.

'I want my mother! I must get in,' she said. Sir Peter slipped his hand into his jacket pocket. He produced the key and fitted it into the lock. The cottage was clean now, they saw. Wood was polished, copper shone——no trace of the empty beer cans and rotting food remained. But Sylvia had gone. Rosamund hurried in distraught haste, from one room to another. She opened the

wardrobe in her mother's room. It was empty——and so were the
dressing table drawers—-and the photograph of her father, had
disappeared from the wall. Now at last, she acknowledged the
truth of what Hermione had gently told her. She broke down,
sobbing as though her heart would break—-and Peter opened his
arms and lifted her up. She was soaking wet——and freezing, hair
plastered to hr forehead with half melted snow. He carried her
outside. Roberts had the car waiting and opened the back door.
The child clung to Peter now, her sobs coming spasmodically. He
pulled a cashmere rug about her. They were back at the house in
a very few minutes. Hermione stood at the door waiting for them.
She had seen the Rolls coming up the drive from the window.

'Is she all right, Peter?' her eyes were anxious.

'Yes——but we must get her out of these wet clothes.'

'Take her up to my room. Harrington——ask Elsie to run
a hot bath!'

Half an hour later, Rosamund was tucked up in bed, looking
pale and thin against the silken pillows. Her wild outburst of grief
had subsided. Only a slight, dry sob still racked her chest.
Hermione sat beside her bed on a tapestried chair, holding one of
the thin hands.

'Darling child——I know no words of mine can really help you
in what you are feeling now. Only hold onto one thing,
Rosamund————your mother loves you very much—and I
am learning to love you too, as is Peter. You will truly be part of
our family now. I promise you that we will always care for you,
and happier times lie ahead. Now try to sleep. I will close the curtains.'

'How is das kleines madchen,' asked Ernst, as Hermione came
into the room?

'Sleeping! It's probably good that she did break down—-man-
aged to pour out all the hurt. She is just exhausted now, and no
wonder. Young Elsie is sitting in the room to watch her and will
let me know when she wakes.' She turned to Peter. 'I see you

managed to change your clothes Peter!' He nodded absently.

'Yes. You know it is going to be quite a responsibility, caring for her. But she is a courageous little thing——you can't help liking her. Do you think she will accept the situation now?' He looked at Hermione questioningly.

'We will know that later, when she awakes,' replied his mother. 'Come——let's go into lunch.'

Later, Ernst was seated before the Steinway. A Strauss melody filled the room with its entrancing melody, as the old musician's hands flew lovingly over the keys. Hermione sat on the oyster silk couch, watching Peter, as he lifted his violin. Soon the strains of the music penetrated Rosamund's consciousness. She stirred on the pillows and frowned, as she tried to recollect what she was doing there. Then realisation flooded back and with it, the pain. She sat up in bed.

'Are you all right, Miss?' The young maid looked at her sympathetically. News of what had happened had spread in the servant's hall and Harrington had informed the staff, that Miss Rosamund was now to be treated as one of their employer's family. 'You stay there now, Miss Rosamund——and I will call Lady Hermione,' she said. The child shook her head. Her eyes were calm now, their expression grave.

'Don't do that, Elsie. I just want to get dressed.'

'Well, Miss——I know there are some new clothes waiting for you in the wardrobe. So you slip out of bed then, and come and choose.' Rosamund's feet sank into the soft carpet, as she looked into the wardrobe, with as much interest as she could muster. Early this morning, the clothes would have delighted her——now, they only served to remind her, that all that was familiar, had disappeared from her life. She lifted a corn gold trouser suit and turned to Elsie.

'This will do.' She dressed absently, listening to the strains of the music——then was drawn almost automatically in the direction of the music room. She came in quietly, before they were aware of her. She was carrying her violin. Sir Peter was standing behind Ernst. The 'Tales of the Vienna Woods' lilted through the room. Rosamund lifted her bow—and Hermione gasped softly, as the child started to play. The men heard—almost missed a beat, but continued to play, without looking round. A spot of colour burned in Rosamund's cheeks, as the sheer joy of the melody sought response in her breast. Yes, she thought—-her mother had gone—-but she would find her again one day. In the meanwhile, there was this thing of music, in which you could lose yourself— and these people were after all kind. Perhaps this new life had much to offer, and certainly, it would do no good to cry any more. When her father had died, she had found solace in her music and would do so again now. Peter turned at last and looked down at her.

'Well done,' he said. 'But you should never start before first tuning. Give it to me——-there.'

'Thank you, Sir Peter.' She took the instrument back.

'Drop the Sir Peter——Peter will do'

'Thank you, Peter, ' she said softly. Ernst smiled at her. He had listened to her accompaniment with interest.

'What was that piece called,' she asked?

'Tales of the Vienna Woods. Yes, Mein liebchen——-it is about my own dear Vienna. How would you like to visit me there, Rosamund? I fly back in a few days——and I have invited Peter and Lady Hermione to accompany me. We will spend the New Year in Vienna, city of dreams! It will do you good to get away from this place for a while. What do you say?' His kind old eyes smiled into hers, seeing the grief so bravely disguised.

'But Vienna is in Austria, isn't it——Mozart's city,' cried Rosamund.

'Yes indeed, I will take you to all those places associated with our most famous musician——we will go to Salzburg, where he was born. You will love Vienna, Rosamund. We will visit the palace of the Hapsburgs—the cathedral——go to concerts, where

you will have the opportunity to meet famous musicians. Now——
—pick up that bow again!' It was almost as though the intense
vitality flowing from the old pianist, swept through her veins,
releasing creativity.

'Come here, Rosamund. Stand by me.' Peter had positioned
the music stand in front of Natasha's portrait, placing the same
page of manuscript on it she had played on her first visit to the
house. 'Now play.' She hesitated, glanced up at the painting of the
beautiful woman above her, seeing the proud carriage of
Natasha's head, the pearls gleaming in the dark hair, at ears and
graceful throat, the luminous quality of the skin——then down to
the single red rose, held lightly between the delicate fingers. No
wonder Peter loved her. She was incredibly lovely, this woman in
whose memory he was writing his concerto. For the first time, she
considered what she herself would look like, when she grew up.
Would any man ever love her———care for her so much, that he
would dedicate his music to her? She turned her head and looked
at Peter. He was staring upwards at the portrait, the most tender
expression curving his usually stern lips——and Rosamund fetched
a sigh, for she knew that she was plain—even her fingers were
ugly, with their chewed nails. A sudden twinge of jealousy for the
gracious woman, who even dead reigned in her husband's heart,
jerked through Rosamund's spirit—to be immediately ejected as
unworthy and as though in retribution, she drew in a deep breath
and commenced to play.

Ernst Morgenstern had risen to his feet in amazement, for the
music that rose wildly to the air, held a poignancy of grief, tempered with throbbing intensity of love, drawn deep from within
the human soul—that a child was able to instil such finely tuned
emotion, was incredible. He realised that the girl standing before
him held the seed of genius. His eyes met Peter's. They
exchanged glances. Then Peter's Stradivarius brought richness of
tone to the music he had created, the soaring melody sweetened
to moment of lingering joy, as Peter played a further part of the

movement. There was absolute silence as man and child, lowered their bows. Then Ernst gravely took Rosamund's hand, lifting it to his lips in salute. He did not immediately release that hand, but stared down at the slender fingers musingly, seeing beyond the bitten finger nails to the bones and sinews, extension of that something mystical within the heart of the true musician.

'That was wonderful, liebchen. One day, these small hands will charm audiences around the world. But years of practice and self discipline lie ahead. There may even be times, when you will feel like giving it all up—but you won't. Yours will be the dedication needed to succeed.'

Rosamund stared up at him broodingly. 'Thank you,' she said softly. 'Thank you, Herr Morgenstern. I think I have always known that music was to be my life.'

'It is—will be. Now do not call me Herr Morgenstern child. I would prefer that you call me Ernst——perhaps Uncle Ernst?' His wise old eyes smiled down into hers, the wrinkled cheeks creasing to happiness as she nodded her head. Hermione blinked away the quick tears that had risen to her own eyes, at the little exchange. She also realised the latent talent in this strange child, who was to become her ward. Just as she had tended a similar talent in Peter as a boy, so she was resolved to do all within her power to assist Rosamund. But how was it possible to achieve that, if the girl were to remain here at the local school? True the headmistress was wonderfully sympathetic and had been fostering the girl's talent as best she could—and yes, the violin tutor was dedicated, but much more than this would be needed in the future. She placed a hand on her son's arm and drew him aside. 'Peter, I must take her back to London with me. Perhaps we can get her into the Guildhall School of Music?'

'Not the Guildhall, although it is truly excellent. Fritz Klein may be prepared to take her. It is an academy for young violinists. She will receive a good general education there——but more importantly, as it caters only for about twenty youngsters, she will have a specialised training. I know the principal Madame Ouvetsky. Rosamund will have to audition of course, but I do not foresee any difficulty there. The school is in Kensington, so you will be able to keep a close eye on her, without too much trouble.' Peter looked at Hermione. 'What do you think?'

'Marvellous—-the perfect answer.' She nodded her head in agreement. Life was going to be full of fresh interest, moreover Peter would have a distraction from his whirl of concert engagements. Perhaps caring for the child might foster urge to have a child of his own——marriage? Garnford might one day have the heir it needed. Hermione watched as Peter walked over to Rosamund and Ernst, looking at the girl with proprietary interest.

'Well Rosamund——it's time for dinner, and as this is Christmas Eve, I think you will find that cook has excelled herself. You will probably want to retire to your room, to change——I believe my mother has a special dress for you to wear!' She stared at him, puzzled. What was wrong with her trouser suit? But if Hermione wanted her to change—-!'

She followed Hermione out of the room.

'Why do I have to change,' she asked, perplexed. 'My clothes are clean—this suit very nice.' Hermione smiled. She had just come back into Rosamund's bedroom, with a large, expensive looking box in her arms. She opened it, and held out a green velvet dress, with cream lace at neck and cuffs.

'Try this on, Rosamund. I had meant to keep it for Christmas Day—-but we have guests arriving for dinner. Let me see how it looks.' She breathed a sigh of satisfaction at the transformation and blessed the inspiration, which had induced her to make these purchases for the girl, before leaving Knightsbridge. There were soft green kid sandals to go with the dress. She brushed Rosamund's hair to shining blond cap and led her to the mirror. Rosamund shook her head in bewilderment.

'It doesn't look like me,' she whispered. 'I hadn't realised clothes could change a persons appearance so much!' Hermione laughed.

'Well—-that is one lesson you have learned already! But I must go and change myself. I won't be long.' Rosamund sat quietly on the end of the bed, thinking of all that had happened in the last twenty-four hours. She had lost her mother—had no idea where Sylvia might be, or when if ever, she would see her again. She was entirely in the hands of these wealthy people, who were to care for her. She had always hated wealth and privilege. Was she now to be part of that world she had always despised? Being transplanted, into this entirely different strata of society, was but part of the problem. In addition there was the challenge of having to prove that her love for music was not just fancy born of conceit, but a deep and strong love, for a power of expression that went far beyond the eloquence of mere words. A phrase of the Rose Concerto came into her mind and instinctively she lifted her violin from the table. In his own room, Peter paused as he straightened his tie and smiled.

Rosamund sat between Peter and Hermione, trying not to appear nervous before the richly dressed men and women, who were viewing her curiously. Those who were seated around the huge oval mahogany table, dark shining surface reflecting the silver bowl of richly perfumed red roses and flickering fine wax candles in handsomely wrought silver candelabra and the gleam of crystal goblets, were drawn from wealthy county families. She stared back at them, the men in their impeccable dinner suits, the women beautifully gowned, décolleté necklines displaying glittering jewellery, hair perfectly coifed, faces carefully painted—-and she bristled. Hermione sensed Rosamund's unease and wished she had not issued invitations for this particular dinner——yet it had been traditional, for the Garnford family to give a Christmas Eve dinner. Peter had introduced Rosamund as his ward and to begin with, the company although intensely curious, had accepted this. Now, at the conclusion of the dinner, comfortable from the superlative meal and relaxed from the wine they had consumed, they turned their eyes back once more, on the child with the unusual green eyes, who sat erect,

pale face solemn.

It was Helen Delaney-Smythe, red lips pursed, black brows drawn together, who voiced what all were wondering.

'Your young ward is charming, Sir Peter——absolutely charming. But who is she—a young relative perhaps?' The handsome, forty years old woman sat forward in her chair, fixing Rosamund with inquisitive stare.

'Rosamund is the granddaughter of Melissa Lake, the late American violinist. Rosamund shows sign of future talent——will be studying at the Fritz Klein Academy,' said Peter smoothly. Rosamund gasped. Why had Peter introduced her by mentioning only her grandmother, whom she had never met? What of her dead father—and her mother? Then she realised that possibly they were not of sufficient status to impress this roomful of affected individuals. She rose to her feet, flushing hotly.

'If you want to know who I am, then why do you not ask me,' she exclaimed. 'Yes——-my grandmother was Melissa Lake and my grandfather is the actor Dryman Lake. I never met either of them. But my father was Tristam Lake, a farm worker on Sir Peter's estate, until he died when his tractor overturned and crushed him. My mother's name is Sylvia. Perhaps some of you may have met her——at the Bull Hotel, serving drinks—if you go to pubs that is! Only she has gone away——-and Sir Peter and Lady Hermione have taken me in. So now you know! Excuse me——-.' She pushed her chair back and stalked angrily out of the room, leaving a hushed silence behind her. Hermione rose to her feet.

'I apologise for Rosamund's outburst,' she said quietly. 'You see——it was only today that her mother left her and she is deeply distressed. I should not have included her in this party—but felt it better for her to get used to a new way of life at once, rather than leaving her in her room to mope.'

'Sylvia Lake,' mused Colonel Carrington, stroking his droop-ing, silver moustaches. 'Yes, I remember her. Pretty woman with red hair. Looked out of place at the 'Bull'. It may surprise that young firebrand of yours, to realise that some of us do frequent pubs, from time to time!' He chuckled. 'It took courage you know—to face all of us like that and stick up for her parents. I wish you well with the child Peter. How will you cope though? After all, you spend most of your time travelling from one conti-nent to another—and you, Hermione have a busy social life in London!' The colonel turned his admiring gaze on Hermione, who was looking particularly regal in a gown of midnight blue, her son's gift of sapphires shimmering at neck and ears. He won-dered how Hermione would cope with this precocious child.

'I consider myself to be extremely fortunate, to have the joy of a young daughter, at my time of life,' she said evenly. 'Perhaps under the circumstances, you will excuse me for a few minutes, while I go to her. Helen, will you take the other ladies to the blue drawing room, while the men enjoy their cigars. Later, we have a treat for you. Ernst Morgenstern has consented to play for us—and I hope to persuade Rosamund to join us for that.'

Rosamund looked up as Hermione knocked and entered. Her expression was stormy, her eyes bright and it was obvious that she had been crying. Hermione sank down on the bed next to her and slipped an arm about the slim shoulders. Rosamund tried to pull away.

'I suppose you are disappointed in me now, Hermione—want me to go away?'

'How could you think such a thing! As it happens, my guests admire you for the way you spoke protectively of your parents. I know we must all appear very different, perhaps very formal, to you. But Rosamund, you are going to have to mingle with peo-ple from all walks of life—and learn to respect people for what they are as individuals, not because they fit into a preconceived idea of the sort of person you are willing to accept because of their background. In other words dear, you mustn't dislike people just because they are rich or titled. I won't pretend that there isn't much unfairness in the way wealth is distributed in the world—-but you will find that there are some wealthy people who are kind and good—-just as there are some poorer people, who are just the opposite. Yes, there were a couple of people in that room, whom I do not like particularly myself—snobs if you like—but most are old friends, who have joined us for this annual party. Now Ernst is going to play for us shortly. I won't order you to join us, Rosamund. In fact, if you would rather stay in your room, I shall quite understand—-but it would make me exceptionally happy, if you were to walk downstairs with me now!' She waited for Rosamund's reaction.

'I'll come,' said Rosamund. 'I'm sorry Hermione—-it was just that they all looked so artificial—the men dressed like penguins and the women trying so hard to impress each other! But you are right—-I know it is Christmas Eve,' and she bit off a sob, as she thought of other past happier Christmases. 'Daddy always used to take us to midnight service at the local church—for the carols,' she said wistfully. Hermione looked at her. She could not remember when last she had been near a church——-but if it would make Rosamund happy!

'I will ask Peter to drive us down to the village church for midnight service,' she said quietly and hoped Peter would understand. Rosamund brightened. She smoothed the folds of her velvet dress and walked over to the mirror. Her face showed traces of tears and she hurried to the bathroom, to splash them away.

No-one seemed to notice unduly, when Rosamund slipped quietly into the music room with Hermione, for Ernst was already playing and the chords of the 'Moonlight Sonata' hung like magic on the air, but the old musician smiled as he saw the little girl. She found a stool and set it close to the piano

She no longer noticed the people. All that mattered was the music that fell like healing balm on her ears. Pachelbel's gentle

Canon followed—-and then some Grieg. Peter breathed a sigh of
relief, as he saw the strain had disappeared from her face and he
understood, for it was only in music that he had found solace
from the pain of Natasha's death.

Hermione brought the evening to an early close, by ushering
the party into the green drawing room, dominated by the huge
Christmas tree. Each of the guests received a small gift—-a final
toast was drunk—-and Harrington led the departing guests
downstairs. Hermione and Peter waved goodbye at the door, then
returned to the drawing room, where Rosamund was standing
before the blazing log fire, looking wonderingly at the enormous
tree—but thinking of the much smaller one her mother had decorated a year ago. She looked up, as they walked in.

'I have a small gift for you, Rosamund. Something which I
brought back from America—-but which actually came from
much further afield.' He produced the jewel box in its gold wrapping. The paper rustled to the floor, as she opened the box—-
and stared at the delicate green jade pendant. He told her the
story of the Chinese princess—-that the pendant was carved to
represent a tear for her dead lover—-and that it was supposed
to be four hundred years old.

'Here is an antique chain to wear it on,' said Hermione. 'May
this jade tear, be the last tear of your life—-may there be only happiness for you in the future, dear Rosamund.' She bent and kissed
her. 'Well, Peter—-I have promised Rosamund that we will
attend the midnight service in the village.' He swallowed, saw the
child's face turned on him eagerly and nodded with as good a
grace as he could muster.

As they drove through the snow, the lights shining through the
stained glass windows of the church gleamed like jewels and the
night was frosty with twinkling stars. Their feet crunched through
the snow, as they walked the last few yards towards the old
church.

Rosamund knelt. Her prayers were for her mother—-for her

father's soul—-and also for her new family and the way ahead. She rose to her feet, as the organ started to play, the strains of 'Holy Night' filling the church, and Peter Bagshaw felt an unaccustomed choke at the back of his throat.

CHAPTER FOUR

Five years had passed, years in which Rosamund had blossomed from thin, diffident schoolchild, to lovely girl, on the brink of womanhood. The fair hair had darkened to tawny gold and her green eyes beneath dark lashes were expressive of the emotion that welled up from deep within her soul, to flow from fingertips into the vibrating strings of her violin. Sir Peter was proud of his ward's progress and knew how much of her new self confidence was a result of Hermione's devoted care, for his mother's life had entirely revolved around Rosamund, since that Christmas Eve, when she had taken the girl into her arms and her heart.

It had not been an easy task. To begin with, Rosamund had been resentful of a fate that had robbed her first of her father, followed by her mother's apparent desertion. It could not have been easy for the child, mused Hermione, as she sat under the hairdryer in the fashionable La Roche salon——yet she had adapted well. Perhaps the decision to take her on that early visit to Austria, to stay with dear Ernst had helped. Rosamund had been thrilled to see the birthplace of her beloved Mozart, at Salzburg. How excited the girl had been to get her first glimpse of those snow clad mountains——how sombre Peter's mood when he saw them and remembered Natasha's death. Returning to Vienna then, with its beautiful buildings and wonderful shops—and of course, the Opera House. The week they had spent there had opened up a whole new world for Rosamund.

Her French hairdresser inclined his head and lifted the hood of the dryer.

'Just another five minutes, my lady.' She sank back into her reverie. She remembered their return from Austria, preparing a room for Rosamund in her Knightsbridge flat——then Peter arranging an audition at the Fritz Klein Academy, Madame

Ouvetsky, her eyes showing little emotion as Rosamund sight read a fragment of Brahms. Rosamund was then allowed to play a piece of her own choice, and taking a deep breath, she had played a hauntingly beautiful melody. Only when the last note had died away, did they realise how sad it was. 'What is that piece, my child,' Madame Ouvetsky had asked curiously.

'I call it—"Loneliness",' Rosamund had replied. 'I wrote it after my father died.' Madame Ouvetsky had drawn Peter to the other side of the room—they had spoken animatedly together, and Rosamund had been enrolled.

And so it had started, the long road that was to prepare Rosamund for this special April day, when she was to play her first solo at the Albert Hall. It was for this occasion that Hermione was preparing now. A reluctant Rosamund was having her hair blow dried on the other side of the salon. Although the girl had a wardrobe of beautiful clothes, she was never happier than when wearing jeans, with her hair held back from her forehead with an embroidered band, Indian fashion. Hermione sighed satisfaction, as she saw Rosamund's reflection in the mirror, hair curling under on her shoulders in shining cape. That was better! Now there was only one new problem remaining—-whether Peter would manage to get here in time for the big night. His flight was booked and Roberts was taking the Rolls to meet him at the airport. Hermione looked up, as the hairdresser returned.

Rosamund was showing signs of nervousness, pacing up and down the lounge, staring out of the window every so often. She had been dressed for the last hour, and was looking extremely lovely, in a sculpted white dress, that fell in soft folds from the hips. The jade tear pendant hung poised at the apex of the V neckline. It was the only trace of colour and echoed her extraordinary jade eyes, now fixed in exasperation on Hermione's face.

'He will come, won't he? You said he would!' Weeks of practice had gone into this first appearance at the Albert Hall. She was aware that Madame Ouvetsky was expecting a superlative per-

formance from her——and other tutors and the rest of the school
to be present for this competition for 'Young Musician of the
Year'. Some competitors were even coming from as far afield as
Russia. But she could only do her best and knew that the Castel
Trophy would open many doors for the successful contestant.

'I'm sure he will arrive in time. We have to leave soon though.
All competitors have to be present one hour before the concert—
-and it's almost seven. Now stop worrying, darling. You are looking charming! Your hair suits you like that.' Hermione smiled
encouragingly at her. She remembered going through similar
scenes with her son, in his early days as young musician. How
long ago all that was now——how strange to be reliving such
times, with the young girl she now loved as a daughter.

'I'm sorry, Hermione. I know I'm being a bore! But it does
mean a lot to me, to have Peter present at such an important concert. But even if he doesn't make it—-well, you will be there——
and that is so important too!' She smiled at Hermione, thinking
how glamorous she looked in her gold lame gown, with her hair
piled high. She never seemed to age—always charming and con-
siderate. She knew how much she owed to Hermione's love and
support over the years. She remembered many occasions when
she had behaved outrageously, trying to shock with boorish
behaviour, always disliking privilege in any form——and how
Hermione had shown amazing patience, dealing with the way-
ward, talented youngster with tenderness and understanding.
Now a close bond existed between these two, which was to draw
even closer. For Rosamund at near seventeen, was feeling the first
stirrings of tender emotion for Hermione's son, the man she had
first resented, then hero worshipped for his stature as musician—
-and now over the last few months, had come to love.

Not that Peter had any idea of the disturbance he had created
in Rosamund's heart. To him, as she well knew, she was still a
child. A talented child perhaps—-one to be shown off to his
friends—to be treated with a rough camaraderie. Only when they

played music together, did she feel that he was close to her in spirit. Did Hermione guess what she felt? She cast a quick look towards her.

'I love him, you know,' she said softly.

'What was that, Rosamund?'

'I said——that I love Peter!' Rosamund looked at her, from earnest green eyes. Hermione nodded her head, face serene.

'Of course you do, darling—and he loves you. We both do.'

'That's not what I meant. I love Peter——want to marry him one day!' There ——it was out! She looked at Hermione apprehensively. The woman smiled and put an arm about Rosamund's shoulders knowing she had to tread carefully. In a few minutes, they had to leave for the Albert Hall. Rosamund was tense and this was normal. As for this sudden declaration of her feelings for Peter, it was probably a surge of girlish emotion at a time when she was fast approaching maturity. So far she had shown no interest in the opposite sex, all her time being devoted exclusively, and with complete dedication to her music. Yet even as she looked at her, Peter's mother realised that Rosamund with her usual directness, was indeed giving voice to firm intent. She really had made up her mind, marry Peter one day!

'Rosamund——you are very young. Peter is close to early middle age——and as you know, has never really got over Natasha's death. I have always hoped that he would marry again one day———and that Garnford would have an heir. But so far, my hopes have been in vain. Who can tell what may happen in a few years—-when you have finished your training. In the meanwhile, dear child, let us take things as they come. There now—-it's seven and we must leave. Where is your wrap?'

Rosamund took one last look up the road, before getting into the Bentley. Robert's son, Bernard, was driving them tonight, while his father collected Sir Peter from the airport. The car purred up Exhibition Road and in minutes they had arrived before the domed building, where Sir Peter had given so many

performances. She had to be worthy of him tonight. She took a
deep breath as she stepped out of the car, treading carefully, so as
not to catch her long dress.

'Competitor, Miss?'

'Yes———-Rosamund Lake from Fritz Klein.'

'Come this way, please.' Rosamund whispered goodbye to
Hermione and followed the official. In the dressing rooms at the
back, the other young musicians were chatting nervously, each
measuring up the competition. Rosamund looked in particular at
a tall young man, with intense dark eyes and thin lips. She
thought she recognised his features from a recent photograph in
the evening paper. Was this was the pianist, Leopold Heine? She
had heard mention, that he was perhaps her most serious rival. As
though he sensed her gaze, the youth turned and looked full at
her———-as he did so, his eyes narrowed.

'Fraulein Lake,' he inquired?

'How did you know my name,' asked Rosamund?

He clicked his heels together. 'Leopold Heine! I have heard
much about you———-and found that all the others had arrived,
except you—so really a process of elimination. They had not told
me that you were beautiful!' He stepped forward and lifted her
hand to his lips in swift salute, and turned away.

Rosamund found herself blushing. She felt a moment's irritation———-then everything else was forgotten, as the organisers began
speaking with the young people. Lots had been drawn to establish the order of appearance. She had been drawn eighth out of
the ten contestants. Leopold was tenth!

She had tuned her instrument—and now slipped forward to
peer from the wings into the fast filling concert hall. Her eyes lifted upwards to Sir Peter's box. Hermione was sitting there, but of
Peter, there was still no sign. She had been noticed and was called
back. For a moment she felt deflated, hurt. Then a well remembered voice was calling her name.

'Rosamund———-Liebchen!' It was Ernst Morgenstern. He had

marched forcefully behind the stage and now stood staring at her in delight. He had never seen her dressed like this before. This was no child standing before him in the white gown, that sweetly outlined her young figure, but a young woman and for the second time that night, Rosamund felt a man's lips caress her hand.

'Uncle Ernst! Oh——this is wonderful! I didn't know you were to be in London this week!' Rosamund's eyes were bright with pleasure, as she smiled at the old pianist.

'Do you think I would have stayed away at such a time!

I had to come to wish you good luck, Liebchen. You will do well——I am confident of it! All right——I am going,' he said testily to an attendant. Then to Rosamund——'I will be in Hermione's box!' She stood staring after him, smiling, the tension broken. A voice behind her made her swing around.

'Wasn't that Maestro Ernst Morgenstern——the famous Austrian pianist,' asked an awed voice? It was Leopold.

'Yes, you are right,' replied Rosamund. She looked at the young man, sensing his excitement. His brown eyes glowed in the smooth oval of his dark skinned face. He turned his head to gaze in the direction in which Ernst had disappeared and she saw his profile, the hooked nose, the high forehead crowned with luxuriant waving black hair, swept back and worn slightly long. It was an arresting face, giving evidence of his Semitic origins.

'You called him——Uncle?' He looked at her curiously. 'Forgive me——but Ernst Morgenstern is Jewish——and you I think, are not?' As he blurted the question out, Rosamund raised her finely arched brows in surprise. She had never given thought to Ernst's race or religion; to her it was of no importance, only the fact that he was her cherished friend, who had brought comfort and hope into her life, during her blackest hours. Even though she didn't see him too often, he was always there in her mind——Uncle Ernst of the wise eyes and great shock of silver hair, whose wonderful fingers swept over the piano, lifting even the most sophisticated audiences to hushed silence.

'He is not a blood relative,' said Rosamund slowly. 'You could say, that we adopted each other. I have visited his house in Vienna many times——and at other times, he comes to stay with my guardians, Peter and Hermione Bagshaw, at their Hampshire home, Garnford.' He looked as though he would have asked further questions, but Rosamund inclined her head and moved slowly away, to speak with another girl, who was nervously fingering a flute.

'Waiting is always a bore, isn't it,' said Rosamund gently. 'What's your name? Mine is Rosamund Lake.' She extended a hand as she spoke. The serious red haired girl with the flute gave a grateful smile. She took the hand.

'I'm Olwen Jones——and I'm from Anglesey——North Wales, you know.'

'Pleased to meet you, Olwen.'

'This is the first time I've been to London. It's just huge, isn't it——and everyone is in such a hurry, pushing and jostling in the streets. But the shops are wonderful.' She gave a small grimace. 'Forgive me for prattling on—but I guess I'm just a little nervous!'

'Don't be,' said Rosamund. 'It will be all right when you start to play. When do you go on?'

'I'm drawn second.'

'Well——that's good. Not so long to have to chew your nails,' laughed Rosamund, and the red haired girl managed a small smile in reply.

'Silence please! The curtain goes up in five minutes. Competitor number one, come forward. Karl Wasserman—— French horn!'

Rosamund listened intently as the beautiful Mozart horn concerto stole on the air, transporting her to a woodland glade. He was good, that Karl! A tremendous round of applause——and then Olwen took his place. Vivaldi——light, fresh——perfection— —ah, perhaps a slight hesitation there? Then the applause again.

As competitor after competitor took their place, before the dark-ened audience, Rosamund found her thoughts returning to Peter. Had he arrived yet?

?Are you ready, Miss Lake? You are next——this way please.'

The Rolls halted before yet another set of traffic lights and Roberts sighed in frustration. He knew how important it was to get to the Albert Hall by eight——and it was already five to, and they still had several miles to go.

'Hurry man——hurry!' Sir Peter leaned forward in the back seat, almost ignoring is companion, whose heady perfume was fill-ing the interior of the car. Roberts glanced at her reflection in his mirror, as he waited for the lights to change. She was beautiful, certainly——wealth of black hair wound high on her head, face subtly painted, eyeshadow echoing the rich turquoise of her silk trouser suit——unusual necklace and earrings of turquoise and lapis in filigree gold setting. His eyes studied her face again. There was no warmth in her blue gaze—and that mouth, although it could smile so winningly at Sir Peter, nevertheless had a slightly sulky cast to it. What would Lady Hermione make of her, he won-dered——then switched his full attention back to the road, as the lights changed.

It was twenty-five minutes past eight, when they finally arrived at the Albert Hall. Peter's face was dark as a storm cloud, as he assisted the beautiful woman he had brought from America, out of the car. Then he hurried her up the steps and into the build-ing——up the stairs—ignoring her protests at this undue haste.

'Peter, honey——simmer down! That little girl of yours will understand that the flight was late——and that man Roberts is a fantastic driver. He couldn't have gotten us here any faster than he did! Wait—I haven't even had time to tidy up! I need to go to the washroom.' She almost panted, as she tried to keep up with him. But her complaints were of no avail and she sighed in exas-peration.

Hermione lifted her head in sheer relief, as Peter appeared in
the box. Ernst too, gave a sigh of delight.

'Peter, darling———oh, I'm so glad! Rosamund is third to last.
She was so anxious that you should be here and I told her that—
—,' Her voice tailed off uncertainly, as the gorgeously clad female
figure stepped into the darkened box—and even by the dim light,
Hermione could see that the woman was extremely lovely. There
was a moment's silence. Then Peter spoke awkwardly.

'Mother—-Ernst, dear friend——may I present Lois Challoner.
We have become good friends, if I may put it so, during these last
three months in the States.'

'Lois,' he turned to his companion, whose musky perfume
wafted towards them. 'Lois———-my mother, Lady Hermione
Bagshaw——and   my   esteemed   friend,   Maestro   Ernst
Morgenstern.' Hermione took the proffered hand in shocked surprise, but immediately rallied and produced a welcoming smile.

'It is always a pleasure to meet my son's friends,' she said evenly.

'Especially when they are as charming as you, dear lady,' managed Ernst with a bow. He turned a quizzical stare on Peter, then
nodded towards the stage.

'See——another competitor is about to commence—a cellist.'

Lois Challoner did not sit immediately. She stared at Peter's
mother, out of cool blue eyes. 'I'm sure glad to meet you, Lady
Hermione,' she said with southern drawl. 'And you know,' she
continued———-'I hope soon to be able to address you less formally——as mother!' Having dropped this bombshell, she gave Ernst
a wide smile, handed her sable wrap to Peter and seated herself
next to Hermione, whose face had whitened in shock. Then all
eyes were fixed on the stage, as the fair-haired Hungarian youth,
bowed and seated himself. He had chosen the Adagio from
Dvorak's Concerto in B minor——and Hermione's confused
feelings were temporarily lost in the artistry of the young musician, who so finely captured the composer's grief for his home-

land. His performance drew animated applause from the audience and she realised how vary talented were all those performing here tonight. Her thoughts went out to Rosamund, who had blurted out her tender feelings towards Peter. How would she react to this disturbing new influence in his life? She felt very uneasy. True, she must not prejudge—-and after all, had she not spent the last few years, trying to persuade Peter to seek a new wife. But why such a one as this?' Perhaps there was a surface resemblance to Natasha, she mused—the hair colouring—build. But where was the delicacy, the breeding? Instead of these, had been disturbing brashness.

Hermione's attention was once more drawn to the stage. A harpist this time, the musician a dumpy girl from Ireland—-but when she started to play, the audience were absolutely still. As the last notes plucked on the strings dripped aching melody in the air, the applause was thunderous. Peter frowned. She was going to have to be very good indeed, with the competition so keen. He had totally forgotten the beautiful woman at his side, in his total absorption in the events on the stage.

It was time. She stood alone on the stage, the spotlight pooling down on her white dress, turning her tawny shoulder length hair, into a darker gold. She stood absolutely still for a minute, then inclined her head to the audience, tucked the violin under her chin and raised her bow. As the music soared in wild cadences, exploring the hidden places of the heart, the man in the box leaned forward holding his breath. She was playing the Brahms, having chosen what must surely be one of the most beautiful passages ever composed——one that was taxing in the extreme—and he felt sudden tears come into his eyes. It was only as the last note hung quivering on the air, that he took in Rosamund's changed appearance——saw her for what she had become, a very lovely young woman.

'Oh, Peter——,' breathed Hermione. 'Wasn't that wonderful!' The audience seemed to agree. They were on their feet. The applause was thunderous for the startlingly beautiful girl, who had played with all the confidence and artistry of a seasoned musician. Her lips parted to a smile, as she looked upwards to Hermione's box, not knowing whether Peter had arrived to hear her—-but that dear old Ernst was definitely there. She inclined her head again, and as the clapping gradually ceased, she walked off still with utmost poise, nor was it until she was behind the curtains, that she took a shuddering breath of relief.

'My homage,' said a guttural voice. Leopold, who had been listening to every note, came forward and stared at her. 'That was very fine,' he said simply. 'One day, Miss Rosamund, you and I will share a concert stage together—-and also a bed. When I have proved myself—-I shall ask you to become my wife.' Rosamund stared at him dumfounded. Neither of them noticed the oboist walk past them, to take his place out front, but as the notes of the oboe, smoothed into the silence between them, he smiled at her expression of outrage. 'The Haydn—quite good——but not good enough for the prize—-which I shall take!'

'You are—impossible,' she said stiffly.

'So I am frequently told. But I meant every word of what I said.' He gave a quick bow and went to stand ready at the side of the stage. The applause alerted him to the fact that his turn had come at last. He flashed a quick smile at Rosamund, nor heard her almost reluctant——'Good luck!'

In Hermione's box. Lois Challoner was having whispered conversation with Peter, before the final contestant commenced. Ernst was watching with keen eyes, as the young man with hooked nose and high forehead, took his place at the piano. He had heard of this boy—-that he had studied in Berlin, but was now living in Israel. He glanced in slight irritation at Lois, who was still attempting to talk to Peter. Leopold's fingers arched over the keyboard, as he threw back his head in dramatic pose. Then—
—-as Chopin's exquisite nocturne flowed from his touch, Ernst let out a slow breath. He was good, this young man——very

good. It would be a close match between this Leopold and his
darling Rosamund.

'You told me she was a child,' hissed Lois, refusing to be quiet.

'So she is,' replied Peter firmly. 'She has not yet had her seventeenth birthday. Now please be quiet Lois. I wish to hear this
boy.' With that, he leaned his face on his hand, watching
Leopold's flying fingers. He is not just playing the music—he is
living it, thought Peter. This one will go far—but he is not quite
as good as Rosamund—but almost—almost. As Leopold's fingers
hung poised over the keyboard for the last time, there was
silence—-then tumultuous applause, as he rose, smoothed down
the tails of his evening coat and bowed. At the back of the stage,
Rosamund knit her brows together—then Leopold was there
beside her, his face triumphant. He at least it seemed, was sure of
the result.

There followed what seemed to be an interminable wait—-
then at last, a name was called————-and it was Rosamund's!
She gave a sigh of relief—then gave a glance of sympathy towards
Leopold, who was standing crestfallen, head bowed. She walked
from the wings, back onto the stage.

'By unanimous decision, the Castel Trophy for Young Musician
of the Year, goes to Rosamund Lake.' The chief adjudicator
smiled encouragingly at Rosamund and continued.

?But it must be said, that pianist Leopold Heine, came a very
close second.' He held out the trophy—a beautifully wrought
hand in bronze—to the girl in the white dress. The audience came
to their feet with roar of approval and it was obvious, that she was
their choice too. It was customary for the winner to play an
encore and the adjudicator held whispered conversation with
Rosamund. He announced into his microphone—-

?Rosamund has asked that her fellow competitor, Leopold
Heine, join her in a duet!' At this, there was a round of applause.
Leopold cast a grateful glance at the girl, as he returned to the
stage.

'What shall we play,' he asked, watching her beneath quizzical brows. Rosamund, whose heart had been touched by his earlier disappointment and was trying in this way to make amends, thought swiftly—-something light-hearted.

'Tales of the Vienna Woods,' announced the official. Leopold seated himself and Rosamund tuned her instrument—-then the lovely Strauss waltz floated round the hall, a lively and spirited finale to the evening. They took a bow together as the lights went up. Rosamund's eyes flew straight to Hermione's box. He was there—-Peter was there! He had heard her after all. A delighted smile curved her lips, which changed slightly, as she became aware of the woman at Peter's side——a beautiful woman with dark hair, in vivid turquoise outfit. Now the other competitors were on the stage with her, Leopold taking position to her immediate right.

'So—Miss Rosamund,' he murmured. 'The first part of my prediction has already come about—that we would share a stage together, and that at your own suggestion. Do I take it that the second half of my prophecy will come about also?' His dark eyes narrowed in amusement, at the annoyance on her face.

'How dare you think that I had that in mind,' she whispered crossly. They took several curtain calls, Rosamund taking the final one alone, holding the Castel Trophy——and then it was over. Madame Ouvetsky, the principal of Fritz Klein embraced her.

'Well done, my child——well done! Is your guardian here?'

'Thank you, Madame——Oh, thank you.' Breathed Rosamund. Praise from Madame Ouvetsky's lips was a rare treasure. 'Both my guardians are here—-Sir Peter as well as lady Hermione——and Uncle Ernst!'

'Uncle Ernst?'

'Maestro Ernst Morgenstern——here they all come. Excuse me, Madame' She looked expectantly towards Peter, who was hurrying towards her, with the strange woman in tow.

'Rosamund—-dear child——that was superb! Madame

Ouvetsky—good evening. What do you think of your pupil?'

'That she has made an excellent beginning to her professional career. Perhaps you could call at the school within the next few days, as there are several points I would like to take up with you, concerning Rosamund's future.'

The Russian woman smiled briefly at Rosamund. It was not often that she had a youngster of such rare genius—-indeed she doubted whether she would ever be so blessed again—but then, even to have had such a pupil once, made all the painstaking work with less gifted pupils, worthwhile. Her eyes sped past Sir Peter and his companion——and to Ernst Morgenstern.

'Ernst——,'she said softly. 'It has been so many years——.'

'Svetlana—-what a pleasure! Are you then that Madame Ouvetsky of whom Rosamund has spoken so often? It is to you that she owes her talent.' Madame Ouvetsky shook her head.

'No. She doesn't owe me her talent, as you will be aware. It is something she has been born with, and that I have had the pleasure in fostering in her. I never guessed that you were involved with Rosamund, as well as Peter. She is a very lucky girl indeed.'

'We must meet again and soon, Svetlana. Where can I contact you?'

'Either at the school——or here is my card, with my home number.' She smiled up into his eyes and Rosamund realised that her Principal was really an attractive woman for her age. She was dressed tonight in black velvet, her silver hair swept high on a Spanish jewelled comb. She wondered how these two had met in the past——-had there been a romance, perhaps?

'Rosamund————-darling! Congratulations————I knew you could do it.' Hermione slipped her arms about the girl, hugging her happily.

'Well——and isn't anyone going to introduce me,' asked Lois? She had been standing silently by, cool blue eyes busily examining Rosamund. She held out a braceleted arm. 'My name is Lois Challoner——I come from Florida, but I have a home in

New York as well. I flew over with Peter today to meet his family——Hermione and—you. Only I understood that you were just a little girl. Seems I was mistaken. I bought you a present—it's in the car——a doll! I guess I will have to find something more appropriate.' She leaned forward, and placed a light kiss on Rosamund's cheek. 'Congratulations on winning your prize. That was surely very well done.'

Rosamund had suffered that kiss with a slight distaste, for instinctively she didn't like this woman.

'I am pleased to meet you, Lois,' she said politely. 'I hope you enjoy your time in England. Where are you staying?'

'I'm booked into the Savoy for the next twenty four hours——after that, I believe Peter is supposed to be driving us all down to his country house——let me see, what's it called——ah, yes——Garnford!' She gave a meaningful smile. 'From all that Peter has told me about it, I am sure I will feel very much at home there!'

Rosamund and Hermione exchanged dismayed glances. There was a sudden silence. Ernst Morgenstern aware of the slightly uneasy atmosphere sought to diffuse the situation.

'Rosamund, liebchen——I would like to meet that young pianist, Leopold Heine. Do you think you could find him for me?'

'But of course,' said Rosamund and hurried in search of him. As soon as she had gone, Ernst took Peter to one side.

'Tell me,' he said gently———'Is it true——you and this American woman?'

'I may be going to marry her,' said Peter expressionlessly.

'You say that as though it were an unpleasant draught of medicine you were contemplating taking!' Ernst considered his friend thoughtfully. 'Obviously this isn't the place to talk. All I will say is though——be careful of young Rosamund in all this. Tonight is her big night. Let her enjoy it, before you make any dramatic announcements. Is it agreed?'

'Do you think I want to hurt the child?' Peter's eyes were moody as he drew his heavy brows together in displeasure. 'Next to my mother, she is the most important person in my life!'

'Peter—-lieber freund——I am at the Dorchester. Come to my apartment tonight, so that we can talk——I think you need to. Ah——here is our young pianist!'

'Leopold Heine, Maestro. It is a great honour to met you, sir!' Leopold clicked hid heels together and bowed low, his intense gaze fixed almost reverently on this man whose playing was legend. All his life, he had dreamed of meeting the great man—-and now it had been made possible by the lovely girl, to whom he had given his heart this evening—-for although Leopold had spoken light-heartedly to Rosamund, he had meant every word that he said. One day, he would aspire to marry her. That they came from vastly different backgrounds and were of different faiths worried him not in the slightest.

'Young man——I enjoyed your playing tonight. They tell me you that you have come from Israel?'

'Yes, Maestro. I have lived there for the last year. I needed to go there, to find my racial roots I think—-to discover my real self. I have been living in Jerusalem.' He stood looking uncertainly at Ernst. Did the old musician understand what he was trying to say? He did.

'And have you found yourself in the Holy City,' he asked gently. The boy shook his head.

'No——I realise now, that I will only find this through my music. On the other hand, my travels through Israel have been spiritually rewarding. What I have experienced there, will always remain in my heart to sustain me.' He was speaking seriously now Rosamund realised, all the brashness gone. He was a much deeper person, than she had at first imagined.

'Well, Leopold——I have a suggestion to make to you. How would you like to return to Vienna with me, as my pupil? No——-don't answer too quickly. I can be a hard taskmaster, for I require nothing less than perfection of those who are able to give it!' Old man and young looked at each other——and a bond formed between these two who had been strangers.

'Maestro,' whispered Leopold humbly————'I am honoured to accept—and I promise you, that you will never regret this kindness.'

'Good——good. That is settled then. I return to Vienna in a week. You may as well move into the Dorchester with me tomorrow—-there is a spare room in my apartment. Be there at eleven tomorrow morning. Goodnight to you, my boy.' He watched as the young man bowed and turned away—but before he was swallowed up in the crowds, Ernst saw Leopold look at Rosamund. There was no mistaking that look. 'So,' breathed Ernst softly. 'The little Rosamund has an admirer.' His eyes sped to Rosamund's face. She had not noticed Leopold's yearning glance, for her own eyes were only for Peter—and suddenly Ernst felt very troubled. Rosamund was looking at Peter, not as a girl does a father, but rather as a woman looks at the man she loves. Lois saw that look as well, and her blue eyes narrowed.

'Well, I'm sure you will excuse me, lady Hermione, If I borrow Peter to take me to my hotel. I'm shattered after the fight and I'm looking forward to a shower and an early night.' Hermione breathed a sigh of relief, that she was going to be relieved of Lois company at least for the night, but watched with a knot of anxiety forming in her breast, as Lois brazenly took Peter's arm and pulled it round her shoulders.

'Peter, honey————I want to get to that hotel—the Savoy it's called? Let's go——I want to shower and relax!' She pouted seductively, but Peter merely detached her arm and smiled awkwardly at his mother and Rosamund.

'I will settle Lois in her hotel—-and drive back to your flat mother. Later, I have promised to go to the Dorchester, to speak with Ernst.' He nodded and shepherded Lois quickly away.

Hermione smiled at Ernst. At least she thought, if Peter was going round to the Dorchester, then he would not be spending the night with Lois.

'I think it is wonderful, the way you have taken that young pianist under your wing. I thought his playing was quite brilliant. Now I take it that you will be coming to Garnford, Ernst?' She looked at him pleadingly. She was going to need all the support she could muster. He nodded and she continued. 'Bring Leopold along too.'

'Hermione——I look forward to coming, but before I do so, I would first like to contact Madame Ouvetsky. Do you know, I never realised the principal of Rosamund's academy, was an old friend of mine! We were very close once, but she married another——we lost touch———and that is life I suppose.'

'Why, but it's quite amazing that you know Madame Ouvetsky. Look Ernst, the academy is closed now for Easter. Why don't you invite her to come to Garnford too? You would like that, wouldn't you, Rosamund?' She turned with a sweet smile to the girl, including her in her plans.

'Yes. It would be great to have Madame come——I'm not so sure about that boy though.'

'Why ever not?' Hermione looked perplexed.

'Well———it's only that he said that he wants to marry me!' But Rosamund was laughing as she told them this. Obviously she hadn't taken Leopold seriously, nor indeed could he have been serious, thought Hermione, for they had only met briefly tonight—
—but again, perhaps this young man would have to be watched!

'I expect there will be many other young men, who will want to do that,' said Hermione gently. 'I will see that this one behaves himself——and so will Ernst. Now look Rosamund, that young girl with red hair is waving to you. Isn't she one who played the flute?'

'Yes———it's Olwen. Excuse me!' Rosamund hurried off to see her new friend, giving Hermione the opportunity to speak briefly with Ernst.

'Oh Ernst—I'm so worried! That woman is quite wrong for Peter—I know she is———and there is something else. Rosamund is growing up. She confided to me this evening, just before the concert, that she is in love with Peter and wants to marry him! If only she were older and perhaps Peter a little younger, there is nothing I would like better. But she will only be seventeen in May—and now—-this woman! I don't know what to do!'

'Dear Hermione———-do not worry! I will be speaking to Peter tonight. He does not love Lois. Of that I am sure. As for the little Rosamund, she is growing up fast—-on the brink of lovely young womanhood. We must be very careful that she doesn't get hurt—-the emotions are very strong in a first attachment and if Peter goes ahead with marriage to the American, then tremendous hurt could come to Rosamund. We must do all in our power to prevent this. But see—-she is coming back!' He stepped away from Hermione.

'I must say goodnight to you, liebchen—-until tomorrow.' He gave her a smile that was very tender. 'You did very well——a wonderful evening. Always remember that whatever happens to us in life, we musicians always have the comfort and the strength of our music.'

As the old man walked away, Rosamund looked after him with serious eyes. She fingered the jade tear pendant. Oh Peter, she thought——is this jade tear of a centuries dead princess, symbol of what is going to happen in my life? Then with a quick shiver, she bent to pick up her violin.

'Shall we go, Hermione.'

CHAPTER FIVE

The pageboy deposited Lois bags in the suite and she exclaimed in satisfaction at the luxuriance of her surroundings. Yes—-this would do very nicely. Peter tipped the youth and closed the door after him.

'Well Lois——I have a very busy evening in front of me, so I am sure you will understand if I leave you. You have only to ring and the hotel will see that you are provided with everything that you need.'

'But surely you are going to take dinner with me?'

'I'd like to Lois—-but it is not possible tonight. I have business to attend to.' His tone was firm and she pouted. Then her expression cleared and she gave him a warm smile.

'That's OK, Peter, but let's sit down for a moment. We'll just have a quick drink together before you go. Now that's all right, isn't it?' She smiled again. 'You ring room service and order the drinks brought up—-and I won't be a moment.'

He sighed and walked over to the phone. When he put the receiver down, he heard the sound of water in the bathroom next door. It was too bad. Why couldn't she wait to take a shower until after he was gone————-and then he gasped! For Lois had come through the door, black hair cloaking her shoulders, a soft pink towel about her middle—-which she let slip. He looked at her—-and then lowered his gaze.

'Well, darling————!' She lifted her arms and stretched like a sinewy cat. 'I just thought that we might enjoy ourselves before you rush off to all your business affairs!'

Lois had a spectacular figure, although it was noticeable that she had lost quite a few pounds recently. She was thirty, admitted to twenty-six, but could easily have passed for a year or two less than that. She had spent the last ten years enjoying life, sharing her charms with any man rich enough to offer the style of living that she considered necessary. But the time had now come, when she had decided she wanted to marry and settle down——and for that, she wanted a mate who could give her a certain position in life as well as presenting a challenge.

Sir Peter Bagshaw, famous composer and musician filled her programme exactly. The fact that he didn't share her enthusiasm for a future together didn't worry her over much. As things were, he would marry her for one very good reason——but at the same time, it was galling that he did not respond to her charms. She walked towards him now, arms outstretched.

'That's the waiter, bringing the wine. You had better put a gown on'. He opened one of her bags, luckily choosing the one with her robe. He tossed it to her.

'I will tell the waiter to bring the wine in——and you can tell him, if there is anything else you want. Goodnight, Lois.'

As he shut the door firmly behind him, he heard a scream and the sound of something being thrown at the door.

'I think Madame dropped something,' he said to the waiter, who grinned as Peter strode off along the corridor. Peter's thoughts were confused as he got into the Rolls.

'Where to, sir? To Lady Hermione?'

'No Roberts——not yet. I think I will go straight to the Dorchester to speak with Ernst. Do you want to take yourself off home and let me drive myself?'

'Wouldn't dream of it sir. You must be very tired after your flight and that long concert tour. You relax.' Roberts always took a fatherly attitude with Peter and he was touched by the chauffeur's solicitude. He had been in Hermione's employ, since Peter was a small boy, many years ago. 'Wonderful news, sir——that Miss Rosamund took the prize tonight! I'm so glad that I got you there in time——I would never have forgiven myself, if you had missed her performance.'

'It wasn't your fault my flight was so late. You drove very well, to get to the Albert Hall when you did.' He looked out of the window. They were proceeding along Park Lane, passing the Hilton. Trees glittered, festooned with light bulbs in the dark night and a few people were afoot along the street. Ah—here it was—-the Dorchester, with its fountain outside.

'Have you eaten tonight, Roberts?'

'Not yet, sir.'

'Well——lock the car and I'll arrange something for you inside. I'll probably be a couple of hours.' Roberts smiled gratefully, for he was indeed hungry.

Ernst welcomed him with a warm embrace. 'So—-I'm surprised you managed to tear yourself away so quickly, from the beautiful Lois. I have ordered a light supper, a cold collation, as I was not sure at what time you would arrive. Wait and I will ring.' He continued to make casual conversation, as they waited for the supper to be served. The waiter knocked. Peter smiled as he saw what the man had brought. There was leberwurst, a selection of salami, sauerkraut, gerkins and olives—-brown bread, and a cheese board. The waiter deftly poured two foaming tankards of German beer, bowed and retired..

'Ernst—-you are incorrigible! You could have any delicacy you wished here at the Dorchester——so what do you order? Salami! Ernst old friend—-you are wonderful!' Peter let out the first real laugh that had passed his lips in months.

They set to in companionable silence at first, enjoying the simple fare. At last, their appetites assuaged, they sat back in their chairs sipping a second tankard of beer and looking at each other. Ernst noticed that there were new lines of strain around his friend's eyes, a slightly haunted look.

'So—-do you want to tell me about it? Explain perhaps, why you are going to marry a woman you do not love!' Ernst ran a hand through his shock of silver hair in obvious perplexity. 'Come on then——-tell me, in your own words!'

Peer stroked the rim of his tankard and sighed. It would be a relief to be able to unburden himself—-even though he knew Ernst would say that he was all kinds of a fool.

'It was the usual hectic tour,' he began. 'From every point of view, it was going very well——except that I was getting progressively more and more tired. You know the feeling. You just don't want to walk onto that stage, because you are exhausted—-but you do—-you go on—-and then the adrenaline takes over, the music holds you in its spell—-you and the music become one, there is the feeling of exultation, as the audience joins with you—applauding the final climax! Then you go home—-to the hotel—-or a friend's house—and you flop out in a chair or on the bed. Added to this, there is the round of inevitable parties, as fashionable hostesses present you to their friends, almost like a trophy! You know how it is, Ernst, for you have been doing it for far more years than I have——and I realise now, with far greater strength and vitality.'

'Yes, my friend—-I understand all of this. The problem is that you have been pushing yourself too hard—taking on one tour after another. The body is after all a machine—-the most wonderful and complex machine its almighty Maker could devise—-and like all machines, it needs rest and attention from time to time. But continue.' Ernst sat forward, listening.

'At one of those interminable parties, I was feeling very tired. It was being held in her Florida villa, by Lois Challoner. She had invited other musicians there and the composer, Andrei. There was a lot of champagne flowing. It was a hot night—-and I was thirsty——I drank too much. All I can tell you, my friend, is that I remember nothing more of that night, until I came to the following morning in a double bed——with a naked Lois next to me. I had a blinding headache! I literally could not remember getting into that bed and certainly, I could not remember making love to the beautiful woman, who was smiling so seductively next to me on the pillow.' Peter swallowed miserably. 'She invited me to make love to her again—-and I replied, that I did not remember having done so before. That I must have taken too much wine and asked her pardon.'

Ernst chuckled at this. The woman would not have felt very flattered by such reaction, he thought. Then his face became serious.

'You really had no recollection at all of getting into that bed— or of embracing the woman?'

'No! I promise you——I had no slightest memory of it. She is lovely, admittedly, but not the sort of woman who appeals to me——-apart from which, I have not slept with a woman since Natasha's death——-have no wish to.'

'So what happened next? Did the woman suggest marriage, because you had compromised her?' Peter nodded sombrely.

'Yes—-she did——and I refused. A couple of months passed. Lois started to follow me wherever I went——Washington—— New York! She was at every concert, every function that I attended, always charming, always telling me how much she loved me. Then one night, she came to my hotel room. She was distraught. She told me she was pregnant and I was the father of her future child. I told her this was impossible——-but she said that I was definitely the man responsible, as she had not had a serious affair, for two years.'

'But you only have her word for that?'

'Yes. But there again——I have always wanted a child. But I suspected a trap, that she might not even be pregnant—so I asked her to get a doctor's confirmation of her condition. Well, she brought me a specialist's statement the next day, to the effect that she was three months pregnant. She said it was up to me, whether my child should be born legitimate or otherwise————-and how would it look in the national newspapers, if Sir Peter Bagshaw refused to marry the mother of his child!'

'But that was blackmail!' Ernst was truly horrified.

'You could say that Ernst—or perhaps a desperate mother, trying to get a decent life for her baby. I mean——-I just don't know.

If only I could remember what happened that night in Florida! But I can only repeat, that I have no memory of fathering that child. So, what do I do, Ernst?'

'Have you promised to marry her?'

'No. When she knew that I was about to leave the States, she came to me again and threatened to go immediately to the New York Times with the story, unless I brought her over to this country, to meet my mother. I couldn't stop to argue——I had to be back for Rosamund's big night. Maybe I should have called her bluff——but if she had gone through with it, can you imagine what would happen to my career. Worse, can you think what the shock would do to my mother and young Rosamund?' Peter put his face in his hands and gave a short groan. Ernst shook his head in dismay.

'Peter. You are like a son to me——and I advise you now like a father. You must not marry this woman, whatever her threats, not feeling the way you do about her——only disaster could follow such a match. Now—let us take one point at a time. If she is truly pregnant, then there is I suppose, the remote possibility that you might be responsible. Truthfully, I think this most unlikely, as for a man in the state of exhaustion you have described, a few drinks too many would just produce heavy sleep——not the sudden sexual urge which Lois attributes to you. When her baby is born, you merely have to ask for the child to have a blood test, to establish whether you could possibly be the father. You may find that even this demand may discourage her, for if another is the father, she obviously won't want you to know this—and will refuse the test.'

'I had not even thought of such a thing,' said Peter, lifting his head hopefully.

'I also have a question for you, Peter. Can you remember the names of any of the musicians present at the party? You mentioned the composer, Andrei?'

'Why yes——-then there were Lucullus and Rosenbaum——and Chris Wade.'

'So! Chris Wade, the American cellist? This is quite amazing. It may interest you to know that he is in this hotel at the present moment. I met him earlier and even took note of his room number. He is playing at the Elizabeth Hall in two day's time. Have you any objections to my phoning him to come to this apartment?'

'Of course not! But what possible good can that do?'

'I'm not sure yet——just an intuition that he may be able to help. Excuse me!' Ernst rose and walked over to the phone.

'You will——-a thousand thanks! I will see you in a few minutes then!' He turned triumphantly to Peter. 'He is on his way to see me. Now my friend, I want you to go into my bedroom, so that I can speak with this young man alone.'

Peter nodded and dutifully disappeared. He could hear the rise and fall of the voices on the other side of the door, without being able to distinguish the actual words. At last, there was a rap at the door. He opened it, to see Ernst smiling broadly.

'Come here, Peter. Chris Wade has something he wishes to tell you.' He gestured towards a young man with short cropped, blond hair and a wide grin.

'Why——Hallo, Chris,' said Peter awkwardly, not knowing exactly what Ernst had been saying. The young man smiled and held out his hand.

'Sir—-it is an honour to meet you again. The maestro has been telling me, that you have had a few problems following Lois Challoner's party in Florida, where we last met. It may help you to know, that you passed out towards the end of that party, sir. Andrei and I could see that you were terribly tired, even when you first arrived, Lois was pushing champagne at you. I saw her put one last glass into your hand——and well——you just collapsed in your chair. Andrei Weiss and I were at your side at once and asked Lois where there was a spare room to let you rest—-and in fact, one of the other guests, an elderly doctor followed us through to the bedroom Lois indicated, and checked you over.

He was afraid you might have had some sort of seizure. When he was sure it was nothing serious, he told us to leave you to sleep. As for Lois——well to be honest——she was casting some languishing glances in my direction and I am only human! We spent the night together. She left my room at about eight in the morning.'

'You slept with Lois that night,' said Peter incredulously. 'That is the truth?'

'It sure is——if you want any proof, the lady has as I remember, a mole just below her left breast.' He gave Peter a quizzical look. 'Lois was after that Spanish painter—Martinez, last year,' he said inconsequentially. 'Well, I hope I have been of some help to you, sir?' Peter looked at his open young face and swallowed. He did not know how to express his relief.

'If ever I can help you, Chris Wade,' he said, holding out his hand.

'Sir——I'll bear it in mind,' said Chris cheerfully. 'Goodnight to you both!'

?Ernst! There are no adequate words to thank you,' blurted out Peter, as the door closed behind the American. 'But the whole situation is so incredible! Why should Lois have lied to me in such a way? She must have realised that the truth might come out one day!' He shook his head. He could hardly believe that the nightmare was over.

'She was probably gambling on the fact, that as man of honour, you would take her word for what apparently happened—-that by the time the truth was known, you would be married. My friend—-you have had a very lucky escape, from a very shrewd and calculating woman.' He put an arm about Peter's shoulders.

'Peter—-you look terrible. Let me ring Hermione and tell her that you will take the other bedroom in this suite and stay here tonight. I will also let your man know. As it is late, Roberts can have a couch in this room, if you like?' And so it was arranged. Ernst rang Hermione and told her that Peter would stay at the

Dorchester and see her in the morning. If he thought that Hermione sounded a trifle strange, he put it down to a bad line. When he went to bid Peter goodnight, the younger man was already asleep.

Hermione drew a sigh of relief, as she saw Lois step into the Rolls, as a sombre faced Peter slammed the door on the other side. Ernst too had disappeared. The greater part of the audience had also dispersed, only friends and relatives of the young performers still lingering. Bernard drove the Bentley forward as he saw them. He helped Hermione in, then as her guardian was seating herself, Rosamund heard her name being called.

'Rosamund——Rosamund! Over here.' The girl looked around her, puzzled. The voice was strangely familiar—it sounded like—but that couldn't be! A figure detached itself from the side of the building and beckoned her. The girl gave a startled cry, as she realised who this was. Sylvia's once attractive face was thin, the hands she held towards her daughter, emaciated. With a cry, Rosamund ran towards her mother and would have embraced her—but Sylvia shook her head.

'No, Rosamund,' she whispered. 'Don't let anyone know you have seen me. Here—take these flowers. I bought them for you. Oh, my darling—you were wonderful tonight. My heart is too full to tell you how very proud I am of you. I saw your name in the paper—that you would be competing here tonight and couldn't resist the urge to come.'

'Oh, mother—mother,' cried Rosamund brokenly, taking the small nosegay of violets. 'Where have you been? Why did you leave me?' Then as she looked properly at her mother's face, saw it was that of a very sick person. Again she made to embrace her mother—but Sylvia merely pressed a piece of paper into Rosamund's hand.

'This is my address. But I want your promise, that you will never let Sir Peter or Lady Hermione know that I have contacted

you again. Now go——before you are missed!' And before
Rosamund could stop her, she disappeared into the shadows.
Rosamund considered running after her, but knew she would be
hampered by her long dress and the violin she carried, yet only the
knowledge that she held her mother's address in her hand, made
her turn away and step up to the Bentley.

'Who were you talking to, Rosamund?' Hermione looked curiously at the girl at her side, for she sensed the tension in her
ward—but put it down to the effect Lois had produced on them
both.

'A woman gave me these flowers,' said Rosamund softly.

'Violets! Who was she?'

'Someone who liked my playing.' Rosamund pushed her nose
into the damp sweetness of the flowers, her mind fraught with
worry. Her mother had looked ill. It was not just that she was five
years older, the once beautiful features were sunken, lines of pain
about the mouth, that had curved to a smile.

Once inside their home in Hans Crescent, she made murmured
excuse to Hermione, saying she wished to change and went
straight to her bedroom. She unrolled the piece of paper she had
screwed up in her hand, as she placed the violets on the dressing
table. The address was in Paddington——Shirland Road. She
determined to go there, as soon as she could. She dropped the
small piece of paper in the bin by the side of the dressing table and
went into the bathroom to fill a small shell shaped vase with water
for the violets—and arranged them with utmost tenderness. All
the resentment towards her mother that had grown over the
years, for the way in which she had deserted her, now disappeared
as she placed the violets on her bedside table. Only then, did she
strip off the white gown, toss it onto a chair and get into jeans and
sweater. That was better.

Hermione had also changed into something less formal than
her gold lame and was wearing an embroidered caftan. Her face
looked very tired, Rosamund thought. She reached out a hand in

sympathy.

'She was awful, wasn't she, Hermione!'

'Yes——-quite unsuitable. What a shame you took your white dress off. I would like Peter to have seen you in it.'

'He did,' said Rosamund shortly. 'But I hardly think he noticed my appearance——but then, after all, he did manage to arrive for my big night and I know I should be grateful for that. But what did you mean by saying she was unsuitable,' questioned Rosamund and Hermione bit her lip. Of course, the girl had been unaware of Lois bald statement that she intended soon to be able to call Hermione mother.

'As a houseguest, I mean. She is not right for Garnford.'

'And certainly not right for Peter,' exclaimed Rosamund. 'I'm not blind, Hermione——-that woman's after him, isn't she!'

'Yes,' replied Hermione. She bowed her head, then said—— 'But Rosamund darling, whatever we may think of Lois, if she is Peter's choice—-well!' Her voice trailed off sadly. 'Let's talk of you though Rosamund. Tonight has opened an exciting future for you. It is possible you may get offers from many well-known orchestras. Madame Ouvetsky wishes to speak with Peter about this. I do hope she agrees to come down to Garnford with us. I was planning on driving there tomorrow—but I wonder whether I should postpone it for another twenty- four hours. We'll discuss it when Peter arrives. Hopefully he should be here soon.' As she said this, they heard the doorbell ring. 'That will be Peter now,' she exclaimed. 'He must have lost his key!' They heard the maid Marie, talking with someone.'

'My lady——there is a Miss Lois Challoner to see you,' said the girl and Lois heavy perfume suddenly suffused the room, as she stalked in. She was wearing a tight, leopard skin patterned, trouser suit, whilst a scarf of matching material, was twined in her dark hair. Bracelets and gold chains jingled as she moved towards them with studied grace, greatly resembling the jungle cat whose covering she emulated.

'Lady Hermione,' she purred, opening her hands in expressive gesture, 'I ask your understanding, for calling at such a late hour, when both you and little Rosamund must be feeling so tired after the concert——-but I have been longing to meet you properly, so that we could talk!'

'Yes——well, it is indeed late,' said Hermione————'And surely I heard you tell my son that you were very fatigued after your flight and wanted an early night! Where is Peter?'

'Oh——he had some business to attend to——-but you know how he is!' As she spoke, her eyes were on Rosamund. She had noticed the way in which the girl's attention had been focussed on Peter, when they met, and had realised intuitively that Rosamund's affection for him, was perhaps of a different nature to that of ward and guardian. She would have to watch this attractive girl, who shared a touch of that same genius on the violin that was Peter's in such abundance.

'Well, may I offer you coffee——-or a sherry?'

'Not alcohol I think,' drawled Lois. 'It might be bad for the baby! Oh well, perhaps, just a very small vodka?' She had dropped her bombshell with an air of complete innocence. Hermione reached for the back of one of the armchairs for support, face white with shock.

'What did you say,' she asked unsteadily?

'Oh————I'm sorry! It just slipped out. Peter had really wanted to give you the news himself——-that you are to be a grandmother.' She raised her shoulders in contrition. 'We plan on an early marriage. He once mentioned that you had always dreamed of becoming a grandmother——-so no wonder you are surprised that your dream is soon to come true! I hope that we may become very good friends, Hermione.' She walked forward and planted a light kiss on Hermione's partly averted cheek.

'It's not true! It can't be. Peter wouldn't behave like that.' Rosamund's eyes sparkled, outrage stamped on every inch of her face. 'You're lying!'

'You think so? Ask Peter then. Obviously that expensive academy of yours has neglected to teach you manners, even though they may have helped you to express some smattering of musical talent.' Lois words were chosen to sting and they did. She turned a cool smile on Hermione. 'I'm sorry, Hermione, but the child has to learn.'

With an exclamation of disgust, Rosamund turned on her heel and walked to the door. She swung about. 'Excuse me please, Hermione. Perhaps you would explain to this——lady, that loose moral standards are most definitely not taught at my academy—-hence my surprise at coming in contact with them from a mature woman from whom I might have expected better!' She closed the door behind her, after nodding her head in defiance at Lois.

There was a moment's silence. Then Lois chuckled.

'Ouch! Fiery little thing isn't she. I certainly didn't want to get off to a bad start with her—-or with you. I had thought that I might possibly have waited here, until Peter arrives, so that we could all have had a cosy little chat together. But perhaps that might be better postponed until we go to Garnford tomorrow. I must say, that I am longing to see Peter's mansion—my future home.' Hermione was going to retort with the truth, that Garnford was hers and would only devolve to Peter upon her death, but she merely turned a bland smile on the woman, whose advent into their lives was causing such distress.

'Peter may be extremely late,' she said, 'and I am certainly very tired—-so you will excuse me, Miss Challoner, I have no doubt we will see each other again soon.' She walked gracefully over to the door and called for Marie.

'This lady is just leaving, Marie. Will you please see her to the door!'

She waited until she heard the door bang and then dropped into a chair, with a cry of relief.

What an awful woman! How could Peter, who was so discriminating, have selected such a person to replace Natasha? True you should never make comparisons between people—each person is unique. But having acknowledged that—-why someone of this sort; someone who obviously would take an abrasive attitude towards Rosamund? Hermione smiled slightly, as she remembered her ward's spirited retort. She sat long, turning the matter over in her mind, then sighing, rose to her feet. She must go to Rosamund. The child must be feeling terribly upset. Not knowing quite how to deal with this new crisis in their lives, she resolved to show as much understanding and tenderness as possible, whilst trying to lighten the event that marred what should have been one of the happiest moments in Rosamund's life.

The telephone rang and she paused—and picked it up. It was Ernst.

'Hermione, dear friend——-Peter is over tired and so I am insisting that he sleeps here tonight. He has much to discuss with you tomorrow.'

'Thank you for telling me Ernst. And yes—-I am sure he has indeed, much to discuss tomorrow. Please wish him goodnight from me.' She replaced the receiver.

She tapped gently at Rosamund's door.

'Rosamund. May I come in dear?' There was no answer. She knocked again and again received no response. She hesitated. Should she go in? Perhaps Rosamund had gone to bed and fallen asleep in exhaustion after the excitement of the evening. She sighed, and went to bed.

Back in her hotel, Lois paced restlessly up and down on the plush carpet. The phone rang and she rushed to pick it up. Surely this must be Peter.

'Miss Challoner? This is Ernst Morgenstern. We met earlier tonight, at the concert.' Of course, she thought, this was the elderly Austrian pianist.

'Why, hallo there. This is very friendly of you to call, Ernst. Peter has spoken of you as his best friend and I am charmed to speak with you again.'

'You may not be quite so charmed, when you have heard what I am going to say to you, dear lady. Peter has put me completely in the picture regarding your relationship——in every degree—— you understand? I must admit that I have met some unscrupulous people in my life, but no-one to equal you. Well, what I have to say is this. I have spoken with the man with whom you really spent the night at your villa.'

'I don't know what you can mean. I do not want to pursue this conversation.'

'Nor I assure you, do I. But I would strongly urge you to return to the States. To remain, would obviously be embarrassing for you, as Peter is now aware of the deception you employed to ensnare him into marriage.' She slammed down the phone, her eyes bright with anger. So that was that! Or was it? She pulled the smallest of her suitcases towards her, her fingers impatiently fumbled the concealed in the lid and she withdrew a brown envelope. She opened this and smiled at its contents. Then she reached for the phone.

'I wish to speak to your editor please. It is a matter regarding Sir Peter Bagshaw——yes——that's right, the musician. This is his fiancée speaking.'

'Oh——-hallo? I would like you to send one of your feature writers round to the Savoy, to speak with me——and I have a very special photograph which I am sure you will agree, will look just great on your front page!'

She replaced the receiver and sat down to wait.

Morning dawned and Peter stretched and looked around him blankly. Of course, he had spent the night in Ernst's apartment. He went to the bathroom and ran a bath. When he returned to the bedroom, it was to find a grey suit laid out on the bed for him. Ernst stood there smiling.

'Your man Roberts——he's very thoughtful. He remembered you were wearing your evening clothes when you arrived, so he took your bag from the boot and brought these clothes up for you, after the hotel had them pressed.'

'Wonderful. Give me a few minutes to dress——then I have to get round to Lois hotel, to have a word with her about the changed situation.'

'You may find that she has already left!'

'What do you mean, Ernst?' He listened as Ernst told him of the phone call he had made last night.

'Why——what can I say——except that you are a marvellous friend! I think we will just drive round and see my mother and Rosamund then.'

As the Rolls drew up outside his Hans Crescent home, and he stepped out of the car, he was suddenly besieged with reporters. He was well used to a warm welcome by the press and smiled.

'Good morning, Sir Peter,' called a tall, sharp eyed blonde.

?Congratulations on your engagement sir! Can you let us know when the wedding will be? Will it be here——or in the States?' A barrage of questions followed from other reporters. Peter's face whitened in shock. He looked at the reporters in bewilderment.

'I am not engaged. You are mistaken,' he said stiffly.

'Oh, come on sir——what about this then?' One of the reporters pushed a newspaper in front of him. It was one of the more lurid tabloids he realised. On the front cover, was a picture of Peter in bed, with a ravishing shot of a naked Lois bending over him. The caption——'Famous musician, Sir Peter Bagshaw in whirlwind romance with beautiful American socialite Lois Challoner.' He felt a sick feeling at the pit of his stomach.

'May I have that,' he asked and took the paper. 'Please excuse me,' he continued and ran lightly up the steps of the mansion flats, with Ernst hurrying behind him. There was a groan of protest from the waiting reporters who set themselves to wait for him to come out again.

Hermione had seen the Rolls arrive and was at the door to greet him. Her eyes were swollen from weeping and Peter stared at her in dismay.

'Mother! What's wrong? Is it that you have seen this rag?' He indicated the paper he was holding. Hermione shook her head.

'I haven't seen a paper this morning. Oh, Peter——its Rosamund. She's gone. I went into her room this morning. The bed had not been slept in——and there was a note on the dressing table.' She held the piece out to him, He scanned it in alarm—then handed it silently to Ernst.

'Dear Hermione—I know Peter has every right to marry any-one he chooses. But that Lois is just too awful. I know I would explode every time I saw her——and that just wouldn't be fair to Peter or to you. I hope the grandchild will be a boy, for I know this will make Peter happy. But I cannot think that she will give him any lasting happiness. Do not worry about me. I have some money on me, my violin and a few clothes and I will be quite all right. I will get in touch with you fairly soon. Hermione, I just want to say thank you for all the care and love you lavished on me—and give my love to Peter and Uncle Ernst. I shall miss you all, but what I am doing is for the best————Love—-Rosamund.

Peter had dropped the newspaper, when he had taken Rosamund's note. She bent to pick it up, as Ernst now read the note——and her eyes caught the caption——and she saw the photo-graph. She gasped and looked at her son in dismay. How had this compromising photograph come to be in the paper——how indeed had such an intimate photograph come to be taken in the first place?

Peter saw her looking at the photograph and his expression became grim.

'Mother—-you can ignore that photograph. There is not time to explain this now, but Lois is a very determined woman. Things are not as they seem—and I can only tell you, that I will definite-ly not be marrying that woman. If she is indeed pregnant, then the child is not mine. You will just have to take my statement on trust, when I tell you that there was never opportunity for this to have taken place.' Hermione looked into Peter's eyes and read the truth there.

'I believe you, Peter,' she said quietly.

'Have you any idea where Rosamund may have gone? I will never forgive myself if anything has happened to her.' He swallowed. Hermione shook her head.

'Perhaps she may have gone to stay with the family of one of her fellow students.'

'True. That may be a possibility. Have you looked in her room for any clues?' He made for Rosamund's bedroom, his mind turbulent with worry, all thoughts of Lois devastating behaviour put by. He looked at the charming room, with so many little touches that betrayed the girl's personality—glanced at the bedside table with its splash of colour—the deep purple of the violets. He walked over to the flowers—-and then stared at a framed photograph of himself. The silver frame was in the shape of a heart. The fragrance of the violets rose sweetly to his nostrils.

'Who gave her these flowers, mother?'

'I don't know. An unknown admirer after the concert—a woman I think.'

'I should have given her flowers myself,' he said chastened.

'Yes—-you should. What are you doing?'

'Looking in this bin——there's a bit of crumpled paper here.' He picked it up. And smoothed it—-303, Shirland Road, Paddington. Could it be that this was where she had gone? Hermione looked over his shoulder, as did Ernst.

'Who lives at this address? Do you know?'

She shook her head, puzzled. Then a thought struck her.

'Marie empties that bin every morning. So Rosamund must have dropped it there after coming home from the concert, which might mean that it has some connection with someone she met there——or——I just wonder, whether it is possible that the person who gave her the violets, might also have given her this address?' Peter brightened. That made sense! Then his eyes

returned to the newspaper in his mother's hand. How could he
go to Rosamund if she had seen this wretched article! He groaned
and reached for the paper. The thought came to him——how had
Lois managed to have that photograph taken? Surely any reason-
ing individual would realise that no sane person allows a photog-
rapher into the privacy of the bedroom. It brought home to him
the duplicity of the beautiful woman who had so degraded him,
her innocent victim, as nothing else had. What redress did he have
in law? How could he prove his unwilling participation in that
photograph?

'Ernst——I have to have Lois make public acknowledgement
that what this revolting snap shows is a fraud deliberately perpe-
trated to force me into an unwanted marriage.'

Ernst looked at him in sympathy. He took the paper and studied the photograph. It was noticeable that Peter's eyes were
closed in sleep, whilst Lois was flamboyantly awake and glancing
towards the camera.

'Peter, lieber freund——-Chris Wade mentioned that a doctor
examined you, when you were put to bed that night——as it was
thought that you might have had some sort of seizure. We must
find out the name of this doctor and see if he can be persuaded to
give testimony of the state in which you were put to bed. This
plus Chris Wade's evidence, that he spent the night with Lois, will
I think be sufficient to make Lois retract her statement to the
press. She can make another, perhaps acknowledging that she had
the photograph taken for——-fun shall we say——-admitting that
she allowed a practical joke to go too far!' His eyes gleamed with
enthusiasm for this idea. 'May I use your telephone Hermione?'
She nodded and he immediately phoned the Dorchester.

'I wish to speak with one of your guests——Mr Christopher
Wade. This is Ernst Morgenstern.' A short conversation ensued.
Then Ernst placed an international call, which proved to be a
lengthy one. When he replaced the receiver, his face was triumphant.

'Why did you want the number of my fax machine,' inquired Peter, face bent curiously upon him. For answer, Ernst merely told him to be patient. Some fifteen minutes later, the fax machine in Peter's bedroom began to produce evidence that was to set him free of his unwelcome relationship with Lois. Ernst gave a sigh of satisfaction and pocketed the paper. He asked that Roberts should drive him to the Savoy. He waved to the waiting crowd of reporters as he went.

Lois was dressed in, a clinging, scarlet jersey, trouser suit, set off by her usual dramatic gold jewellery, dramatising her lovely body. Her long eyelashes flirted in amusement, as she received the elderly musician. She knew that she had won her battle and Lois was inclined to be gracious to a defeated adversary.

'Good morning, Maestro,' she said in her slightly mocking tones. 'Have you come with a message from Peter? I guess he must be feeling a little riled today, but as a sensible man, he has no doubt decided to accept the situation!'

Read this,' said Ernst sternly. He offered her the faxed message. She took it negligently in her hand—-but as she read it, her face paled under the makeup. The eyes she turned on him were dark with fury.

'How did you come by this?'

'A matter of simple deduction at first. Chris Wade mentioned that a doctor had examined Peter when he became unconscious and had to be put to bed. I managed to contact that doctor, as you can see. What I could never have hoped for, was that after examining Peter and finding him in a condition that baffled him, the doctor picked up Peter's last glass of champagne—-which you had poured, Madame——and seeing traces of powder in the dregs, took it away with him for analysis. Perhaps the fact that Doctor Lewis had worked for many years for the police in forensic medicine had given him an abnormally suspicious mind. His findings—-that a sleeping draught had been mixed in Sir Peter's champagne, caused him some puzzlement. But by all accounts,

Peter had suffered no ill effects and so he shelved the incident, merely making note of it in his diary——-and thought no more about it, until I contacted him this morning. You have his report in your hands. No! Don't tear it up. To do so, would be useless, for you see, he sent a duplicate. Ah, Madame——-Madame! Such language!' Ernst put his hands to his ears, his eyes shining in merriment.

'OK——-you win! But do not think that Peter Bagshaw has heard the last of me,' she raged! Ernst thought he had never seen any human being show such fury.

'Of course, you realise that Peter could have you brought to court for your actions. He does not wish to do so——but he does absolutely insist, that you contact the newspaper that bears your photograph and explain how it came to be taken——and that it was merely a joke, that you allowed to go too far!'

'And if I refuse?'

?This faxed document will be published, plus a statement from Chris Wade to the effect that he spent the night in your arms. I feel that this might place you in a rather foolish light.'

'I'll ring the paper——but later, when I have thought how to phrase things.' Her face puckered with worry. How could she retrieve the situation with any dignity?

'You will ring the paper now. I will obtain the number for you.' Ernst reached firmly for the phone—and asked hotel reception to get the number.

'Your editor please.' He waited. 'Ah, yes——good morning, sir. This is Maestro Ernst Morgenstern. A dear friend of mine featured in a story on your font page. The story was false. Yes—— that's right. I refer to Sir Peter Bagshaw. The lady in question went into Sir Peter's bedroom in the morning, before he wakened and had a friend take that compromising photograph, merely as a joke. Why? My dear sir——I do not pretend to understand the female mind. But Lois Challoner is by my side and wishes to speak with you. Now, Sir Peter does not wish to sue your paper, for he has always a most cordial relationship with the press——but he does insist that you print a story refuting the conclusion that all your readers will have come to. Yes——I know the lady will be embarrassed——but perhaps she should have thought of that, before trying to make a fool of one of your countries most prominent musicians! He handed the telephone to Lois.

'Yes——I'm sorry. I'll say whatever you want me to. You're sending a journalist round. Is that necessary? Oh——I see. You want to hear it from my own lips. OK. But make it snappy—— I'm taking the next flight to New York!' She slammed down the phone.

'Satisfied,' she asked Ernst?

'I will be——when I have heard you repeat this to the journalist.' He studied the beautiful angry face objectively. 'Why did you tell Peter that you were pregnant,' he probed?

'Because I am. I thought he would be happy——even if the child were not his. After all, he would never have known.' She gave a sudden vicious smile. 'You know——people will talk. When the baby is born, there may be those who will gossip and wonder about the paternity of the child.'

'But, dear lady, a simple blood test would prove that Sir Peter was in no way involved,' said Ernst gently. He felt slightly uneasy, as she drew herself up like a leopard about to spring and for the first time, Ernst began to realise that the woman before him, was not normal. His heart began to beat faster as he confronted her. Then there was a discrete tap at the door. The anger seemed to die down in her eyes, as she opened it to admit the reporter. Ten minutes later, Ernst left the Savoy at the reporter's side.

'What a woman,' sighed the journalist. 'If I were Sir Peter, I would be flattered to have one as glamorous as that after me! But he has obviously been completely innocent of any involvement with her. What a strange affair! I promise you sir, her denial of the romance will appear on the front page. I have her signed statement, that it was just a joke!'

Ernst smiled approvingly at the young man. 'I am sure I can leave it in your capable hands to clear Sir Peter's name, from this woman's machinations.' As he sat back in the car, Ernst shoulders slumped. He felt very tired. Not for the first time in his life, Ernst had come into contact with someone he had known was completely evil. He was grateful he would never have to see her again. No premonition of those tragic events that lay ahead disturbed the old musician's thoughts.

CHAPTER SIX

The taxi drew up outside the terraced house in Shirland road. Rosamund paid off the driver and picked up her suitcase and violin. On the other side of the road, two drunks shouted at her and made an obscene gesture. She walked briskly up the steps and glanced at the small panel bearing the names of those who lived at this address. A cat yowled and shot past her, as someone opened the door, with its peeling paint.

'Oh—-good evening. I am looking for 303A.' She stared at the middle-aged woman with a cigarette hanging from the corner of her mouth, who had just sent her cat out for the night.

'Downstairs maisonette, dearie. Entrance in the basement— Mrs Lake.' The woman jerked her head towards dark steps that led downwards. The drunks were crossing the road now and Rosamund's heart beat faster as she hurried down the steps the woman had indicated. She rang the bell and waited apprehensively. Would the door never open? The men were at the top of the steps now, shouting down at her and Rosamund felt very frightened. But she held her head serenely erect. At last the door was cautiously opened and the girl saw that it was on a chain.

'Mother?'

'Rosamund——-child! Oh, wait.' The chain was undone and the door opened. Sylvia saw the two men leering down at Rosamund and hastily pulled her inside and shot the bolt and locked the door. 'What are you doing here? I asked you never to let Sir Peter or Lady Hermione know that I had been in contact with you.' Sylvia began to cough——a desperate, rasping sound that seemed to tear her chest apart. Rosamund dropped her belongings and set her arms about the sick woman.

'Oh—-mother——mother! You are ill!' He young face was taut with worry. 'I thought you looked unwell, when I saw you outside the Albert Hall. Have you a doctor I can call?'

Sylvia shook her head, the spasm was passing and she indicated that her daughter should follow her along the narrow passage. She opened a door that led into a bed sitting room. It was lit by a central light in a fringed yellow lamp shade that threw a cheerful light upon a couch with faded chintz covers and a brown armchair. Along one wall, there was a single bed, covered by a biscuit gold candlewick bedspread. A small battered oak table bore the remains of Sylvia's supper. A gas fire spluttered in the hearth.

Several attractive country scenes in cheap frames adorned the walls. Sylvia watched as her daughter walked over to one of the pictures and stared at it wonderingly. It was Holly cottage, where they had lived in happier years.

'It's the cottage,' cried Rosamund.

'Yes, dear——I painted it! Over the last years, I have developed a talent I had at school. I manage to make enough money to get by on.' She smiled at Rosamund's obvious surprise. 'But come, let me show you this little home of mine,' she said.

Rosamund followed her, first inspecting the narrow kitchen with its bright red enamelled saucepans and bundles of herbs—— then was shown the bathroom, with its long, old fashioned bath with claw feet, then on along the passage way into a small room.

Sylvia switched the light on and Rosamund gasped. The walls were hung with canvases——and more were stacked on the floor. An easel was set next to French windows that seemed to lead out into a little courtyard.

She stared, for on that easel was the portrait of a man with strangely compelling eyes. Rosamund walked over to it, drawn by the look of love and compassion in the man's eyes——dark eyes that seemed to shimmer with golden light. His hair and beard were dark chestnut, the lips bore a tender smile. One hand was outstretched in welcome—the centre of its palm bore a dark stain.

'Oh, mother——-it's—-the Christ!' She turned wondering eyes on Sylvia.

'Yes. As I see Him,' said Sylvia softly. 'I still have some work to do and will never be able to express all that I want to——but at least, it is my best work.' She smiled at Rosamund. 'Come child, let's go back to the sitting room. We have to find you somewhere to sleep.' She switched off the lights in her studio and beckoned to the girl to follow her. She opened a cupboard and pulled out sheets and blankets and proceeded to make up a bed on the couch. 'It's the best I can do, dear. There are another two rooms upstairs, but they are unfurnished, as I've had no use for them. Can you manage on the couch?'

'Why——its marvellous,' smiled Rosamund. 'But I want to talk some more, before I sleep.'

'Well first, let me get you something to drink. Will cocoa do?' She walked out into the kitchen and was soon back with two steaming mugs and a tin of biscuits. 'Rosamund——I haven't touched alcohol since I left Holly cottage. I joined AA when I came to London. It was hard at first——very hard. I missed you terribly, but I knew I had taken the right decision and that the Bagshaws would give you a good home and help you with your wonderful gift of music. Many times I almost weakened and was on the point of contacting you——but I knew it would be very selfish to disturb you, once you had settled to a new life. Perhaps I shouldn't have let you see me tonight——only the temptation was so great.

Darling——I was so proud when I saw you on the stage—listened to you playing so wonderfully. When I saw you receive your award——heard the clapping——well, my heart was just so full!'

'I am just so thankful that you did speak to me.' Rosamund's eyes were wet with tears. All the bitterness towards her mother that had crept into her heart over the long years evaporated now, in the joy of her presence. Only a nagging fear, that her mother was quite ill, dented the perfect happiness of the reunion. One question remained.

'That man——did you ever see him again?'

'Who? Oh——you mean Bert Hampton. No. I never saw him again. There will never be another man in my life now, Rosamund.' Her eyes travelled to a framed photograph of Tristam, on the mantle piece. Rosamund followed her mother's stare as she too looked at the handsome face of her dead father.

'Do I look like him at all,' she wondered?

'You have his eyes——the same extraordinary green colour. Then your look of concentration at times——-he had that. As for the rest of your face, I think perhaps you favour your late grandmother, Melissa.'

'I didn't know that you knew her, mother.' Rosamund looked at Sylvia curiously.

'I met your father's parents only once,' said Sylvia slowly. 'Dryman Lake was a very handsome man, with a head of thick silver hair, worn slightly long and a silver moustache. He was a very well known actor then——- and I believe, still takes parts in films today. I can remember his slightly haughty stare, when your father introduced me to him——-and to Melissa.

Tristam had been up at Cambridge, and taken a degree in art. Then there had been a camping holiday in Hampshire with some college friends. We met and well, we fell in love——and married all within a few weeks! It was such a wonderful, deliriously happy time. What more natural than that Tristam should have wanted to take his wife back to the States, to meet his parents!' Sylvia's head drooped on her breast for a moment, as she remembered that traumatic meeting.

'What happened mother? Didn't they like you——or what?' Rosamund came and sat on the arm of her mother's chair and took her hand.

'They were very polite at first—although distant. They were obviously very annoyed that Tristam had married without first telling them. I had the feeling that Melissa would have liked a grand wedding.' She stopped again.

'Go on——go on.'

'They asked about my parents—-my background. Rosamund, I had to admit that I had grown up in a Children's home. My mother had abandoned me at birth, so it seems. I have no idea who she was—-or my father!'

'Oh, mother! Why on earth didn't you tell me all this before!' Rosamund looked at her mother with eyes brimming with sympathy—-and a dawning understanding of what it must have been like, for a young girl growing up in an orphanage, not knowing who she was—-having no-one to love her.'Melissa asked me to wait in another room. They wanted to talk privately with Tristam. It was wrong I suppose, but I listened at the door. I heard them telling my husband to get a divorce——I was totally unsuitable. They would make a settlement on me, so that I would be—comfortable—-yes that was the word!' Sylvia bit her lip.

'What did father say?'

'He said—-that he loved me—and that I was all that mattered to him in the whole world. They asked him to make a choice, If her didn't divorce me, they would disinherit him. They were very wealthy you know, and had been supporting him through University.'

'How could they behave like that! It was cruel. Why——they didn't even know you. I thought that in America, it was what you were like as a person that counted!' Rosamund's eyes were bright with exasperation.

'Well, your father suddenly came bursting through the door, into the room where I was waiting. He seized me by the hand. He said we were flying right back to England. Further studies at the university were now out of the question. We rented a terraced house and both got jobs—-your father as a general assistant in a small museum—-whilst I found myself work as a typist. Then after just one year, you were born dear. I had to give up my job and Tristam was earning very little at the museum, although he liked the work. We struggled on for three years—-and then the rent of the house was put up to such an extent, that we couldn't cope.

Someone mentioned a job on a big estate—with a tied cottage.'

'Garnford?'

'Yes! Tristam was quite frank and told the estate manager that he had no previous experience of farm work, but was willing to learn. They liked each other—-and your father was employed! I remember how happy we both were when we moved into Holly cottage. There was never much money, yet we were very happy! When you were about four, we saw a headline in the paper. Melissa Lake had died. There was a photograph of a large group of musicians at the graveside and the caption—-"The music world honours Melissa Lake, famous violinist."

Tristam was full of grief. He rang his father, asking if he could come to see him. I was standing by the telephone—and could hear that overbearing voice. Dryman Lake said——'Do not call yourself my son——I have no son!'

'He said that?'

'Yes. I often wondered whether it was grief at his wife's death that made him behave so. Your father said to him——'So you have no son! Well, perhaps you might just like to know that you have a little grand daughter. Her name is Rosamund——and it is your loss, that you do not know her.' He put down the phone and never spoke of his father again. The rest you know. You started to show an interest in music—-a recorder first, at school. Then your father bought you your first small violin, when you were six. That was how it all started. I only wish your father could have lived to have heard you play tonight dear. He would have been so proud.' She gave a tremulous smile.

'Mother——it must have been so terrible for you, when father died! I can understand so much better now. You had no family——could not even go to his! Then we had to leave the cottage and you had to go to work in the pub. It must have been absolutely shattering for you.'

'Yes——it was. But you see, when Sir Peter arranged for us to return to Holly cottage—in a way it was even worse. Because it was the same home—-but there was no Tristam. And every time I looked at you—at those green eyes, so like his own—well, my heart almost broke all over again. I suppose I will never be able to forgive myself, for becoming involved with Bert Hampton. Grief can make people behave I strange ways, Rosamund. You seek to fill a gap—hurt yourself, even degrade yourself, because nothing seems to really matter any more. I was so full of self-pity that I didn't stop to think what reaction my behaviour was having on you. All my feelings were blunted by grief—-and by alcohol. When Bert Hampton broke up our home that night—-and Sir Peter arrived, threw him out and took you to the big house, I just sat there. Then a woman came, a Mrs Duff. Sir Peter had sent her to help me clear up the mess. When she saw the empty beer cans—wine bottles—-dirty plates and the whole horrid mess that the cottage was in, a kind of black despair came over me. What had I done to Tristam's home—-to your home! I had sullied it. I wrote a letter and gave it to Mrs Duff. I told her to give it to Sir Peter the next day. Then I packed my clothes—and your father's photograph—-and hitched a lift to London.'

'Have you been here ever since?'

'In this flat——no, only for the last two years. I tried several jobs to begin with—-typing, selling. I started to put a little money by. In the evenings, I attended Art College and to my amazement, was commended by my tutor. I started to sell my paintings. At last I was making enough money to live on my painting alone. It was difficult to find a studio—-London is so expensive. But two years ago, I found this place. I know the area is a little rough, but it has character. The little courtyard is lovely—-there is a fountain and a rock pool and a small gazebo!'

Suddenly she started to cough again and Rosamund could see the pain it caused her. She ran to the kitchen for some water. When she got back, Sylvia was standing and clutching onto the back of a chair. She forced a smile when she saw the girl.

'Drink this. Mother——you are ill, aren't you. I mean—-really ill?' She stared apprehensively at Sylvia, longing for her to deny it, but she nodded.

'Yes. I could lie to you. But I won't. The doctors have given me six months. That was why I wanted to see you again.' Two tears ran down her sallow cheeks, but the smile on her lips was one of courage. Rosamund gave a choking cry, pulling her mother into her strong young arms.

'No! No! I won't believe it. I will get you the best specialists——Hermione will know what to do!' Her eyes were distraught.

'No——it would do no good. I have cancer. They thought it was just one lung effected at first——but it seems it was both. No, don't weep child, because I'm not. I have my painting——my lovely little courtyard—and now, the sheer joy of seeing you again. Now darling——I'm very tired, and I'm sure you must be. So why don't we both go to bed and talk more in the morning.'

She tucked Rosamund up on the couch, with a look of tenderness in her eyes, as she took joy in the presence of the daughter she had feared she would never see more. Now they were together again, the hurts of the past had been washed away, a new deeper understanding between them, than she would ever have thought possible. She switched off the light and slept content.

Rosamund wakened, to the sound of her mother singing. She rubbed her eyes and sat upright on the couch, eyes adjusting to her new surroundings. There was the delicious smell of freshly brewed coffee.

'How do you like your coffee, Rosamund,' asked Sylvia with a smile?

'White please——and one sugar.'

'There you are then. You enjoy that——and then perhaps you would like a bath. I'll run the water. I can't open the curtains in this room until you are dressed——people have a bad habit of peering down into basement windows as they pass!'

Later, dressed in jeans and an Aztec sweater in gorgeous colours, Rosamund entered her mother's studio for the second time. Today the sun streamed in through the French windows, the light pooling on the painting on the easel. Rosamund was again drawn to it——those eyes! How had her mother captured that extraordinary expression, a questioning look, full of tenderness—and more—almost an examination of the soul of the one who stood wonderingly before the portrait.

'What are you going to do with this—when you have finished,' asked Rosamund. Sylvia came to stand beside her.

'It is going to hang in a church. The pastor is a dear friend of mine. He and his young wife Sue, saw me through the dark days, when my cancer was first diagnosed. His name is Michael Howard and he is coming here today, so you will be able to meet him.' A sudden fit of coughing caught her unawares. Rosamund rushed off to get her a glass of water. When she returned, Sylvia seemed already to have recovered, but she took the glass and set it to her lips. She opened the French windows and invited Rosamund outside.

'Why——but this is really lovely, mother! It's so small, but so perfect. I wouldn't have believed that a little courtyard could be so enchanting!' She looked in surprise at the rockery, bright with the gold, white and purple flowers of spring, the cascade of water trickling into a little pool, in which a fountain played. The rest of the courtyard was tiled and set with flowering shrubs in stone pots and at the far end, a gazebo's metal frame swarmed with vines and roses, providing leafy privacy to the bench set within.

'It's really a little too early in the year, to sit out here,' said Sylvia. 'But I should have the lovely months of summer to look forward to. I have put a lot of work into it—and I only hope that the next person to live here—after I——that is, when I no longer need it, will care for this garden I have put so much love into. Come into the Gazebo for a moment. I want to talk to you.' She patted the worn velvet cushions she had placed on the stone seat and indicated that Rosamund should join her.

'Now my dear. What happened yesterday? I know that you

would have come to see me fairly soon anyway, after I had given you this address. But when you arrived late last night, you were deeply upset—-I could sense it, but thought I would let you tell me about it in your own good time, after a good night's sleep.'

'Mother—-there is so much I have to tell you of the last few years. I was enrolled at the Fritz Klein Academy by Peter and Hermione, where I first had to audition and was fortunate enough to satisfy Madame Ouvetsky's exacting criteria. A whole exciting world opened up around me. A world of hard, unrelenting work—-scales and arpeggios at first—-practising until my fingers hurt—but oh the joy, as I acquired perfect mastery of my instrument. Music filled my whole life. True there were wonderful holidays in Austria with Uncle Ernst. He is the famous Austrian pianist and has adopted me as a sort of niece.

We would return to Garnford during Christmas, Easter and the summer, when Peter would return for brief periods from his never ending concert tours abroad.'

?He was there last night, at the competition, wasn't he. I saw him in his box.'

'Then—-did you see the woman sitting next to him?'

'Yes I did, when the lights went up——a glamorous looking creature with black hair. Who was she?' '

'Her name is Lois Challoner——and she is going to marry Peter. She—she's having his baby!' There, she had said it! Put into words, the pain that had niggled as she had fallen asleep last night, pain that had returned to pierce consciousness with throbbing hurt this morning.

'Are you telling me that sir Peter had been having an affair? I cannot believe it!' Sylvia shook her head in troubled surprise. 'Not that there is any reason why he should not remarry. His first wife has been dead for many years now and I suppose he needs love, as we all do.'

'But I love him!'

'What did you say, Rosamund?'

'I said that I love him. I know I am still young—–I'll be seventeen next month——but I'm old enough to know that I love
Peter, with a love that will never change.' Rosamund's eyes glittered through tears as she said this. Sylvia shook her head, bewildered. She still looked on Rosamund as a child. But of course she
wasn't—or at least, had now entered that period between girl-
hood and womanhood, that was fraught with emotional perils. Of
the fact that Rosamund meant every word she said, Sylvia had no
doubt—–but her daughter was so young and had no experience of
the world.

'That's why I will not be going back to Hermione. I couldn't
bear to be around, when Lois marries him. She doesn't like me
anyway! I'm afraid I was rather blunt with her last night!' The
words came tumbling out then, as she related all that had so
recently happened—even mentioning the advances of the young
pianist, Leopold Heine and that Ernst Morgenstern was taking
him back to Austria with him. Sylvia restrained a smile, as
Rosamund told her exactly what Leopold had said—–and that he
was accompanying Ernst together with Hermione and Peter,
down to Garnford for few days.

'He sounds a very forceful young man,' she said mildly. 'But as
for your feelings towards Peter Bagshaw——darling, it is quite
possible that this is a mixture of hero worship and natural affection for a man who has taken your father's place in your life. If he
married this Lois Challoner, although it will hurt for a while and
you may resent her, eventually it will open the door to a relationship with someone else——perhaps someone nearer to your own
age!' She turned wise eyes on her daughter.

'Mother—–when you met father, had you ever been in love with
anyone else?'

'Why, no.'

'Did you have any doubts when you found that you loved him,
that he was the right person for you?' Rosamund's straight gaze
precluded prevarication. Sylvia smiled. She knew what was com-

ing next.

'Then please accept that in the same way, I know that Peter will be the only man in my life——-and as Lois is having his baby, there is nothing I can do!'

Tears of frustration sparkled in her eyes. She jumped up from the seat. Sylvia rose too.

'Rosamund, I do not know what to say to you at this time——except to counsel patience. If you really do care for Peter, you will not want to distress him by disappearing and causing anxiety both to him and to Lady Hermione, whom you have told me, has been so very kind to you. Just think what she must be feeling like this morning——her son involved with someone brash and unsuitable—and you, whom she looks on as a daughter, disappearing instead of giving her the support at this time when she so badly needs it!'

'I hadn't thought of it that way!'

'Well—do! Now I must just go round to the corner shop for milk and bread for our breakfast.' She moved towards the French windows and as she did so, a violent fit of coughing, caused her to hold onto the doorframe. She recovered, but her face showed the pain it had caused her.

'I'll go to the shop for you,' said Rosamund. How could she have forgotten her mother's health, in selfish absorption with her own problems. 'Which way is it?'

'Turn right at the crossroads. It's a little general store—they open early.' Rosamund found the shop easily enough and paid for her purchases. As she was waiting for her change, her eyes fell on the daily papers laid out on the counter——then she gasped at what she saw. She picked up the tabloid bearing the picture of Lois and Peter, face frozen with shock. She took her change, paid for the paper and walked back to her mother's flat.

'Look at this,' she said and handed the paper to Sylvia. Her mother studied the picture and the caption——then read the short report, based it would seem on details supplied by Lois Challoner.

Her eyes returned to the picture, baffled. Something was wrong—that she instinctively knew. Peter Bagshaw, cool and fastidious, would never knowingly, have allowed himself to be photographed in such a compromising situation. In some way, which she could not yet fathom, Lois had contrived this situation. She looked at Rosamund's blank face, saw the shock in those green eyes—the hurt.

'Rosamund——I know what I see—-but I do not believe what I see,' she said quietly. But Rosamund wasn't listening.

'How could he,' she whispered. 'The whole world will be laughing at him now, after seeing that photograph. As for that Lois—-I hate her!'

'You mustn't hate, darling. If as I feel, she had engineered this whole affair, then it will ultimately only rebound on her own head!' She went into the kitchen and returned with two mugs of coffee and handed one to Rosamund, and stared at the girl. 'Rosamund—-do you really believe that the Peter you know, would have deliberately have put himself into such a flagrantly compromising situation with any woman?'

'It certainly is against all his normal forms of behaviour. But perhaps when people are in love, standards alter,' replied Rosamund. Then she shook her head. 'But you know mother, even then I cannot believe that Peter would have allowed himself to have been photographed in such—-well—-in bed with that woman!' She forced herself to study the photograph, her eyes narrowing in concentration. 'Look—-Peter is asleep!' Her thoughts were interrupted by the sound of the doorbell ringing.

'That must be the Pastor,' said Sylvia. 'He certainly is early!' Rosamund hardly noticed as her mother went down the passage to answer the front door. She was still trying to fathom an answer to the puzzle. She heard voices. She recognised Peter's voice. Before she could turn to flee, Sylvia had opened the sitting room door and Peter stood in front of her. He glanced at the paper she held in her hands and walking towards her, took it firmly away and ripped it up.

'Rosamund——that wretched article deserves to be flung in the rubbish bin. What you have seen and read there, is totally untrue!' She saw the anguish in his eyes. 'When I found out that you had gone away, I was worried out of my mind! My mother has been crying her eyes out and Ernst is distraught.' He made to take her hand, but she snatched it away.

?If Hermione has been crying, perhaps it is because of Lois—- and that article! But what you do, is of course your own affair——and I realise that. But I don't want to be involved in a situation where I have to be in contact with Lois Challoner—you know of course, that she told Hermione last night, that she is having your baby!'

'If Lois is having a child, then I swear to you, that I am not the father! Mrs Lake,' he turned to Sylvia, who had followed him into the sitting room. 'I can tell both you and Rosamund, that Lois is a scheming woman, who for her own devious purposes, drugged me whilst I was a guest at her house—-and then when I was sleep- ing, deliberately had the photograph taken. Ernst has made sever- al telephone calls to the States. The whole situation is too compli- cated to tell you in one sentence——but glance over this fax mes- sage if you will. I think you will find that it bears out all I have said.'

'I told you that I didn't believe it,' breathed Sylvia, as she looked over her daughter's shoulder, at the thin paper. Rosamund shook her head in amazement.

'But why? Why did she drug you—-and try to make you marry her? What would have been the purpose, if she knew you didn't love her? It doesn't make any sense!'

Peter lowered his eyes I thought. 'She is a beautiful woman and some might say very desirable. I can only imagine that she thought I might eventually return her feelings. I do remember her asking me in front of friends, if I had any children—and that I replied that my wife had died childless and that my mother would

have loved an heir for Garnford. Perhaps her designs on me, originated from that time——I cannot say.'

'Has she seen this fax,' asked Sylvia?

'Yes. Ernst took it round to her hotel. She is flying back to the
States today, so you will not have to see her again ever. Oh yes——
——and she has made a retraction of this article, which will appear
in the paper tomorrow and I imagine in most of the other papers.
It may have made me look a little foolish, but her more so.' He
smiled wryly.

'Oh, Peter——I'm so glad you are not going to marry her,'
breathed Rosamund and would have said more, but Sylvia hastily
intervened.

'Breakfast! That is what we all need. You will join us, Sir Peter?'

'Thank you, that would be very kind. I certainly haven't eaten
so far this morning—and please, just drop the sir. My name is
Peter.'

They had eaten now and Rosamund led him to her mother's
studio, whilst Sylvia was clearing up. He looked around him
amazed, as he saw the pictures lining the walls, stacked on the
floor—one propped on a chair. And then he saw it—the picture
on the easel, and as he walked towards it, he drew in his breath.

'She painted—this——your mother? It is unbelievable.' For
minutes, Peter just stood in front of the portrait, completely
enthralled. 'This is the most beautiful painting I have ever seen,'
he said sincerely, 'And I have visited all the great galleries in the
world and seen many wonderful private collections. Why did you
never tell me, that your mother is an incomparable artist? I am
beyond words!' He didn't even turn towards Rosamund, but continued to stare at the painting.

'She says that it is her finest work——and oh, Peter——that it
may well be her last!' Her voice broke on a sob.

'Why, what can you mean?' Now he did turn to her, fixing his
slate grey eyes on her pale young face.

'Rosamund means that I have an inoperable cancer,' said a quiet voice. There was no self pity of Sylvia's worn face, only a calm acceptance. 'The doctors have given me a few months—-perhaps until the end of the summer, if I am lucky. I may paint another few canvases, but this one will speak for all the other paintings I will never do.'

'Mrs Lake——Sylvia. I am so sorry. Why, oh why, didn't you contact me when you first became ill? Even now, there are some wonderful surgeons in the world. I promise I will get the best advice for you—the best treatment money can buy!' His face was warm with sympathy and she was touched by his obvious deep concern.

'Peter, you are kind, but you know, there is nothing to be done. It was because of the short time I have left, that I weakened and decided to contact Rosamund. I had already half intended doing so—-and when I heard her play last night, saw her looking so beautiful in her white dress, I just couldn't restrain the impulse! I will never be able to thank you and Hermione, for what you have done for my daughter. God bless you, Peter Bagshaw.'

'May I come in,' asked a deep voice and startled they looked round. 'You left the front door open, Sylvia, so I let myself in. Shall I go? I didn't realise you would have company.' Pastor Michael Howard smiled at Peter—then his glance lingered questioningly on Rosamund. 'Forgive me——but aren't you Rosamund—Sylvia's daughter?' She nodded and he turned back to Peter——'And you surely are Sir Peter Bagshaw?' He held out his hand in warmly spontaneous gesture. Peter grasped it. 'My name is Michel Howard,' continued the pastor, shaking Rosamund's hand in turn. Then he looked interrogatively at Sylvia. 'So you did decide to contact Rosamund!'

'Yes, Michael—-and oh, I'm so happy!'

Peter looked at Sylvia curiously. She was dying of cancer, her wonderful talent to be cut short in the height of its flowering— and yet, there was no regret, no sadness. Indeed, her sallow cheeks were tinged with slightest touch of pink, her eyes shining.

Surely even the joy of being reunited with Rosamund again, could not be responsible for the obvious spirit of happiness that seemed to flow from her, to suffuse her very being. In his first urgent desire to rectify the misunderstanding with Rosamund, he had given scant attention to the woman who stood next to him. He remembered their last meeting, when sullen and ashamed of her liaison with Bert Hampton, her face bearing traces of the man's violence, she had lowered her eyes before him in distress. This was a completely different person—vibrant, with a strange inner glow, that showed in her eyes and even more so, in the incredible painting on that easel.

'Sylvia,' said Peter gently. 'Forgive me for saying this——but you seem so different. Its as though you have found your real self—-been reborn!'

'That is because she has been,' said the pastor with a smile. 'She has found God, Peter Bagshaw.' Then he turned to Sylvia. 'May I see it now,' he asked?

'I suppose so. Yes.'

'It is two months since you let me look at it and it was wonderful then.' He walked over to the easel—-then drew in his breath in awed delight. 'Why——Sylvia————-how did you manage to paint those eyes—that expression. It is as I myself have always imagined the Holy One to have looked. Our little, church will be rich indeed to house such a gift. Whenever we look at this, we will remember the love that went into painting it.' He took one of her thin hands in his and patted it gently.

'You intend this for a church,' asked Peter? 'Surely it should rather be shown in one of the major galleries. I have contacts and know I could arrange this for you, Sylvia.' He looked at her expectantly. To hide this painting in some obscure church would surely be a sin. But Sylvia merely shook her head.

'This was painted especially for Horeb,' she said. 'Perhaps one day, I will explain why.'

'Will it be ready for Easter,' asked Michael hopefully?

'I really wanted to do a little more to it——the background. The actual figure is finished—-and then and should be allowed to dry for a period of time and it has to be varnished.' She looked at it critically. Perhaps the slightly misty background should not be touched. It seemed in fact, to throw the figure out in more dramatic relief, than the dappled shadowing she had envisaged. 'You shall have it for Whitsun, and that is a promise,' she said finally. She smiled, as she noticed Peter's rueful expression. 'I'm sorry,' she said. 'I know you meant well, Peter. Have you seen some of the other paintings.' She said this to distract him and he started to examine them with rapt attention, working from one side of the studio, to the other. When he had finished, he looked at her, puzzled.

'Sylvia——here is something I do not understand. The paintings on this side of the room are—well, good—-but not exceptional. Then on the other side of the room, there are these others, which almost seem to be painted by another hand.' He stared at her interrogatively. 'What happened to change you from a reasonably talented painter, into someone who produces such wonderful work?' Rosamund also looked at her mother, because she also had been examining the paintings with Peter and noticed the same thing. It was Pastor Howard who replied.

'Sylvia gave her life to Jesus——became as the saying is—'Born Again'. Following this, it was discovered that she had cancer—yet as she herself will tell you, a wonderful joy was born in her, which graces all her paintings. It was as though this gift had been especially given to her.'

For a moment, there was complete silence, for Michael Howard was describing something beyond the musician's ken, but about which he felt dawning curiosity. But he also knew this was not the right time to discuss the subject, when Hermione was waiting so anxiously at home, to find out whether Rosamund was safe.

'Pastor Howard—-I would like to meet with you again one day. There is much more I would like to know. Alas, I now have to return to Knightsbridge and from there, to Garnford. Would you perhaps like to join my family there for a few days?'

'I thank you for the invitation, but I shall also be much engaged in the approach to Easter——but I am sure we are going to meet again, Sir Peter. But I must go, as my wife Sue will be waiting for me——we have some hospital visits to make.' He shook hands with Peter and gave Rosamund a warm smile. 'If you ever need me—this is my address.' He handed her a little leaflet, giving details of Horeb and the name and address of its pastor. Then he was gone.

'Did you like him,' asked Sylvia, addressing them both?

'Yes——he is an interesting man,' said Peter. 'I really would like to see him again. Now Sylvia——I want you to do me a very great favour. Would you please consent to come to Garnford with Rosamund for a few days? We will be a small party——my mother, Ernst and his new pupil, Leopold——Rosamund's tutor, Natasha Ouvetsky and ourselves. Will you come?' At first she was going to refuse and he saw it in her eyes.

'The painting has to be finished. I promised Michael to complete it as soon as possible.'

'How long will it take?'

'Well——it really only needs a few more touches. I suppose I could be ready by tomorrow. It will in any case need to dry before varnishing.'

'Then it is settled. I will drive the others down to Garnford today and return for you tomorrow. What about you, Rosamund, will you come with me now, or wait until tomorrow with your mother?'

'Tomorrow, Peter. I have only just found my mother again. I want to be with her. But please give Hermione my love.' Then with a quick impulse, she moved swiftly to his side, and raising her arms, pulled his face downwards and placed a quick kiss on her lips. 'I'm so glad you are not going to marry that woman, Peter Bagshaw, because you see, you are going to marry me one day!' Then blushing scarlet, she broke away and ran of into the bathroom. 'Go now,' she cried and wonderingly, he did.

CHAPTER SEVEN

Sylvia and Hermione stood together, looking from the drawing room window. Beneath them, banks of daffodils and narcissi swayed, beneath the shimmering, massed, pale pink haze of flowering cherries. Beyond, a fresh April breeze was spanking the surface of the lake into a myriad dancing wavelets. To the far left, tender green buds of spring, on the avenue of sturdy beech and oak, were finely etched against the bright blue sky. It all looked so idyllic.

'In London, you hardly notice the changing of the seasons, unless you stroll through one of the parks,' said Sylvia reflectively. 'If it were not for my little courtyard, I don't know how I would cope.'

Rosamund mentioned how beautiful you had made it—and that you have a fountain and a small rockery. May I visit you, Sylvia?' Hermione smiled at her, finding it hard to recognise the once attractive red haired young mother, in the tight drawn features of the serene figure at her side.

'Of course—I hope you will come and often.' She looked down and sighed, realising there might not be much time for Hermione to make those visits.

'Rosamund told me—everything,' siad Hermione gently. 'It almost broke my heart, when I learned how badly your husband's parents had treated you—-and then of course, you lost your dear Tristam so very early. But you know, Sylvia, although our circumstances have been so very different, in this we share a similar bond. I lost Peter's father when he was a small boy of five. My husband was killed in a car crash——and then I made Peter all of my life.'

'As I should have made Rosamund mine. I can never thank you enough, for all you have done for her. It hardly seems possible, that she will be seventeen in two week's time.' She looked grave-ly at Hermione. 'She is very fond of Peter, you know.'

'I do know. But she is so young—-and we don't want her to be hurt. Peter seems to have room for nothing in his life now, except his music—-yet perhaps that same music may give them a close-ness they would find with no other partner. Sylvia—-Rosamund has told me of your illness. I am more sorry than I can express in mere words——and it is because of this, that I feel that we two, who love both our children so much, should perhaps share our thoughts on their future?'

Sylvia looked back, at the beautiful, poised woman at her side, saw beyond the carefully coifed hair and still youthful face, enhanced with carefully applied cosmetics, to the honesty and strength in the level gaze. This was a woman she could trust, not recklessly as she had done all those years ago, without due thought for the child she had entrusted to this patrician woman's care——but as one who would always be a good friend and who truly loved Rosamund.

'Rosamund kissed him—and told him that she wanted to marry him,' confessed Sylvia, with a gesture of helplessness. 'Has he mentioned this to you?'

'No—-he hasn't,' said Hermione slowly. 'But on the night of the competition, Rosamund told me she was in love with him. It was for this reason, that she was so terribly upset over the Challoner woman!' She stopped and thought.

'He was unusually quiet at dinner last night,' she said. 'He did-n't seem to be paying his usual attention to Ernst or the others. I thought it was just reaction, after escaping from the clutches of that scheming woman. She really was awful, Sylvia!' She paused—then, 'I sensed something strange about her too——a sort of imbalance—-a cruelty perhaps. But I suppose I am being fanciful.' Hermione gave a self-conscious smile.

'No you're not. Rosamund said something very much the same about Lois. But at least, neither of you will ever have to see her again!' The two women returned to sit on the sofa, exchanging confidences, opening up to each other in growing friendship. At last Sylvia asked it they could go into the garden, for she had never seen the grounds of Garnford house. They started down the stairs and Sylvia paused, as they passed the first of the portraits of the Bagshaw ancestors.

'That is Peter's father. It was painted only months before his death,' sighed Hermione. 'I have asked Peter on several occasions to have his own portrait painted, but he has always refused——just as he has, every time I have suggested that he remarry to provide an heir for Garnford.'

'Perhaps he felt that there has to be a more important reason for marrying, than just producing a son to carry on a tradition,' said Sylvia with more truth than tact. 'Was Lois Challoner the first woman he had shown an interest in, since his wife's death?'

'Yes. Something froze inside his heart, when Natasha died. I feel that perhaps he has always blamed himself in some way for her death. And yet, he certainly has nothing to reproach himself with. She was killed in an avalanche, whilst deliberately taking a danger- ous decent, even though Peter tells me that he shouted to her to stop. He did mention that she was very upset before they started out that day, because she was unable to give him a child.'

'Poor girl! Did she want a child very badly?'

'She had taken the decision not to become pregnant, for fear that any child of the marriage would be born with haemophilia—- -it ran in her family. Peter deferred to her wishes in the matter—- -but I feel deep down, that he always wanted a son. I remember there was one occasion after Natasha's death, when I brought up the suggestion of remarriage, that he asked me whether musical talent could be an inherited factor——whether two gifted musi- cians would produce a similarly gifted child.'

'What did you say?'

'What could I say——-I don't think anyone could answer a question like that. Nor would it have been a proper reason for

choosing a wife—-merely selecting her on that basis.' Sylvia nodded agreement and they walked on.

They entered the great hall and Sylvia paused again, staring up
at the succession of portraits—and a wry smile crossed her face.

'Looking at all this—-an unbroken line of Bagshaws, I think I
can begin to understand why you have wanted a grandchild so
badly. Well, who knows what the future may hold.' She gave a
sudden exclamation.   'Surely——that's a Kneller!' She stood
below the portrait, eyeing the dark haired man in powdered wig,
red velvet coat and ruffled shirt.

'Yes——and on the other side, you will find a Holbein—-its a
bit dark and needs restoring. Perhaps Peter will have it done one
day.' Hermione looked at Sylvia, a speculative gleam in he eyes.
An idea had just struck her.

'Sylvia, my son has told me that you have become a most wonderful artist. I have heard all about your painting of the Christ and
would really like to see this so much. What I want to ask you now,
you may refuse—-and if so, please do not worry about it. But
Sylvia——would you consider painting Peter's portrait?'

'Oh, no. I couldn't—-at least——I don't think so.'

'I shouldn't have sprung the suggestion to you in this way.
The idea just came into my head, as we looked at these portraits
of Peter's ancestors. He probably wouldn't sit for you anyway.'
Hermione sighed and looked down. Sylvia frowned. She suddenly thought of all the kindness this woman had showered on her
daughter. Was this really so much to do in return? But with so few
months left, was it even feasible to undertake such a work?

'I'll think about it, Hermione. Let's go out now!'

An hour later, they returned to the house. Harrington came to
meet them. The butler hardly seemed to have aged at all in the
last years, reflected Sylvia.

'My lady—-we have a visitor. Senor Rodrigo Mendes is in the
music room with Miss Rosamund and the others—-and she asks
that you both join them there. I believe Sir Peter is waiting for

your arrival, before playing to the company.'

'Thank you, Harrington. We will go up' She took Sylvia's arm, steadying her, for the younger woman was shaken by one of her coughing fits. 'Harrington—-bring some water—-quickly!' Sylvia sank down on the stairs, face pinched with pain. She took the glass, with murmured thanks. At last, she rose to her feet and managed a slight smile.

'I'm sorry, Hermione. I'm all right now.'

'Oh, my dear——I blame myself. I shouldn't have walked you so far in the gardens. How are you feeling now?'

'Do you want me to be polite—or truthful! But as for the walk, I loved it. I shall always remember the pathway of the fountains, as you call it—it's like a scene from a dream.

Well——I suppose we had better go to the music room. I'm ready now.' She took Hermione's arm and they walked slowly up the stairs, Harrington pacing beside them, with anxious glance at Sylvia.

The sound of a piano duet greeted them, as they paused outside the music room. As Harrington opened the door, they saw Ernst and Leopold seated side by side, young face and old enrapt in their playing. Rosamund stood next to a stocky man with thick, black hair, receding slightly at the temples, luxuriant moustaches lining his full lips. His dark eyes were shining as he listened intently to the two pianists, whose fingers flew over the keyboard in this rendering of one of Liszt's poems. Peter also was giving his attention to the music, although his fingers were rustling through pages of manuscript.

'That was wonderful,' cried Hermione, as the last chord died away. They came to their feet as they heard her voice, Leopold bowing courteously. Ernst chuckled benevolently.

'He has possibilities, this young one,' said Ernst, eyes twinkling. Then his eyes fell on Sylvia. He had never met her before, but having heard all about her, knew who this must be. He came forward now and gently lifted one of Sylvia's thin hands to his lips.

'Dear lady—-you are the mother of Rosamund? My name is Ernst Morgenstern. I am very pleased to meet you at last. You have a wonderful young daughter.'

Hermione quickly made the other introductions, to Leopold on whom Sylvia's eyes rested curiously—to the conductor, Rodrigo Mendes——and to the woman they hardly noticed at first, as she sat so quietly on a chair in the corner. Svetlana Ouvetsky looked inquisitively at Sylvia. So this was the woman who had abandoned her daughter and disappeared completely from her life. Svetlana was used to assessing her fellow human beings; had perhaps been ready to be critical of one who had caused so much grief in the life of her favourite pupil——yet as she looked into the spiritual gaze of the sick woman, her automatic reaction was one of sympathy. She drew Sylvia to her and placed a quick kiss on her face.

'It has been a privilege to teach Rosamund,' she said softly, as her pupil watched dumfounded. It was the first time she had seen Madame show any emotion. Tears came into Sylvia's eyes, at the kindness with which she had been received by all, for she had been partly dreading facing them. Yet it had all passed off so naturally, just as though she had never gone off, leaving a bewildered child with strangers.

'Mother,' said Peter, cutting through the poignant silence that had fallen. 'For the last few years, Rodrigo has been pressing me to set a date for the first public performance of the Rose Concerto. I have had a special reason for delaying that performance. I was waiting for the time when Rosamund would be ready to join me on the concert platform. When I heard her perform at the recent competition, I realised I need wait no longer. Rosamund—-I want you to play the duet in the slow movement with me. I want your mother to hear it.' He was standing beneath Natasha's portrait and Sylvia lifted her eyes to it. What a beautiful work! The eyes shone with a soft light, the lips half parted in a smile, the cream skin gleamed——and the treatment of that single red rose, held lightly in the slender hand.

Of course—-the Rose Concerto! The portrait completely dominated this room. Did the dead woman still dominate his life? She came to a sudden decision. Peter and Rosamund had taken up their violins and were tuning up. Sylvia called softly to Harrington.

'Please—-would you do something for me?'

'Anything, Mrs Lake.'

'Then go to my room. You will find a sketching pad and charcoal on the dressing table. Will you bring them?' She smiled gratefully as he turned to go.

She watched objectively, as Rosamund stood next to Peter, as he placed the manuscript on the music stand. He was smiling down at her, with a slightly quizzical glance and Sylvia knew he was thinking of Rosamund's impulsive declaration to him. She wondered if Peter were now seeing the girl, not merely as the talented child he had encouraged over the years—but as a young woman, lovely and vivacious. If only Rosamund were a little older. They started to play and she realised that this did not matter. The lovely theme soared, was taken from one bow to the other. The movement was full of tenderness and passion—-now a throbbing despair, that changed to wistful hope, and pulsing through it now, a vibrant joy, an almost unearthly happiness. All eyes were on Peter and the young girl, whose playing held a mastery to match his own. No one noticed Sylvia start to sketch the two figures as they stood so close together. As the last lovely notes vibrated through the room, Sylvia slipped the pad beneath her chair and joined in the applause.

Rodrigo was ecstatic.

'Five years ago, dear friend, I sat her with Adrian Moulting. We both knew then that what you were composing was a masterpiece. Having heard what I have today, I forgive you for that five years delay! But it has whetted my appetite to hear the whole work—and indeed, to start rehearsals with you. When, Peter——when?' His sibilant voice was husky with emotion, his eyes burning with excitement. He knew the power of the music he had just heard, and the impact it would have on the music world. It was a work of genius.

The next hour passed in animated conversation. Through it all, Sylvia watched Peter's face, bright with animation—and her daughters, her unwary glances betraying her tender feelings for him. Someone else was watching those glances. Leopold's eyes were darkening, as he saw the way Rosamund was looking at her guardian. Sylvia felt a cough coming on. She signalled to Hermione.

'I want to go to my room. There's a pad—-under the chair Bring it when——!' The last words were caught in her coughing, as she excused herself and left. Rosamund ran after her anxiously.

'Mother—-are you all right?'

'Yes—-darling. I'm all right. You played so wonderfully just now. I'm very proud of you. Now—go back to them. I'm going to lie down for a little.' She managed a smile and relieved, Rosamund returned to the music room.

It was evening when Sylvia wakened. She had only meant o rest on her bed, but had fallen asleep. Next to her, lay the sketching pad. She sat up and stared at the sketch critically. As she did so, she saw in her mind's eye, the finished portrait, as it would be. But it would need such a lot of work—and she would need photographs of Peter—-a violin for detail—-sketches of Rosamund—-and yes, if possible, to paint her in the white dress she had worn for the competition. Her face started to flush with anticipation. There was a quiet knock at the door. It was Hermione.

'I let you sleep. I came in before with your pad. Oh, Sylvia—-does this mean you will undertake the portrait?'

'Yes. But it will show both of them! I shall paint them as I saw them just now, playing their violins together. But I shall need your help, Hermione.' She told her what she wanted and Hermione nodded. If she had reservations about the portrait being of Rosamund as well as Peter, she let no sign of this appear on her face, for she saw how much Sylvia was set on it.

'But can you really paint from just this quick sketch—and photographs?'

'I'll try. I cannot promise what the result will be. Hermione—would you think me very ungracious, if I said I would like to return to London tomorrow?'

'If that is what you really want.'

'If I am going to work on this portrait, then I must start immediately.' They exchanged glances, for they both knew why this must be.

'I'll drive you back tomorrow myself. As for the photographs, I'll look out as many as you like for you. I have plenty—-and of Rosamund as well. A violin will be no problem either.'

'There is one other thing, Hermione. Rosamund has said, that she wants to spend as much time as she can with me, over the next few months. I understand this—-but want her to continue with her own life as much as possible at the same time.' She looked at Hermione and her eyes were sad. She wished so very much, that her daughter would not have to face the sorrow of separation so soon.

'Rodrigo has arranged with Peter, to start rehearsals on the Rose Concerto within the next few days. They intend to use Derwent Hall in West London for rehearsals, so Rosamund will be close to your home for the foreseeable future.'

That is good. Perhaps I can manage to slip in at some of those rehearsals, to make further sketches,' said Sylvia in satisfaction.

'We are going down to dinner soon. You will join us won't you?'

'Providing I can return to my room, if my cough becomes troublesome!' Sylvia managed to look strangely beautiful that night. She wore a dramatic green and gold caftan, trimmed with glittering gold sequins. She had bought it on impulse, several years ago and had never had a sufficiently important occasion to wear it—until now. She noticed Leopold Heine's eyes lingering on her thoughtfully. She ate sparingly of the excellent dinner, so beautifully prepared, and drank a little of the white wine, which for all that it seemed light, set her blood pulsing. She fingered the crystal goblet and stared at Peter, who sat at the head of the table. The years had been kind to him, she thought. Perhaps the silver peaks at his temples were more pronounced than when she had first met him, the lines at the sides of his mouth, more deeply etched. Otherwise, the slate grey eyes flashed as imperiously as ever, above his hawked nose—yet the old sardonic smile was missing from his lips tonight, replaced by a gentler smile, as he looked at Rosamund. Sylvia realised that Peter was now treating her daughter as a woman, and an attractive one.

'Excuse me, sir—but was your Rose Concerto named for Miss Rosamund,' asked Leopold unexpectedly?

Peter looked at him in surprise and was about to shake his head. Instead, he said slowly-'It was indeed named for another rose—yet the one you mention is as fair as the petalled variety, so perhaps my concerto can be tribute to Rosamund as well!' It was nicely said and Hermione relaxed. But she stared at Leopold with a slight frown. When they had been in the music room, she had noticed the boy staring fixedly at Natasha's portrait and at the single red rose, in the painted fingers. He must have realised the true dedication of the concerto—so why ask Peter this question in front of Rosamund? Then as she saw the look on his earnest young face, she knew why. This boy was in love with Rosamund and jealous of Peter. She exchanged glances with Sylvia and saw that she also had taken measure of the situation. Well—Leopold would be accompanying Ernst to Austria in a few days and then would be so heavily involved with his music that he would have no time to dwell on romance.

Ernst was exchanging some very friendly glances with Svetlana Ouvetsky. The years fled away as they recalled a passionate interlude in their lives, before Svetlana had married the handsome colonel, after whose tragic death, she had returned to her music, finding in creativity, the solace so many find in this way.

'Why don't you come to Vienna for a few days,' Ernst was say-ing. 'Your academy is shut for a whole two weeks. What do you say?' His eyes shone, as she nodded, her cheeks flushing slightly. 'Das ist wunderbar! Svetlana—-you make me very happy!'

When she slipped tiredly between the silken sheets that night, Sylvia was still thoughtful. She felt contented that her daughter's life was going to be happy and fulfilled. She thought of Rosamund's fast approaching seventeenth birthday—of the party to be held in Hermione's flat in two weeks time—and she won-dered whether perhaps Peter would propose marriage before the summer was out? Or was she merely romancing. Perhaps his heart was still with his dead wife's ghost. She sighed and turned her head on the pillow.

The following day, Sylvia kissed her daughter goodbye and slipped into the back of the Rolls, next to Hermione. Roberts was to drive them. The powerful car slid effortlessly through the beau-tiful Hampshire countryside and Sylvia looked around her a little wistfully. How fresh and lovely it all looked, tight buds beginning to unfurl and pale primroses starring the banks, dark ploughed fields, contrasting with the soft green of the Downs. Then her thoughts returned to her daughter and Peter—-and to that por-trait.

'Did you manage to find some photographs,' she asked Hermione?

'I certainly did——-and I have one of Peter's old violins in the boot!'

'Well done,' she breathed. Hermione gave her a slight conspir-atorial smile as they chattered happily together. London soon wrapped its dusty garment around them, taxis vied with red, dou-ble-decker buses and heavy container lorries rumbled between impatient cars, shop windows were elegant with the pale green and yellow of the latest spring fashions, whilst at street corners, flower sellers offered daffodils, tulips and anemones. Every sweet shop seemed full of stacks of brightly coloured Easter eggs and tiny yellow chicks. Spring was in the air and people's faces bore the bright impatience of those anticipating a holiday. Tomorrow was Good Friday.

'We'll stop at a restaurant for lunch and then drive to your flat,' said Hermione. She indicated an expensive looked restaurant where she herself sometimes ate.

'Why not let me cook something for us—-if you trust my cooking, that is!'

'If you prefer—-yes, I'd love that,' said Hermione. Roberts eased the Rolls to rest outside the basement flat. In minutes, curtains were drawn aside, as neighbours, frankly curious, stared as Sylvia was helped out by the chauffeur, to stand beside the elegant woman, who looked so totally out of place in this street of crumbling buildings. Roberts opened the boot and lifted out Sylvia's case, together with the violin, swathed in a car rug.

'I didn't want Peter to see me take the violin, in case he wanted to know why,' explained Hermione. She followed Sylvia down, glancing back to the top of the steps, where Roberts was surrounded by a swarm of small children, all exclaiming at the Rolls. He managed to evade the youngsters and followed them down. Hermione waited as Sylvia used two keys to unlock her door and then walked in behind her. The children were shouting down to them, asking if they could ride in the car.

'Put those things in the hall, Roberts—-and I think it would be better if you were to return to Hans Crescent. Perhaps you could come back for me later, in say—three hours?'

'Certainly, my lady.' Roberts looked slightly relieved as he hurried back up the basement steps and they heard the car draw away. Hermione was very thoughtful as she looked about the shabby little flat. Everything bespoke lack of money and yet the place had a character of its own, was cosy and gay and reflected the defiant courage of its tenant.

Sylvia was a very good cook. She quickly produced a risotto, followed by apple crumble and cream. As they sipped their coffee, Hermione's eyes lighted on the painting of Holly Cottage and exclaimed in surprise.

'Yes. I painted that a few years ago. It is not very good—but it reminds me of happier days with Tristam.' She indicated the photograph on the mantle-piece. Looking at the handsome face staring reflectively out of the frame, Hermione realised the look was one she had often seen on Rosamund's face.

'She is very like your husband, isn't she,' said Hermione gently.

'So much so, that when he died, I found it very hard to look at her sometimes, for she reminded me so of Tristam. She also has a look of Melissa—her grandmother.' They finished their coffee. Hermione insisted on helping to wash the dishes and at last, was able to ask what she had been longing to, since she entered the flat.

?May I see your paintings now, Sylvia—-in particular, the one which Peter told me so much about—the Christ.'

'Come this way. Oh yes—-and you must see my little garden!'

Hermione looked about her in amazement, astonished at the sheer amount of canvases in that small studio. Then her eyes were drawn to the portrait on the easel and she drew in a deep breath. Sylvia looked at her friend's face interrogatively. What would the portrait communicate to this sophisticated woman at her side? To her surprise, tears sparkled in Hermione's eyes, spilling down the carefully rouged cheeks. Hermione's hands rose, to be clasped in almost supplication and her eyes seemed to be seeing beyond the compelling, gold flecked gaze of the painted face.

'There are no words to express what you have created here,' whispered Hermione at last. 'You have captured the Son of God in all his holiness and humanity. Oh, my dear——this gift of yours will touch the hearts of many.'

'You really think so,' said Sylvia huskily?

'Yes. You are a wonderfully gifted artist, Sylvia.' She slipped an arm about Sylvia's thin shoulders. 'If I may put it so——your

whole life is fulfilled in this painting. It says more than the most
eloquent sermon I have heard preached. It searches out the hidden places of the soul.'

'Come out into the garden——and I will tell you how it came
to be painted,' said Sylvia. Then there, in that little courtyard, sitting in the gazebo, hearing the trilling of a blackbird, and the soft
splashing of the small fountain, Hermione sat enthralled, as Sylvia
told her the extraordinary story of a life full of emptiness and pain.
A constant struggle against alcoholism, a daily battle; a coming
into contact with others sharing the same illness; finding strength
in supporting new friends afflicted by the same addiction——and
then, at last crying out to an all caring God, for his help and forgiveness.

Addiction had been taken completely away from her, new purpose burgeoning into her life, a determination to learn to paint
and to eventually support herself through the sale of her work.
There had been struggles at first, but a growing sureness in her
brushstrokes as she sought for perfection. But at last, her work
had indeed started to sell and she had found this little flat, which
provided a studio—-and started work on the courtyard, which at
the time, had been a repository for accumulated rubbish thrown
there by previous tenants.

'You mean to say, that you created this beautiful garden from a
rubbish dump?' Hermione was amazed.

'Yes. But you see, it was merely a parallel to what my life had
been previously—-before I came to God.'

'How did that come about——if it is not too personal a question?'

'It is indeed very personal—but I will willingly share it with
you, Hermione. I just fell on my knees one night, in the quiet of
my room and poured my heart out. I said——'If you are real—
—if you are there—-then please forgive the mess I've made of
everything! I want you to take over in my life, for I can no longer
manage on my own. Father—-please help me!' I don't know how

long I stayed on my knees, only that my eyes were bathed in tears
and a feeling of warmth and peace stole over me and seemed to
envelop me.

The next day, I woke with a song on my lips and a wonderful
sense of release. Although I hadn't taken a drink since I left Holly
Cottage, the temptation, the need for a drink had always been
there. Without AA I do not think I would have made it. But now
it was different. I no longer wanted a drink——you could say that
I was cured of alcohol.'

'But that was marvellous. What happened next?'

'I looked for a church. Instinctively I knew that I didn't want a
big showy church, but a quiet place. I found a small Pentecostal
church, not far from here, called Horeb. Peter met its pastor—
Michael Howard, when he visited me here. I slipped into the back
of the church and was struck by the fervency of the worship, the
feeling of peace and joy—it was like no service I had ever attended before. I listened to the young pastor as he spoke of Jesus
Christ. Then he asked if any wished to make a commitment to
Jesus, they should come forward. I felt my feet taking me to the
front of the church—I knelt down and the pastor prayed with
me——and then something else happened, something so wonderful, that it is difficult to put it into words. As I prayed, the Holy
Spirit of God seemed to be all about me. I had such a sense of
awe—of deepest reverence—and as I raised my voice in praise, I
realised that the sounds that fell from my lips, were not just ordinary words—but that I was speaking a different language, that
later I was to learn was called tongues!' She paused looking quietly at Hermione, to see if her friend understood all she had been
saying.

'I have heard of this phenomenon,' said Hermione thoughtfully. 'Surely it is what happened to the disciples of Jesus at
Pentecost? When tongues of fire appeared on them?'

'Yes. You are right! They spoke in other tongues as the Holy
Spirit came upon them, empowering them in their service, as He

does with us today.'

'This is all a bit too much for me to take in,' said Hermione. 'It seems so far removed from the average service on a Sunday in the village church.'

'It turned my life right about. I felt a new confidence. I had already taken an evening course at art college and been praised by my tutors and had managed to sell some of my work——but I knew my paintings lacked that special something which sets the true artist apart. Now however, in the quiet of my little studio, it almost seemed as though my inner joy flowed through my brush strokes and all my new work, showed this quality of what I can only call enhanced awareness.'

'Sylvia————-what you are telling me—that your experience of the reality of God—-of Jesus, so changed your life—-this I can almost understand. I envy you your faith. What I cannot comprehend now, is how you have continued to show faith and love for God, in the face of your present illness.' Hermione had tried to phrase her words carefully.

'When the doctors diagnosed cancer—-there was shock—deep shock at first, almost unbelief. Then when I was told that I had only months to live, there was sadness, that I would never now be able to regain my daughter's love—to see her as an adult—to tell her how much I loved her. What you do not know, Hermione is that according to the doctors, I should have died fifteen months ago!' She spread her hands out in resignation. 'I know I am living on what some would call borrowed time—but I believe, that it is time especially given to me, to finish that portrait and to get to know Rosamund again.'

'Then—-you still believe in God? You have no bitterness that life is to be cut short, just as your true talent is becoming so wonderfully evident?'

'I can only answer that Hermione, by telling you, that I have a peace about it—-and no fear. After all, I will be going to that same precious Saviour, who brought such healing and happiness into my life.'

For a moment, there was absolute silence. Hermione had been touched to the very fibre of her being, by the matter of fact way, in which Sylvia had explained her faith——the key to the peace and quiet acceptance that al at Garnford had found in her. Sylvia broke the silence by inviting Hermione to return to her studio, to look at some of her other paintings. Hermione got up with alacrity, for she was anxious to see that special portrait again and to find out what materials Sylvia would need, for the painting of Peter and Rosamund, for surely the least she could do, was to provide Sylvia with all that would be required.

'Its all right. I have several canvases left and enough oils. Where you may be able to help, is in providing a frame of the quality you would deem necessary, for a painting to hang at Garnford. But that of course, will come much later. Now——let me see the photographs you have brought!'

And so it started, the long painstaking work—preliminary sketches—transferring the preferred layout in charcoal onto the prepared canvas. She found she was rising to the challenge of this commission. In spite of being told that Sylvia lacked nothing in the way of art materials, Hermione arrived one day, with a beautiful cabinet, which when you opened its doors, displayed a set of drawers, each full of row upon row of paints and an assortment of brushes. Sylvia looked at it mutely. It would take months to use even a fraction of these paints—certainly she would never empty that cabinet. But she brightened, as she had to admit how wonderful it was to have everything she needed at her fingertips.

Two weeks had passed. Rosamund stretched and leapt out of bed, as she realised that this special day had dawned at last——for it was her birthday and she was seventeen! But she also knew that it would be no different from any other day, as far as rehearsals for the Rose Concerto went, nor would she have wished it to be.

She dressed and hurried down to breakfast, to be greeted by a warm embrace from Hermione.

'Happy, happy birthday, darling!' She released Rosamund and handed her a little package. 'Open it,' she said quietly and looked tenderly at the girl as she did so, opening the flat suede case, to reveal a pearl necklace with particularly beautiful rose lustre. 'My mother gave this to me, on my seventeenth birthday,' she said simply. For reply, Rosamund kissed her. She would always treasure this gift, had seen this necklace about Hermione's own neck several times and knew how she had loved it.

'Thank you Hermione. It's lovely. But are you sure you really want to part with something which as well as being extremely valuable, is part of your life?'

'It is because it is so full of memories of my own youth, that I now want it to belong to one whom I love as a daughter,' said Hermione softly. 'Now—-your breakfast is ready. Peter left early this morning and said to wish you 'happy birthday' from him. He will see you at rehearsals.' If Rosamund felt disappointment that Peter had not thought it important enough to wait to say happy birthday to her personally, she tried to let no vestige of this appear on her face.

At the Derwent Hall, the full compliment of musicians were already present, some chatting in small groups others tuning up. Peter was standing at the piano, talking to Rodrigo Mendes and Ivan Martinchyck. He gave a cheerful wave to Rosamund as soon as he noticed her, but continued his conversation. Rosamund walked over to him.

'I hope I'm not late, Peter?'

'No. I merely wanted to make an early start. I believe birthday congratulations are in order.' He bent and planted a light kiss on her forehead, in the fashion in which one would salute a child. Others standing around called out congratulations, and the day was underway. They had a brief pause for lunch then continued at the same gruelling pace. Rosamund hugged the small hurt to her, that this most important day was being treated of no account by Peter and tried to fill her thoughts with the music, which was not

really difficult as the melody swelled, its deep sadness gradually
giving way to flood of purest joy. No musician could have done
other than experience these emotions from their innermost being.

'We should be ready by Whitsun,' said Rodrigo, wiping the
sweat from his forehead. His face broke into a smile. 'Tomorrow,
Peter, we will play the concerto straight through, without inter-
ruption from me. I want to check what I now feel is true——that
we are almost ready to give the performance of a lifetime. One
that will truly make musical history!' His dark eyes glowed with
enthusiasm, as he laid his baton aside. 'Now my friend Peter,' he
continued with a gleam of amusement in his eyes,'——'I think it is
time for you to prepare for your own evening performance!'

'What's the time?'

'Seven.'

'Why——I'd no idea it was so late.' Peter gave a nod to
Roberts, who had been sitting unobtrusively at the back of the
hall. Suddenly the whole crowd of assembled musicians leapt into
unexpected activity. Chairs were moved to the side of the hall and
benches erected at one end. At the same time, waiters started to
arrive with covered trolleys of food. On their heels, a sea of flowers were carried onto the stage, banking it so that it was trans-
formed into a cradle of multi coloured spring blooms, their fragrance filling the air.

Rosamund looked about her in bewilderment. Then she saw
her mother and Hermione standing at the door. She ran over to
them, still holding her violin.

'Mother——Hermione! What a lovely surprise! Does either of
you know what is going on here?' As she asked this, she realised
that Sylvia was wearing that beautiful green and gold caftan and
Hermione her gold lame.

'Come Rosamund——into one of the changing rooms at the
back of the stage. I have your white dress there!' Hermione seized
her arm and hurried her, still protesting ward forward. Still utterly confused as to what was going on, Rosamund washed herself

quickly at the small sink in the dressing room and changed obediently into the white dress. She brushed her hair loose onto her
shoulders and then turned impatiently to Hermione.

'Now——what exactly is going on? Is Peter going to play for
someone special?'

'You'll see,' said Hermione exasperatingly and Sylvia was equally unresponsive. They left the dressing room and made their way
back to the hall. As Rosamund entered, the musicians raised their
instruments and the strains of Happy Birthday filled the hall.
Rosamund started to laugh.

'Oh, no! This cannot all really be for me!' Suddenly tears filled
her eyes, as she looked at the stage banked with flowers, the
benches covered with white damask cloths bearing an exotic cold
buffet, arranged with artistry and colour. Peter came to greet her.
She noticed that he had changed into an evening suit, a red rose
in his buttonhole. This time, instead of chaste kiss on her forehead, he bent his lips over hers—and as his lips caressed hers,
Rosamund trembled.

'Happy birthday, Rosamund darling,' he said huskily. He took
her hand and led her up onto the stage. All eyes were on them.
As she glanced at the sea of faces below her, she noticed most of
her fellow pupils from Fritz Klein, together with Madame
Ouvetsky and her other tutors.

'Friends and colleagues,' he began——'and you, my dearest
mother——and Sylvia, mother of this young lady we are honour-
ing tonight, as you all know, Rosamund is celebrating her seventeenth birthday today. So far, it has been a typical day in the life
of a musician——hard work——exacting work——but work that is
the breath of life to us. But even musicians have to play sometimes——and that is not meant to be a pun!' for the whole hall
exploded into laughter.

'So now,' he continued, 'I invite you to raise your glasses——
once the waiters have poured the champagne.' At this point there
was the noisy popping of champagne corks, and he waited until

everyone had a glass in their hand. 'Ladies and gentlemen, I give you, Rosamund Lake——to whom I formally dedicate my 'Rose Concerto'! And now Rosamund——here is my more specific gift to you!' He turned to Rodrigo, who had been holding something behind his back and now produced a violin case.

'Oh, Peter——a new violin!' Rosamund was almost choked for words, for she had been deeply touched by his words regarding his concerto, which she knew very well, had been written for his late wife. What did this new dedication to her portend? She reached for the violin case and opened it.

'Not a new violin, dear Rosamund——but a very old one. It is a Stradivarius, my dear!' His eyes were very tender as he saw the awe with which she lifted the old instrument out. He noticed that her hands were trembling slightly. 'Give it to me,' he said and taking it tuned it, then returned it to her. 'So now, Rosamund—— the slow movement, one more time.'

He produced his own violin and side by side, they lifted their bows and their fingers swept deftly over the strings——and the music rose as never before, in throbbing intensity. As the last poignant notes vibrated on the air, there was total silence——then the whole hall exploded into applause, nor was it mere politeness, but an accolade from seasoned musicians to something they acknowledged was extremely fine. As the clapping died down, Peter led her down from the stage to the flashing of cameras. People approached the buffet tables and the party started. A band appeared on the stage, and as their appetites were satisfied, couples started to dance. It was a happy, light-hearted occasion.

'Rosamund——here is my small present to you,' said a soft voice, as Sylvia held a package to her daughter. Rosamund took it, and opening it, found a beautifully painted miniature of her father, his eyes smiling, just as she remembered him from her childhood.

'Oh, mother! What a truly lovely gift! I will never part with it— -it is Daddy, just as I see him, whenever I close my eyes. Thank you for this——and for the wonderful painting that went into mak-

ing it!' She embraced Sylvia warmly. Then she gave a delighted
cry.

'Uncle Ernst! I didn't know you were here!' She ran to the old
Austrian pianist, who now came towards her, hands outstretched.

'Liebchen! Did you think I would have forgotten your birthday! Your playing just now was magnificent. May I examine your
new violin?' He handled the shining wood, smooth with age, with
reverent fingers. Yes—-it was an instrument worthy of her. 'Now,
meine Liebchen, I give you my own small gift.' He held out a
beribboned package, saying gently—-'Open it with care.' She did
so, and exclaimed in delight at the beautifully painted casket,
which when she opened it, turned out to be a musical box. Inside
it, lay a small book. 'These are some small verses of mine, written
over the long years. Dip into them sometimes, child and who
knows, they may speak words to your heart, when you most need
to hear them!'

'Uncle Ernst—-it's a beautiful casket—-and I shall read those
verses when I am alone. I did not know that you are a poet as well
as a musician!'

'An indifferent one, I fear. But Rosamund, this casket, which in
reality is a music box, like your violin, is not new. It had another
and most famous owner.'

'Why—who?'

'Wolfgang Amadeus Mozart! Ach——don't drop it!

It's very fragile. No—don't thank me. It has been one of my
most treasured possessions, and now I would like to think that
you will feel the same way about it.' He patted her cheek and
turning to Sylvia, asked whether she would look after her daughter's gifts, whilst he demanded a dance of his niece. Then to the
strains of a waltz, Ernst whirled her about the room. At it's conclusion, and almost breathless, she found herself in Peter's arms.
It was the first time she had danced with him, and as she found
his hand pressing lightly at her waist and his very closeness, her
heart beat faster and she glanced upwards into those slate grey

eyes, that were now burning with so tender a light.

'Rosamund—-you are very lovely tonight!'

'No, I'm not. It's just the dress!' He laughed at that and bending, he placed a swift kiss on her cheek.

'Rosamund——-Rosamund! You must learn to accept compliments gracefully—-when they are meant—are true.' When the dance came to an end, he beckoned to a waiter and took two glasses of champagne. He led her to a quiet corner of the room.

'I lift my glass to you, Rosamund—my little wild rose, who had so many thorns!'

'And I lift my glass, to a very special man, Peter Bagshaw.' They touched glasses and drank. Then he took the glass gently from her. He took her hand.

'Rosamund——I have another gift for you—-but only if you wish to receive it. A few weeks ago, you told me that you loved me. Now I know you are still very young—-compared with you, I am an old man—-no—no. Don't interrupt. When Natasha died, I thought I could never love another woman—not even to assuage the loneliness I felt. Then in recent months, as I have watched you grow from talented child, to lovely young woman, I have found the ice in my heart cracking—and in short, I have done what would have seemed impossible. I have fallen in love with you. You are still very young and I have no wish to take advantage of that youth and inexperience—but one day, I shall ask you to do me the very great honour of becoming my wife." As he said this, he offered her a small box. In it lay an emerald ring, surmounted by diamonds in an antique setting. 'It is a family piece,' he said with a smile. 'I leave it to you, to decide on which finger you will wear it.'

'Oh, Peter! It's beautiful! Please will you put it on the fourth finger of my left hand!' He did so and suddenly she was in his arms, laughing and crying all at once. 'I can hardly believe that you really do love me! Yes—I may be young, but old enough to know that you are the man I love and want to marry and to honour as dear husband.' He took her in his arms at that and kissed her.

Then he raised her to her feet and walked with her to the middle of the hall, for the dancers were resting while the band enjoyed some refreshments.

'Ladies and gentlemen, I have an announcement to make tonight, that fills my heart with happiness. Rosamund has just agreed to become my wife. We are engaged!' Amongst the people pushing forward to congratulate them, were Sylvia and Hermione. He stretched his arms out to them in apology. 'I should have told you first, mother——asked your permission, Sylvia. But say that you give us your blessing!' He had that slightly guilty look in his eyes that he had so many times as a small child, when he had done something wrong, thought Hermione fondly. As for Sylvia, she looked into those level grey eyes and read the strength of the man there. With him, she knew Rosamund would be safe—and that also, she would be most deeply loved.

'God bless you both,' she said softly, tears in her eyes.

'Oh, my darlings, I'm so happy for you,' faltered Hermione, the suddenness of it almost taking her breath away. Her eyes fell on the ring on Rosamund's finger. It looked so right there, she thought. Ernst came forward, embracing first one of them and then the other, in a bear hug.

'And you told me nothing first! But I am so happy for you—so very happy. This is indeed a night to remember.' He called to Madame Ouvetsky to join them. The smile she gave Rosamund was one of genuine affection. She opened her arms and Rosamund slipped into that embrace wonderingly. For Svetlana looked different——indeed smelt different. She was dressed in a long skirt and matching bolero of burgundy velvet, and a cream lace shirt—and was wearing a hint of make-up that warmed her skin and enhanced her slanting dark eyes——and surely that was Chanel perfume?

'Well, Peter Bagshaw,' said Ernst, his eyes twinkling. 'I ask your indulgence to make another announcement to your guests!' Peter stared down at him intrigued. He sensed a subdued excitement in the pianist.

'Why—-what can you mean,' wondered Peter?

'This evening, I asked Svetlana to marry me! And miracle of miracles—she has accepted!' He drew Svetlana away from Rosamund and held out her left hand to Peter. It bore a large ruby, set in pearls in delicate gold setting

'Ernst! You dark horse!' The two men were in each other's arms, pummelling each other. 'So that was why you decided to spirit Svetlana away to Austria! I couldn't be more delighted for you both. Congratulations!' He turned to Svetlana and raised her hand to his lips, looking at her with new eyes. Yes—this woman who had taught Rosamund with such devotion over the years, was in fact a very handsome woman. Why had he never noticed it before? Taking Svetlana and Ernst each by a hand, he called out for silence.

'My friends,' he cried——'It would seem, that tonight we have a double celebration. My dearest friend, Maestro Ernst Morgenstern has become engaged to a lady well known to most of you—a lady both talented and charming, and one who shows the utmost patience with budding members of our profession—- I refer to the Principal of Fritz Klein Academy—-Madame Svetlana Ouvetsky!'

Cameras flashed again and congratulations poured in, as both couples were surrounded by well wishers. This certainly was a most extraordinary night! Then the dancing recommenced and once again, Rosamund found herself in Peter's arms, her face pressing against his, as he bent his head over hers. She smelt the spicy tang of his after-shave, the roughness of his chin, for he had not shaved since this morning and her breath quickened. He was to be her husband, with whom she would spend all the days of her life—-and her nights. As she thought of this, she half closed her

eyes. Would there be children? Would she be able to give him the
son he so much desired? But would a child interfere with her
musical career? To her own amazement, she found knowledge
coming, that loving Peter and bearing his children, was of far
greater importance than even her music.

If her thoughts were in tumult, so were Peter's. Was he being
unfair to the lovely young girl in his arms, expecting her to marry
a man more than twice her age? After all, there was that young fellow that Ernst had taken under his wing—Leopold Heine—
whom his mother had told him was infatuated with Rosamund.
He was so much nearer her age, had fire and ambition. But his
every sense rebelled at the thought of her being touched by this
or any other man. No. He loved her and could only be appalled
at his blindness, that he had not realised this until lately. But then
of course, he had always only regarded her as his ward—-almost a
daughter. Was it morally wrong to take this young life to blend
with his own, when she had never had a chance to spread her
wings in the world—to experience the normal complexity of eval-
uating the myriad characters she would come across in life's tapestry? He looked down at her with troubled eyes as the dance
came to an end. Perhaps she sensed his thoughts, for she rose on
her toes and whispered in his ear.

'I love you Peter Bagshaw—-and I will, until my last breath.'
He slipped his arm about her waist and walked her over to
Hermione and Sylvia.

'May I see your ring once more,' said Sylvia, taking Rosamund's
shapely hand into her painfully thin one. 'Why, it is truly lovely,'
she said softly. She attempted to say something else, but suddenly was seized by the most horrific fit of coughing, that convulsed
her form. Rosamund looked horrified at the blood welling from
her mother's mouth, as Sylvia collapsed.

'Peter!'

'Out of the way——I'll lift her. Someone call an ambulance.
Hurry! Hurry'

Peter carried her onto a bench, staunching the blood as best he could with his handkerchief. She was deathly pale, but breathing. It seemed an incredible time before the ambulance men entered the hall and came towards them. They glanced from Rosamund's frightened, tear stained face, to Peter's stern one, as they bent over Sylvia's inert form.

'Are either of you relatives, sir,' the older man inquired?

'I am her daughter,' replied Rosamund. 'She has cancer of the lungs. Please get her to hospital as soon as possible.' The second man took out a book and quickly took a few details, as his colleague opened the stretcher. Peter took Rosamund's hands as the men lifted her mother onto the stretcher. He called to Ernst and Hermione to explain matters and continue with the evening's festivities. But as soon as the little party had left he hall, people began to disperse a sombre mood descending like a blanket upon them.

The hospital sister was calm and reassuring.

'The specialist is with her now. I will have tea brought for you, while you wait his report. One of the nurses will take you to an empty side ward, where you can sit. Now——I must go to the bedside.' She smiled and walked to her office door—then she hesitated. 'Forgive me,' she said to Peter—-'But aren't you Sir Peter Bagshaw, the famous musician?'

'Yes, I am Peter Bagshaw,' he replied.

'Well—let me tell you, that on the rare occasions that I manage to get away from my duties, listening to your concerts brings the greatest joy into my life.' The words were said quietly and with deep sincerity. He bowed slightly, feeling suddenly very humble, that his music should so stir this woman, of whose existence he had been unaware of, until tonight.

'We had just become engaged,' said Rosamund brokenly. 'Perhaps the excitement of the party was too much for mother. I knew she was very ill, but she never seems to show it——and I suppose I have tried to pretend that it wasn't true.'

The sister looked at the woebegone face, glanced at the long white dress and then at the important emerald on her hand and sensed the tragedy of her mother's collapse on this very important night.

'Miss Lake—Rosamund,' she said firmly. 'Your mother is an all together remarkable woman. It is only her tremendous fighting spirit and her deep inner faith that have prolonged her life thus far. Help her now, my dear, by showing a similar bravery—-wipe those tears away—there is a bathroom two doors along—and when you go to your mother's side, encourage her with a smile!'

'You are right. I will,' said Rosamund, shamefacedly. 'Excuse me, Peter.' As she washed the tears away, she murmured a swift prayer to God, to help her mother. As she did so, she suddenly realised that her mother would need the comfort of Pastor Michael Howard. She remembered the little leaflet he had given her, with details of Horeb and his private address. She hurried through to the room where Peter was waiting.

'I think we should get her pastor here, Peter. This is his address and telephone number.'

'I'll ring at once,' he replied and hurried off to do so. Mercifully, Michael Howard was at home and said he would come immediately. He was as good as his word, and his very presence brought calm to Rosamund and Peter. As they spoke quietly together and he realised they had just become engaged, Michael asked whether they would mind if he were to pray a blessing on their pledge. The words he spoke brought tears to Rosamund's eyes again and even touched the sophisticated heart of Peter Bagshaw.

'Michael,' said Peter softly. 'I know this is not the time to discuss such things——but I would be most happy if you would agree to conduct our wedding ceremony.'

'I am touched that you should ask me to do so—-and of course I will,' replied Michael. Then as they looked around as they heard the sister's voice. She came in, accompanied by a tall, grey haired man, wearing a white coat, a stethoscope about his neck. He inclined his head courteously to them.

'Sir Peter—Miss Lake—-Pastor. My name is Roger Holliford. I take it that you know some details of Mrs Lake's case——-and the prognosis.' As they nodded, he went on quietly. 'She has regained consciousness and is asking to see you all. Indeed, she is talking about returning to her home. This I cannot allow at this time. I would like her to rest here for at least a week, so that we can carry out certain tests. But I know that she has an indomitable will—— is an amazing woman. So may I ask, that you add your persuasion to mine.' He walked back along the ward to Sylvia's bed, the other in his wake, with sister bringing up the rear. Sylvia was propped up on pillows, her extreme pallor making the yellowish tinge of her face, more apparent. She gave Rosamund a warm smile, turning in greeting to Peter and Michael.

'I'm so sorry that I spoiled your special night,' she said in slightly hoarse voice, then with a determined smile, 'But I promise not to repeat the offence on your wedding day!' Rosamund swallowed and bent and kissed her mother. It seemed thing impossible, that she was sitting up and discussing their wedding. Peter reached down and took one of Sylvia's hands.

'June is the month of roses,' he said 'I would like to marry Rosamund then—-if you agree?' Sylvia smiled up at him, with an impish smile.

'Perhaps you should ask my daughter that, Peter! But I think a June wedding would be wonderful! Well, darling?' She turned her head to Rosamund.

'Yes,' replied Rosamund huskily. 'We will set it for the second week in June.' She would have said more, but did not trust herself to speak.

'Good. Then that is settled,' said Sylvia in business like tones.

'So then, Sylvia. Your specialist prefers that you remain here for about a week. You need rest you know. We have to have you fighting fit for June.' Peter spoke authoritatively, his slate grey eyes holding Sylvia's gaze.

?I will only say, that I will stay here as long as I feel that I must.'
And with that he had to be content. She then murmured that she
wished to be alone with Michael Howard and they went, promising to return the next day.

'But only after rehearsals,' she called after them.

When her specialist and the sister had also retired, she looked
up levelly into the Pastor's eyes.'Michael—-I sense that I do not
have much longer. But there are two things I want to accomplish,
before going to a loving Saviour's arms. I want time to complete
the painting of Peter and Rosamund—-and I do so want to be
present at their wedding. Peter knows how short time is—-which
is why he is having such an early wedding. I want Rosamund to
have the comfort of a husband's arms about her, when I die. Will
you pray with me for this?' And Michael Howard did, his simple
words throbbing with the fervency with which he made his prayer.
As he finished, Sylvia opened her eyes and smiled a little tremu-
lously.

'As you prayed, Michael, I heard a voice in my mind, say quiet
clearly——"Yes. It shall be as you have asked." So now I know it
will be all right!'

'Thank you, Lord. Thank you, Jesus,' said Michael softly. They
smiled at each other then. And he went.

Sylvia was home within four days, working at her easel.

CHAPTER EIGHT

A month had passed. Sylvia's courtyard was ablaze with flowers of early summer. The gazebo's frame was entwined with budding roses and richly perfumed sprays of cream and bronze honeysuckle.

Amazingly a duck had arrived from somewhere and landed on the small pool, where framed by gold and purple irises it splashed happily. Sylvia stood at her French windows, brush in hand, and watched in amusement, which turned to dismay, as it dived beneath the water——her goldfish! It surfaced, the sun intensifying the dark green and tender beige of its feathers, so that she itched to paint it.

'Shoo,' she cried and with indignant squawk, it took to the wing. She looked at the flowers and the fountain, heard the musical tinkle of the water and longed to be out there, but turned resolutely back to her studio.

At last, she stepped back critically from her easel, and her eyes narrowed, trying to view the painting objectively——and even according to her own exacting standards, had to admit that it riveted the attention, with its lifelike depiction of its subjects. It possessed a compelling quality, with beauty and energy equally mixed. Peter Bagshaw's slate grey eyes, were half turned on the girl at his side, standing slender and shapely in her flowing white dress——but the painting's power lay in the sheer mastery, that produced the feeling of movement, as man and girl drew their bows over the strings of their violins.

Somehow, this untaught woman had entered into the world of the musician——angle——position of the fingers on the strings—— the sound of music almost flowed into the studio. At Rosamund's feet, on the cream carpet, a single red rose lay, it's crimson petals glowing in velvet tribute.

Her hand stretched out to touch further highlights into a fold of the dress—-then lowered her brush instead. Although there was much more she could do to the painting, instinct told her to leave it now. Any further seeking after perfection might mute the drama of its appeal on the senses. Yet she could hardly bring herself to admit, that it was finally finished. True, it would have to dry and eventually be varnished and then framed. But its actual creation was now complete.

Suddenly tears flooded into her eyes, as she stared at the painting. Now at least, whatever else happened in life, Rosamund would have lasting and poignant memory of the flowering of her love for Peter—-the shining days that come to the heart of one enmeshed in the net of tender emotion. It was indeed fitting tribute to her daughter and the man she loved.

'I hope you don't mind—but you left the front door ajar!'

'Michael! Of course—I went out to fetch the milk in.'

'Well, you should remember to keep it shut. Its sad that we should have to take these extra precautions these days, but—-,' and he shrugged. 'Poor Mrs Higgins at the corner of the road, was broken into last night, beaten up and robbed. I have just come from her bedside in the local hospital.'

'Why, but that's terrible,' cried Sylvia in distress. 'I only know her slightly, from having spoken with her at the local shop.' She made a mental note to visit the hospital and see the old woman. 'How could anyone want to hurt a frail, elderly lady—and one who has so little of this world's goods, judging by her appearance.'

'Probably youngsters wanting money for drugs. That's the usual—although the viciousness of the beating she received has even shocked the local police. It's a spiritual sickness, Sylvia, a malaise that is spreading its tentacles into all branches of society. People are crying out to fill a need, which they are unable to give a name to—-are seeking to slake that need by resource to alcohol, drugs, promiscuity and violence, with all too many now turning to occult practices!' Michael Howard's eyes were flashing, as he grew more impassioned.

'You're right,' aid Sylvia softly. 'What they really want is love--and God is love.' Michael looked at her as she said this, and took one of her paint stained hands in his.

'You speak the complete truth. These days, people are searching into this extraordinary umbrella movement which they loosely call 'New Age'. It's a conglomeration of worthy objectives, such as attempting to slow down the terrible damage man is doing to God's beautiful world. Mixed in with this, what they see as an opening of their senses to outside forces, through meditation, crystals, yoga—-ancient philosophies, worship of an earth goddess, not realising that by doing so, they are making themselves vulnerable to satanic attack, through their involvement in the occult.'

'How is that young boy, Stephen, now? The one who was messing around with ouija boards?' She withdrew her hand as she spoke, smiling as she saw his own hand was now sticky with paint. She handed him a wet turps cloth.

'After ministry, Stephen is now at peace with himself. He says that he had months of the most terrible nightmares, after those Ouija sessions—was too scared even to go to bed sometimes.' Michael shook his head, remembering the tormented youngster who had come to him for help. 'I will introduce you to him at church tomorrow, Sylvia. Since he accepted Jesus into his life, he has become another person, and in his turn, is reaching out to many of his young friends, who are as disturbed as he once was, through turning to tarot,

I-Ching, and astrology, and to mediums. One of the most rewarding features of my work Sylvia, is seeing immediate release from bondage as they turn their lives to Christ—-to find inner healing and peace—-happiness!'

'I would like to meet Stephen.'

'Then you shall. Sylvia——when he was through in the vestry,

he saw your wonderful painting of the Christ. You remember you told me to keep it there until it is absolutely dry—-well, he looked at it—-this was before ministry, and he asked who had painted it. I told him about you. He said—-'If Jesus is anything like this lady's vision of him, then I want to know him.' I truly believe that you had very special help when you painted that picture.'

'Thank you,' said Sylvia simply. 'Yes—-I know that I did,'

'Well, that brings me round to what I have come round to ask you. Tomorrow is Whit Sunday——-Pentecost! May I take it, that it is time to display that painting in the church?' Michael looked at her expectantly.

'Yes.'

'Wonderful!' Now at last he turned from Sylvia and saw the painting she had been working on——and he drew in a deep breath. Although no connoisseur of the art world, he nevertheless knew instinctively, that he was looking on a very fine work indeed. One that would live on years after the painter was gone. Long he stared at it and turned back to Sylvia, unable to find words suitable to express what he felt. If the painting of the 'Christ' was the shining crown of her life, then surely this other painting was its sceptre. All the love of a mother's heart, had flowed into this portrayal of her daughter and Peter Bagshaw, the power of its execution ensuring that future generations would marvel at its artistry.

'Sylvia—-you prayed for time to paint this picture——and the result is beyond my poor words to express. Congratulations, dearest friend. I feel very proud to know the painter!'

'Thank you, Michael! You are the first person to see it. Hermione has been asking repeatedly——but I wanted to finish it first. Lack of confidence, I suppose. I knew it was quite good, but was afraid I might spoil it. An artist can do too much to a painting, you know. The secret I think is to know when to put down the brush.' She smiled self-consciously. 'Well—-let's go into the kitchen and have some coffee.' He followed her, as she continued talking. 'Oh——and by the way, Michael——Rosamund has given me tickets for you and Sue for Monday night. It's the first performance of the 'Rose Concerto' at the Albert Hall. You have a box next to Hermione's.'

'Why—-how very kind of her. I would have gone in any case—-but the price of a box, would have been an extravagance beyond my purse. I must say that I am looking forward to it tremendous-ly——and Sue loves music, as you know!' He took the cup of cof-fee from her. She started to cough. He put the cup down and was just in time to catch her, as she collapsed.

Rosamund and Peter bent over the couch. Sylvia was lying very still, too weak to move yet, but her smile was as warm as ever. Michael stood by the door, talking to the doctor, who was just going.

'Its no good getting her into hospital. She just won't stay there and to be honest, I think she is better left here in her own home, until she herself decides otherwise. She is an extraordinary woman, Pastor.'

'True. If you are passing my church tomorrow, come in. You will find one of her paintings displayed there. I would like you to see it, doctor.'

'Really? Then yes, I will. I have known that she paints of course, but have only seen the few landscapes on the walls of this room.' The doctor looked at him curiously.

'Then you are in for a surprise.'

Horeb church was in fact a long meeting hall, positioned beneath the local branch library. Its worshippers in no wise dis-turbed by the rumbling of the underground trains, which passed far below. Its dark, wood panelled walls had been lovingly waxed, the ceiling was cream with dark wood beams. There were no pews, but chairs were set in a semi circle about a low platform. There was no altar, just a simple table, set with a white cloth. Above it, Sylvia's painting in a plain wood frame.

Michael Howard stood before the Bible, set on his lectern, and stared across at his congregation. The seats were full, with many standing. In the front, sat Sylvia and next to her, Rosamund, Peter and Hermione. Behind them, he noticed to his amazement, Ernst Morgenstern, together with Svetlana Ouvetsky and a serious young man with Semitic features, whose eyes were fixed on Rosamund's back To Michael's left, several young people were grouped around a piano. A violinist started to play softly, his soaring notes now taken up by the other young musicians. The people started to sing————'Come, Holy Spirit, come.' The singing was beautiful, full of emotion.

Rosamund listened to it and turned to Peter to see his reaction, for the people were now pouring out their hearts to God, in spontaneous melody that rose and fell, and was not in English. She began to realise that what she was hearing, must be what Sylvia had described to her as 'tongues.' Peter's face was intent. He drew in a deep breath. What was this——sensation stealing into his harshly disciplined sophisticated heart. No——it was more than mere sensation. This was a presence. Peter felt himself start to tremble——tears came into his eyes and he closed them in prayer.

Sylvia lowered her head, as Michael spoke to the people about the painting now hanging at the top of the church, saying that although no one had any idea what the Lord Jesus had looked like, when he had walked the dusty roads of Palestine. That nevertheless, the beautiful painting Sylvia had donated to Horeb, was one that would touch every heart, focussing their thoughts on the Holy One, their Living Lord, whom one day, they would truly see in all the power of his Majesty.

Then Michael Howard started to preach on the power of the Holy Spirit, sent by the Father to cleanse the hearts of men, to fill them with his power and love, to help them in all aspects of their lives. All eyes were fastened on the young pastor, whose eyes flashed with the fervour of his message. Then he asked if any present wanted prayer for anything specific. A young black woman, clutching a toddler, put her hand up. Michael asked her to come to the front.

'What is your name,' he asked her?

'Jenny Johnson—-and this is my baby, Tommie. Tommie, well he was born deaf, Pastor. I want him to be able to hear, when the other children call to him——to be able to hear my voice—and yours!' She stood erect before Michael, holding the child in her arms. Rosamund and Peter stared at the scene in surprised amazement. What did the woman expect Michael to be able to do?

'Do you believe that Jesus can heal your little boy,' asked Michael? The woman looked at him steadfastly.

'Yes, Pastor—-I do. I believe the Lord can give my little boy his hearing.' All eyes were riveted on the young woman in the violet coat. Michael bowed his head in prayer, then placed his hands on the little boy.

'Tommie——in Jesus name, receive your healing,' he said to the child—-and as he spoke, the child lifted his head, to stare at Michael. The pastor walked behind the woman. 'Don't let him look round,' he said. Then he clapped his hands sharply. The child turned his head. Then Michael took off his watch and held it to the little boy's ear. An interested smile spread across his small face and he started making clicking noises with his tongue, in time with the ticking of the watch. Michael stood immediately in front of him.

'Mum,' he said.

'Mmmm,' enthused the child. Michael went behind him.

'Mum!'

'Mmm! Mmmm——Mmmm!' Suddenly the hall was full of people praising God for the miracle that had just occurred in their midst. As for Jenny Johnson, she was on her knees, Tommie standing wonderingly at her side. Then he toddled over to Sylvia and held out his little hands.

'Tommie. Tommie,' said Sylvia.

'Tumm,' said the little boy. Then his mother laughing and crying and praising God, swept him up into her arms, and went back to her place and the service continued. Then, after the last hymn of praise, the people filed out, to go round to a smaller hall, where they were to have coffee. Sylvia and her party left, to drive to Hermione's flat. They sat in that luxurious lounge, thinking of the bare meeting hall, in which they had just witnessed what could only be described as a miracle—-and they besieged Sylvia with questions.

'He is a very wonderful young man, that preacher,' said Ernst. 'I have never seen such a thing before.'

'He is indeed a greatly blessed man of God,' said Sylvia softly. 'But you know Ernst, he is only a channel for the wonderful healing power of God. Of himself, he could do nothing.'

'Have there been other healings,' asked Hermione?

'Oh, yes! People delivered from cancer—deformities—arthritis and many other infirmities. People have been set free from alcoholism and drug addiction, gambling—-and from the evils occurred in dabbling with the occult.' Her thin, sallow features were flushed with emotion, as she shared her knowledge and faith with these others.

'You once told me, that Michael had prayed for you,' said Peter, watching her curiously. He did not add, that she obviously had not received healing from her cancer, but she read his thoughts.

'Yes, Peter. Michael and the whole church prayed for me—still do. True I have not been healed physically, but the most tremendous joy has flooded through my life, and you may judge for yourself of Our Lord's hand upon my brush,' she exclaimed, with a smile and Rosamund took her mother's hand, blinking back tears.

'May I say what a superb painting you created for that church,' said Leopold. 'I am a Jew—-but I must admit that I was deeply touched by that face—-those eyes! I intend to return to Horeb one day, to look at that painting again—-and to speak with Michael Howard.' His dark eyes fixed her with their intense stare. 'Perhaps I might call upon you also, dear lady?'

'Of course, Leopold—-but perhaps you should come soon,' she

replied quietly, so that only the youth heard her words. Then the conversation became general until lunch, after which the party split up, Peter and Rosamund driving Sylvia back home, for she was extremely tired. Then they hurried off, for a last but one rehearsal of the Rose Concerto, which was being performed for the first time in public, on the following evening.

Rosamund stood in front of her dressing room mirror. She was wearing a new white dress similar in style to the one she had worn when she received the Castel Trophy—only now, that magnificent emerald adorned her engagement finger, setting a seal on her new maturity. A few months ago, she had been competing against other talented young musicians—-now she would be playing at the side of the world's acknowledged premier violinist, said also to be the greatest composer this century. As she considered this—-the responsibility she carried on her shoulders struck her with insidious force. This concerto was she knew the peak of Peter Bagshaw's achievement. Suppose she did less than justice to that beautiful theme, in the part of the work, where she would stand at his side, to play that poignant duet. A dozen negative thoughts assailed her.

'Miss Rosamund—-Sir Peter asks you to wear this!'

She took the rose the attendant offered her, lifted it to her nostrils and inhaled its sweetness. When she fastened it to the front of her gown, so that it nestled between her breasts, all doubts had fled.

The great concert hall was packed, every seat taken, the topmost gallery jammed with those standing. The world's press was in attendance, wondering if this new concerto would be able to contend with his 'Peace for the Nations'. Hermione was seated in her box, looking regal in amethyst satin, with a pearl and amethyst necklace gracing her still youthful neck, matching jewels at ears and wrist. Her cheeks were flushed with happiness, as she looked down at the stage, where the curtains now revealed the orchestra. Her eyes sought out Peter and Rosamund.

'It's like a dream,' murmured Sylvia, who was sitting at Hermione's side, wearing her favourite caftan. 'I can hardly believe that Rosamund—my little daughter, will be playing here——and with Peter!'

Hermione took the thin hand in hers and squeezed it—then both women were silent, as the opening chords of the concerto, stole on the air. Rodrigo Mendes baton quivered, instructed, implored, as the magic of the music held the audience spellbound. Fire, passion——tribulation, throbbing notes of utmost despair. A flute sounded a note of purest love and hope, stirring all hearts, its message taken up by the horns and then the full orchestra! Then the tempo changed. Peter Bagshaw and Rosamund lifted their bows and a waterfall of cascading notes throbbed to rousing crescendo——and it was the interval. The applause was sustained and deafening.

The second half started dramatically, its throbbing heartbeat vibrating with mesmeric intensity. The audience sat absolutely motionless, the passion of the music holding them in thrall. Wilder now and full of longing, the tension of music built up, tearing at the senses. Then magically, gently at first, Peter and Rosamund started on that beautiful theme, which was the climax of the concerto. The sounds that lilted almost eerily around the hall became charged with emotion. All eyes were fixed on their bows, as the music poured in waves. Wildly despairing at first, the anguish giving way to hope, until the air was charged with purest joy, the throbbing strings vibrating with a happiness that transmitted itself to every person absorbing this most unusual and beautiful of works.

Many eyes were damp with tears. An absolute stillness greeted the conclusion of the concerto. Then the applause broke and it was thunderous! Rodrigo Mendes dark eyes flashed with triumph! He took bow after bow——but it was for Peter Bagshaw that the audience cried themselves hoarse——and for this new star to rise on the musical horizon, vivacious and it would seem with

a talent that would almost seem to match Peter's own—-
Rosamund—Rosamund Lake! That duet had been the most
incredibly beautiful movement any could remember hearing, and
so they shouted their praise, clapping until their hands stung from
the effort.

Rosamund took a final bow, with Peter at her side. The stage
was littered with bouquets—-and now, as she looked almost
uncomprehendingly at the great sea of faces turned upon them,
she looked inquiringly at Peter, eyes shimmering with tears.

'They are calling for an encore, Peter,' she said.

'No. It would detract from that which they will now carry away
in their hearts,' said Peter softly. 'But we will give them something
to remember this evening for, as well as that which they already
have had,' He held his hand up for silence.

'Ladies and gentlemen. We thank you from the bottom of our
hearts. The concerto you have just heard was started five years
ago, born of deep distress at a personal tragedy. It was finished
three years ago—but I decided to withhold its first public performance, until this young lady at my side, was ready to fulfil her
early promise, which I think you will agree, she has done so wonderfully tonight. It is to Rosamund, soon to be my wife, that I
have dedicated the 'Rose Concerto'. He took her hand that bore
his ring and lifted it to his lips, and then in spontaneous gesture,
she lifted her lips for his kiss.

The hall exploded into applause. Suddenly a familiar figure was
walking towards them on the stage, bearing a huge basket of red
roses. Maestro Ernst Morgenstern placed the basket at
Rosamund's feet then clapped an arm about either waist and
hugged them to him. Rodrigo Mendes joined them for a last
bow————————-and the evening was over!

Champagne flowed at Hermione's flat, as toasts were drunk to
Peter and Rosamund. Rodrigo let out a sigh of deepest satisfaction. Tonight was the fulfilment of a life's ambition, to conduct
the most inspired new work of the twentieth century. Only one

small thing dented his complete joy in the evening—-and now he spoke of it.

'My friends—-perhaps we could drink a silent toast, to one who should have taken part in this evenings performance——but is no longer with us. I refer to that wonderful cellist, Adrian Moulting—-rest his soul.' His dark eyes were sad.

'We all knew he was very ill,' said Peter soberly. 'Otherwise I would never have allowed the performance to go ahead without him. He was a good and faithful friend, a comfort to me in my dark days. I heard this morning, that he had died in a Los Angeles clinic. If I had realised just how ill he was, I would have flown out there, to be with him.'

'You met him on you recent American tour, did you not,' asked Hermione?

'Yes. He was at home when I called at his lovely old house—-sitting on the veranda, in his wicker rocking chair, sipping his favourite orange brandy liqueur, a bright patchwork quilt over his knees. He looked ill, emaciated——but he greeted me with all his old warmth. I bitterly regret now, that I didn't spend more time with him——perhaps have persuaded him to return to this country to get specialist advice.' Peter's voice was sad. 'He died of pneumonia, didn't he. If only that stupid woman, Lois Challoner, had not been giving me so many problems, I would have tried to do more. I shall never forgive myself.' His voice was dejected and Rosamund slipped onto the side of his chair and slipped an arm about his shoulders. He squeezed her hand gratefully.

'But there was nothing you could have done, Peter my friend. It may have been pneumonia that finally killed him——but surely you knew that Adrian was suffering from AIDS?'

'What?' Peter's face blanched with shock. 'But he was not homosexual.'

'No. But he had a very pretty young mistress, a South American girl, who was a heroin addict. Carmelita died eighteen months ago—-of AIDS. Man or woman can contact HIV through normal

heterosexual relationship, Peter.' Rodrigo shook his head sombrely. 'The scientists are only now beginning to understand the full
extent of the danger with which AIDS threatens mankind. So far,
there is no known cure.'

'Surely it started in the homosexual community in America,'
said Peter, his face still frozen with shock.

'Yes. But I have heard that before that, it was in evidence in
Africa. It started to take its toll slowly in the States. The American
government seemingly took no immediate action, considering it
to affect only a few members of society, with a certain life style.
Then as year succeeded year, it began to spread at an alarming
rate——noticeably so in the entertainment world. Actors and
musicians started to find colleagues laid low by it. Some famous
names began to be mentioned in the press and the world took
notice——but I fear, too late. We are sitting on a time bomb,
Peter!'

'But surely, it is only those who are particularly promiscuous
who are at risk,' ventured Rosamund, her young face tense with
concern.

'Those, certainly. But also––young sons and daughters, who
mess around with drugs, using infected needles. Then there are
those unfortunate ones, haemophiliacs, who have received infected blood transfusions—a death sentence. A husband or wife who
is maritally unfaithful, may contract it, and then pass it on to their
innocent partner.'

'From what I have heard,' said Sylvia, who had so far been listening silently, 'A person who becomes HIV positive, only
becomes aware of his or her condition, when after a few weeks,
there is a slight illness, with inflammation of the lymph glands.
This clears——and apparently there are no further symptoms for
some considerable time. Unless there is early diagnosis, the affected person can pass on the disease to anyone with whom they have
sex, unaware that they are doing so.'

'How do you know so much about it, Mother,' asked

Rosamund in surprise?

'Pastor Howard is presently counselling several people in our area, who have the disease—-and is also visiting unfortunates in prison, who are infected, as well as liasing with their worried relatives.' Sylvia spoke with a tremor in her voice. She did not let them know that she often accompanied Michael and his wife Sue, on their prison visits.

Hermione gave a quick shudder—-then forced a smile back onto her face.

'What a sad topic of conversation, for such a wonderful night,' she said. 'Let's fill our glasses and drink another toast! This one to the future—-to Peter and Rosamund on their forthcoming marriage!' As the champagne cork popped violently, it seemed to clear the air of the heaviness that had fallen on the little group. As the golden bubbles caressed their throats, the problem of AIDS receded to the back of their minds.

Rodrigo smiled and lifted a guitar he had brought and started to play some spirited flamenco music. Rosamund's cheeks burned with excitement, as the second glass of champagne loosened inhibition. She stood up and clicked her fingers. She had learned a few of the spirited Spanish dances, when Hermione had taken her on a month's holiday to southern Spain. They had rented a villa in a small village in the mountains, where time had stood still. She would always remember the intense violet of the mountains in the twilight, against a smouldering sky. There had been that quaint restaurant, stuffed birds and animals lining its staircase, and the candles guttering on the tables during occasional power cuts! A fire had blazed in the open grate. And she had watched the young couples who had leapt to their feet, at the prompting of the ancient guitarist, with his face of creased leather. The dancing had been wild and uninhibited, and Rosamund had loved it. At fifteen she had identified spiritually with the emotion of the Spanish people—-had learned their dances.

She lifted the skirt of her long white dress—-and began to

dance. Rodrigo watched her in delighted surprise. His fingers moved faster and he began to sing, the guttural words thrown with sibilance into the air, as Rosamund's feet beat furiously on the parquet floor, avoiding the carpet. Her body curved and swayed, as she flashed her green eyes seductively at Peter. Faster and faster the music rose, compelling them all to their feet.

'Come, Peter—-come,' she cried and seized his hands. He shook his head in amusement.

'I wouldn't know how, my dear,' he cried.

'But I do,' said a laughing voice. Leopold Heine tossed off his evening jacket and stood on his toes, his hands above his head. He looked towards Rodrigo, who struck up another rhythm. It was the dance of the bullfighter. Rosamund was still panting from her earlier efforts. She glanced towards Peter, whose face was expressionless—-then advanced to Leopold, as together they danced and swayed in the age old drama. Automatically, the whole room started to clap in time and Rodrigo's voice rose with the music as he both played and slapped his guitar—then with last throbbing chord, his voice hoarse, he set aside the instrument. Leopold looked down at the laughing girl at his side and raised her hand to his lips.

'Salute,' he said. She stared back at him. His black eyes were burning with desire and for the first time, she felt a slight apprehension, at something she read in those eyes. Then with a bow, he resumed his seat, to the applause of the party—-and Rosamund had to explain how she had acquired this hitherto unknown accomplishment.

'I didn't know you could dance like that,' said Peter slowly. His eyes flickered in Leopold's direction. 'I would prefer that you keep this accomplishment for my own private delectation in future!' It was said in teasing tones, but Rosamund saw the cold look he directed towards Leopold and knew to her surprise, that Peter was jealous. She kissed him contritely.

'I will dance especially for you—-on our wedding night,' she promised him and saw his eyes darken.

The evening drew to a close. Ernst and Svetlana left first, accompanied by Leopold. Then Rodrigo took his leave and finally, Peter drove Sylvia back to her flat. She stumbled as she entered the hallway——and Peter caught her and helped her into the sitting room. Her face was grey with pain and he ran to the phone.

'No, Peter——I will be all right—I'm just tired. Don't call them. I want to keep going until the wedding. After that, my dear, it will be in God's hands. Now——go back to Rosamund. Watch over her carefully, this dear child of mine. Soon she will need all her strength,' she said——and Peter knew what she meant. He lifted her hand to his lips.

'You are a very gallant woman, Sylvia Lake,' he said quietly—and left.

If Hermione was a little sad, that Peter and Rosamund were not to have the fashionable wedding she would have liked, she hid the fact from them well. She decided that if they were determined to hold a private ceremony at Michael Howard's church, then she would do everything she could to make all go smoothly. It was at least to be a white wedding, but with only a few of Peter and Rosamund's musical friends present. The press had been ringing Hermione's flat periodically, to try to find out where the ceremony was to be held—but to no avail. So they checked with all likely churches——even getting touch with Garnford's village church, where the vicar informed them regretfully, that Sir Peter had at no time discussed a possible wedding there.

Rosamund sat quietly in her bedroom, the night before the wedding, looking at the gorgeous white dress hanging on the outside of her wardrobe. She could hardly believe that this was the last night she would spend on her own. She sipped the milk drink that Hermione had pressed on her, insisting that it would help her to sleep. Dear Hermione——how would she have got through these last years, without the support of this second mother. Then her thoughts sped to Sylvia, her own dear mother. She thought how frail she had looked, when she had kissed her good-night. As she closed the door of the flat in Shirland road, Rosamund had been caught by a terrible pang, as the knowledge forced itself into her mind, that perhaps one day soon, the flat would be empty——the flower filled courtyard left untended. She could not bear to face that knowledge and pushed it from her. Tomorrow was her wedding day——and surely a June wedding was the dream of every bride.

She slipped into bed, but it was some two hours before she finally slept, to dream of Peter. What would it be like, tomorrow night? Would he like the way she looked? Would she satisfy him, in the way a woman had to, with the man she loved? She did not ask herself whether Peter would fulfil her own needs. She didn't have to, for instinctively she knew that he would.

Morning broke and the sun streamed in through her window. Hermione appeared with a kiss and a cup of coffee. The ceremony was to be early, at 11am, so that the party could then motor down to Garnford, where the wedding lunch would be served. Peter had spent the night at the Dorchester, with Ernst, who was to be his best man. Hermione had forbidden him to appear at her flat that morning——he was not to see Rosamund until they met at Horeb.

'I am going to drive round to your mother and collect her now, while you have a quiet breakfast,' said Hermione. She hugged Rosamund fondly. 'The hairdresser will be here in half an hour's time,' she said and was gone. Rosamund showered and slipped into a pale green kimono, while she drank some coffee and played with a croissant. She was too excited to eat. All that was happening seemed like a dream. A scant few months ago, the most important thing in her life had been to work for the Castel trophy——now, not only had she received acclaim as a fine musician in her own right, but was to marry the man she adored. It all seemed too good to be true—unreal.

'Good morning, Darling!'

'Mother! Oh, you look beautiful!' She stared in amazement at Sylvia, who was wearing a rose pink dress, with loose panels that hung from her shoulders, drifting with her every movement, disguising the painfully thin frame. She was skilfully made up, cosmetics hiding the dark eye sockets and yellow pallor and a hat with soft fall of small ostrich feathers, in matching rose, framed her face. She smiled gratefully at Rosamund's praise, as she opened her arms to her daughter.

'Happy—-happy day, my dearest one,' she murmured softly.

'The hairdresser is here,' called the maid. Time sped by—-she stood as Hermione and Sylvia arranged the folds of her dress, looking at herself in the mirror, in almost disbelief. Surely this couldn't be her—-the once thin child with bony knees and wispy hair, who had screamed defiance at Sir Peter! The lovely young woman, who stared back at her from the cheval mirror, seemed like a mysterious stranger.

'Rosamund——-you can't wear your jade pendant with that dress,' said Hermione. 'You need your pearls.'

'But I've never taken the pendant off before!'

'Well—-I'll tell you what to do,' said Sylvia with a smile. 'Pin it to the inside of your dress! Something old, something new——now for something borrowed and something blue!

'Yes. And both the pendant and the pearls are old,' said Hermione.

'Here is something new,' said her mother. 'I found this little butterfly in a Bond Street jeweller. It is so tiny you can pin it on your head-dress.' The fragile filigree wings were set on an invisible spring, so that they quivered from the pearl and gold body——an exquisite work. Rosamund exclaimed in delight. She kissed Sylvia and lowered her head, as they settled the veil on her hair. The little butterfly nestled amongst the circlet of orange blossom.

'Something borrowed,' said Hermione, handing her a wisp of a lace handkerchief!

'And something blue,' laughed Rosamund, lifting the folds of her dress, to display the frilly blue lace garter. Then Roberts was knocking at the door————and it was time. Rodrigo Mendes was giving her away and sat beside her in the Rolls, with Hermione and Sylvia following in the Bentley. People poured out of their doors at the sight of the white beribboned limousines, which drew up before Horeb's door, where Pastor Michael Howard was waiting, with his wife Sue at his side, a broad smile on his face.

'Rosamund, you look extremely lovely,' said Michael gently——but it was really Sylvia he had come to the door to look for, and seeing her looking so radiant in her rose dress, he sighed in relief. He took her hand briefly and murmured a quick blessing, before disappearing back into the church. The strains of the wedding march sounded within, and Rodrigo offered his arm to Rosamund.

'Rodrigo————I'm scared!'

'Don't be! You must be strong to give strength to Peter. He has been biting his nails all morning,' siad Rodrigo with a grin. Biting his nails? He would never do that! Then she started to smile, thinking of her own habit, only recently overcome, and the tension broke. She walked up the aisle on the Spaniard's arm, with grace and confidence. She drew level with Peter and suddenly she was trembling.

'Darling————,' he whispered huskily————'I love you.'

Michael commenced the simple service, with a congregation drawn from Sylvia's humble friends, who were all there. Yet the lovely praise hymns, accompanied by the strains of a violin, played by Stephen, soared with joy and solemnity, as these two were joined together in bond of love, in the sight of God. Ernst eyes were moist with emotion, as he handed Peter the ring.

'With this ring I thee wed————,' he said. As he mouthed the lovely old words, promising to love and cherish his bride, his voice almost broke. Then he continued firmly. As he kissed her, she saw that his eyes were damp.

'My darling wife,' he whispered.

'My beloved husband,' she murmured back. Then music stole sweetly through the church. Ernst had dispensed with tradition and seated himself at the piano, paying his own special tribute to his friend's marriage. Peter lifted his head and glanced towards Sylvia's picture of the Christ and the eyes seemed to smile at him. Michael saw that look.

'After I return from honeymoon,' said Peter quietly, 'I want to come and see you. I think I want to become a Christian.'

'Why then——praise the Lord,' replied Michael with a smile, his eyes full of joy. A brief pause in the vestry, swift movements of a pen and then they were walking down the aisle together, to cries of congratulation. They posed for photographs, Hermione looking gorgeous in jewel blue, gently supporting Sylvia, who had swayed slightly.

'Ernst,' called Hermione. He saw the need and supported Sylvia on the other side, as Svetlana hovered, close behind. At last the photographs were over, confetti flung and the Rolls drove slowly away, a collection of old shoes incongruously bobbing behind. They helped Sylvia into the Bentley, where she sat frail and still beside Hermione, but with a smile of utmost happiness on her face.

'She was a most beautiful bride, wasn't she Hermione?'

'The most beautiful in the world,' replied her friend, brushing her cheek with a kiss. 'And you were the most beautiful of bride's mothers!'

'I'm so happy, Hermione. God answered my prayer——to let me live to see my daughter married.' She turned painfully, to glance back at the little church, as the car started out.

'Well——-I want to tell you now, that your picture of Peter and Rosamund is hanging in the music room at Garnford! I had the portrait of Natasha removed——placed in one of the guestrooms. I supervised the men hanging it, because I know you told me it has not had the time to dry out properly yet. The frame you chose looks just right. Oh Sylvia, it's a wonderful painting, really it is!'

Sylvia looked troubled.

But should you have removed the portrait of Natasha, without Peter's permission? Suppose he is angry?'

'He won't be——not when he sees what's hanging there instead! Besides, it was time to lay the past at rest. I have put away all those photographs of Natasha as well——replaced them with those of Peter and Rosamund. I've changed the furnishings too!'

'Oh, Hermione! Yet—-I'm sure you are right. I can't wait to see everything!' The distraction seemed to have given new strength to Sylvia, who began to look quite animated. But as the long journey continued she seemed to weaken again.

Harrington was on the steps, together with all the staff, to receive Peter and Rosamund. As the couple stepped from the car, the butler signed to them and a triumphal arch was formed, as they held garlanded frames festooned with June roses, over the newly weds heads. Now Harrington was helping Hermione out of the Bentley and with utmost gentleness, assisting the sick woman to her feet.

'Do you wish to go to your room, madam,' he asked Sylvia?

'No. Harrington——but thank you.' His kind eyes swept over her, seeing behind the carefully painted face, to the pain beyond. It must have taken courage of a very special kind, to have taken part in this morning's ceremony and then endured the long drive from London. No wonder she looked exhausted. Lady Hermione had already warned him just how gravely ill Sylvia Lake was.

The wedding lunch was served——and it was delicious. Cook had excelled herself—the wine cool and invigorating. Then the cake was brought in. Rosamund looked at it in delight, for the two tiny figures atop it, were holding miniature violins!

'Let me help you to cut it darling,' said Peter. He placed his hand over hers, and her perfume stole into his nostrils and his breath quickened. A camera flashed as the moment was caught. Then they all quietened as Hermione stood to make an announcement.

'Sylvia has a special present for you both. It is in the music room,' she said.

Harrington opened the door and wonderingly Peter and Rosamund made their way to the music room, with the others close behind, Sylvia leaning heavily on Harrington's arm.

Peter gasped! What had happened? The room had changed! Instead of oyster pale furnishings, all was now in delicate shades of green, with graceful ferns in beautiful white and gold urns. Then he saw it—-and his mouth dropped. He was speechless. It was an amazing likeness of himself and Rosamund. It dominated the room——their bows seeming to move—some kind of optical illusion perhaps. Sylvia had captured all the arrogance of his features, whilst allowing a look of deep love to shine from those slate grey eyes, as he stared challengingly down at Rosamund. She was responding to his glance, with passion in her own extraordinary green stare, as their joint love of their music, seemed to flow from the strings. It was an incredible painting.

'Sylvia! What can I say!' He turned at last in utter amazement to his mother-in-law, glancing at Rosamund, to see her reaction.

'Why——-mother! It's a most beautiful painting,' breathed Rosamund, touched beyond words by what she saw. How had Sylvia managed to paint it, ill as she was? How had she managed to paint the violins like that—-the movement of their hands—— but above all, how had she captured their love for each other, with such tenderness?

'Do you really like it,' asked Sylvia diffidently?

'Like it? It's superb. However did you manage to capture that moment—position of the hands—the feeling of energy and the quality of——?' He sought for the right words.

'Of love,' said Rosamund softly.

'Well—-you see, I wanted to give you a lasting memory of your dawning love for each other, with all the challenge of the years ahead—-combined with memory of my love for you both,' said Sylvia. The others were exclaiming at the picture, standing back and viewing it from different angles. Sylvia listened to their praise with a grateful heart—but it was the response from Peter and Rosamund that was reward enough for all her hard work. She was indeed content. She turned to Harrington.

'Please—-would you help me to my room now,' she asked him. 'I really do feel rather tired.' As the man started to support her, she leaned on him, and Rosamund hurried to her side, concern on her face

'It's all right, Rosamund darling. I'm just very tired.'

She turned a laughing countenance on the girl. 'Don't forget to come into my room to let me see your going away outfit, before you leave for Scotland,' she said.

'As though I would forget! Are you sure you will be all right though? I don't like the idea of leaving you!'

'I don't think Peter would appreciate his mother-in-law coming on his honeymoon,' said Sylvia lightly, and at those joking tones, Rosamund relaxed.

True to her word, she came into her mother's room, wearing a suit of forest green, a jaunty knickerbockers outfit chosen with the Highlands in view. Peter came in behind her, in sports jacket and cords. They looked supremely happy and Sylvia smiled. She was too full for words now. It was accomplished. Rosamund was married to the man she loved and who loved her. The future was bright and full of promise————and now at last, she could relax—-let go!

'Be happy, my darlings,' she breathed gently, as they kissed her and went out of the door————and then she fell into exhausted slumber.

As Peter and Rosamund climbed into the helicopter, specially hired to fly them to the little village of Kinloch Rannoch in Perthshire, Sylvia started to give in to those forces in her own body, that were drawing her towards a very different kind of journey.

CHAPTER NINE

It was the first time that Rosamund had travelled by helicopter. She soon found that she enjoyed the sensation. It had been Peter's idea that they should honeymoon is Scotland. If by any chance, Sylvia should get any worse, they would be able to return quickly. The pilot, whose name also was Peter, told them of his wife Laura, who was expecting their second baby soon. At the mention of babies, Rosamund's eyes became very dreamy, as she tried to imagine what it must feel like to be a mother. Perhaps Peter guessed her thoughts, for he squeezed her hand.

'We are approaching Kinloch Rannoch now,' said the pilot, at the end of four hours, and Rosamund gasped as they hovered over a long sheet of water, set between hills and mountains. One peak in particular caught her eye, for it seemed to rise to a point.

'That is Schiehallion, the 'fairy mountain',' volunteered the pilot. 'Now over there, you will see a Timeshare estate, whilst on the other side of the loch, a few miles along, there is a well known boy's school.'

'That will be Rannoch School,' asked Peter?

'Yes, sir. We are coming in to land now——in that meadow!' the helicopter circled and came gently down. A couple of ponies took to their heels in fright, as the blades set every bush and wild flower in trembling motion. When Rosamund stepped out, she found it strange at first, to be standing on firm ground.

Peter was taking their luggage from the pilot——and their violins. She looked around her. Two hundred yards away a tall house stood perched on a hill, surrounded by rhododendrons. In the late evening sunlight, the house looked as though it were set in a jewel casket, for the rhododendrons were in full bloom, their massed mauve, pink and purple splashed with occasional white and wine red, making spectacular garland against the dramatic back cloth of the hills. All around peaks rose steeply to the sky, their lower flanks covered in birch forest——and a few hundred yards away, the waters of the loch sparkled, ruffled by the soft wind.

'Well—-that's the house you want,' said the pilot. 'I would help you with your cases, but I don't really want to leave the copter.' He jerked his head towards several young boys climbing over the fence. He shook hands with Peter and Rosamund, wished them much happiness and climbed back into his craft, which took off. At last they were alone.

'Kiss me,' said Peter. She did so shyly. 'Now——I'll carry the bags and you take the violins.' They set off across the field and climbed over a small style. The field was bordered by a narrow winding road and across from it, was the driveway to the house, two irregular weirdly shaped stones perched on its gate pillars. A heavily built man walked down the drive towards them. He inclined his head courteously.

'You'll be the Bagshaws,' he asked?

'Yes—-Peter and Rosamund Bagshaw.' Peter held out his hand. The man shook hands with each in turn, lifting the cases that Peter had set down. He glanced at the violins, which Peter now took from his wife.

'You'll be musical, then,' he asked? Peter looked at him incredulously. Was he joking? But he obviously wasn't. For once, Peter had not been recognised, in spite of giving his real name. He found it amusing——indeed, refreshing!

'We are having a ceilidh in the village tonight,' the man continued. 'It might be that you would like to give the lads a hand with the music?'

'Why, yes——I'm sure we would enjoy that very much,' smiled Rosamund, 'Wouldn't we, Peter!' Her own eyes were bright with merriment.

'Well——that's settled then. Och, and by the way, my name is Jimmie Munro, though some call me the bear——-a nickname just.' He glanced upwards at the fast disappearing helicopter, which had circled in farewell. 'Now I see you came by helicopter—-so what about a car while you are here? There is a good little garage a quarter of a mile away in the village.' He turned his ruddy face towards them interrogatively, the sun's rays polishing his bald head.

'The helicopter was the fastest way of getting here,' said Peter mildly, for he had detected a hint of criticism in the man's words. 'We were married this morning,' he added.

'The English are always in a hurry——-. Er, what was that you said though? You are just wed? Why then, my heartiest congratulations!'

They entered a wood panelled hall and followed Jimmie up a wide, curved staircase. Stag's antlers and rich folds of red tartan decorated the walls, the stair carpet a dark red.

'This is the dining room——and the lounge is next door,' said Jimmie, throwing the doors open. Fires crackled in both hearths, blazing a welcome. A huge crystal chandelier hung from the lounge ceiling and pictures of birds and animals caught their gaze——-but their attention was then drawn to the dramatic painting over the fireplace of a kilted highlander, red hair and beard jutting above his beruffled shirt, a deer hound at his feet. Above his head, a curiously shaped hill was shadowed in dull purple.

'The sleeping giant,' said Jimmie, as they walked over to the picture.

'He looks quite wide awake to me,' quipped Peter!

'The hill, I mean. The man is the owner of this house——-Sir Percival Bruce. He is English like your selves despite his surname. One of the many absentee landlords with whom our country is plagued!' His brows drew together in acute displeasure as he spoke and they began to realise why he was called 'the bear'. With a final look at the room's good solid furniture, obviously of a previous century, they followed Jimmie up another flight of stairs. He opened a door. This is your bathroom——-the water will be guid and hot. And here is your bedroom!'

Rosamund gave a cry of delight, as she saw the old fashioned four-poster bed, hung with velvet——the two comfortable armchairs and curtains in gold damask. Again a fire crackled in the hearth, while a French ormolu clock, ticked beneath the huge gilt Venetian mirror.

'Why——this is perfect,' she breathed and walked to the window. The sun was sinking and was painting the sky in the most extraordinary shades of flame and bruised violet, the colour flooding over the waters of the loch. It was perhaps the most beautiful sunset she had ever seen, the whole exquisite scene to be indelibly printed on her memory.

So absorbed were they in each other, that they hardly noticed their fellow guests in the dining room that evening, as together they enjoyed the wonderful flavour of the freshly caught salmon, They finished the spicy fruit dumpling, served with cream, then sipped their brandy appreciatively. They became aware of Jimmie watching their table.

'Was the food to your liking,' he asked?

'Wonderful, Mr Munro. Did you manage to sort out a car for us?'

'It is what I came to tell you. There is a black BMW waiting in the drive for you. I took it upon myself to choose it on your behalf. You can see the garage tomorrow.'

'Why, that is splendid.'

'I suppose——you'll be wanting your fiddles for the ceilidh,' prompted Jimmie. 'I rang the folks at the hall, to tell them you would be coming!' Taking the hint, they rose from their table and went upstairs to collect their violins. Rosamund had already changed into a calf length skirt of black velvet, with frilled white shirt and black bolero, while Peter wore a dark green wool plaid shirt with his cavalry twill trousers. Jimmie offered to lead them to the hall in his car, although there was little chance of getting lost in a village of only three hundred people.

As they got out of their car, sounds of music were borne to their ears, from the village hall. Jimmie signalled to someone standing by the door, as they approached—-and the sound of the music ceased abruptly. Instead, there was the skirl of pipes, and as they entered, they saw a solitary piper standing on the stage, playing a hauntingly beautiful tune.

'It is for you——for good luck on your marriage,' said Jimmie gruffly. 'The composition is Roddy McLean's own!' He smiled as he saw the warmth of their reaction.

'Oh, Peter—-isn't it just wonderful,' whispered Rosamund. 'What a lovely thing to do.' Then she looked around at the crowd of laughing village folk, who all pushed forward to wish them happiness in their new life together. Then two accordionists and the keyboard player commenced to strike up a spirited jig.

'Strip the Willow,' said Jimmie. 'Put your fiddles up there on the stage—-they will be all right. Now take your places with this set.' Rosamund's cheeks were flushed scarlet with the exertion of the dancing, as somehow they managed to follow the instructions shouted at them by the other dancers, as they wove and swung at breathtaking pace. At the conclusion of the dance, she looked up at her husband. This was a new Peter, relaxed and carefree. He seemed to have shed at least ten years!

One of the accordionists climbed down from the stage and introduced himself to them.

'Hugh Macdonald. My wife Allison is on the keyboard—and that is my son Iain with the other accordion. My congratulations on your marriage, Mr and Mrs Bagshaw. Now I understand you play the fiddle—-so would you like to join us in a tune or two?' He ushered them onto the stage and a whispered conversation ensued.

'You start—-and we will follow you,' said Peter. 'Then we will play a duet for them—an old fashioned waltz. Will that do?' And they were off. Rosamund thought she had never enjoyed herself so much. They quickly caught the rhythm and the tune of the

eightsome reel and received relieved looks from the band that
they could indeed play, which deepened to respect.

'Tales from the Vienna Woods,' inquired Peter, glancing questioningly at Rosamund. She nodded. It was a favourite of theirs
on account of Ernst! As the couples took the floor, Peter and
Rosamund looked into each other's eyes, as their fingers quivered
on the strings and the music that soared from their bows, clear
and beautiful, made many a head turn upwards to the stage. They
had a rare touch on the strings, these two!

They alternatively danced and played their way through the
evening and the locals took them to their hearts, It was a warm
and marvellously friendly occasion. As Peter held Rosamund close
to his heart in the last waltz, her breath quickened—-nor was it
caused by the twirling dance. It wasn't a dream, all of this——-
but real! This man staring down into her eyes in a way that made
her heart pound, was her husband, in whose arms she would soon
lie.

Peter was drinking a night-cap with Jimmie Munro in the
lounge—-Rosamund had gone up into their room ahead of him,
asking to be allowed ten minutes on her own, to which he smilingly acceded. Jimmie viewed him curiously over his whisky glass.

'She is younger than you, I think—-and very bonny. You are
a lucky man, Mr Bagshaw. My own dear wife died some eleven
years ago and I miss her now as much as I did in those first weeks
and months. A good wife is a treasure greater than wealth or position, always remember that.' His bright blue eyes held Peter's
authoritatively. 'Treat her well,' he said.

'I will,' said Peter. 'And yes—-I do know how lucky I am, unbelievably so. I was married before you know, many years ago. My
first wife died in a skiing accident and for years I felt a gnawing
ache—a sense of utter loneliness, which I tried to fill with music.
I never thought I would ever know real happiness again—beyond
satisfaction in my work.' Peter's eyes were grave.

'So, You sought solace in music. For myself, I tried to lose myself in this!' He held his whisky glass aloft.

'Did it work?'

'No! All it did, was to make me lose something else—-this house and estate! I had to sell——should have moved far away from Dalrannoch House! But you see—-there were memories of my wife here—-of our children's growing years. They all live abroad now. I took a position with the man I sold to, as manager of this place, so that I could remain here. Not a very edifying story!' He gulped the rest of his whisky and poured another. He made to refill Peter's glass.

'Not for me, Jimmie.' Peter placed a hand on the other's shoulder, eyes dark with sympathy. 'You have had a difficult time—and are a brave man. It must have taken courage, to remain under such circumstances.'

'Aye—-it did. Well now——away off to that fair young wife of yours. The room I have given you, was the one where Fiona and I spent our first night together—-and all the years thereafter. It is a good room to start a marriage in, Peter Bagshaw.'

He closed the bathroom door. He had changed into the short burgundy robe he had hung there earlier—-then opened the bedroom door. She was standing by the fire, looking incredibly lovely in a gossamer fine lace negligee of shimmering white, caught together in front by silken ribbons. She had turned the lights out, but the leaping firelight licked her beauty with flame, as she turned towards him, arms outstretched. He advanced towards her—-stood still in front of her—-then lifted her hand bearing his wedding ring, to his lips.

'Rosamund——dearest, dearest wife,' he murmured huskily—- then caught her to him, seeking her lips. His hand pulled gently on the ribbons holding her negligee—and it fell open—-slid to the floor. He gazed at her loveliness.

'Wife——you are beautiful!' For answer, she lifted her arms and pulled at the cord of his robe. She gasped. He let it fall on the fire rug and lifting her, carried her over to the bed. He caressed her with the delicacy and innate tenderness with which he brought such exquisite notes from his violin——and then, when she was ready——-! She cried out once. He held her close—then as the soft winds of Rannoch soughed about the house, she cried out again, in ecstasy and joy. That night, their child was conceived.

The days sped by like a dream—days of hill climbing, listening to the music of waterfalls—-making love in a secret glade amongst the sweetness of myriad wild flowers—canoeing on the loch—-attempting to windsurf! Each day brought fresh activities——-wandering on the desolate splendour of Rannoch Moor, where a hundred small lochans gleamed bright blue beneath the June sky and mosses were jewel green amongst the wakening heather. They caught glimpses of deer, shy as the wind, saw birds they did not know, lay beneath a huge boulder, dreaming and planning for the future——-then drove back, staring in wonder at the scattering of ancient rocks, looking as though some giant hand had tossed them. Rannoch, wild and beautiful, a place of mystery, that they would never forget!

But the dream came to an abrupt end, with a telephone call from Hermione. Sylvia had been taken to hospital, on the night of the same day that they had set out for Scotland——-but had not wanted them to know. Only now the doctors advised that time was short, if they wished to see her. Rosamund broke down, as Peter told her the news as gently as he knew how. He held her close, trying to comfort her.

'We have to return to London, Peter,' she sobbed.

'Yes, my darling. Jimmie is booking our flight from Edinburgh and wants to drive us to the airport himself. Let's pack. Remember this——-your mother wanted our happiness more than anything. She planned for us to enjoy this wonderful honeymoon, before facing the inevitable. When we come to her, let it be with the same courage, that she has shown.' Her sobs gradually subsided and she straightened up and started to empty the wardrobe and drawers. He helped her. They took a last wistful look around the room, where they had experienced such unbelievable happiness. Would it ever be the same again?

Jimmie helped them with their cases, going with them to the departure lounge. He grasped their hands, his face working with emotion.

'Goodbye, Peter and Rosamund. God go with you,' he said. 'Don't forget Rannoch——and those who care for you!' Then he was gone and they felt a sense of loss, missing the strength they had found in this lonely Scotsman.

Roberts met them at the airport and drove them straight to the hospital. When they arrived there, they made immediately for the ward where they had visited Sylvia before. Sister came out of her office, as they hesitated at the top of the long ward.

'Sir Peter—-Lady Rosamund. Come in for a moment. Sit down.' She sat at her desk, facing them.

'Sister—-she's not—-?' Rosamund could not frame the word and just looked appealingly at the sister, who shook her head.

'She is very weak and I have the feeling, that she has been holding onto life long enough to see you both again. We have managed to keep the pain as much under control as possible and she has been sleeping for long periods. But she is completely lucid—-and has the most wonderful feeling of peace about her. All my young nurses have been remarking on it.'

'May we see her, sister,' asked Peter huskily?

'Perhaps you would like a cup of tea first, while I see if she is ready for visitors. The nurses may be attending her at this time, for there are screens about her bed.' She called an orderly and asked her to bring tea for the couple, while she went down the ward. They made a token of touching their lips to the cups, faces tense.

They heard their names being called and looked up.

'Peter——Rosamund! I was just going to see her, when I caught sight of you in here.' It was Pastor Michael Howard, face was warm with sympathy. 'She didn't really want us to tell you—

—didn't want to interrupt your honeymoon, but I think she realises the time has come to make her farewells.'

'Oh, Michael——I don't want her to die! I love her!'

'She knows that you do so, dear Rosamund. And that love buoyed her up over all that she has endured over these last few weeks. However hard it is, attempt to show that same happiness in each other, that was shining on your faces on your wedding day——for it will help her very much indeed. If you try, God will give you the grace to be strong.' He placed a hand on each of their shoulders as they sat there, and prayed softly for a few minutes. He straightened up, as sister came in.

'Why——hallo, Pastor. I am glad you've come.' She turned to the couple quietly. 'If you are ready——? She knows you are here and is looking forward so very much to seeing you.' They followed her into the ward. The screens were around the first bed on the left. 'She is here. I will leave the screens. You will have more privacy.'

Rosamund gave a soft cry, as she saw Silvia propped up on the pillows. In one short week, her mother had become gaunt in the extreme, her skin held a waxen pallor—but the eyes that smiled up at Rosamund had the glow of happiness in them. Her lips moved—the words barely audible.

'Rosamund——my darling daughter. I am so sorry to bring you back—from your honeymoon.' Her eyes searched Rosamund's face. 'You are happy, child. Yes, I can see it. Peter——come here.' She turned her head slowly to stare up at him. 'Take great care of her. But then you always have——and I know you always will.' They thought she was going to sleep. But she roused herself and looked at them again, a faint smile curving her lips. 'Was Scotland beautiful,' she asked?

'Oh, mother——Kinloch Rannoch is a magic place. A loch shimmering between woods and mountains——wild roses, blushing red against a blue sky, banks of bluebells between fresh young bracken fronds——rocks as old as time. People who take you to their hearts.' She tried to paint a word picture for Sylvia, who sighed in satisfaction.

'It sounds lovely, dear.'

'It will always remain in our memory—-as will the wonderful old house where we—-became one,' said Peter softly, taking one of her thin hands. 'Sylvia—-mother—-if I too may call you so—-you have given me the greatest gift in this world—my beloved wife!' He raised the hand to his lips and she smiled up at him. Rosamund bent over the bed, and pressed her lips down onto her mother's face.

'Don't cry, darling. I'm not. I am going to be with your father—-with Tristam. You mustn't grieve for me, when I am gone—for we will meet again one day, where there will be no more pain—no more partings. You do believe this, don't you?' She searched her daughter's face.

'Yes, mother——I believe this,' said Rosamund brokenly. Then Michael, who had been standing back, came closer to Sylvia, so that she could se him.

'Hallo, there, dearest friend,' he said softly. 'How is it with you?'

'Michael! I'm so very happy——and oh, so————tired.'

She closed her eyes again—a spasm crossed her face. Then her eyes fluttered open again. Michael took her hands in his and started to pray—-wonderful words. Her lips moved with his. She drew a hard rattling breath——and they thought she had gone. But her eyes opened again—-and she attempted to sit up. An expression of purest joy crossed her features, as she loosed Michael's hands and held hers out in front of her.

'Lord Jesus——-,' she whispered. 'The light————-the glory————-!' And the brave spirit of Sylvia Lake sped on its way, to the Saviour she adored. Michael gently closed her eyes.

'What do you suppose she saw,' asked Peter through stiff lips.

'The risen Lord in all His glory! Now her happiness is complete.' He looked compassionately at Rosamund, who was sobbing as though her heart would break. He prayed again——and Rosamund's sobs gradually ceased, as Peter held her close. At last, when she felt strong enough, Rosamund placed one last kiss on Sylvia's face. 'Tell Daddy I love him,' she whispered, and then with Peter's arm about her shoulders, walked from behind the screens. Michael remained, still praying, but with a look of joy on his face.

Hermione welcomed them back with relief that swiftly turned to sorrow, as they told her of Sylvia's passing.

'I thought you might come here first——waited for you. I should have realised that you would have gone directly to the hospital. I was with her earlier today. She was——wonderful.' Hermione was fighting back tears, for she had come to love Sylvia Lake as a sister. Her death would leave a gap in Hermione's life. She looked at Peter——saw the concern for Rosamund on his face——the love. Then she took the girl in her arms.

'Cry if you want to, darling——let the tears flow. It will help. But once you have finished grieving, remember this. She was the happiest person I have ever met. She had a joy and peace that no money can buy——and no slightest fear of death. Her faith was the most wonderful thing about her. When you go back to Garnford——look at that picture she painted of you both! It is full of life and love and painted with tremendous courage. She will always live for you both, in that painting——and that is why she spent her last strength completing it!' Hermione patted Rosamund's shoulder.

'You're right, Hermione. I know she wouldn't want me to cry——but I am going to miss her so terribly.' Peter's dark eyes were brimming with compassion. He took his weeping young wife from his mother's arms, cradling her to his heart.

'Rosamund——on an earlier occasion, your mother told me she wanted you to have the love and reassurance of a husband, when this inevitable parting came. She knew it would be hard for you——but also, that you would have a similar courage to that which she had so selflessly shown on all occasions.'

'I will try——-really I will.' She took the handkerchief he offered her and blew her red nose hard, mopping her eyes. 'I'm just going to wash my face,' she said quietly. Once in the privacy of the bathroom, she perched on the side of the bath and cried again——great wracking sobs, that shook her body. Gradually, she found control returning. She thought back to that time at Garnford, when she found that her mother had deserted her, the tears——-panic and feeling of exhaustion. But then——the solace she had found in her music, even as a child. Instinctively she knew that she would find that same healing in her violin. She splashed her face over and over with cold water and glanced helplessly at the swollen features that stared back at her, red eyed from the mirror. Why was it, that in books, heroines always managed to cry without showing trace of it, she thought illogically! She took a deep breath and went back into the sitting room.

'Peter——where is my violin?'

'In the hall I think——Roberts put all of our luggage there. I'll get it for you,' and with a wondering look he went.

'Here you are, dear heart.' He looked at her understandingly. She took the violin from the case and went with it into the bedroom. He glanced at Hermione and as they exchanged looks, they heard the sound of Rosamund's violin, the strings exploring some of the praise songs, that Sylvia loved to sing——blending the tunes into a multi coloured skein of soaring praise to God. Peter listened amazed. Then he took his own violin and gently opened the bedroom door. The music that now poured to Hermione's ears, was that of throbbing praise and adoration——not a note of melancholy in it, as these two played lilting farewell to the departing spirit of Sylvia Lake.

Slowly, painfully, Rosamund adjusted to a world that went busily on. Her mother had wished to be cremated and her ashes interred in the village churchyard, close to Holly Cottage. They followed her wishes. Then her paintings were carefully crated and taken to Garnford, together with all her personal possessions. She had left everything to Rosamund, but had asked that if it were possible, Peter should arrange for the flat which was only rented, should be leased to Michael and Sue Howard——as she knew they would tend her garden courtyard. Peter made a point of visiting the estate agents managing the flat. He put in a bid to buy the property, which was promptly accepted. Michael Howard was amazed when he was told, that he and his wife could move in whenever they wished——and that there would be no rent to pay——the only stipulation, to care for the garden.

Sue Howard's pretty face, framed by its cap of short dark curls, was full of emotion, as Peter and Rosamund stood with her in the little courtyard, listening to the soft splashing of the fountain.

'I promise you that I will keep it as Sylvia would have wished! It will be a privilege to care for a place as lovely as this——with so many memories of a brave woman we all loved.

Our present flat is on the third floor. In London, a garden is a precious oasis. How can I ever thank you both!'

Rosamund kissed her and smiled at Michael who joined them now. He had been standing in what had been Sylvia's little studio, thinking of the many times he had seen her painting there.

'Look, Peter and Rosamund——if there is ever anything we can do to help you in any way, then it will be a great pleasure. God bless you both for your kindness!' His face expressed the happiness he felt, at the amazing help this free accommodation was to afford. Now he could direct those monies he had previously had to pay in rent, to helping the needy in his church.

'Perhaps I can come and see you tomorrow——alone, Michael,' said Peter quietly, as the two girls spoke together.

'I shall look forward to seeing you. I am free at 11. Is that too early for you?' Michael's face creased into a smile, for

he knew what   Peter wanted to discuss——-and so it was arranged.

It was middle September. The weather continued hot and

sunny and Hermione swung in a hammock, slung between two of Garnford's ancient oaks, enjoying the slight breeze pouring off the lake. Peter and Rosamund were supposed to be arriving some time today or tomorrow. She sighed contentedly, stretched out her dainty sandalled toes and let her face sink back into the soft cushions. A blackbird trilled his urgent song, a robin chirped, bees buzzed amongst the lavender bushes and roses—-and she fell asleep.

'Hermione!'

'What——Oh! Rosamund!' She sat up, realising the sun was low in the sky. How long had she slept?

'We have been here for two hours now. But you looked so peaceful, that we decided not to disturb you——-only it is getting a little cool now!' The girl smiled at her teasingly, then her face became more serious. 'Hermione——I wanted to speak with you on your own, before Peter joins us.'

'What is it child?' Hermione swung her legs over the side of the hammock and invited Rosamund to join her on it. They sat in companionable silence for a few minutes, gently pushing themselves gently back and forth with their feet. Then at last, Rosamund spoke.

'Darling——you are going to be a grandmother I think!''What was that!' Hermione almost fell off the hammock. She took Rosamund's hands in her own—searching her face. 'Are you sure, Rosamund? Why——-but that is wonderful, wonderful news!'

'Well——it is three months since——! I have been feeling squeamish in the mornings too!' She returned the pressure of Hermione's hands. 'I am going to see a doctor at the weekend—have an appointment. Will you come with me, Hermione?' Hermione kissed her, laughing and crying at the same time.

'Of course, I'll come with you! Does Peter know?'

'Not yet. I want to be absolutely sure first——-but—well, it seems fairly certain!' Rosamund's face held a dreamy look.

Mr Patterson smiled at Rosamund. He had been at the pre-

miere of the Rose Concerto at the Albert Hall and greatly enjoyed
the artistry of the young girl now sitting up on the examination
couch, in her short white gown.

'Yes——you are definitely pregnant, Lady Rosamund.
Congratulations!'

'I had the feeling that it had happened, the first night that Peter
made love to me, on our honeymoon at Kinloch Rannoch!'

'When was that?'

'The third Monday of June!' She looked at him expectantly.
?When do you think I will have the baby?'

'Well——if you are right——and I am sure you are, mothers have
an instinct about these matters, well, the third week of March!'
Now, if you will go with nurse and have yourself weighed—and
then there will be a blood test——and we will need a urine sample.'
He helped her off the couch and the white uniformed nurse, led
her into a side room. Later, when she was dressed, she answered
questions about her general health.

'I have never been ill in my life——except for German measles
when I was very young——and chicken-pox.'

'How about your family's health? Your mother, for instance?'
The doctor was busily making notes. He looked up, as he did not
receive an immediate answer to his question.

'My mother died of cancer, just after our honeymoon.' There
was a slight catch in her voice and the eyes in the doctor's lined
face, expressed sympathy. 'I am very sorry to hear that, my dear.
But perhaps this sorrow will be assuaged in the new joy of
approaching motherhood! A life you treasured has gone——but a
new young life is growing inside you. In six short months, you
will hold your little one in your arms!' He saw from her expression, that this was a baby that would be welcomed into the world.
All too often it seemed these days, young women weighed possible abortion, as an alternative to having their child. True he was
usually able to help them to accept their pregnancy—managed to
put them in touch with those who cold help and advise, where the

circumstances were difficult, as when the mother was very young and unmarried. But it was always a real delight to him, to find a patient who joyed in her condition and didn't allow pressure of career or financial difficulty to detract from the wonder of a new young life forming in the secrecy of her womb. He continued with his questions.

'What about your father?'

'He died in an accident when I was a child. But he was a very healthy man.'

'Do you have any other living relatives, my dear?' he continued to write.

'Only a grandfather in America, whom I've never met—-nor want to! His name is Dryman Lake. He is a film actor.' Her voice was cool and detached.

'Why——I've seen several of his films. Surely his wife was Melissa Lake, the violinist?' He looked at her curiously.

'Yes. She died a few years ago—-of a heart attack. I never met her either.' Her voice didn't invite further discussion and he went on to other matters. Later, as he bowed Lady Hermione and Rosamund from his consulting room, he wondered briefly what had made her choose him, rather than an obstetrician from Harley Street. Curiosity made him inquire how she had come to him.

'My friend, Sue Howard told me you are looking after her.' He stared at the two beautifully dressed women in surprise.

'You mean Pastor Howard's wife of course?'

'Yes. She is a dear friend of mine. She said that you delivered her little boy Mark.' She turned to go. He still felt puzzled. Surely the wife of someone as famous and wealthy as Sir Peter Bagshaw would have selected the most fashionable name in obstetric circles and felt very touched, that the young girl had come to him, on account of her friendship with Mrs Howard. He turned back to his office to meet his next patient, young, heavily made up and looking very apprehensive. Rosamund was forgotten.

'Rosamund darling———we have a tour booked across Europe

that will take us up to Christmas. So——back to Garnford for the festive season, then on to the States for three months!' Peter's face was animated, as he broke the news to his wife. 'Well——aren't you pleased?'

'Of course I am. Only you have made the arrangements rather far ahead. Does that mean that the tour in the States will carry into March?' She viewed him seriously, trying to keep the imp of mischief out of her eyes.

'Yes. We should be back for Easter though!'

'Well, Peter——it's just that I shall be otherwise engaged in middle March! Furthermore, it is an engagement that cannot be broken.' He stared at her, puzzled. Had Ernst perhaps invited her to Austria?

'But Rodrigo says they are crazy to hear the Rose Concerto. They were putting pressure on, that we should go there first, before Berlin, Paris and Vienna——but Rodrigo had already made those bookings. You will enjoy the States, Rosamund! There is so much to see and do. We will visit the Grand Canyon, climb the Rockies and maybe take a trip to the Bahamas——!' She put a hand over his mouth, to stifle further plans.

'Peter dear—apart from the fact that we would never have the time to see those places in the middle of a demanding tour—'

'We would——.'

'As I was saying then, do you really think it is a good idea, for your future son or daughter, to be born on an American concert platform!' There——it was out——and she had told him! Peter sprang up from the couch, to stare down at her. Did she mean it? She wasn't joking? He saw from her eyes that she wasn't, and he bent forward taking her hands, lifting her to her feet.

'You mean——you are going to have a baby!'

She drew his head down to hers and opened her mouth to his kiss.

'Yes! I had an examination today——and it's definite! Baby is due some time in the middle of March. You are pleased, aren't you—-even though it disturbs your bookings?' She pulled back to look at him and found his eyes were full of tears.

'Darling, darling Rosamund. I didn't feel I could be any happier than you have already made me, by becoming my wife—-for now, every new day is a joy to wake up to! But a child, to love, to cherish—-to carry on my name—-it is the most incredibly wonderful seal on our marriage!' He took her gently in his arms, kissing her over and over again. She relaxed against him, eyes shining with happiness as his lips caressed her mouth, her forehead, and her hair. Gradually Peter's mind came back to terms with practicalities.

'I will arrange for you to be attended by the best obstetrician in Harley Street. My own doctor, Sir Charles Nesbit will be able to advise on it. Now how are you feeling—-shouldn't you be resting? Of course the European tour will have to be cancelled—— perhaps I can fit in just a few performances. The States of course, is right out!'

She raised a hand to his lips, blocking further words.

'Now listen Peter——first the doctor! I already have one. He is the man who delivered the Howard's little boy. I like him—-know I can depend on him and he has already made a booking for me at the 'General' where my mother received such wonderful care.'

'But that is ridiculous! I know your mother received good attention there—but this is my son! I want you both to have the best money can buy!' His tone carried authority. His face bore the slightly stubborn expression that usually presaged stiffening of opinion on a particular subject. Rosamund took a deep breath. It was the first time that she had asserted herself in the marriage, but knew it was essential that she didn't knuckle under his forceful manner, if they were to have a harmonious relationship, where each acknowledged the views of the other. The finely balanced duet of the Rose Concerto had to be re-enacted in their real lives.

'Peter——-first, our little one may be a son or a daughter.' She put emphasis on the word our. 'Secondly, I am the one who is going to give birth and accordingly wish to select an obstetrician with whom I am comfortable at a hospital I am familiar with. Now don't look so worried Peter! Having a baby is a perfectly natural process. Thousands of babies are born every day.'

'But sometimes there are complications!'

'True——-but I am sure that Luke Patterson is well equipped to deal with any emergency.' Her voice was calm and reasonable. He smiled a little doubtfully, but nodded grudging acceptance.

'Now as for the European tour——when do we start? I am perfectly capable of playing with the orchestra, for at least the next three or four months.' She looked at him levelly from her green eyes. 'I promise you that if I feel any undue exhaustion, I will immediately let Lawrence Lindeman take my place!'

He brightened. Perhaps it would be possible to attempt the tour, providing that she would allow Lawrence to take over from her fairly often, for certainly the young man had ability, would one day be a powerful musician in his own right, even if he did not possess Rosamund's natural genius. His black brows relaxed and he started to smile.

'On that basis then——-and providing that you get regular check-ups wherever we happen to be——and, if your doctor agrees that it is reasonable for you to continue with what is as you know, an exacting and sometimes very tiring occupation.' And so it was agreed.

During the following two weeks, before they were due to leave for Berlin, Rosamund was totally involved in the early prepara-tions for the baby. She chose paint and wallpaper for the future nursery at Garnford——the room where Peter himself had spent his first few years.She went with Hermione on a shopping spree, purchasing nursery equipment in pale yellow—the colour of Spring sunshine, as she put it—going on to select a rocking horse and a veritable zoo of soft cuddly toys. Hermione made no attempt to restrain her, for it was good to see the girl animated again and full of enthusiasm, after the painful months of mourning her mother. Next came the layette, with Hermione helping her to choose the tiny garments with loving care.

'Now———-what about yourself, Rosamund?'

'What do you mean?'

'It is early days to be thinking of such matters——-but maternity clothes. Some of the modern designs are marvellous, darling——-not like the shapeless garments of my young day.' Hermione smiled to see Rosamund's face express lack of interest.

'I will wait until I begin to lose my waistline,' she said. 'Besides——-I can always pick up clothes in Paris or Vienna. After all, I will only be a little more than six months by Christmas, and I will be back home by then. I certainly will need some comfortable dresses for the States though.'

'But surely you do not want to continue with your music after Christmas?' Hermione looked concerned. 'You will need to take a certain amount of rest then!'

'We'll see,' was the best she could get from Rosamund.

Germany——-France———Austria, a whirl of stringently rehearsed performances, that brought accolades raining down on their heads——-on to Rome———and then an unexpected invitation to Moscow! It was the second week of December and bitterly cold. But Rosamund was well wrapped up in furs, her face bright with interest, as they explored the strange onion shaped palaces. Peter was beginning to feel the tiredness that usually attended the near close of a busy concert tour. His face under the fur hat showed traces of this——-but all his concern was for his wife, who stubbornly refused to allow anyone else to stand in for her, despite his protests.

Rosamund had already made up her mind, that once her baby was born she would stay at home, devoting all her energies to her little son or daughter. In the meanwhile, she was determined to enjoy her music to the uttermost. When she stood at Peter's side, she now possessed a confidence to match his own. With their deep love for each other and their commitment to the music they adored, the couple seemed to lead a charmed existence.

The Moscow audience warmed towards them, the throbbing emotion of the Rose Concerto stirring the terrific depths of feeling within their Russian hearts. The fact that Peter Bagshaw was married to the beautiful girl at his side—that the concerto was dedicated to her touched them greatly. Now, as the last note hung wistfully on the air, they rose to their feet, giving the couple the most thunderous applause they had received on their busy tour. Rodrigo Mendes dark eyes flashed in triumph, as he bowed again and again, standing back for Peter and Rosamund to receive the huge bouquets of scarlet roses.

'A very important person wishes to meet you both,' he murmured to them, repeating the message just brought to him—-but as his lips uttered these words, Rosamund swayed and crumpled to the floor.

She looked around herself uncomprehendingly. She was lying on a couch in a white, clinical room, where Peter stood in anxious speech with woman wearing a white coat. She had strong angular features and calm eyes. They were both looking at her. Rosamund pulled herself upright on the couch.

'Peter! What's happened? Where are we?' He hurried to her side, bending over her.

'You fainted. This is a clinic, quite close to the concert hall and this lady is an obstetrician.' He took her hands and looked at her earnestly. 'How are you feeling now?'

'I feel fine. Whatever caused me to faint? I have never done that in my life before!' She looked amazed, her expression chagrined.

'Young lady,' said the doctor in heavily accented English, 'As you know, you are expecting a baby. It seems that you have been pushing yourself in a way that would have proved taxing to one not pregnant. Your blood pressure is far too high. You must rest—otherwise there is danger to the baby and yourself.Providing you are sensible and take life at a normal pace, all will be well. You are a healthy young woman. It is up to you!'

Her shrewd eyes glanced down at Rosamund, seeing the rebellion in the girl's green eyes, that was subdued as her fingers stole to the mound beneath her breast that was her growing child

'Must I stop all concerts now, doctor,' she asked quietly? The doctor surveyed her shrewdly and qualified her earlier statement.

'Perhaps one or two more concerts——after a period of calm and sustained rest. Be guided by your own physician when you return home.' She nodded to Peter. 'You must look after her. You are a lucky man,' she said.

The next day they were on their way back to Britain, the Leningrad concert cancelled. Rosamund had vainly suggested that Lawrence take her place, in order that those who had booked their seats should not be disappointed. But Peter was more intent on getting her home for medical check-ups, than in furthering the brilliant success that had so far attended his concerto. So it was with an expression of resignation, that Rosamund boarded the plane, whilst promising herself that one day she would return to this great land, where however deep the frost and snow, the people had such warm hearts. For years in common with many in the West, Rosamund had thought of Russia as a hostile place, now however briefly she had seen its true face, where a people long repressed, bore their problems with stoicism and courage. Music and art know no boundaries——-thus she reflected, as they left the Soviet Union below them, beneath the clouds.

Hermione was all solicitude, as Rosamund sat ruefully on the sofa, while Peter spoke of cancelling the tour in the States. She could see how deep the girl's disappointment was.

'Peter——-what I suggest is this. Rosamund's doctor has said there is no immediate worry. Her blood pressure is now only slightly higher than it should be—and this after only a few days rest! We will have Christmas at Garnford, as already arranged—and then, if Rosamund still remains in good health, I will accompany you both to the States. Rosamund could then play with you in New York—maybe a concert in Washington——-and perhaps in Los Angeles. Then you could let me take her on to Florida, to get some good healthy sunshine, which can only be good for her, rather than facing the rain and mists of an English winter. This way you can still continue with your other bookings, instead of fussing around Rosamund like a broody hen!'

'Really mother! What a picture you paint of me!' Peter tried to scowl, but looking into Rosamund's laughing eyes, smiled instead. 'Now be reasonable, both of you. What are a few short months—-weeks——when Rosamund's and the child's life are at risk!'

'But they are not,' replied Rosamund equably. 'I promise you most solemnly Peter, that if you take me——and if my blood pressure shoots up again, I will return immediately with Hermione, whilst you complete your concert tour. After all, you have already cancelled the bookings for middle March. But I really would like to play in New York—that at least!'

He looked into the green eyes turned so imploringly on him—-and was lost. The decision that was to have such a profound effect on their lives was taken.

'Very well then,' said Peter Bagshaw. 'I agree, on these terms—-but you are only to participate in two or at the most, three concerts!' Hermione smiled as she rearranged the roses Peter had bought for her, and a petal dropped on the carpet.

CHAPTER TEN

They arrived at Garnford to a warm welcome by the staff. It was now common knowledge that young Lady Bagshaw was to have a child in the Spring and some of them had visited the pretty little nursery, that was soon to house Garnford's heir. It was to this little room, communicating with their own bedroom that Rosamund made her way. She sat down in the wicker rocking chair, with it's gay Mexican cushions and stared about her.

As she looked at the tiny crib, set on rockers—and the bigger cot, painted with teddy bears and with beaded sides, she began to ache to hold the little one in her arms. Everything looked so perfect, from the hand painted wooden train and colourful tiny roundabout, that played a tune—to the shelves of cuddly toys— the abacus——and of course, the red saddled, white maned rocking horse.

How she knew it was going to be a boy, she was not sure— only that it was. She wondered whether Peter would allow her to name him Tristam after her father. Sitting here in the quiet nursery, she suddenly considered whether she was being unreasonable in demanding she accompany Peter to the States. But at least, it would make the waiting time pass more quickly——and she had never been to America, Besides, if she were to forgo this opportunity, it might be some considerable time before she got another chance, once the baby was born!

She roused herself from her reverie, as she heard the sound of music——the piano. Only one person could play Chopin like that!

'Uncle Ernst! Darling———I didn't know you had arrived!' she ran to him, to be carefully caught up in his arms.

'Liebchen! What is all this I hear about your having been unwell? You certainly show no trace of it——-motherhood only makes you look more beautiful,' he said gallantly. As he released her, she became aware that there was another person in the room——Leopold Heine was standing beneath Sylvia's painting of Peter and herself. He bowed gravely, eyes sweeping across her thickening waistline, just discernible in her dark tartan dress, with its froth of lace at the neckline. Gone was the slender unsophisticated girl, who had stood beside him, at the competition for the Castel trophy——a lifetime away it now seemed, but in reality, less than a year. The poised, beautiful young woman, who now smiled at him in greeting, glowed with the secret joy of maternity.

'Leopold——welcome! We missed each other when I was in Vienna——for you had already gone to Leningrad. How did your performance go? I'm sure it was brilliant. Uncle Ernst told me he was delighted with your progress—that already you have achieved a standard that required little help from him!'

'Be careful, liebchen——-or you will make his head swell,' protested Ernst. But his smiled benignly on his protege.

'If I can ever approach your stature, maestro——I will then begin to be satisfied,' exclaimed the young man.

'Never be satisfied, Leopold. When you are satisfied—-then you will be empty of that seeking after perfection, that ever drives true musicians on. Do not merely strive to match my poor achievements—-but to surpass them!' Then Ernst turned whimsically to Rosamund.

'I have a confession to make to you, that I have already made to Peter.'

'Why—-what can that be?'

'That two weeks ago, Svetlana and I were married. It was a very quiet ceremony. We didn't want the press to know. You were both in Rome and were going on to Moscow. We didn't want to interrupt your tour—-but would like to hold a small party in London, so that you can celebrate our happiness with us.' He smiled contritely at Rosamund, knowing that she would, be disappointed not to have been at the ceremony. But all he saw in her eyes, was spontaneous joy at his happiness.

'Oh——Uncle Ernst! What wonderful, wonderful news! Where is she? Where is Svetlana?'

'Sitting with Hermione, indulging in women's talk! Peter is busy arranging some special entertainment for this evening. He said to be sure to tell you to rest!'

'Oh, really——-he would wrap me up in cotton wool if he could,' exclaimed Rosamund in exasperation. She glanced back at Leopold, sensing that he was looking at her. The look she intercepted was mixture of longing and pain. She stiffened. Surely he no longer harboured that infatuation for her, that he had displayed months ago? His expression changed to one of polite interest and she relaxed. She had been imagining things. The door opened and Svetlana came in with Hermione. She stared in amazement at her one time Principal, for Svetlana had changed out of all recognition. But it was not the new short hair style and Parisian gown that announced the change, but the unmistakable expression of a woman fulfilled in love, irrespective of age.

'Svetlana——I am so happy for you,' said Rosamund softly, as they embraced. Peter had indeed arranged something special for that evening. He had invited all their county neighbours, and to entertain them, had engaged a group of actors, to put on a show in the Great Hall. They were dressed in costumes of Tudor England and the actor who portrayed Henry Vlllth gave a tremendous performance. Peter explained to their guests, that the dinner and performance were to take the place of the traditional ball——as his wife needed to rest after the rigors of their recent tour. So they filed into the drawing room to receive their gifts from the glittering tree, one day earlier than usual. Many had brought gifts for Rosamund of baby clothes and toys for the future baby. As they waved goodbye, Rosamund remembered guiltily, her earlier dislike of Peter's friends, when as hurt child, she had stormed out of their presence. Now she was able to accept them as normal people, despite their wealth and privilege. Sylvia had taught her that she must allow her love to flow out to all people, however rich or poor. What was it that Sylvia had said? 'God has no favourites!'

She stood staring up at the glossy tree, every branch looped with tinsel, sparkling with frosted baubles and winking fairy lights——and thought of the care that had gone into preparing it—-and wondered who decorated Garnford's tree, year after year. She must find out and express her gratitude. How easy it was in life to take for granted the work of others, without which life would be so much poorer. She must ask Hermione what provisions were made for the staff at Christmas. Perhaps for the first time, she realised that her position as Peter's wife, carried its own responsibilities. She resolved that she would start to take up these duties, which until now, Hermione had still shouldered.

Christmas Eve dawned stormy and wild. Rain lashed across Garnford's windows, wind boomed down its chimneys, but inside all was warm and happy. Rosamund and Hermione worked together, wrapping the gifts for the staff, and as they handled each parcel, Rosamund asked for details of the recipient. She found to her dismay, that Hermione's own knowledge was sketchy about most except the key members, such as Charles Harrington, butler and friend, Roberts, their faithful chauffeur————and of course cook, Mrs Honeyset.

'I feel ashamed that I really know so very little,' said Hermione softly. 'It is no excuse, that I spent most of my life in London——-and Peter until now, has passed most of his adult life travelling the world. I suppose we have tended to use Garnford merely as a place to return to for holidays.' She paused reflectively. 'I believe that during the lifetime of my late husband's parents, things were very different. But they were already dead, when I married Peter's father——scarlet fever. My husband and I spent those first wonderful years here at Garnford—-after his tragic death, I spent most of my time in London——-music college for Peter, making a few friends of my own, mostly as I realise now, bored society women.'

'Hermione—-you devoted your time almost exclusively to Peter. He owes you so much——but I also know that you have a deep love for this place. Perhaps between us, we can focus much more attention on Garnford.'

'I agree. It will be a wonderful place for you to bring up your child———maybe other little ones later! In the meanwhile, we will both take a closer interest in those who work here.'

'Well——I tell you what we will do,' said Rosamund thoughtfully. 'We'll ask Harrington to come in and tell us what he can about the other members of the staff—-whether they have families—any special needs.' The caring attitude she was showing was to reap dividends in the years ahead, in a way she could never have envisaged.

Rosamund wanted to attend midnight service in the village church and so it was agreed that they should all go. Before this, there was the traditional Christmas Eve dinner——albeit on a smaller scale this year, as there was not the normal gathering of county folks. Although Rosamund had said she could easily cope with the annual ball, she had to admit that she had acceded to Peter's determination to cancel it, with alacrity. The exhaustion of her European tour combined with her pregnancy, had laid a certain toll on her, try to ignore it as she would.

The dinner was superb———-roast duck garnished with mandarin, served in a delicate source—-the sherry trifle delicious, with fruit and walnuts and whipped cream. Toasts were drunk in the fine German wine—-and then they warmed their toes round the huge log fire inn the drawing room, sipping their brandy.

'What's that I can hear,' cried Rosamund suddenly?

'Just the wind, my dear. It is still wild out there.'

'No, Peter—-I can hear singing!'

'Oh—-of course, the carol singers! Harrington——send someone down to invite them in. See that they get hot punch and mince pies.'

'And after that, Harrington——ask them to come in here and

sing to us,' said Rosamund. Later, as the crowd of wet, rosy cheeked village folk trooped into the room, the sounds of 'Holy Night, Silent Night' rose sweetly into the night. Peter went out and returned with his violin and Rosamund's. The next three carols were accompanied by the strings of their much travelled instruments—and suddenly, the very spirit of Christmas seemed to be captured, as the beauty of the music mingled with the lovely simplicity of this outpouring of love, for the Christ child.

Later, when the carol singers had gone, with a generous donation by Peter, they all made their way to the Christmas tree. The exchange of presents began. Rosamund waited as Peter slipped the gold signet ring, she had ordered from a Bond Street jeweller, onto his finger.

'Press that minute button on the side,' she instructed and as he did so, the top of the ring sprang open, to reveal a tiny rose of filigree gold and red stones. 'They are garnets, not rubies,' she said softly. 'If you look on the shoulders of the ring, you will find our initials entwined there.

'Why Rosamund—-it's a lovely thing. I will never take it off my finger.'

'The craftsman is the brother of a friend from Fritz Klein.' She took the gift he offered in return. As the rustling paper fell to the floor, she cried out in wonderment, for in her hands, she held an icon—-and from the painting of the Virgin and Christ Child, she could see that it was very old.

'I bought in Russia, when we were there. I was looking for something unusual that would have meaning for you. It's twelfth century. I was going to have bought you jewellery—-a tiara, but—-.'

'Oh, Peter, you couldn't have chosen anything I would have loved so much as this icon. I feel very privileged to own something so very special that must have been used in worship, by so many.' She rose on her toes and kissed him. And so it went on, the joyful exchange of gifts, carefully chosen. Then when the last

wrapper had been removed, Rosamund glimpsed Leopold standing alone at the side of the room———and a pang of dismay
touched her heart. None of them had known that Leopold was
coming———although of course, it might have been reasonable to
expect it, when Ernst always made a point of spending Christmas
at Garnford. What could she do? She had no gift for him. Then
inspiration came and she slipped out of the room. When she
returned, she was carrying a small package, hastily wrapped.

'Leopold——this is for you——from Peter and me,' she said.
Intrigued he took it from her. As his fingers removed the gilt
paper, he found himself staring at a painted miniature of
Beethoven, showing the famous musician as a young man. 'It was
given to me when we were in Berlin,' said Rosamund softly——
and I know Peter will join with me in wanting you to have it.
Perhaps as a pianist, you will draw inspiration from a great master.' Peter raised his eyebrows as he saw her give the young man
this costly gift——but looking at her love gift on his finger, he said
nothing, merely nodded to Leopold.

'Rosamund——Thank you,' said Leopold and raised her hand to
his lips. 'This is for you.' He handed her a scroll, which when
released from its red ribbon, proved to be a manuscript. She
glanced through its pages, pleased and surprised. It was scored for
violin and piano. Her eyes raced over it, her head nodding the
beat.

'Its called———Rose of Sharon,' said Leopold expressionlessly.

'I want to play it,' cried Rosamund 'Come on everyone——let's
go to the music room!' Leopold seated himself before the piano.
'You permit, sir,' he said to Peter.

'Of course,' said Peter stiffly, feeling an unreasoning resentment
towards the younger man, but not wishing to appear churlish.
Rosamund had not noticed her husband's slight coolness and
stood at Leopold's side. He raised his hands——held them poised
over the keys———and then those lean, dark skinned fingers, started to explore the introduction, a plaintive theme, oriental, richly

ornamented and romantic. It was totally unlike anything Rosamund had ever heard before and she sighed in expectation, as she raised her bow. The duet that followed, embodying the sultry rhythms of the East, began shyly, almost delicately—then exploded with mounting passion, into wild, emotional finale. In spite of himself, Peter had to admit that it was a remarkable composition. He glanced curiously at Leopold's face——saw him looking at Rosamund with undisguised admiration, which faded, as he became aware of Peter's stare.

'What did you think, sir,' he asked Peter, his eyes including Ernst in his question?

'Its good——very good. Did you receive help in its composition?' Peter glanced towards Ernst. But Leopold shook his head.

'No. Only from the emotion that gave birth to it——a love of country that has called to me through the centuries, in my blood.' He looked as though he would have said more, but dropped his eyes, after a last swift glance at Rosamund.

'My boy——it is a fine piece——very fine. I congratulate you,' said Ernst, walking over to him and clapping him on the shoulders. 'I for one, found it very moving. Perhaps this could be expanded one day, into a complete symphony!'

'That——only time will tell,' replied Leopold softly. He rose to his feet, to receive congratulations from Hermione and Svetlana——then Peter announced peremptorily, that it was time for them to leave for the midnight carol service in the church.

As they walked the short distance from the car to the church door, the freezing rain stung their faces, drenching their clothes in its onslaught. But once inside, as the service started, Rosamund found peace stealing into her heart. Memories of her mother, drifted through her mind——loss, mixed with extreme thankfulness that her mother's pain was over, that she was indeed released into the joy of her Lord. Peter knelt at her side, shame for his resentment of Leopold stealing over him. He decided that he would ask Hermione to introduce some eligible women to the pianist. As he looked sideways at his wife kneeling beside him, he felt he wanted to share a similar happiness. Also——he wished that he had made that total commitment, that Michael Howard had told him was necessary, to become born again! How did you decide to let that God, who had only been part recognised in past life, as shadowy, awesome—-yet unreal—-to become what He really was—the pivot of your life—-indeed, the giver of life, mighty father, guiding, loving——for so Michael had described him. In the last few months, Peter Bagshaw had now secretly acknowledged that God was indeed very real. But to give your whole life over to this mysterious, all powerful God—-to hand over the reins as Michael had said—-how did you actually come to decision on this? What happened to ambition—to pride in accomplishment? Peter had read John's gospel, knew that God was mirrored in his son Jesus. In him there had been no pride, his dedication only to healing the sick in mind and body, as he spread God's message of love, wherever his feet brought him.

He stood up with a start, realising he was the only one still kneeling. As they sang-'Little town of Bethlehem', Peter knew that sooner or later, his decision had to be made.

In bed that night, as he drew Rosamund gently into his arms, she touched his face, stroking the small knot between his brows.

'Peter?'

'Yes, darling?'

'When we were in church tonight, I felt you were trying to make a decision. Forgive me——but I know you went to see Michael Howard—-but I do not know what happened between you. Matters between a pastor and any other person are completely private. But I would like to ask you now—-do you believe in God—in Jesus?' Her voice faltered to a stop. For a while he did not answer her, his breathing deep and agitated. Then he said-

'I believe. Yes, Rosamund——I believe. But I feel the time has not yet come for me to make final commitment. There is so much in life I still want to do.'

'But why should this stop you? Many well known musicians, writers, artists are Christians—find their faith the well spring of their creativity!' She raised her self on her arms, to look down on him. He shook his head slowly.

'I only know that I'm not yet ready. No——-speak no more to me on this subject just now, Rosamund' He closed her mouth with a kiss. When after their lovemaking, he kissed her and turned over in sleep, she remained awake, in troubled thought. Then she too slept.

The morning broke with glittering sunlight pouring across the lake. Birds sang in the bare branched trees. Rosamund finished her breakfast and looked at Peter.

'I am going for a stroll in the grounds. Will you come?'

'Perhaps later. I have to make certain alterations to our original schedule for the States and will have to spend some time on the phone. You go——but do not over tire yourself.' He smiled at the grimace she made, then hurried off to the library.

Rosamund sought out Hermione, whom she found in the drawing room with her head bowed over fashion magazines with Svetlana. They both smiled as the girl came in.

'Who feels like a walk in the grounds with me?'

'Not just yet, Rosamund. The sunshine is bright, but it's still extremely cold——perhaps if it warms up later.' Said Hermione absently, as the two women considered the new spring fashions. So Rosamund pulled a fur lined hooded jacket over her trouser suit and set off alone.

There certainly was a bite in the wind, which was whipping up the waters of the lake——but it was good to be out in the open air. So much of the last few months had been spent in one hall after another, rehearsing and performing. As she walked in the general direction of the lake, Rosamund looked about her consideringly. She had decided that the baby would eventually need a safe play area, where she could have a swing and a slide erected——and perhaps a climbing frame and a sand pit. She selected a position close to Hermione's favourite spot, where her hammock hung in the summer months. It was not too far from the house.

'Good morning, Rosamund! You forgive that I join you? I saw you from the window of the music room.' It was Leopold. She looked up, startled. 'Why were you staring so intently at that tree?'

'Not at the tree——but at this area generally. I am looking for the right place to make a playground, for my future little son or daughter.'

'Why——-but need for that is a year or two ahead, surely?' Leopold's face was sad as he spoke, for to speak of her forthcoming child, was to acknowledge the impossibility of a future with the lovely girl at his side, whom he loved with all the passion of his aching heart. If only he had been more forceful at that first meeting, when they had both been so young, life a challenge. Now with Rosamund married to the world's most famous violinist and happily so, a baby on the way to seal their marriage, there was obviously no chance for him. But a tiny flicker of hope refused to be extinguished in his breast.

'Did you really like my 'Rose of Sharon'? Did it speak to your heart in any way,' he asked? Rosamund looked at him in surprise.

'Of course I loved it——always will. I am flattered that you should have dedicated it to me, for it truly is a beautiful work, full of wild emotion—a joy of life!' She smiled at him. 'Surely you realised how much I appreciated such a gift. I know how much work——how much of you, went into it!'

'Do you really know, I wonder? Did you understand that my Rose of Sharon, is Rosamund of the green eyes and bright spirit? Did it speak its message from my heart to yours?'

He had not meant to say the words. They just burst out and he lowered his eyes in confusion, knowing that he had crossed that invisible line between close friendship and deeper emotion. For a moment, her own eyes softened momentarily, as automatic reaction to his declaration throbbed through her own heart. Then reason and the deep love she bore her husband, took over. When Leopold looked up again, her face was composed.

'Perhaps we musicians are prone to deeper emotion than stirs others, and this allows us to express it in moving fashion in our music. But we also have to harness our feelings, discipline them, Leopold, where expression in certain situations, can cause disruption in the lives of those we care for. But I thank you for your gift—-and that which prompted it. No——don't say anything more. Let's go back to the house.'

'I should not have spoken. Forgive me, Rosamund. Well at least you now know how I feel. However, I will never speak of it again—-but I hope you will allow me to remain one of your friends—and one who will always help you, if ever occasion arises when you need that help.' He looked into her eyes and she saw the longing in those dark eyes and the sadness.

'Dear Leopold. You will always be my friend, almost part of my family and I know, a true friend to Peter.' She spoke the words firmly. They walked back to the house in silence, with Rosamund in troubled thought. If she loved Peter as much as she truly did, why then had her heart beat so fast when Leopold admitted his love for her? Then Peter came hurrying towards them.

'Rosamund——go and pack my dear. We leave tomorrow!'

CHAPTER ELEVEN

Six weeks had passed——exciting, triumphant weeks for Sir Peter Bagshaw. American audiences were enchanted by the Rose Concerto and took the young mother to their hearts, as she played so poignantly at her husband's side. New York, Washington, Boston——-and on, across the great continent, moving from one famous concert hall to another. The pace was gruelling, but Rosamund remained so full of energy, delighting in their success, that Peter's fears for her health, were lulled into false security. True he made token protest, that he had agreed to her performing in three concerts only, but with everything going so smoothly, his pride in his concerto and her dedication, displaced the very real concern he had evinced for her in the period before Christmas.

They were in Florida. Hermione was speaking seriously to Peter.

'She cannot be allowed to continue at this pace, Peter. If you have any real concern of Rosamund and your child, you will put your foot down, however much she may resent this. For it seems to me, that you have both lost touch with the reality, that Rosamund is to become a mother in a few weeks time.' Peter glanced at his mother in surprise. He had never heard this note of iron in her voice before.

'So——-what do you suggest? That I cancel the last four concerts?'

'No. Not that! But that you allow Lawrence Lindeman to take over from Rosamund.' He looked at her silently and his face expressed contrition. How could he have been so uncaring, so obsessed by his music.

'All right, I agree.'

'What do you agree to?' asked a laughing voice, as Rosamund

came into the hotel room.

'That you do not play any more on this trip darling. No——
don't look like that!" You agreed to only three concerts, when we
came here. I have been abominably selfish expecting you to continue so late into your pregnancy.' He put his arms around her,
drawing her gently to him. 'I suggest that you take a week or two
by the sea, just relaxing and enjoying the sunshine. I will continue, with Lawrence in your place for another two weeks, to complete out engagements and then we will fly home together.'

Rosamund sighed, then nodded. If she were honest, she had to
admit that she was really tired. She thought for a moment.

'If you allow me to play tonight, for one last time, then I will
do as you ask.' He kissed her in satisfaction. One last performance
would not cause any problems as far as he could see, for she had
shown no signs of the stress condition that had caused him such
anxiety on their Russian trip.Rosamund played as never before
that night, but as she bowed to the audience at the conclusion of
the work, accepting their plaudits with Peter and Rodrigo
Mendes, seeing the familiar bouquets of red roses tossed and carried onto the stage, something happened. A veiled figure came
towards her from the wings, and thrust a black, silk rose into her
hand and hissed a few words into Rosamund's ears before disappearing as quickly as she had come. Peter and Rodrigo glanced at
Rosamund in surprise. Who was the woman? What had she said?
Even as they looked at her, Rosamund swayed and collapsed.

For the second time, Rosamund came to on an examination
couch, to see a strange doctor smiling down at her reassuringly.

'Hey——now don't you worry, young lady. You are fine. You
fainted! I've been telling this husband of yours, that you must not
perform in any more concerts, until after your baby is born! Your
blood pressure is way up——uncomfortably so. I am ordering you
bed rest for at least a week.'

'Who was she,' whispered Rosamund, totally ignoring the doctor's words?

'What do you mean,' asked the doctor perplexed?

'Rosamund—-do you mean the woman who rushed over to you on the stage? What did she say to you?' Peter bent over her in concern. He had never seen that look of fear on Rosamund's face before.

'The veiled woman——-she said——-"Don't think you have won! He will not be yours for long. You are both going to die!"' She sat up on the couch and looked at Peter beseechingly. 'Who was she, Peter?'

He shook his head slowly, his expression baffled, trying to recollect the appearance of the veiled intruder.

'I don't know who she could have been, Rosamund. Inevitably you get some deranged persons at public occasions, as well as publicity seekers and those working out their own private fantasies. Be sure of one thing though—-you will never have to see that woman again. You mustn't let the incident upset you.'

'There was something evil about her. Although she was only close to me briefly, I sensed this most strongly.' She gave an involuntary shudder. The doctor frowned. He walked over to his medicine cabinet.

'Drink this, my dear. It's a mild sedative. Obviously you have had a nasty shock, which combined with the pressure of your work at this time, necessitates complete rest.' He took Rosamund's pulse. 'Would you consider going into a clinic for a few days—-just to make sure you really do relax.'

'That won't be necessary, doctor,' said Peter firmly. 'I have decided to fly home with my wife, on the next available flight!' As he spoke, the nurse opened the door was to admit Hermione.

'Rosamund! How are you darling?' She turned to the doctor. 'How is she?' Her face was tense with anxiety.

'This is my mother—Lady Bagshaw,' put in Peter.

?Both she and the baby are fine—-but she has to slow down and have complete peace and rest. Your son has just said he will return to the UK with her—-otherwise I was suggesting admitting

Rosamund to a clinic.' He smiled reassuringly at Hermione, who was quite white.

'Look Peter——I am quite prepared to go home immediately, if that is what you want——but on one condition only.' Rosamund's tone was firm now, almost brisk, as she slipped her legs over the side of the couch.

'There are no conditions, Rosamund'

'Oh, but there is just one.'

'And that is?'

'That you remain and give your remaining performances. Lawrence can take over from me, as already arranged. This way, hundreds of people won't be disappointed. Hermione will come back with me—won't you darling? So you see, I will be all right!'

Peter hesitated. He knew in his heart, that he really should drop everything ands return with his wife—-but on the other hand, if Hermione was to travel with her. The doctor saw the indecision on his face, knew that this talented musician wanted to stay, that the young woman now sitting so serenely on the couch, seemed to be in complete possession of her self now.

'May I make a decision, Sir Peter?'

'What is that, Doctor Maybury?'

'That a qualified nurse travels with your wife and mother.'

Peter's face brightened. He glanced at Rosamund, who nodded.

'Could you arrange that for me, Doctor?'

'It will be a pleasure, sir.'

He embraced her fondly in the departure lounge and she clung to him. It was to be their first parting, but both knew it would be a very brief one. Peter sighed, as he drove away from the airport in his hired car. He scowled as he thought of the veiled woman, who had caused so much upset and wondered whether it was worth mentioning to the police, then decided against it. After all, he wasn't even going to remain in the area. His next engagement was in San Francisco.

That night, Peter tossed restlessly in his hotel bed. He missed his wife's golden head on the pillow. After two hours, with sleep still eluding him, he got up and pulling back the curtains, stared out into the night. The hotel building was set back from the road, on the banks of a creek, surrounded by flowers and shrubs. Tall trees were festooned by hanging mosses. All this was plainly visible by the light of the full moon pooling down and by the strategically placed subdued floodlighting of the grounds. He unbolted the glass doors that led onto his balcony and stepped out. Above his head, the stars glittered like jewels and the hot night air warmed his face. He realised just how good the hotel air conditioning must be. How beautiful it was here——what a shame that Rosamund was not able to enjoy it with him.

As he stood gazing into the night, at peace with himself, seeing the moonlight reflecting on the rippling waters of the creek, he found his brain weaving a new illusive theme into a web of golden notes. How long he actually stood there, he was not sure afterwards, only that the theme became clearer, rich and lovely and full of wistful longing. He must get it down on paper——capture it in ink!

Then it happened. As he turned to leave the balcony, he half saw a figure detach itself from the shadows beneath a tree. From her curves, it was a woman. She called his name.

'Peter! Peter Bagshaw!' He turned back to the rail at the edge of the balcony, trying to focus his eyes on the shadows where she was standing. Then a shot rang out! The bullet passed within a hair's breadth of his forehead. He threw himself back into the room and dragged the curtains close. He was trembling with shock. He grabbed the phone and called the desk.

'This is Sir Peter Bagshaw. Call the police——there is a lunatic out in the grounds——a woman. I was on the balcony, getting some air, when she shot at me——and luckily missed.'

'I'll get someone up to your room right away sir——and the police will be informed immediately Stay away from the window and keep your door locked until one of our people get up there.'

Peter poured himself a stiff whisky and gulped it down. The night duty manager arrived, identified himself and came in. He was wearing an anxious expression. It was an honour to have someone of Sir Peter's standing staying at the hotel and it would not do the hotel's own security system much good, to have it known that a famous musician had been shot at by an intruder. As the two men sat talking, there was a heavy knock at the door and two uniformed police officers presented themselves.

'Our patrol car was only a mile from here, when the call came through,' said one officer. 'Two other cars are on their way. You are Sir Peter Bagshaw, sir—the musician?'

'Yes, officer. Briefly, I was standing out on the balcony——I couldn't sleep. As I stood there, the idea for a new composition came into my mind and I suppose I must have been out there for quite awhile. I was just about to go back into the room, when a woman stepped from beneath that tall tree immediately in line with my window. She called me by name. I turned to see who she was, and before I realised her intent, she raised a gun——and I was lucky! She missed. But it was uncomfortably close.'

'Had you left the glass doors open while you were out on the balcony?'

'Yes, officer.' He watched as the second, younger man walked over to the far wall and exclaimed.

'Here it is, Sergeant! It's embedded high above the picture—see!'

'Right. We'll get downstairs and start a search of the grounds. I very much doubt if we'll get her now though——too much time has elapsed. But at least we'll try. You stay put sir.' The two officers hurried out and Peter walked with the manager, towards the small dark hole high in the wall, where death had passed him by.

'Can you think of any person who holds a grudge against you,' asked the manager? Peter shook his head. He still felt shocked by what had happened. At least Rosamund had not been there——and now he was infinitely grateful that his lovely young wife was safely on her way home to Garnford. He dreaded to think what the shock would have done to her.

'Look,' he said to the manager. 'I don't want any of this getting in the papers. My wife is expecting a baby in a few weeks and the shock might seriously upset her at such a time.'

'You may be sure that none of my people will inform the press,' said the manager, only too grateful that his guest wanted the matter hushed up. Later, the officers were back, this time accompanied by a captain. He started to question Peter, while another officer took Peter's answers down in his notepad.

'Well first of all, sir, I have to ask whether you recognised your assailant?'

'No. She was wearing something dark I would say. She had long hair. Her face looked black. I suppose she could have been wearing a mask. It was all so quick—-like a camera flash.'

'Now I understand she called your name out. Is that right?'

'Yes, captain. She called out—'Peter——Peter Bagshaw!" So I turned automatically, and she stepped forward from under the tree——-and shot!'

'OK. Now, I want you to think very carefully. Did you recognise her voice?' His eyes bored into Peter's.

'No. It was high pitched——with what I would call a southern accent.'

'Well——-that's not a bad description. Do you know of any woman, who would hold you a sufficient grudge to want to kill you? Any disgruntled musician say——or more likely, an old flame?' Peter shook his head. It was all so incredible.

'I know of no musician, male or female who would want to harm me in any way——-and as for your second suggestion, Captain, I am happily married and my wife is expecting our first child very soon. I have never been what I believe is referred to as a ladies man.' Suddenly his face tightened and he looked at the captain from eyes that had darkened with anger.

'I must be an absolute fool,' he cried. 'There was an incident at last night's concert——a most distressing event that caused me to send Rosamund back to England. I just didn't connect the two things——because I thought the woman was some kind of crackpot.'

'Perhaps you would explain what you are talking about, sir!' The captain stared at him intently. Peter told him as succinctly as possible, of the woman who had rushed onto the stage and given Rosamund the black rose. He described how his wife had fainted, but he had not realised until she came to in the doctor's examination room, that the woman had spoken to her. He repeated the words Rosamund had revealed. The officers exclaimed in amazement.

'You informed one of our departments, I suppose sir?'

'Well, no. I thought the woman was deranged——-or maybe on drugs, or something of that sort. My first concern was to get my wife back home with my mother. Her blood pressure was very high. I wanted to go with her——but she persuaded me to complete my tour——I have only four concerts to go. The baby is not due for few weeks and so Doctor Maybury arranged for a trained nurse to travel with Rosamund and my mother.'

'Can you describe the woman. She probably is the one, we're after!'

'She was veiled——and dressed in something long and black. People were bringing bouquets of roses up onto the stage——-congratulations were coming from all sides. It was only when Rosamund collapsed, that I realised anything was wrong——-and even then, I only thought it was overwork causing a faint. It had happened to her before——-in Moscow.'

'So what we are left with now, is a death threat to both of you, by an unidentified woman, who attempted to carry out her threat on you tonight. Can you give me no clues, sir? Is there no woman in the States, who has cause to dislike you?'

'Well——-there is a woman who wanted me to marry her a year

ago——but it was only a fleeting affair, with no encouragement from me. I met her at a party. She attempted to compromise me and indeed insisted on accompanying me to England. If I tell you of this, I hope it will be kept entirely confidential. I am absolutely sure that Lois Challoner could not possibly be involved in anything like this.' He swiftly sketched in events that had led to Lois putting her compromising article in the paper———and her subsequent withdrawal of all she had suggested, when confronted with the truth.

'I know of this woman, Sir Peter. She is wealthy and as you say, extremely beautiful———and she is constantly photographed in the papers, accompanied by one well heeled man after another. We'll check this out, Sir Peter. It seems unlikely———but what do they say about a woman scorned!' He turned to the young officer who had removed the bullet from the wall, carefully dropping it into a plastic bag.

'Do you think she will try again?' Peter was suddenly aware that this could be an ongoing situation. Then another thought struck him. Would this deranged woman attempt to strike out at Rosamund, in the peace of their Hampshire home? His anxiety burst into words.

'You have to find this woman———and find her soon! Suppose she follows us to England, with the terrible danger to my wife and unborn child?' The captain turned back from his quick glance at the bullet, to stare at Peter sympathetically.

'We will do our utmost to track her down, but with so little to go on, this may be difficult. Perhaps we should check out Lois Challoner first.'

'If you must. But I assure you it couldn't be her. I know—— why don't I ring her now! If she is at home, then it could not possibly be her. She would never have had time to drive over a hundred miles back from here'

The captain nodded. It made sense.

'She may not be too happy at being disturbed at this hour in the morning. It is 3am. Go ahead sir.' He watched as Peter reached for the phone. It rang for some minutes before Peter's eyes narrowed, as he heard that well remembered husky voice.

The captain drew closer.

'Lois Challoner! If that's you, Gunther, then you can get lost! I had a real nice meal waiting for you——-lobster a la Creole—- candles and champagne! You'd better have a good excuse for standing me up, otherwise you can get lost!'

The captain, who had his ear next to Peter's, grinned as the tirade continued. 'I waited for you until two o'clock——then I thought as you had missed dinner, you might like me instead, for desert——so I had a bath and had my maid massage some of Guy Delecroix fabulous new perfume into my skin, and I've been wait- ing in my bedroom for you ever since!'

'Lois——this isn't Gunther, whoever he may be—but Peter.'

'Peter who?'

'Why——Peter Bagshaw.'

'Oh——-that Peter! Well, that's sure some surprise! If you want to pick up where we left off last year, then forget it! There's noth- ing so dead as last year's disappointment, as far as I am concerned. Anyway——-didn't I hear that you married that little child prodi- gy of yours? No accounting for taste, of course——but I would have thought she was a little insipid for a real man, but then—— -you hardly fit that category!' There was light mockery in the tones.

'Rosamund and I are very happy, Lois. Did you by any chance attend any of the concerts we have been giving in the States?'

'What? You expect me to attend one of your concerts? You must be joking! I've given up on all that classical stuff. I'm back with jazz now. Where are you ringing from, anyway?'

'Just outside Orlando.'

'You don't say! So near and yet so far——and it will always be too far for you now Peter! What are you ringing me for at this hour?'

'We musicians keep long hours, Lois——so I apologise. I was working on a new theme——suddenly thought of you and that perhaps you might like tickets for the concert in San Francisco in two day's time.' He improvised a reason, as best he was able, but guessed it must sound rather lame. Lois apparently thought so too. He heard a snort on the other end of the line.

'Let's get one thing clear, Peter Bagshaw. I don't want anything to do with you, or your precious music—-not now or at any time in the future! I would rather you didn't ring me up again either. Goodnight!' He heard the sudden click and knew that she had slammed the phone down and he grinned, in sheer relief. At least she was in no way involved in the shooting—but then of course, he had known that she couldn't be.

'So——-we drew a blank there,' said the captain. 'I take it that you recognised her voice, sir?'

'Only too well,' replied Peter feelingly. 'I wonder who the unfortunate Gunther is?'

'That will be Gunther Ottermeir, the industrialist,' said the captain. 'Saw them pictured together in one of my wife's glossies recently. Now, Sir Peter——you get to bed. I am posting a man outside your door—just in case and another two officers will patrol the grounds. I'll see you again in the morning. Meanwhile, I will contact San Francisco and arrange security for your concert there. Now just let me know where you will be staying—anything else, I can get all that from you tomorrow.' He signed to his men, who called goodnight and left.

Peter's mind was in turmoil, when the officers departed. Amazement that anyone should have wanted to kill him, together with worry for Rosamund made sleep impossible. He wondered whether he should fly back to her, to protect her, until the realisation dawned, that by staying and keeping to his announced schedule, he might be able to draw the attacker out into the open. For an hour he paced——then little by little, he found the notes of the fragile melody he was grasping at on the balcony before the

incident, becoming clearer in his mind. He started to hum——
and a flood of cascading notes drifted on his inner ear and he
gasped in quiet joy. All night his pen flew over paper and the concerto to be known as the Golden——or Last Concerto was born!

It was another two hours, before he contacted Rodrigo, whose
room was on a lower floor of the hotel, to share with him the
traumatic events of the night. The conductor listened in troubled
amazement to hear that Peter had nearly lost his life, demanding
to know why his friend hadn't called sooner and listened, expression still hurt, as Peter explained that he had first had to come to
terms with the attack. He told Rodrigo not to inform the other
members of the orchestra, of his close shave with death. Nor was
he to mention it to anyone else, in case word of it got to the press.

The commander of the San Francisco branch of FBI listened in
silence to the detailed account given to him personally by Captain
Morton, who had been instructed to appear here, in this private
but busy office, where matters warranting top priority were dealt
with. A world famous musician of Sir Peter Bagshaw's status certainly came within that category. Accordingly the grizzled individual in the light grey suit, listened with extreme care to the account
given to him by the regular police captain from Orlando.

'So——it would appear that our only known suspect has a complete alibi for the time in question. Can you be sure, that it was
indeed Lois Challoner who answered the phone to Sir Peter?'

'He recognised her voice sir. But in spite of that, I arranged
with the police in her area, for a watch to be kept on her villa, during the rest of that night and the following day. Nobody was seen
entering the house in that period——and Lois Challoner herself
came out of the house at 11am and drove off in her car. She was
followed and merely went to a hairdresser. She had obviously
been in her villa all night. There was no way in which she could
have driven over two hundred miles in less than an hour——the
time between the attack and Sir Peter's call to her.'

'It was quick thinking to have contacted her local police to keep watch on her. Well done, captain!'

'I also visited the doctor who attended Lady Rosamund, following her collapse at the close of the concert. I wanted to check on the exact words the veiled woman had said to her.'

'Good thinking. What did he say? Was he able to remember?'

'Yes, sir. The words reported as being used, were——"Don't think you've won. He will not be yours for long. You are both going to die!" The doctor said these were the exact words Lady Rosamund mentioned that the woman said to her.'

'Hum. "Don't think you've won." That sounds exactly what a rival for Sir Peter's affections might have said, especially combined with the phrase—-"He won't be yours for long!"

Yet you tell me that Sir Peter has not been involved with any woman, other than this Lois Challoner. Is he a truthful man, would you say?' His shrewd eyes held those of the uniformed officer.

'I'd bank on him sir. He struck me as a man with only two loves in his life—his music and his wife—perhaps, but not necessarily in that order! I say this, because whereas any other husband concerned over a young wife's high blood pressure, in the last weeks of her pregnancy, would have returned home at her side, he elected to remain here in the States to complete his tour. Of course, he says that it was not to disappoint his public who would have booked seats for the Rose Concerto.'

'I would say he has done her a favour, wouldn't you? If this mystery woman intends to have another go, then its just as well the pregnant wife is safely out of the way. Now let's go over the programme we've laid out for his security in this city. He and his orchestra are all booked into the Melford Hotel, and we have that well covered. Our men will be stationed in the concert hall tonight, covering every entrance and the stage—-with officers also placed high above in the lighting galleries. Then again, his route will be watched by squad cars. It seems as foolproof as possible. OK Captain Morton. You can return to your own neck of the woods now——unless you would like to have a seat at the concert tonight?' He smiled understandingly at the uniformed officer. 'Incidentally——what did you say the name of Lois Challoner's expected late night visitor was?'

'She called him Gunther. It so happens that my wife recently pointed out a photograph to me, of this Lois Challoner, with the industrialist, Gunther Ottermeir. My June just loves keeping tabs on all the glamorous types in so called society—I guess it's a harmless enough hobby. I remember glancing at the picture in one of her glossies, just to please her, which is why it stayed in my memory.'

'Hold on, Captain. Gunther Ottermeir is in Washington for trade talks with the Japanese delegation. I remember seeing it in the business columns of the New York Times! Now if I am correct on this, how come Lois was expecting him for a midnight supper last night? It doesn't make any sort of sense!' The two men looked at each other, faces baffled.

'Maybe he had forgotten the trade mission when he arranged that date with her——or again, perhaps she knows another character called Gunther.' The captain shook his head as he made the two suggestions—-they sounded feeble and he knew it.

'It smells, doesn't it,' said the FBI chief. 'I know it doesn't make it possible for Lois Challoner to have been in two places at once—-unless there is some factor we haven't tumbled yet. But she lied during that phone call, and was providing an alibi for herself to anyone who might have called her—and it just happened to be Peter Bagshaw. It could have been someone from our department. What do you think?'

'That perhaps we should try to contact Ottermier and just check with him whether he had forgotten a date with her last night. I realise the chances of her knowing someone else called Gunther, have to be pretty slim.'

'We are onto something, Captain—but just what, I'm not yet sure. I will have an immediate check made on the lovely Lois—-a detailed report on anything the department can dig up on her.'

In the meanwhile, Peter and Rodrigo Mendes had arrived with their party at the Melford, to find a tight security net being thrown round the famous violinist. Not that Peter allowed it to disturb him in any way, for his mind was now full of the new work he intended to embark on, as soon as the present tour was over. He had already played a fragment of what he intended to call the Golden Concerto, to Rodrigo, who was all enthusiasm.

'It has warmth—-a richness—-combined with an intriguing sense of mystery. It is unlike anything else you have composed before. My friend you must progress with this new work——nor I implore you, must you wait five years this time, before allowing me to conduct it!'

Peter gave a hearty laugh at Rodrigo's plaintive remark and it released some to the tension that had built up inside him.

'For some reason, I feel an urgency to get down to some serious work on this concerto—-a compulsion to finish it as soon as possible. It will also serve to occupy me during the baby's first few months.' He was silent for a moment, as he stared out of the hotel window, down onto the busy street, being careful not to expose himself to anyone below, as advised by the police. He was suddenly seized by an intense anger, that some demented woman should have the power to so complicate his life. Who was she? Why did she seek to kill him———and what possible reason could she have for threatening Rosamund?

'Come and have a drink, my friend—-you look as though you need one,' said Rodrigo shrewdly. 'Are you concerned for security during the concert tonight?'

'I would be less than human, if I didn't have a few qualms,' grunted Peter. 'But I would far rather that the attacker came out into the open now, than risk her travelling to England and putting my wife at risk!'

'It certainly is a most extraordinary affair!' Rodrigo shook his head. Then they toasted the forthcoming performance—-dis-

cussing the ability of young Lawrence Lindeman, who was to play
the duet with Peter.

The concert went extremely well, although Peter felt much of
the lustre of the performance was missing with Rosamund's
absence. This was in no way an aspersion on the playing of
Lawrence, which he grudgingly conceded was brilliant, yet the
young violinist lacked the emotion which Rosamund poured into
her own interpretation. However technically skilful a musician
was, without the deeper gift of emotional perception, he would
never hit the heights of genius. However the audience reacted
with predictable enthusiasm at the conclusion of the concerto.

Bouquets were carried up onto the stage amidst the huge roar
of approval and sustained hand clapping. Those who presented
flowers to Sir Peter had already been checked by police standing
unobtrusively in the wings. Now, as Peter Bagshaw took his last
bow, a slim young man, dark skinned and bearded, white turban
as bright as the frilled shirt of his evening suit rose from the stalls
and leapt up onto the stage. He was carrying a sheaf of dark red
roses, which he proffered to Peter, bowing respectfully. The officers in the wings drew their pistols and held the stranger in their
sights. But he looked harmless. Then, as Peter reached out a hand
to take the roses, amidst another burst of applause, the young
man appeared to say something to Peter, whose face registered
shock. Suddenly the slim tanned hand slid amongst the roses, to
produce a knife, which glittered in the footlights. A gasp of horror shuddered through the audience, who watched in fascinated
horror, as the knife rose and descended, plunging into Peter
Bagshaw's breast! Simultaneously a shout had pierced the troubled silence.

'Drop it—-or you're dead!'

The shot entered the man's back, even as he struck home. He
fell face downward across Peter Bagshaw's inert form, withdraw-
ing the knife from the wound in reflex action. The blood that
welled from his chest, mingling with that which poured from the

musician's side. Cameras flashed and police converged on the stage from all directions. A doctor who was in the audience, hurried to the front. When he called out his profession, willing hands pulled him up onto the stage. His first move was to help Peter. Rodrigo assisted him to remove the blood soaked jacket and shirt. The doctor had already given the keys of his car to one of the officers, with instructions to bring his bag and call an ambulance.

'I believe he is lucky. The knife struck a rib and hopefully was deflected. I cannot be sure. It's a nasty wound————but with luck, he may live!' He heard a hoarse laugh as he said this. He packed the wound and bound Peter's chest and swiftly turned his attention to the man who had almost robbed the famous violinist of life. The police had already dislodged the assailant less than gently from his supine position across Peter, where he had been thrown by the force of the bullet. Amazingly, he still seemed to be alive. The doctor asked one of the officers to remove his jacket and shirt.

It's a woman! A white woman!' The officer had roughly jerked the turban off the attacker's head. A wealth of dark hair uncoiled, to lie in glossy profusion on the wooden floor. He pulled at the beard—which came off, revealing the white skin beneath. At this moment, Peter Bagshaw opened his eyes and moaned in pain. He tried to focus on those around him. Rodrigo slipped an arm under his head and shoulders.

'Gently, my friend. You have a knife wound————but it's not fatal!

'Wrong————wrong!' The words were forced in gurgling gasp from the lips of the woman who lay next to Peter Bagshaw. She managed to turn her head towards her victim.

?Your wound is fatal! You will die————whatever the doctors may do. But it will not be a clean death now!' The horrible laugh was cut off, as blood bubbled between her lips and Lois Challoner lost consciousness.

'Lois————Lois Challoner!' Peter recognised the voice. He

looked bewildered. The doctor was attempting to staunch the woman's blood, which was still flowing and had previously soaked through Peter's clothing, before gathering in a dark pool on the stage.

Another doctor and a team of paramedics arrived at the scene. They lifted Peter onto a stretcher————-the woman onto another, as the police instructed the audience to vacate the building immediately.

'He is out of theatre now, sir————but he will be in intensive care for at least another twenty-four hours.' The orderly gave the news to Rodrigo Mendes, adding that the surgeon, Mr Charles Sylvester, would talk with him soon.

'Will he live, Mr Sylvester?' Rodrigo's dark eyes were full of anguish as he looked at the surgeon's grave face. The surgeon nodded, but his grim expression seemed to belie his words.

'Surgery has been totally successful, Mr Mendes. Sir Peter will have to stay in intensive care for a day or two at least. Heart surgery is a major trauma—-even in these days. He will need a couple of weeks in this hospital————then certain checks may have to be made.'

'What do you mean, doctor?' Rodrigo searched the surgeon's face. The tired, green gowned figure countered his question with another,

'Are you aware that Sir Peter's attacker is also here in this hospital. Some of my colleagues are still working on her' He watched Rodrigo as he spoke. 'Is Sir Peter well acquainted with Lois Challoner?'

'As far as I know sir, she is one of those rich, bored social butterflies who flit across life, seeking nectar at many sources. A year ago, she made life rather unpleasant for Peter, by throwing herself at him and trying to entrap him into an unwanted marriage. Now Peter had never shown interest in any woman, following the tragic death of his first wife, many years ago—-until that is, he recently married Rosamund. He definitely would never have chosen a woman of Lois Challoner's type to marry!'

'This explains a lot. The next question is one you may not care to answer——but one which I have good reason for asking. Did Lois Challoner have sexual relationship with Peter Bagshaw—as far as you know?'

'A strange question indeed! As I am assured from conversations I have had with Peter——emphatically not! But surely these are matters for the police to inquire into, where relevant—-not—-others!' Rodrigo regarded the surgeon with indignation, reproof in his tone. The surgeon ignored Rodrigo's reaction.

'You are a good friend of Sir Peter Bagshaw, Mr Mendes?'

'His best, I would say——apart from another whom you may have heard of—-Maestro Ernst Morgenstern. He has always been like a father to Peter, whose own father died when he was a child. But why these questions/' The surgeon seemed to come to a decision.

'Come with me. We cannot talk here.' Utterly bewildered, Rodrigo followed the man. Something was wrong he knew—-but what? The surgeon opened an office door and signed to a nurse who was writing something on a pad, to leave them. He pulled a black leather seated chair forward and signed to Rodrigo to sit and then faced him across his polished desk .At last he spoke.

'I know Sir Peter is married, because the papers have carried glowing accounts of his young wife's musical genius—-and the fact that she is soon to be a mother.'

'You are right. Rosamund is a truly lovely person. Everyone who meets her cannot help but warm to her. Peter brought her up as his ward. His own mother treated Rosamund as a daughter long before they fell in love and then married. He is most won-derfully happy now—and it shows in his music.'

'What kind of person is his mother?'

'Lady Hermione? Why—-vital and very supportive. When his father died, Hermione brought Peter up—-fostered his love of music in his early years and helped him through the dark days, when his first wife Natasha, died in an avalanche. It took Peter years to come out of that deep sorrow that furrowed his soul after her death. We all tried to help—-but his mother's love—- and his music brought him through pain, into new joy in life.'

'So——-and Rosamund? Is she a courageous person, would you say?'

'Strong? Yes——I have seen her push herself to the point of exhaustion in a concert tour—yet never snap at a colleague in irritation, or allow any sign of stress to show. Her baby is due in a month's time. She only returned to the England a few days ago, after she collapsed at Orlando, following a performance, when a veiled woman came onto the stage and uttered threats against her and Sir Peter.' He told the surgeon exactly what had been said and added———'I suppose the veiled woman must have been Lois Challoner! But why—-oh why, would she want to kill Peter, just because he didn't want to marry her? Rich and beautiful as she is, she could surely have had any other man who took her fancy!'

'I believe that this woman who threatened Rosamund, was already very sick. Now before I go on, I must have your word of honour, not to breathe a word of what I am going to tell you, to another soul—-at least, not until I say that you may. It is only because of the unusual circumstances surrounding this case, that I am breaking patient doctor confidentiality.'

Rodrigo drew a little crucifix he wore about his neck, between his fingers.

'You have my promise, sir.'

'A routine blood test on Lois Challoner, has shown that she is suffering from AIDS!' A look of horror passed over Rodrigo's face, as the surgeon continued—-'Even if we bring her out of the coma she is in—-well!' He sighed, then continued. 'The bullet fired by the police officer, entered her back and tore its way through, leaving a gaping wound in her breast——and she fell it would seem, right across the body of Peter Bagshaw. Her blood, Mr Mendes, flowed across Sir Peter's chest——and inevitably some would have entered the knife wound!'

At last comprehension flooded across Rodrigo's features and he pulled his hands over his face.

'Ah———no! Not Peter——not Peter with AIDS!' He broke down, great tears falling between his fingers onto the desk. At last his sobs subsided and he stared through blurred eyes at the surgeon. 'But perhaps———perhaps he may have been lucky? Her blood may not have infected him?'

'I wish I could share that hope sir. I cannot. So we have the job of monitoring his health——running checks on him——and further more, of having to tell him the situation in case he inadvertently infects his wife.'

'So that explains why you were asking me all those questions about Rosamund——and Peter's mother, inquiring if they possessed an inner strength!' He drew a tired hand across his forehead

'Just so. They will need all their strength and resilience to give support to Sir Peter, courage to face the road ahead!'

'To face his death, you mean!'

'All men must die one day, Mr Mendes. It may be quite some years, before Sir Peter Bagshaw dies. Hopefully a cure for the scourge that is AIDS will be found.' He paused and looked encouragingly at Rodrigo. 'Once we have established that he is indeed HIV positive, then apart from some minor early symptoms, which rapidly disappear, he may carry the virus in his blood for many years, before it develops into what is sometimes referred to, as full blown AIDS. His life during the first period may be to all intents and purposes, fairly normal. But under no circumstances, must he have sex with his wife——or anyone else. Nor must others come into contact with his body fluids at any time. Apart from this, he will constitute no danger whatsoever to those he comes into contact with. As far as we know, you cannot possi-

bly contact AIDS through saliva——so using their cup—or indeed
kissing a patient, is without any risk.'

'Are you going to tell him?'

'I think I must do so——for the sake of others——his wife.'

'Poor Rosamund! They are so deeply in love. I have never seen
a couple with such joy in each other.' He shook his head despair-
ingly.

'Love is the greatest force in this world, Mr Mendes. Indeed,
it is often said—that God is love. We will just leave this matter in
his Almighty hands.' He got up from his desk and extended a
hand to Rodrigo. 'I have to go. Others need me. Keep in touch
with me, sir.'

The FBI commander glanced up from his papers as Captain
Morton entered.

'Ah, yes——-Captain Morton. You are leaving this morning? I
am glad to have this quick word with you first though.' He peered
keenly at the uniformed officer.' You know of course, that Sir
Peter is now out of danger?'

'Yes. Sir——-and that Lois Challoner is still in a coma and the
hospital offer no hope.' He hesitated. 'Did you contact Gunther
Ottermeir, sir?'

'Indeed I did. As we guessed, he had no arrangements to meet
with Lois that evening. He said that she was an amusing companion, but no more. I have also had Lois Challoner's villa searched.
The force at Orlando, were most co-operative and their report is
of an unusual nature. They found a room there, obviously used
for what would be called occult practices——-black candles, gowns
with cabalistic signs and all the paraphernalia associated with
Satanism. Her maid was closely questioned about it——-she comes
from Haiti incidentally——-and divulged under examination, that
her mistress had been involved in the occult for many years. They
also found a diary belonging to Lois Challoner. It is being sent
here——-but I understand that she pours out her rage and frustration that Sir Peter Bagshaw had rejected her.'

'Well——at least we know some of the answers now. What a strange case, sir!'

'You think so? Well——try this on for size now. Lois Challoner has AIDS. She says so in the diary. I've passed word of it to the hospital—-but they already knew it from routine blood testing.' He looked in concern at Captain Morton's face, for the officer had a look of deep dismay across his aquiline features. 'Hey—— what's wrong then? Surely you are not too upset to hear that a would be murderess has AIDS?'

'It's not that, sir——although to be honest, I would not wish it on any human being! But she fell over Sir Peter, sir, when your guy shot her—-and they were both bleeding!'

'You don't mean? Why——-I hadn't even thought of any possible danger to Sir Peter in this, fool that I am! Not that there would have been anything I could have done anyway. But it does make sense of what one of my officers tell me Lois croaked out, as she lay there.'

'What was that, sir?'

'That his wound was fatal, whatever the doctors could do—- and that he would not have a clean death!' He looked at Captain Morton and whistled through his teeth. She must have realised that she had gotten an even more terrible revenge than she had planned!' The phone rang. He lifted the receiver. 'She's dead! Did he regain consciousness? No? OK. Thank you. Get back to your station, officer.'

'Lois?'

'Yeah. A merciful end for her, I would say. She'd have suffered on slowly, even if a jury had acquitted her——-which no way they would have done. She would have ended her days in jail. It's crazy, isn't it? All that money——and beautiful with it.'

'One thing I still don't understand, sir. How did she manage to shoot at Sir Peter on his hotel balcony that night————and still be back in her own home almost two hundred miles away, within the space of half an hour?'

'Speedboat moored in the creek——connecting up with a helicopter which put her down five miles from her home, near where
her car was parked. She drove the last bit and her maid was
primed to cover for her——but the woman cracked when she
heard what happened to her mistress.'

'Well, as far as we are concerned, I suppose the case is closed.'

'Yes. You can deal with any loose ends back there in Orlando.
Keep me informed if you find anything more that should go in the
records.'

Captain Morton saluted and took his leave. The commander
looked at a photograph of Sir Peter Bagshaw in the newspaper
lying on is desk. It was taken at an earlier concert, with his young
wife at his side. Suddenly the man realised the implications for her
as well as Sir Peter.

'Damn! You were a cruel bitch, Lois Challoner,' he said. The
phone rang again and he put the matter to the back of his mind,
filed with yesterday's business.

Hermione had persuaded Rosamund not to go immediately to
Garnford, when they arrived back In England, but to spend a few
days in London, seeing her obstetrician and buying any last things
she would need for the confinement. So it was, that Rosamund
turned on the breakfast time TV programme and heard the
news—-that world famous composer and violinist, Sir Peter
Bagshaw, was knifed the previous night, by a woman to whom his
name had once been linked, Lois Challoner. Sir Peter lay in critical condition in San Francisco.

She uttered a cry and collapsed on the floor. Hermione heard
that cry as she came into the sitting room and plunged to her
knees beside Rosamund.

'Darling! What's wrong? What's happened?' Hermione's face
was tense with worry. She called to her maid to bring some water.
She splashed Rosamund's face and then glanced up at the television, as she heard her son's name mentioned. More news was
coming through of Peter's attack and this time Hermione paled

with shock——but she looked at the young girl lying so still before her and steeled herself to remain calm. Her mind was screaming with pain as she thought of her only son lying stabbed in hospital thousands of miles away, but she realised what shock this news must have been to Rosamund.

The girl groaned and tried to sit up. Memory flooded back. Peter——Peter was wounded. Lois Challoner had tried to kill him.

'Hermione——have you heard—about Peter?' Her lips trembled.

'Just a few words just now—as I tried to revive you. It said on TV, that he had been stabbed——was now in hospital in surgery. So at least he is not dead darling—that at least!'

Rosamund took a deep breath and stumbled to her feet in ungainly fashion. She put her arms about the older woman.

'We must fly right out there,' she said.

'Of course——I'll ring the airport. You throw a few things into a case and——Rosamund? Rosamund! Are you all right?'

'A pain——a pain in my side, Hermione. I must have got up awkwardly!' Then Rosamund's face paled, as she realised what that pain really portended.

'It's the baby, isn't it. The baby's coming?' Hermione led her over to the couch, her fears for Peter temporarily subdued in her concern for the girl she loved as a daughter. 'I'll ring Luke Patterson!' She ran to the phone and minutes later, was back to sit next to Rosamund.

'He is on his way, darling. Now try not to worry about Peter——I just know he is going to be all right.' She tried to keep her tone light and confident. 'Now you go into the bedroom and lie down, for the doctor will want to examine you. I will get your things together for hospital.'

'No need for that Hermione. I've had a case packed and ready by the side of my dressing table for months!' Rosamund tried to smile, then her face went taut as another pain came.

'Let me help you through there. Lean on me.' Hermione knew

that labour should not be as abrupt as this and a deeper worry
smote her, than her concern for Peter. The baby was coming five
weeks too soon. Rosamund's blood pressure was already uncomfortably high. And now with the shock of Peter's condition?

'Did you hear about my son, doctor?'

'Yes. On the news. I thought about Rosamund as soon as I
heard—-would have come in any case.' He looked at her encouragingly. 'I'm so sorry that you have this worry, Lady Hermione—
-but surgeons in the major hospitals in the States, are amongst the
best in the world. I know it is no good telling you not to worry—
—but at least, try not to let Rosamund see it. She is going to need
your support.'

'I do know this, doctor,' she said simply. Then——'Rosamund
heard the news on TV. When I came into the room, it was to find
she had collapsed on the floor. When she regained consciousness,
she became aware of a pain almost at once.'

'I will go into to her. I have already called an ambulance and
we'll get her into hospital away. Now try not to worry.'
Rosamund had been aware of the slight blur of their voices outside her door, as she lay on the bed and roused herself now, as
Luke Patterson came in.

'How are you, Rosamund?'

'Fine, thank you, doctor.' A faint smile came to her lips as she
realised how the polite reply had come almost automatically. 'I
think the baby is coming,' she added. Hermione helped pull back
the sheets and helped the doctor to raise Rosamund's gown. Even
to her untutored eyes, it was apparent from the hardening of the
uterine muscles, that labour had definitely started. He took
Rosamund's blood pressure and Hermione saw the slight flicker
of alarm in his eyes. But his smile was as reassuring as ever.

'Must I go into hospital right away,' asked Rosamund anxiously? 'I really need to contact the States to se how Peter is. I don't
even know the name of the hospital where he is being treated.'

'I understand, my dear——and if Peter were aware that you

are busy producing his child, he would no doubt wish to phone you. But this is one time when you will both have to be patient——for the sake of a very special little person, who has decided he wants a February birthday!'

'You said—-he.'

'He or she, that is!' He glanced at his watch, as another pain caught her, the contraction obviously harder. Why didn't the ambulance come! Then it did. Rosamund found herself being helped into it by a kindly fatherly ambulance man, who was obviously well used to coping with mothers in labour. He talked with her soothingly, as the ambulance negotiated the morning traffic, with its siren blaring. Luke Patterson was following behind in his own car. The hours that passed were full of pain for Rosamund——not just the travail of childbirth, but the mental anguish of not knowing whether her husband was alive or dead. 'Peter——-Peter——Peter!' The scream rose and fell in her mind, as mentally she saw the knife that had pierced his breast, rise and fall again and again in cruel co-ordination with her pains. Her face was wet with sweat. She pushed away the gas and air mask the midwife tried to guide over her face.

'Peter——Peter!' The moan escaped her lips again and again.

'Rosamund? Can you hear me? Rosamund! It's Michael Howard.' The pastor leaned over her, his face warm with pity. 'Rosamund?'

'Michael.' Her whisper let him know that she had recognised his voice through her anguish. She opened her eyes and fixed them on is face.

'Hermione told me you are soon to be a mother. More than that—-I have welcome news for you! Peter is out of surgery. He is going to live.' She looked at him almost uncomprehendingly and again, he said those wonderful words.

'He is going to live!' Tears came into her eyes and slowly ran down her cheeks, but they were tears of relief.

'Are you sure?'

'Yes, my dear. So now, you concentrate on the joy that will soon be yours, when you hold your baby in your arms. They tell me it will be very soon now.' Her face contorted with another contraction, but as it passed, a smile touched her lips.

'Thank you, Michael. Oh, thank you.' He touched her shoulder sympathetically and then took her hands. He murmured a prayer. Hermione who had stood back, her own heart overwhelmed in relief that her son was to live, now came nearer to listen to the quiet voice that spoke such beautiful words of love.

'Thank you Jesus. Thank you, Lord,' he said quietly and loosed Rosamund's hands. 'I will leave you with your doctor and the nurses now my dear——but I will remain in the hospital until your child is born.' She rewarded him with a smile. Then she became totally absorbed with the forces within her own body. She saw Luke Patterson bending over her encouragingly——heard the midwife giving quiet orders—found her face getting tighter as she held her breath, until she felt her face would explode——then the splitting feeling between her thighs——

'Well done, my dear. Your baby's head has just been born. Wait until your next good contraction—— and then another push!'

'Aghhhh!' the cry burst from her lips and with it came the unmistakable cry of a new-born baby.

'It's a boy! You have a lovely little son, Rosamund!' She heard Luke Patterson's voice through the combined sensations of total exhaustion and joy. She opened her eyes and tried to lift her head from the pillows. She felt an exquisite tenderness overwhelm her, as the doctor laid the tiny body in her arms. Gently she raised a finger to touch the dark hair plastered wetly to the tiny head, as she stared into eyes as dark as Peter's own.

'Tristam. Little Tristam,' she murmured.

'Is that what you are going to call him,' asked the midwife, preparing nametags for the baby's wrist and ankle. Then, they took him from her to clean him and weigh him. 'We are going to put him in an incubator for twenty four hours,' said the midwife, glancing at the doctor for confirmation.

'What's wrong with him,' cried Rosamund in consternation?

'Nothing is wrong with him, Rosamund,' replied the doctor with a reassuring smile. 'Although he is five weeks premature, he is a good weight—six pounds two ounces! He is fine and healthy—but because he was born in rather a hurry, he needs time to adjust to the world he has just entered. You too will need a lot of rest my dear. But you have done very well indeed——and so has Tristam.'

After the afterbirth was delivered and a small repair attended to, she was taken to a side ward. She was asleep before the nurse had finished smoothing the sheet. So it was, that she didn't hear the heated altercation outside the ward.

'I only want to see her for a single minute! I am a good friend of hers. My name is Leopold Heine—the pianist.'

'I don't care if you play a hurdy gurdy Mr Heine. My patient has just been through a very hard labour. She is still far from well and under no circumstances are any but direct family to be allowed to her bedside.'

'Then at least——-tell her that I came as soon as I heard. That I am delighted that she has a son——and that Peter is going to live. Give her these.' The sister took the huge bouquet of spring flowers, their fragrance filling the corridor.

'I will see that she gets your message, Mr Heine——and the flowers.' With a last reluctant glance towards the room where he knew that she lay, Leopold turned away, knowing as he did so, that although the marriage bond between Rosamund and Peter was strengthened by the birth of their son, nevertheless he would love her, until the day of his death. When he had heard the news of Peter's stabbing, he had hurried to Hermione's flat, only to learn that Rosamund had gone into precipitate labour. Now he returned to his hotel, to phone Ernst Morgenstern, to let his benefactor know that both Peter and Rosamund were out of danger—and that a son had been born to them. Tristam! He must find out why Rosamund was naming her son so. He could I admit not know that it was the name of her late father, whom she had loved so dearly.

The sister spoke with her staff nurse, as they drank a hurried cup of tea together. She spoke of Leopold.

'Such a forceful young man, my dear———-and very handsome, with dark wavy hair and black eyes. I would have suspected he was more than just a friend, if I didn't know otherwise, for Lady Bagshaw was constantly crying out her husband's name through her labour, poor thing. What a mercy that mad woman in the States didn't kill him. Such a wonderful musician———and so is she! Mind you, the young man did say he was a pianist—and these musicians are probably very close———like a big family, I suppose.'

'How is Lady Rosamund now? I saw in her notes that it was touch and go at one point?' The staff nurse looked at sister seriously.

'That's true. She is still not completely out of the woods. Her blood pressure remains high and she is very weak. She will be all right, but I want her watched carefully. The baby also is in slight shock and will remain in an incubator for a couple of days———just to be on the safe side.'

Hermione sat talking to Luke Patterson. He looked tired———had been up all the previous night with a girl who had delivered twins. But this kind of tiredness was the best kind, he reflected. Surely one of the most worthwhile jobs on this earth was to help bring new life into the world.

'She will be fine now, Lady Hermione. But we will probably want to keep her in a little longer than usual, until she and her son are much stronger. You of course, can visit at will———but I would prefer that other visitors should wait a few days.'

'I could see from your eyes, that you were worried about her.' Hermione looked at the doctor tiredly. The double worry of her son's perilous condition and Rosamund's difficult labour had taken its toll on her.

'Well—-I admit now, that there was a stage when I worried that we might lose her. It was just before Pastor Howard came and spoke with her.' He smiled. 'It must have been the wonderfully reassuring news that he brought her, that gave her new heart.'

'Yes. But not only that—-when he prayed with her—a peace came around the bed. That is the best way I can describe it.' Hermione was silent for a moment. 'If she is sleeping now, I will go home and shower—-and come back in two hours time.' He watched her go. 'You are quite a lady, Hermione Bagshaw,' he murmured——nor was he referring to her title!

Peter Bagshaw came back to a world that was full of pain and bewilderment. Confused images floated through his mind—-a man raising a knife—-the knife descending—-and a woman's voice. Again and again he heard her words and hoarse and distorted though the voice had been, realisation of whose voice this was—-Lois. Lois Challoner! He groaned and opened his eyes. A nurse immediately bent over him.

'Sir Peter? Are you awake, sir?'

'Yes. Where am I?'

'In State Hospital, sir. I'm Nurse Webster. How are you feeling?'

'My chest—-a lot of pain.'

'I'll get you something for that, sir. But I will just call the doctor first.' He closed his eyes again and only opened them when he heard voices. The man who looked down into his eyes looked kind—-more than that, his face was full of compassion.

'Sir Peter——my name is Charles Sylvester. I am the surgeon who headed the team operating on you the night before last. Do you recall what happened to you—-how you came to be wounded?'

'Yes. I was knifed—-wasn't I? It was like a nightmare. A man in a turban! He was carrying roses——like they all do. Then he produced a knife and I saw it glitter as it rose.' He tried to lift his head to focus on the doctor. 'Aghh, this pain,' Peter groaned. The doctor lifted a syringe from a tray——after carefully drawing new gloves on first. He gave the injection, then put the disposable syringe and the gloves which he stripped off, into a plastic bag and went to the sink to scrub his hands. But Peter had closed his eyes in relief, as the drug started to take effect. The doctor returned to the bed.

'Can you still hear me, Peter?'

'Yes,' came the faint reply.

'The man in the turban, was in fact a woman.'

'Lois Challoner?'

'Yes.'

'She spoke afterwards——in a horrible voice. But I recognised it as hers. I couldn't see her——only heard the voice'.

'Don't try to say anything else right now, sir. You sleep. One thing though——she is dead. You never have to fear her any more.' His words were rewarded by a deep sigh of relief from the bed.

Another twenty-four hours passed. Charles Sylvester called upon his celebrated patient again. This time Peter was fully awake and sitting up, propped up on pillows. He gave a smile as he recognised the surgeon.

'How are you feeling today, Sir Peter?'

'Foul——but glad to be alive! I believe my thanks are due to you Mr Sylvester.' He extended a hand to the surgeon, who took it and then drew a chair to the bedside.

'I have come to give you some news, Sir Peter——both good and bad.'

'So? Well——let's have the good news first. I could certainly do with some!' Peter looked at him curiously.

'You are a father, Peter! Your wife Rosamund gave birth to a son on Tuesday morning your time! They are both doing fine!'

'A son! Why that's the most wonderful news you could possibly have brought me! I wish I had some champagne here to toast such happiness with you.' Peter's face was bright with happiness and the surgeon felt a knot of pity grinding in his bowels for the blow he must now deal this man, who had already suffered so much.

'I have other news for you—-but it is not so good.'

'Is it to do with my recovery? Will the operation affect my playing in some way?' Peter's eyes were apprehensive. But the surgeon slowly shook his head.

'No. It will not affect your playing. You will be stiff for some weeks. There even may be some discomfort for a few months, but it will pass.'

'Then what is it———out with it man?'

'Do you remember clearly what happened to you, when you were knifed.'

'I remember the pain—-falling——a loud report—-a firearm I suppose. Then there was a heavy weight on my chest——and Lois Challoner" voice, sounding strange and distorted——-saying that my wound would be fatal whatever the doctors could do. That I would die—-not a clean death, but horribly.'

'Then let me explain to you, that the weight you could feel, was Lois body falling across you, as you lay wounded and bleeding. She had been shot in the back by the police—but fractionally too late to save you from her attack. The bullet passed right through her body, narrowly missing you——and when she fell on you, she was bleeding profusely.'

'But that's horrible,' said Peter. 'I still find it quite impossible to understand why she intended to kill me. She wanted me to marry her a year ago. I refused to do so——did not love her. I had forgotten all about her. I have been so wonderfully happy with my wife Rosamund. Was this what you wanted to tell me——of how Lois died?'

'I wish that it were all. No, my friend! Lois Challoner had AIDS. The blood that flowed over you, entering your open wound, was virulent with the AIDS virus. I am so sorry—-so very sorry.'

'But——what are you saying? That Lois had AIDS? That her blood has infected me with it? For heaven's sake man, say that I have misunderstood you?' Peter's face was grey with shock. The agony in his eyes tore the surgeon to the heart. But there was nothing he could do, but tell the truth——and then to give what support he could.

'I am telling you, that the AIDS virus has entered your blood stream, Sir Peter.' The cry that burst from Peter's lips, was heard by the orderly, at the end of the corridor. She hesitated, wondering what pain had caused it.

Chapter Twelve

After that wild cry of anguish had passed his lips, Peter lay back against his pillows, a look of absolute despair on his face, his slate grey eyes blank. At last he spoke, his words barely audible.

'Why did you have to save my life? It would have been kinder to let me die!'

'Peter——,' the surgeon deliberately used his patient's first name. 'I want you to think carefully, before talking along those lines. Life is a precious gift from God. My own work is to prolong life wherever possible. You have just heard that you are the father of a baby son——.'

'Whom I will never now see grow to manhood!' interrupted Peter bitterly.

'Perhaps not. But at least you will have the joy of holding him in your arms——guiding his early footsteps. You will be able to see the wonder in his eyes, when you take your violin and play your beautiful music to him. You will be able to embrace your lovely young wife and thank her for the gift of a son!' Charles Sylvester spoke with quiet fervour.

'Rosamund! How do I tell her? She will shrink from me in horror!' But even as he uttered these words, Peter knew them for a lie.

'That is not true, I am sure,' said the surgeon, seeing the slightly guilty expression that crossed Peter's face. 'I understand that your wife was playing at your side until only eight days ago, although then far advanced into her pregnancy. This would indicate to me both courage and dedication——and a real love for her husband.'

'How do you suppose, a young and vital woman like Rosamund, who enjoys the intimate side of married life, is going to cope with a husband who cannot make love to her any more!

Oh yes——-I know enough about AIDS to fully realise that I will never be able to have sex with her again.' Anger now burned in his eyes, a smouldering resentment against a fate that had robbed him of the physical joy of his relationship with his wife at a single stroke.

'It is true that you will never be able to have sexual intercourse with her again——but that doesn't mean that you cannot enjoy great comfort and intimacy with each other.' He paused, and said——'One thing you have to realise is, that if you prove to be HIV positive, then your life will be able to continue in an almost normal vein, perhaps for many years before the illness known as AIDS starts to take effect. Indeed, before that time, it is always possible that a cure may have been found. Scientists feel that eventually they have to make a breakthrough!'

'Huh! They haven't even found a cure for the common cold yet!'

'Perhaps not. But just consider, TB was rated as a killer not too long ago, and now it is easily dealt with.'

'All right——-then how about cancer. You can send man to the moon, but thousands die of cancer every year.'

'And thousands more respond to surgery, when the condition is diagnosed in time. Again, the scientists are close to success in this field also. But I know you will now have to deal with life on a simple day to day basis. Your wonderful gift of musicianship will not be impaired——nor your ability to compose.' The surgeon reached over and took one of Peter's hands, but was shrugged away, the movement causing pain.

'How did you think I can ever compose again, facing a thing like this!'

'I wonder how Beethoven coped with deafness,' pondered the surgeon. 'At the moment you are hurt and angry——and understandably so. But sometimes in life, we just have to go on and accept those things which we cannot change.' He went to the sink, washed his hands, gloved himself and then took a small syringe from a sealed tray. He filled it from a phial and then inject-ed into Peter's thigh. 'There——that should deal with the pain.' He dropped the syringe into a plastic bag and pulling off his gloves, dropped them in after it and sealed the top. Then he scrubbed his hands again.

'I could have withheld the information about your condition from you for a few more days——but you are an intelligent man and I'm sure you would have noticed the very stringent precau-tions that all nursing staff are having to employ when attending to your wound or giving injections. You yourself will have to show a like care in the future, when attending to any cut, or burn, how-ever small——but you will soon find that this becomes automat-ic.'

'How very easily you say that,' whispered Peter.

'Easily? Well perhaps that is because I have seen how well a cer-tain very wonderful person coped with this very situation.' His eyes were sad.

'Who is that?'

'My son. Richard is seven. Two years ago, he fell off his push bike onto some broken glass. He cut an artery—-was rushed to hospital—-not this one. He had lost a lot of blood and they gave him a transfusion. It was infected with the AIDS virus. Richard is a wonderful child—full of fun. But he has learned that when he cuts himself, he must not let other children come into contact with his blood. Sandra—my wife, just puts rubber gloves on, cleans and dresses the cut, then places all materials used and the gloves into a plastic bag and seals it. It is just standard procedure.' Charles Sylvester gave Peter a warm smile. 'If Richard can cope, then I am fairly sure if you are even half the man I think you are, then you will cope too!' Now indeed, Peter Bagshaw reached out his hand and took the surgeon's.

'Forgive me,' he said. 'One day, when I am out of this place, I would like to meet your son.'

'So you shall. He will be very excited, when I tell him that a famous musician wants to meet him! And one day too, perhaps I may meet your own son. What do you aim to call him?'

'I'm not sure. Perhaps I should let Rosamund decide that.' His voice was tired. His eyes started to close as the powerful painkilling drug took effect. Charles Sylvester stood up. He called to the nurse, who had retreated to a recessed area, where she was writing her report.

'Watch him carefully,' he said. 'But I believe he is going to win through,' nor was he talking about the wired rib cage and delicately stitched tissues. The incision in his heart muscle, that had almost robbed him of life.

Rosamund came out of a deep sleep and for a few seconds seemed baffled by the unfamiliarity of her surroundings. Then as she moved drowsily in the bed, she became aware of her lack of bulk—-the mound of her pregnancy had disappeared! Of course—-her baby had been born. Where was he? She sat up anxiously and looked around her. Usually babies were placed in mobile cribs at their mother's sides. Where was Tristam? Then her thoughts flew to her husband, as memory flooded back of the terrible attack on his life.

She drew a deep breath of relief as she remembered the reassurance brought to her by Michael Howard during the most difficult stage of her labour. Had he not said that Peter would live——-he was out of surgery and was going to live? Then the perfume from the massed spring blooms adorning her bedside locker, drew deep sigh of response. They must of course be from Hermione. She reached out a hand and took the card propped against the glass vase.

'Flowers of spring for the Rose of Sharon', was the only indication of the sender. Leopold Heine—-he must have sent them. How had he known that she was here? Then she remembered how Hermione had reported having met the young man in Kensington, shortly after their return to London. She dismissed him from her thoughts, although feeling vaguely pleased that he should have sent the flowers. She pulled the bedcovers back and attempted to swing her legs over the side. How strange and light she felt. She made to walk across the small one bedded ward and swayed, as a nurse who had just entered at that moment, rushed forward and caught her.

'Lady Rosamund. What are you doing out of bed?'

'I want my baby! Where is he? Is he all right?' Her eyes looked fearful. The nurse reassured her and helped her back to bed.

'Don't you remember? We had to put him in an incubator for a little while. It is standard proceeding for a little one who arrives into much of a hurry! Normally the baby takes a certain time to pass from the security of the womb into the outside world. Different muscles are expanding and contracting and he adjusts to differences in pressure. Little Tristam just needs some extra care.'

'I want him now. I want to hold him in my arms!' Rosamund was getting agitated. 'How do I know that something is not seriously wrong!' The terrific stress of knowing her husband to be in critical condition had released a terrible apprehension in her mind. The nurse wound the dark strap of the sphygmomanometer around Rosamund's arm and inflated it. She watched the reading—released it a little—then removed it.

'I will get sister to come and reassure you,' she said comfortingly. 'But I do promise you, that he is absolutely fine. He has a good pair of lungs—-perhaps he will follow in the family tradition and be musical—a singer!' Rosamund forced a small smile at this. When the sister came in, she as pushing a crib.

'Hallo, my dear,' she said. 'I heard that you wee worrying about this young man, and as he really seems to be doing very well, I thought I would bring him to you for a while. Are you going to feed him yourself?'

'Oh——yes, yes! Give him to me!' She lifted her arms out beseechingly. As she held the tiny body next to hers, Rosamund experienced a deep tenderness, totally unlike the love she felt towards her husband. This was her child, born of her body, dependant on her for love and protection. The sheer wonder of stroking the tiny head, running her finger over the firm little nose and dimpled chin, completely absorbed her, until Tristam opened his mouth with urgent demand. With a smile, sister guided the little head towards his mother's nipple and there was peace, apart from small sucking noises. The close bonding between mother and child was taking place——holding him close, Rosamund vowed he would receive all the love she was capable of.

Then at last, as the baby let go of her nipple and fell asleep, she raised her head.

'Thank you Sister. Have you any news of my husband?'

'I gather he is doing well. Your mother-in-law is outside and waiting to see you. She will have more detailed news for you.' She held her arms out for the baby, but Rosamund shook her head.

'Not just yet. I want Hermione to see him.' Sister did not remonstrate, but went to the door and beckoned to the woman who had been waiting so patiently on a chair there. Hermione caught her breath, as she saw Rosamund with the baby in her arms. She thought Rosamund had never looked more beautiful, despite the dark shadows round her eyes, that spoke of the strain of worrying over Peter. As for the baby——

'Oh, Rosamund darling——may I hold him? He is almost the exact image of Peter as a baby!' She looked incredulously at the tiny face. The baby opened sleepy eyes and they were dark as Peter's own, despite that fact that all babies eyes were said to be blue at birth. She held him to her gently, as she murmured——'I can hardly believe that I am a grandmother. What are you going to call him?'

'Tristam——-after my father. I hope Peter will agree.' Her voice was tremulous as she uttered her husband's name. She looked questioningly at Hermione. 'How is he really—do you know?' The sister took Tristam from Hermione's arms and returned him to the crib and wheeled it out. But now, Rosamund did not seem to mind. She was satisfied that her child was safe and now all her anxieties were for her husband. Hermione sat on the side of the bed and embraced Rosamund, her eyes damp with emotion.

'Darling—-he is making a satisfactory recovery from heart surgery. I have spoken to his surgeon on the phone. He will have to remain in hospital for at least two to four weeks. The operation was completely successful—-but the surgeon says he will need complete rest for many weeks to come.'

'We will fly out there,' said Rosamund with determination. The idea of Peter in pain cut her to the heart. All she could think of was wanting to put her arms about him, to comfort him. But Hermione shook her head sternly.

'No, Rosamund. Peter is in good hands. Under no circumstances must you think of travelling with a new-born baby. Your priority now must be your child——-Tristam!' As Rosamund looked into the older woman's eyes, she knew what she said was right, and she nodded her head in reluctant agreement.

'What about Lois Challoner?'

'She's dead.'

'Dead?' Rosamund looked at her in shocked surprise.

'The police shot her as she was in the very act of stabbing Peter. I will tell you everything I have found out.' She proceeded to unfold the story and Rosamund listened in fascinated horror. The whole thing was so bizarre. But at least, if Lois was dead, there would be no future threat to Peter's life—-or her own. She remembered the veiled woman and her words. Of course—-that must have been Lois. She shuddered involuntarily.

'I had a sense of evil about her, when she threatened me that night. But I never for one moment, thought the veiled woman could be Lois!'

'Yes——I remember you spoke about that sense of evil. Rosamund, the surgeon told me something else. The police visited Lois villa and searched it. They found all the paraphernalia of those who dabble in black magic. I know when I first met her, I was repelled by something about her——but I thought it was just my mother's instinct telling me that she was totally unsuitable for my son.'

'I experienced the same distaste,' said Rosamund. 'But why did she want Peter so? What hate him so much that she wanted to kill him? I really cannot understand it.' Her eyes were bewildered.

'She was sick, Rosamund——spiritually sick. But she has gone from both of your lives now and her vengeance with her. Soon Peter will be back with you and you will be able to resume your lives together, with the added blessing of your son. Oh, Rosamund——how Peter will love him! I cannot wait to see him take Tristam up in his arms!' They looked at each other and laughed shakily, in reaction to all that has happened. At least the future was very bright.

After a few days, Rosamund was allowed visitors other than Hermione. Ernst and Svetlana came, bringing a basket of flowers shaped like a crib. Ernst gave her a warm smile and his eyes were moist, when he held Peter's son in his arms. Svetlana kissed Rosamund.

'Dear Rosamund——-I'm so happy for you! He is absolutely charming, your little Tristam. I cannot wait until he is old enough for us to put a bow in his hands!' Ernst lips softened to a tender smile as he looked at his wife.

'There speaks the teacher,' he said. Then he looked at Rosamund again, this time with a more sober expression. 'I am just back from the States, Rosamund. I flew out there as soon as I heard what had happened.'

'What? You have seen Peter? How is he? Oh——-tell me every-thing!' He looked into her lovely, eager face and forced a cheer-ful smile onto his face.

'Why——he is very well indeed, for a man who has been through heart surgery. But Rosamund——you may find that it will take him a little time to adjust back to normal life. Sometimes

People can experience a certain——depression, following a shock to the body.' He paused, seeming to grope for the right words. She interrupted him anxiously.

'Are you telling me he is badly shocked——depressed? Somehow that doesn't sound like Peter. He usually bounces back from a problem. Indeed, he has a wonderful resilience, and—— .' Her voice trailed off, for she remembered Hermione telling her how worried she had been over her son, after Natasha's death and that it had taken many years, before he recovered from his grief. But surely the joy of his son's birth, would outweigh any dark memories of his close encounter with death. Ernst gave her a reassuring smile.

'My child, he is greatly blessed in having such a treasure for a wife. He knows this and absolutely adores you.'

'Have you any idea how long it will be, before he is allowed to fly home?'

'Not at this stage, liebchen. But as soon as he is strong enough, he will be back at your side. So be patient. Ach, that reminds me——you have another visitor waiting outside. Leopold asks if he may come in?'

She smiled and nodded her head and Ernst went to the door and called Leopold's name. Leopold's eyes flew straight to the bed. Rosamund was looking extremely lovely in an embroidered white lace negligee and he lowered his eyes, so that she wouldn't see the desire in them. When he looked up again, it was to give her a stiff little bow and to offer her a small teddy bear.

'For your son Rosamund,' he murmured. Then he saw the baby cradled in Svetlana's arms and he drew his breath in slowly. This was the sealing bond on Rosamund's marriage to Peter Bagshaw. The baby, as though aware of his concentrated stare, moved his little head. Instinctively, Leopold moved towards him and bent over him, touching one of the tiny hands with his finger. Immediately the baby curled his fingers over Leopold's exploring one—and the young man was surprised at the strength in the dimpled hand. He looked down at the baby gravely. This was Rosamund's son—not just Peters, and as such, he vowed that he would do all he could in life to help him. He felt a strange feeling flowing through him and almost reluctantly, moved backwards as Tristam released him.

'Why——he likes you,' laughed Svetlana, but she watched Leopold shrewdly. Both she and her husband were aware of the deep feelings that Leopold had for Rosamund and the impossibility of his ever having them returned, for Rosamund was extremely happy in her marriage. Poor boy, it was a shame! She wondered whether Rosamund realised the havoc she had wrought in the pianist's breast—probably not——and yet, she thought she glimpsed a look of sympathy on Rosamund's lovely face, as the girl rested her eyes on Leopold's bowed head.

It was six weeks since his operation. Peter was allowed to leave the hospital. His case lay open on the end of the bed, as Rodrigo helped his friend to dress in his own clothes again. Peter realised that he had lost a lot of weight, for the waistband of his trousers was very slack. He buttoned his shirt, feeling a degree of discomfort from his ribcage. But he was learning to deal with this and knew that it would lessen as the weeks went by.

'Why—-you really look the old Peter again,' cried Rodrigo admiringly! 'No-one would guess that you were so critically ill so very recently. Those dark shadows round your eyes are the only visible trace—-and they will only serve to attract the ladies to you more, for they add an air of mystery to your face!'

'They will not exactly be attracted to me, when they find out the truth!'

'But nobody will know——unless you tell them! I certainly never will and I know Ernst also gave you his word. Have no fear, my friend. Your secret is safe.' Rodrigo took one of Peter's hands and squeezed it firmly. 'Come now. It is time to go——to start living again!'

'You're the best friend in the world Rodrigo! As for dear old

Ernst, I have always looked on him as a father.' He cast a last look around the safety of the little private ward, that had been all his world for so long and followed Rodrigo resolutely out of the door. The nursing staff and doctors were in the reception hall, to wave goodbye to their celebrated patient. None apart from his own specialist and the nurses who had had direct care of him, knew that he was almost surely HIV positive and their professional integrity sealed their lips.

Rodrigo helped him into the passenger seat in the bronze limousine. Then they were off. The sunshine streamed brightly down on this famous American city where thousands of its citizens carried the same seeds of potential death in their veins, as now circulated those of Peter Bagshaw. But Peter glanced out of the windows unseeingly, his thoughts back in Britain, where an unsuspecting young wife and baby son, awaited his return.

'I'm not going to tell her, Rodrigo.'

'What?' The car swerved to a blaring of horns from outraged fellow road users. He righted it. 'You must be joking, my friend. You cannot expose Rosamund to——.'

'To AIDS! Of course I won't. What kind of a fiend do you think I am? I shall simply not sleep with her. I'll think of some excuse——not wanting her to face another pregnancy, because of her high blood pressure.'

'Have you forgotten birth control Peter? She will merely insist on this, if you prevaricate in such a way.' Rodrigo shook his head. 'You simply must have faith in her, my friend. Wouldn't you expect complete honesty on her side in similar circumstances?'

'I'm not telling her,' said Peter stubbornly———'At least, not until it is unavoidable and then I shall simply go away, to avoid having her face the distress of seeing the way I'll be.' He glanced sideways at Rodrigo, who merely shook his head distractedly.

'Here——this isn't the road to the airport!'

'I know. We have a call to make first.'

'Where to? I'm in no mood for visiting!' But Rodrigo ignored his protests and continued to drive along the road that between attractive homesteads, set in hilly countryside. At last, the car drew into a long, gravelled driveway, and came to a halt outside a large white bungalow, surrounded by a wide veranda, doors and window frames a soft yellow. The surrounding garden was ablaze with flowers, tubs of flowering shrubs lined the steps leading up to the veranda, while creepers festooned the sides of the bungalow with white and purple star shaped blossom. A woman came to the door, holding a little girl by the hand. Beside her, a tousle haired boy bounced up and down in impatience. Rodrigo opened his door and got out. He approached the woman the woman and spoke with her. She nodded and he returned to the car to help Peter out.

'This is the address of your surgeon——Charles Sylvester. I promised him that I would bring you here before we left the country. I believe you know about his son—Richard? Before Peter could protest, he walked him over to the mother and her children.

'Are you the famous musician, Sir Peter Bagshaw,' asked the woman? 'Why, you look much younger than I thought you would!' She gave him a welcoming smile. 'I'm Sandra Sylvester, Charles wife and these are our children, Richard and Mandy.' She held out her hand and he took it almost hesitatingly.

'I'm pleased to meet you, Sandra. I will always be everlastingly grateful to your husband for his skill and wonderful care of me, I'm afraid I've been a terrible patient!' He patted the little girl on the head, but it was to the boy that he looked with unusual intensity. 'You are Richard then,' he asked gently?

'Yes, sir. Dad told me you were coming! Come along——he's round the back in the pool.' He took Peter by the hand and led him through the house and out of glass doors, into a truly beautiful garden, dominated by a large pool.

'Hi———Dad! It's your friend who plays the violin!' Richard jumped up and down to attract his father's attention. Peter smiled as the red haired surgeon pulled himself up and drew a towelling robe about him Richard thrust a towel at him. He made a token gesture of drying his hair, but dropped it almost at once, as he came towards Peter, hands outstretched.

'Peter! You came——-I'm so glad! Sandra——-how about a drink for our guest. What will you have, Peter?'

'A coffee would be most acceptable.'

'OK. Coffee for me too, then darling. What about you kids——shakes?' He watched as Sandra and little Mandy went back into the house. 'Well, Peter. You have met young Richard. Quite a boy, isn't he.' He looked at his son, with pride mixed with tenderness. 'Come——-let's sit awhile.' He indicated a bench set beneath a tree that was adrift with scarlet blossom. 'Now then——how are you feeling? Ready to cope with the world again?' He glanced keenly at Peter. 'I would have been at the hospital to say goodbye to you——-but to be honest, I hoped that you would accept my invitation to see me here, before returning to the UK. I'm delighted that you've come.'

'I'm glad of the opportunity of thanking you personally for your care of me——-which went far beyond mere medical dedication. As for feeling ready to carry on with life——-well, I suppose I have no option but to do just that. My music carried me through an earlier traumatic period in my life and I'm hoping that it will do so again.'

He looked around him. 'Where's Rodrigo?

'I guess that like a good friend, he is making himself scarce whilst we talk. Don't worry. Sandra will be looking after him'

'I fear he disapproves of a decision which I explained to him on our way here.'

'May I ask what that was?'

'To withhold knowledge of my condition from Rosamund, at least until it reaches that stage where it may be no longer hidden. Of course, I will take every conceivable precaution to prevent the slightest risk of infection to her or my son——or indeed anyone else.' He searched Charles face, expecting disapproval, but saw only sympathy on the calm features.

'How will you deal with the intimate side of your marriage, Peter?'

'I will think of some good medical reason why I can no longer enjoy this with her. Treat her as my best and most loving friend, which she already is——try to shower her with affection in other ways——.' His voice tailed off.

'How do you think you would have reacted, had you returned to her in your previous excellent condition of health, to find she was rejecting you——for medical reasons? Would you not immediately want to know what those reasons were——perhaps insisting on independent medical reports to help the woman you love? Think about it Peter. Try to see it from her point of view. Don't you feel that in time to come, she may feel most terribly hurt that you didn't trust her enough to be honest about a situation that involves her as well as yourself?' His hazel eyes sought out Peter's dark gaze. He thought he saw uncertainty there. He looked around for his son.

'Richard!'

'Yes, Dad?' The boy came running.

'Richard——this friend of mine knows that you are HIV positive. He has a friend with the same problem. Would you like to tell him how you manage?'

'Of course!' He gave Peter the trusting smile of childhood. 'You see sir, I have these little bugs in my body. Which are likely to make me feel sickly, from time to time. Lots of people have the same thing——but to be fair to other folk, I have to be absolutely sure, that none of my blood gets near anyone else. If I bleed, I have to tell Mum or Dad at once, if I'm at home here——and tell a teacher if it happens at school. Then again, if I get a snotty nose, and use a tissue, it has to be put in a plastic bag, just like any blood stained cotton wool or lint used to mop up a cut——and soiled dressings, the same thing.' He smiled at Peter. 'Your friend will be able to manage just fine, sir——once he gets used to it!'

'Richard——you are a wonderful boy,' said Peter huskily. Then a thought struck him. 'Do you love your little sister Mandy?'

'Sure I do—-although she can be a pain at times,' came the laughing response.

'Then—-do you ever give her a kiss?'

'Well—-not too often. That would be sissy——but at bedtime, before prayers. Mom always tells us to give each other a kiss before sleeping—-and she gives me a kiss then too.' He gave Peter a very penetrating look. 'Tell your—— friend——just not to worry. There really is no need to. Dad says that one day the sci-entists will find a cure for AIDS and until then, all of us who are HIV positive, just have to be patient—-and careful.' He reached out a small tanned hand. 'Good luck, sir,' he said softly, then as he heard his mother call from the house, he ran off, looking like any other carefree boy.

'He will be eight next month,' said Charles softly, 'But some-times I feel I am speaking with an adult. He has an amazing per-ception.'

'He knew—-that it was me,' said Peter.

'Only instinctively then—for I promise you, I have said noth-ing. Look Peter, will you keep in touch, after you get home. I have this very strong feeling that our lives are going to touch again.' For answer, Peter held out his hand, and with that clasp a firm friendship was born between these two.

Rosamund looked down at the sleeping form of her son with utmost gentleness. He really did look so like Peter. There was the same dark waving hair, high forehead and resolute chin—but the slate grey eyes were now closed in sleep, were almond shaped like her own and fringed with long curling lashes.

'You are going to break some hearts one day, little Tristam,' she murmured. Then she looked up, as there was a quiet knock and Hermione came into the nursery.

'He's back in this country, Rosamund darling! He'll be here

tonight!'

'Oh——Hermione!' She fell into the older woman's arms laughing and crying all at once. The baby gave a small cry and she tried to contain her excitement, as they both stole out of the room. 'Is it absolutely definite now?'

'Yes. He phoned form the airport just now.'

'He phoned?' Rosamund's face was hurt. 'Didn't he ask for me?'

'I said I wanted to call you, but he said he wanted to greet you here at Garnford instead.' She gave Rosamund a reassuring smile. 'Peter has never been one for expressing emotion on the telephone darling.' There was so much to do. A wonderful meal had to be planned——cook spoken with. Harrington's face was warm with happiness as Rosamund told him the news.

'Just you relax, Lady Rosamund. You have enough to occupy yourself with Master Tristam. Garnford will be looking at its best to welcome Sir Peter back!' She looked at him gratefully. He was such a treasure, always calm, always with everything under complete control.

'Just one thing, Harrington——could we have a centrepiece of dark red roses on the dining table!'

The hours crawled by. Rosamund could hardly contain her impatience. She checked her appearance in the huge Venetian mirror of the great hall, as she wandered downstairs yet again. She was simply dressed in an Italian, cream wool dress, with an unusual belt of soft rolled leather, tooled in gold, her only jewellery, her jade pendant. Her hair hung loose on her shoulders like a golden cape. She was looking extremely lovely and knew it. Harrington came towards her, and bowed.

'He will be here soon, my lady,' he said soothingly.

'What's the time, Harrington?'

'Almost 8pm.' Just as he spoke, they heard the sound of a car arriving in the drive. With a quick smile, Harrington made for the door. Rosamund froze, listening. Then she heard that much loved voice again, sounding flat and a little tired, as he greeted Harrington. As he came into the hall, she ran to greet him. He held a hand out.

'Gently, Rosamund––my wound is barely healed!' She drew up short, arms outstretched, looking at him uncertainly. She started forward again and poised on tiptoes, attempting to kiss him, but he moved his head to one side, and lips that sought his own, barely brushed his cheek. 'I'm sorry, darling––I'm starting a foul cold—and I don't want to risk giving it to you, because of the baby! But oh––it's good to see you! Rodrigo sends his best wishes. I left him in London, but he will be coming here in a day or two.' His voice was light—almost impersonal, she thought.

Harrington came towards them with a tray he had already prepared, and Rosamund smiled as she looked at the dusty champagne bottle and the crystal glasses.

'I thought sir, that you might want to toast the new young master,' he said, as he set the tray on the long oak table. 'I would also like to offer you my congratulations on behalf of the staff, on the birth of your son—and your safe return to all of us, after the dreadful events in America.'

'Why, Harrington––that is very civil of you! But there are only two glasses on this tray—please fetch one for yourself!' He waited as the man went to get one. Then Harrington withdrew the cork, the pop sounding loudly in the quiet of the Great Hall. Just at that moment, Hermione came running down the stairs.

'Another glass, Harrington,' cried Rosamund happily. She watched as Hermione also attempted to embrace her son––and again he drew back, murmuring a warning about his newly healed wound and his heavy cold. Hermione drew back in surprise.

'A cold, darling? What's a cold, after all you have been through,' and she attempted to kiss his lips, but again he turned his head slightly, but Hermione hardly seemed to notice, so great was her joy in his return. She took the glass Harrington held out to her. Peter looked at the two women who meant everything in this world to him and raised his glass.

'I drink to you, my wonderful wife Rosamund—-and to you, my dearest mother——and to my son!' he drank his wine slowly, then lowering his glass between sips inquired—'Have you considered a name for him yet, Rosamund?'

'His name is Tristam,' she replied.

'Tristam? Your father's name! You don't think that perhaps the name may carry unhappy associations—-your father's accident!' He paused. 'I had thought you might have liked to call him Peter, after me.' His eyes searched her face. He saw a slight dismay appear. Then Hermione broke in tactfully.

'Why not have him christened Tristam Peter Bagshaw. That sounds really good, doesn't it!' She placed her glass down on the tray. 'Now come along—you have to meet Tristam. He is absolutely beautiful—-and he looks just like you.' She took his hand. 'Come along Peter—-Rosamund has been waiting all day to show him to you!' Rosamund hurried up the stairs in front of them. Surely it was only tiredness—jet lag that was causing this distance in Peter's attitude. Just let him see the baby, hold his much longed for heir in his arms and then all would be well.

Peter drew in a deep breath, as Rosamund stood framed against the nursery window, with his son in her arms—-the child he would never see grow to manhood. He had told himself, that he would not allow himself to be emotionally involved with the boy, for that might make the situation more bearable.

'He is a wonderful boy, Rosamund! How can I ever thank you enough for his birth.' At the sound of his voice, the baby turned his little head and opened his eyes and Peter walked over to look down into eyes as dark as his own. It was as though generations of Bagshaw ancestors stared back at him through his son's eyes.

'Here——take him, Peter!' Rosamund held the baby out to him. Instinctively his hands reached to tenderly to receive the little one. Then his hands dropped to his sides and he shook his head slowly.

'Rosamund—-it's an indescribable experience seeing your own flesh and blood for the first time. I am touched to the very depths of my being. He is absolutely beautiful—a wonderful child! But darling—I will not touch him just now. Not until my cold has cleared up. After all, he was born prematurely and we must take extra special care of him.' Although his smile was the gentlest she had ever seen and his eyes wet with emotion, she felt rejection, both for herself and for Tristam and was hurt and bewildered. Then she remembered Ernst's warning, that her husband might be depressed following the shock of his near death and she forced a happy smile back onto her face.

'Of course you are quite right, Peter. See——I'll put him back in his crib. I've only just fed him, so he'll just fall back to sleep again.' She tucked Tristam up and in spite of himself, he came close to look. How tiny those little hands were. Would they grow large enough to hold their first violin bow, before he died? He tried to push the morbid thought from him. He turned to his mother.

'How do you like being a grandmother?'

'I love it, Peter! It brings back memories of you as a baby. But come—let's go down to dinner. You must be famished1' Hermione looked at him sympathetically. It was so good to have him safely home.

'I am. You two go on down. I will just change quickly—perhaps a shower first. Tell Harrington to give me a quarter of an hour.'

'Shall I put some clothes out for you,' put in Rosamund.

'No! You go on down my dear. I won't be long.' He nodded to them both. His tone brooked no argument. Hermione took Rosamund's hand. They looked at each other when they were in the dining room. Rosamund's eyes were damp with unshed tears.

'What's wrong with him, Hermione? I know he's been through a very serious operation. But it's over! Why is he so uptight?' She looked at Hermione questioningly. Hermione shook her head slowly.

'Rosamund——I only know that you must show extreme patience and not let hurt show. It will be difficult, but eventually, he will be the old Peter again. I want to contact Ernst if I can. Perhaps he can tell us what is troubling him.' She stopped talking as one of the maids came in to say that cook wanted to know how much longer to wait, before serving.

At last Peter came into the dining room with a smile. It froze as his eyes lighted on the centrepiece on the shining waxed table. Set between the silver candlesticks, was a beautifully arranged bowl of dark red roses. He paled. It was the first time he had seen roses like them, since Lois attack on him. Now it all came flooding back to him——the turbaned figure proffering the sheaf of red roses, their perfume sweet on the air——then the upraised knife—the pain————the dark stickiness of the blood——his and hers intermingled as death flowed into his veins! He heard her voice choking out the words——"You will die, whatever the doctors may do——but it will not be a clean death now!" The words beat a refrain in his brain and he uttered a strangled cry.

'Get those roses off the table! Never let me see red roses again!' He stood holding onto a chair, his breath coming in panting gasps. Harrington looked at him in amazement, but acted swiftly. He took the roses from the table and handed them to a surprised maid outside the door, with instructions to dispose of them.

'Mary——go through every room in the house and throw out every bunch of red roses you find,' he whispered.

'Yes, sir,' she said, surprised and uncomprehending. Mr Harrington must have taken a strange turn, she confided to the other servants later. Within minutes, a crystal vase of freesias adorned the table, taken from an adjoining room. Peter saw Rosamund and Hermione staring at him in horrified silence. They must have thought he had taken leave of his senses, he realised.

?When Lois Challoner stabbed me, she was in the act of offering me dark red roses. Can you understand? Red roses and the

pain are all inextricably linked in my mind. I never want to see
those flowers again!' He seated himself at the head of the table.
'We are ready, Harrington,' he said. The prawn cocktail was delicious, but Rosamund merely toyed with it.

'Peter——it is always possible that people will offer you red
roses again, when you play the Rose Concerto. Its almost tradition now, isn't it,' she said gently.

'But I will never play the Rose Concerto again,' he said, nor
appeared to notice their shocked surprise. Then as the dishes were
removed and the next course served, he added——'However, I
have started on a new concerto. I am afraid I will probably have
to spend many hours alone, whilst I'm working on it. Mother will
tell you that I'm like a broody hen when I am composing,' he said
with an attempt at a smile. 'Perhaps it might be better if you were
both to take the baby to London, whilst I'm preparing the
Golden Concerto!'

'This is my home,' said Rosamund in a choked voice. 'This is
where I want our son to grow up——not in London!'

'Yes. You are quite right, my dear. Perhaps I may decide to
move to London myself. When I'm working, my meal times tend
to be very erratic and my temper is not of the best. A baby's crying might be difficult to deal with at such times!' He looked at
Rosamund's hurt face and hated himself for the pain he was
inflicting. 'We will discuss it later,' he said. The meal continued.
The tender roast lamb seasoned with fresh herbs was very good,
as was the sweet that followed, an amazing trifle topped with
grapes, nuts and fresh cream, laced with orange brandy. But the
three round the table, ate without really savouring the food, each
locked into their own disturbed thoughts. At the conclusion of
the meal, Rosamund rose, trying to keep the misery from her
face.

'I will just go upstairs and see if Tristam is all right,' she whispered.

'Of course, my dear.' He bowed slightly. 'Does he wake you up in the night?'

'Why——yes. Inasmuch as he still needs a feed at 2am occasionally.'

'Then Rosamund dearest, you will forgive me if I ask Harrington to prepare a guestroom for me. I need a lot of unbroken sleep at this time. I'm sure you will understand.' He looked down as he spoke. Rosamund tried to reply, but her breath broke on a sob and she fled from the room. Harrington opened the door for her. As for Hermione, she rose slowly from the table.

'I think that perhaps Rosamund needs me,' she said and followed her out of the room. Peter sighed and looked at Harrington.

'Will you prepare a room for me, Harrington. You see—-,' he chose his words carefully. 'Because of the severity of the wound I received to my heart, I am not allowed excitement of any kind. Do you understand me, Harrington?' A look of comprehension crossed his butler's face. His eyes expressed sympathy.

'Perhaps the blue bedroom in the West wing then, Sir Peter?'

'That will do admirably,' came the muffled reply. 'I'm going to the music room, Harrington.' As the musician walked heavily out, Harrington thanked that instinct that had caused him to tell the maid to remove all red roses in the house——for the music room had been fragrant with them. What a homecoming! Poor, poor Lady Rosamund————and poor Sir Peter. It couldn't be easy for him either. But then—-things were bound to improve. At least, he sincerely hoped so. He signalled to the maids to remove the dishes and hurried off, to attend to the matter of the bedroom.

Later that night, the sound of Peter's violin poured its anguish into the night wind that blew around Garnford, with all the forcefulness of early March. Rosamund heard it, as she sobbed into her pillow. Tristam heard it too and uttered a few protesting cries. Hermione slipped out of her room and hesitated outside Rosamund's door. She heard the sobbing and her heart was torn with pity for the girl she loved as dearly as though she had indeed been her own daughter. But what could she do to help? Somehow she knew, that this was a night that Rosamund had to see through alone. She opened the baby's door instead and rocked the little crib until Tristam fell asleep again. He was the only member of the family who did sleep that night.

It was half past nine the following morning. Peter came briskly downstairs and glanced around as he entered the breakfast room. There was no sign of Rosamund or his mother. He walked over to the window and stood watching the still bare branches of the tall trees tossing to the pull of the wind. Early daffodils were unfurling their buds and the sun glinted on the sparkling, steel grey wavelets of the lake. It was Garnford at its most bracing, as winter surrendered to approaching spring. He sighed. Somehow it seemed to have lost its magic for him though

'Good morning, sir. Did you sleep well?'

'Harrington——you diplomat! You must have heard my violin until the early hours——or did you sleep through it?'

'I think I may have heard you at your music, sir——until I dropped off to sleep that is. How are you feeling this morning, sir?' Harrington's face was gravely sympathetic.

'I still have some pain——but its not too bad. I have medication to take for it. Tell me——have you seen any sign of the ladies this morning?'

'Not so far, sir. But then——they often have a tray brought up to their rooms. Shall I ask Lucy to——?'

'No. No,' interrupted Peter quickly. 'I will eat alone I think.' He seated himself, but as he did so, Rosamund came into the room. She was wearing a pale pink jump suit in brushed wool, with a matching hair band holding back her long gold hair. She was looking enchantingly young and pretty—but as she drew nearer, Peter saw that the touch of gold eyeshadow enhancing her green eyes, did not disguise the puffed eyelids, that bespoke a night's weeping. He felt a knot at the back of his throat and longed to take her in his arms and kiss the swollen eyelids.

Instead, he merely rose and gave a courteous good morning to his wife. He waited until she had seated herself, then—

'So—and how is our son this morning? I hope he didn't disturb your sleep too much last night darling,' he said.

'He was very good——but then he always is, and never wakes up apart from his night feed. I did however hear you playing until five this morning.' She looked at him from sorrowful eyes. 'What's really wrong, Peter? As far as I can see, you have no obvious signs of a cold——no red nose, or cough!' Her direct attack discomforted him. Peter had always been a very honest human being and lying did not come easily to him and now he floundered.

'My throat is hot and sore——that's always a sign a bad cold is starting.' He could see that she didn't believe him but turned his attention to the breakfast dishes being carried in. 'How good it is to be back at Garnford. That was one thing I badly missed in the States——a traditional English breakfast!'

'It is good to see that your cold hasn't robbed you of your appetite,' remarked Rosamund as she watched him dispatching his eggs, bacon and kidneys. She had merely taken a plate of muesli and toyed with it listlessly.

'Rosamund——I am full of enthusiasm for this new concerto I am working on. I have just been thinking, my dear. You are going to have your hands full with young Tristam for the next few months, so I might just decide to take a short trip to the Hebrides. I am sure I will find inspiration there——rather as Mendlesohn did with his 'Fingal's Cave'!'

'The Hebrides?' Rosamund was startled. 'What a lovely idea, Peter. I am sure Tristam will be all right, if I keep him well wrapped up against the cold. I have always wanted to see the islands—Skye particularly!' her face was bright with enthusiasm. It soon disappeared.

'You misunderstand me, Rosamund. I intend to go on my own. I need absolute peace when I am composing——and I'm hardly likely to get that with a young baby along!' He spoke crisply, hating himself for the hurt he saw in her eyes.

'It's not the baby you don't want near you—-it's me, isn't it!' She put her spoon down and stared directly into his eyes. Harrington, realising that a very private conversation was about to ensue, discretely withdrew, taking the young maid with him. He closed the door.

'Peter—-let's have some straight talking. I know you have been through a horrendous experience. I sympathise from the bottom of my heart, with all you have endured. I saw photographs in the newspapers—of that woman lying across you—-and all that blood. I just cried and cried! Oh, Peter—-Peter. I know I almost lost you—-am grateful from the bottom of my heart to Almighty God, that He had His hand over you.' As she said this through lips trembling with emotion, she saw a sudden hardening in his eyes. 'So you see, Peter,' she continued, 'I can only guess what deep hurt it must have been, to have realised that a woman who professed the tenderest feelings for you, was prepared to kill you.'

'There was something evil in Lois,' he said.

'The newspaper article also referred to a reputable source having released information that Lois was involved with the occult—-that her home was searched and revealed many articles associated with black magic and that her maid had something to do with voodoo.' She stopped, for he had risen to his feet, searching her face with an iron glance.

'Yes————and what else did this newspaper say about Lois?' He hung upon her answer. But she merely shook her head in bewilderment.

'What else should there have been to say? Do you know something more then Peter? Is there something else which I should know—-because if there is, then for goodness sake just tell me, whatever it may be!' The opportunity was presenting itself to him to be absolutely candid with her and he almost took it. He found his lips forming the words that Lois had AIDS—-but he found it impossible to speak. The moment passed and his resolve hardened again.

'I was merely curious as to what sort of scandal the papers should have dug up about her life. Don't you think, its better just to forget Lois now? After all, she paid for her wickedness with her life.'

'You're right, darling. I will never mention her again. But perhaps it is good that we have discussed it, for I know such a traumatic happening must have left mental scars as well as physical ones.' She spoke boldly, realising that he was distancing himself from her once more.

'In many ways you are right, darling. Look how I reacted to those red roses. I only know that I am not ready to fall back into a normal family relationship right away. Then there is another matter——-,' he paused.

'What is it,' she asked, her eyes filling with tears.

'There are certain medical reasons—-to do with my operation, why I cannot expose myself to a certain kind of excitement. If I do, then there is danger of a heart seizure.'

'What do you mean? What are you saying?' She looked at him bewildered.

'That I am unable at his time, to enter into that wonderfully intimate side of our lives. Rosamund—it wounds me as deeply as I know it must wound you, to say this. But the risk is very real—-and I do not believe you would want me to take it.' He drew a deep breath and forced himself to look at her. He saw her groping with this information that was so radically to change their lives. 'If you feel—-at any time——that you want a divorce, then of course I will make matters absolutely straightforward for you. You and the child could stay on at this place, Hermione would expect it—and there would be a handsome settlement and——.'

'Stop it! How can you talk about divorce! When I married you, Peter, it was to be in sickness or in health—-and my vows mean a lot to me. I thought that you felt the same way. I thought that you loved me!'

'I do!' The words burst out from the agony of his heart.

'Then show it! Surely we can share a bed together—be affectionate to each other, even if we cannot have sex!'

'I'm sorry, Rosamund—-but one thing would inevitably lead to another. I'm only made of flesh and blood you know,'

?Say rather of ice! I find you inexpressibly selfish.' She looked at him helplessly, then rose from the table with as much dignity as she could muster. 'I am your wife Peter. I love you and always will. I hope that in time to come, I will also learn to respect you again.' As she shut the door, she did not hear the cry that burst from his overburdened heart.

'Rosamund! Oh——my darling Rosamund!'

Two hours later, he was sitting next to Roberts, as they started on the long road to Scotland. He had decided not to take the Rolls, but the sturdy Saab. He wanted to avoid attention and would have driven himself had he been physically able. He hadn't said goodbye to his wife or mother. He was in such agony of soul that he simply couldn't have coped with it. Harrington had managed to discretely produce a few changes of clothes for him—-and he had his violin. Anything else he would buy when he arrived at his destination. But exactly where he was going, he was not sure. It was on this very point that Roberts gently probed him, He knew his employer was far from well and was very concerned for him. Sir Peter should be at home with that sweet young wife of his and his lovely young son. Roberts was worried and deeply troubled by this present journey.

'What about Arran, sir? I've heard that it is a beautiful island. Then there is Mull——-or do you want to take a steamer to one of the remoter islands?'

Peter lifted his eyes, his stare blank. Every word he had spoken to his wife was reverberating through his head, How would she react when she found that he had gone? He knew she would be terribly upset and cursed himself for his inhumanity. Yet wasn't this the best way? Certainly it was the safest way for Rosamund and that wonderful baby boy. How he had denied his natural instinct to take his son in his arms, he would never know. As for Rosamund herself—-beautiful, passionate Rosamund—-how had he been able to resist folding her close to his heart? As though the discomfort of his operation scars would have prevented him embracing her with every tenderness. What could she think of him now? It wasn't fair! She had spoken about God having His mighty hand over him——if only she knew! How could a loving God have allowed this horror to destroy his life!

He remembered how animated her face had become when she thought she was going to accompany him to the Hebrides. What was the name of the island she had wanted to see—Skye! Yes, that was what it was, Skye!

'We are going to the Island of Skye, Roberts.'

'Very well, sir. Then I suggest that we stop over at Newcastle tonight and make for the West Coast tomorrow. I wouldn't advise trying to drive to Skye without a break—-it's a long way and you will need rest.'

'Whatever You suggest, Roberts,' came the weary reply and Peter Bagshaw closed his eyes, so that his chauffeur would not glimpse the pain in them.

CHAPTER THIRTEEN

Green waves sucked and slapped against the ferry's side as she drew gently away from the shore. Despite the weight of despair weighing down on his soul, Peter climbed out of the car and went to stand at the rail with other stalwarts who were braving the freezing wind. Gulls screamed around the ungainly vessel that was making such short time of taking them from the little village of Kyle of Lochalsh on the mainland, to Kyleakin on Skye.

'Why—-but its incredibly beautiful,' he breathed, nor knew that he spoke aloud. The middle-aged woman standing at his side nodded her head.

'Aye. You may travel the world and never find any place as beautiful as Skye. Folk say you either love it or hate it—-but never will you be untouched by it,' Her voice held a warm lilting quality.

'You live on the island?'

'Yes. My husband and I have lived here all our lives. Life can be hard at times—-but I would not exchange it for any other place on earth!' As they looked at the snow clad mountains, seeming to rise sheerly up out of the sea, their peaks wrapped in cloud silk, Peter thought he could understand.

'That's Castle Moll,' she said, indicating a ruin to their left. Soon white walled houses, smoke curling out of their chimneys, came in sight. There was a grinding noise as the ferry reached the slip and Roberts called to him to return to the car. He turned to go, with a quick word of farewell to the woman, but she called him back.

'Do you know Skye? Have you somewhere to stay?' Her bright blue eyes in her weather beaten face were kind. 'We normally take paying guests in the summer months only—-but if you would like to come to us, why then, you will be very welcome. Our house is at Braes.'

'Braes?'

'It's a wee village about eight miles from Portree.' She saw from his face, that this second name meant as little to him as the first. 'Portree is the capital of Skye, a fine town enough, where you can buy most things—-but I sometimes go to Inverness for special shopping.'

'What is Braes like?'

'Remote—-no shops——but the bank calls and the grocer calls twice a week and then again, the library calls—-and we have a post office.' In spite of himself, Peter began to smile. The idea of these various establishments paying a call on a village with this unlikely name appealed to him.

'Why then—-Mrs—-?'

'Mary MacLeod of Tianavaig House. My husband's name is Jack, How are you called yourself sir?'

'My name is Peter——-Peter Lake.' He had lied almost unintentionally—but knew he had to protect his identity at this time. Rosamund's maiden name had come easily to his lips. 'Can you accommodate my man Roberts as well?'

'Your man?' she looked at him curiously.

'Why, yes—-my driver. He is a quiet person. He will be no trouble, I do assure you!' He indicated Roberts who was waving to him again. Cars were already driving off the ferry onto the slip-way.

'He will be very welcome too. I will drive ahead of you. That is my car, the yellow one! I will see you soon then, Mr Lake——and I bid you a warm welcome to Skye!'

Warm welcome, he thought, as the Saab drove between banks crusted white with hoarfrost, despite its being early afternoon and the sun shining. The little yellow car braked abruptly in front of them and with an exclamation, Roberts slammed on their own brakes. He peered out of the window, to see what had occasioned the sudden stop. Several small, black faced sheep stood in the middle of the narrow road. It took a blare on Mary MacLeod's horn to induce them to bound up the bank on the other side. To their right, far below them glittered the brilliant dark blue waters of a sea loch, flanked by majestic mountains. It was wild and lonely and unutterably lovely. Something that had been buried deep in Peter's subconscious, since the sentence passed on him at San Francisco struggled to the surface. Shreds of joy fought up in his mind, a faint illusive theme started working away——a blending of something new with that earlier melody, that he had been going to call his Golden Concerto.

They were off again. Soon they were passing a scattering of houses, strung out like the beads of a necklace. A wide bay opened out on their right, dotted with islands and bordered by snow capped mountains on the distant mainland, whilst on their left soared smooth cone shaped peaks, looking like cathedrals carved out of ice, as they flung their heads dramatically against the sky. Peter started to nod his head slightly, as the melody took shape. After what must have been about thirty miles of driving between brooding mountains and wild moorland, the yellow car signalled and turned to the right, following a narrow winding road, not much wider than a track. Peter had the distinct impression that they were retracing their progress, but veering left all the while.

Another seven or eight miles and the yellow car started to slow down. The narrow road divided, one fork dropping down to parallel the seashore, the other lifting upwards. Mary took the right fork and then left even this, to drive up a bumpy track at an acute angle. Again the yellow car slowed and stopped and Mary MacLeod got out to open a gate. She came back to the window of their car

'I am going to drive on and then stop again to close the gate——the sheep you know. The garden is my husband's pride and joy!'

'We will close the gate, madam,' said Roberts. They followed the yellow car slowly past the gate and over a wooden planked

bridge that spanned a roaring burn in a gully below. Peter slipped
out to close the gate. The cars eventually slid to a halt in front of
a large croft house, with picture windows. The garden was girded
by the wooded banks of the burn deep below, and daffodils made
a brave display around the house and along the banks.

But it was at the view that Peter exclaimed, as he climbed stiffly
out of the car for the last time that day, where from this high van-
tage point, waters of a beautiful bay lay before him, glittering silver bright in the afternoon sun. Mountains were behind and
around him in all directions. The land opposite the bay, directly
in front of him was he realised an island—-and another island lay
to its right. In the far distance he could glimpse the mountains of
the mainland.

'Well, Mr Lake—-this is Braes,' said Mary MacLeod. 'That
island you are looking at is Raasay, from which our greatest Gaelic
poet, Sorley MacLean originated——the water is the Sound of
Raasay and that other island is Scalpay.'

'I have been to many places in the world—-but I must admit
that I have never seen any place as wildly magnificent. What is that
mountain called, to the far left—-the one with the crinkly side?'

'Och, that is Ben Tianavaig—-mountain of the little peaks—-
and it is after it, that our croft is named. Wait now until I open
the garage and then Mr Roberts can put your car away.' Minutes
later, she opened the bright, yellow, front door and ushered her
guests inside.

'Jack? Jack——-are ye there?' There was no answer, but a huge
retriever came bounding towards them from an open door. They
had been aware of its barking whilst still outside. 'This is Pasha,'
she said. The dog attempted to jump up, to make Peter's acquain-
tance, but Roberts restrained it with a deft movement. 'He'll no
hurt you,' said Mary, surprised.

'I have recently undergone major surgery,' said Peter, as he
stooped to pat the dog, which had quietened. His hand caressed
the waving golden coat. 'He is a beauty!'

'Do you have a dog, Mr Lake,' asked Mary

'Not now. I did as a boy. I spend much of my time travelling the world, so I haven't had much time for a dog.' Nor would he have much time now, came the unbidden thought. How long did a dog live—-sixteen years perhaps? No, he certainly couldn't consider a dog now.

'They're grand company, the dogs,' smiled Mary. 'Wait now till I find Jack!' As she hurried off, Peter glanced around the comfortable room, with its brown velvet armchairs and gold patterned couch and the ancient rocking chair by the glowing fire. He realised that the pungent smell he had noticed on entering the room was from the peat that was burning. He wandered over to the picture windows—-staring out across the bay, trying to block off the negative feelings invading his spirit.

'Well now—-you will not be meeting Jack tonight after all,' sighed Mary, coming back into the room. 'There was a note on the kitchen table, that he is over to Glenriach to see Lachy. He is taken with the drink again, at his age too. He is a dear old friend of ours, but he has a problem with the whisky. He can go for months at a time without a drink, and then—well—he just doesn't know what he is at. He is almost eighty and he lives alone.'

'A binge drinker,' said Peter sympathetically. 'I had a friend in the music world with the same problem. It is very kind of your husband to help his old friend.'

'Well——that's what friends are for,' retorted Mary. 'I've shown your driver, Mr Roberts, where both your rooms are, for he wanted to take your bag up——and your violin? I saw the case. Are you a musician, Mr Lake?' She looked at him curiously.

'I play a little,' replied Peter. 'Perhaps I could see the room now?' He followed her upstairs, wanting to avoid further questions about his violin. The bedroom was charming. The yellow chintzy curtains were echoed in the bedspread, covering the low divan, yellow lampshades crowned the alabaster beside lamps on the polished oak lockers, there was a Victorian wardrobe and a solid dressing chest and a comfortable armchair facing the spectacular view from the window. This would do. He liked it. Roberts was standing in front of the wardrobe, hanging his clothes up.

'The shirts may need a touch of the iron, sir.'

'I don't think I'm going to worry about a slight crease on a shirt up here Roberts—-so relax!' Peter smiled at this kindly driver who was also dear friend. 'I like this room very much, Mrs MacLeod. I wonder now—-would you think me very rude if I were to say I want to lie down for a couple of hours. The truth is that I feel exhausted after my journey. As I told you, I am just recovering form heart surgery, so I'm sure you will understand.' He saw her face soften in sympathy.

'You poor man! Just you get into your bed and I will get you up a cup of tea—-or coffee. The bathroom is just through there, if you want a bath. I will bring you up a meal, after you have had a sleep.' He hesitated. He really did feel drained. He saw that Roberts had laid out his pyjamas at the end of the bed. Raw emotions were still churning up in is mind. He needed sleep—-needed it badly.

'Roberts will bring the tea up—-and thank you for being so understanding, Mrs MacLeod!' He ran the water into the bath and stepped in, looking in surprise at the brownish water –but it was soft. How long he lay there, he was not sure, but the water was cooling when he stepped out and wrapped a fleecy towel around his waist. He stared into the long mirror, seeing his scarred chest. He ran his finger over the bumpy ridge of the vivid scar. He supposed it would fade with time. Time? How much time did he have? He tried to drive the thought from him. There was a tray on his locker. He smiled at the tea cosy—a long while since he had seen one of those. He poured the tea, slipped into bed and sat drinking from the bone china cup, with its design of bluebells. He felt cared for——felt a warmth in this croft house that emanated from its kindly mistress. He lay back on the pillows and slept.

Some four hours later, he was wakened by a gentle tapping at his door. Mary MacLeod brought in a tray, with something that smelt very appetising. The steak was cooked in a rich gravy and the vegetables were delicious. He set to with an appetite he had not expected. She smiled as she watched him and said she would be back later with his fruit dumpling.

When he had finished his meal and Mary had retired, he tried to sleep again, but couldn't. Thoughts of Rosamund and his son bombarded him relentlessly, thoughts which he had put aside on his first arrival, so exhausted he had been. But now, after the long rest and a meal, his mind was electric in it's over activity, and real-ising that further sleep was impossible, he pulled his robe about him and sat on the end of the bed.

What was Rosamund doing now? What was she thinking? Of course, she must be frantic with worry! What a coward he had been running away—-an unspeakable coward. But wasn't it bet-ter that she endure this pain, than have to face up to the infinite-ly worse one of knowing that her husband was HIV? But from deep in his mind, a thought surfaced. You should have told her. She has a right to know. Go back to her. But stubbornly he ignored the thought. In his mind's eye, he saw the perfect face of his baby son—-and felt an infinite longing for him—-a fervent gratitude for his birth. He patted the pillow with despairing hand. If only Rosamund's hair were spread across it, her breath fanning between her lips in sleep—the sweet curve of her shoulders—-her breasts.

With a cry of despair, he jumped up from the bed and stared out of the widow. Night had fallen. A silvery moon, partly masked by scudding clouds, pooled it's light over the sea—-the moun-tains were etched mysteriously against the night sky——-and his brain responded to that beauty. He went slowly over to the chest of drawers, on top of which his violin lay.

Mary MacLeod paused, the scarlet thread poised above the tap-

estry she was working on as she listened in amazement. Above
her head, the sound of a violin rose through the stillness of the
night, softly at first——then as the beautiful theme expanded,
throbbing with an indescribable sweetness and power. She turned
her head, to look questioningly at Roberts, who was sitting opposite, his head bowed over a book.

'What on earth——that music——it's the most lovely thing I
have ever heard!' He looked up at her exclamation.

'Why, its just Sir——er——Mr Lake, putting in a bit of practice,' he said calmly. 'If his playing annoys you, please let me know
and I will go and speak to him. Music is his hobby, you know,'
and he lowered his head over his book again. But Mary MacLeod
barely noticed his words, so enrapt was she in the melody rising
and falling in such glorious rendition. For twenty minutes she sat
enthralled——then the violin faltered. A passage was started again.
About a dozen times Peter attempted the opening bars of his second movement, but inspiration had left him and with a sigh of
frustration, he set the violin by.

Mary looped her thread, working carefully on her tapestry,
obviously deep in thought. Roberts cast a quick glance at his host-
ess. She must have been beautiful in her youth, he thought. There
was no guessing the original colour of her long hair, caught back
neatly in a bun, but her brows were dark and finely arched above
bright blue eyes, her lips slightly full and chin firm. Before life
placed that fine sprinkling of wrinkles on her face, she must
indeed have been good looking. As though aware of his gaze, she
lifted her head.

'Have you worked for Mr Lake for long, Mr Roberts?'

'For a very long time indeed.'

'He struck me as being very sad——troubled.' She looked at
Roberts inquiringly, but he made no comment. She put her tapestry down and rose to her feet. 'I am feeling very tired tonight
and I think I will go to my room. The kitchen is through that
door, if you are wanting anything. Just make yourself at home.

Oh——yes, and please tell Mr Lake, that if he goes through the dining room, he will find a door that leads to our little music room. It is at his disposal at any time.' With a smile she quietly withdrew. As he heard the sound of her feet on the stairs, Roberts crossed the hallway and went in search of the music room. He put the light on.

His eyes took in the ancient piano, piled up high with sheets of music, then glancing at the graceful curve of the harp beside the window seat. There were several other instruments lying on a low mahogany table, but it was to the stereo unit in the corner that his eyes were drawn——more especially to the pile of records on a stool, for the sleeve of the one on top, bore the portrait of Sir Peter Bagshaw. It was of the Rose Concerto.

He whistled softly and closed the door quietly behind him, as he too went upstairs. What should he do? His first instinct was to tell Peter, for he knew his employer for reasons of his own, wished to conceal his identity on this trip. Yet if he told him, then Peter might decide to leave at once——or first thing in the morning, and Roberts knew that Peter was suffering from extreme stress. This house was the perfect place for him to unwind, its mistress a woman whom he sensed was completely trustworthy. But had she recognised the man under her roof, as the famous musician pic-tured on her record sleeve? He shook his head as he mounted the stairs, hesitated and then hurried back to the music room. He hid the Rose Concerto at the bottom of the pile of records and remounted the stairs. It would be good to stay here!

Peter's face was calm, as he seated himself at the breakfast table, giving no indication of the turmoil in his mind. Roberts and Mary MacLeod had eaten earlier he found, so he sat alone, staring out of the window as he ate. A faint mist gave the surface of the waters an impression of translucent pearl, under the bright sunlight, of this first day of April.

'I think I will take a walk,' said Peter, as he thanked Mary for his breakfast.

'I'll go with you, sir,' put in Roberts.

'No. I want to be alone——but I won't overdo things, so don't worry, Roberts!' He smiled. 'I will probably take a walk along the seashore.'

'What size of shoes are you,' asked Mary?

'Why——eleven.'

'The same size as Jack. That's lucky. Put on these wellingtons then, for those fancy shoes of yours will be useless up here.' She handed him the rubber boots with a firm hand and he did not argue, but pulled them on. All he wanted to do was to walk and walk as he tried to resolve his mental torment.

Soon his feet were resounding on the wooden plank bridge across the burn, as he strode down the path to the road below. Gorse bushes were flecked with early gold, above the rust of last year's bracken and wild daffodils blew amongst the still faded grass. Spring was in the air, in the sweetness of bird song and in the clean breath of the wind flowing in off the sea.

He reached the road—walked to the point where it forked and took the branch that ran close to the sea. He continued to walk for another half mile, until he was level with a narrow neck of land that sliced out into the sea. Mary had referred to this as the 'Aird'. He tramped across a marshy track, where bog cotton blew, until now, he was panting as the track rose higher and he was some two hundred feet above the sea. He carried on, the spiky grass now interspersed with rocks. He walked more carefully now, along a narrow ledge, that broadened out again——and so on, the track now lost amongst bare rock. Then at last he had to stop, for he was at the end of the Aird.

He peered down, where far below him the green water swirled and boiled among the sharp rocks flanking the Aird's base. An army of gulls took to the wing, screaming their displeasure at his untimely presence at nesting time. His eyes dropped to the water sucking and crashing below him, drawing him with its hypnotic movement. Then Peter opened his mouth and shrieked his anguish, as he had not been able to until now, completely alone in this solitary place.

'Rosamund! Oh, Rosamund! I need you——Rosamund—-my dear, dear love! It's not fair——how can there be a God, when man can walk with living death in his veins. What point is there in life, when all a man holds dear is withheld from him?' He let out a cry of utmost despair and stared wildly down at the heaving, ice cold sea. Within it's cold bosom he would find peace. He threw his arms up wildly and stepped into space!

The jolt that stopped him, caused excruciating pain in his chest, as newly healed bone and tissue screamed protest. The hand that seized his waxed jacket held him firmly, pulling him inch by painful inch back onto the cliff, to lie moaning on the lichened rock.

'Gently, my friend,' said a deep voice, with a soft lilt. 'Whatever your trouble, it cannot be solved in that way.' Peter found himself staring up into eyes of an intense blue—-perhaps the kindest eyes he had ever seen.

'Why? Why didn't you let me do it? I don't want to live!' Peter's eyes were full of pain. Who was this stranger—-and by what right had he interfered with his inalienable right to take his own life!

'But God wants you to live friend——that is why He put you on this earth. Whatever sorrow afflicts you cannot be so bad, that God is not able to help you——-if you will hand it over to Him!' Peter looked back at him blankly, a faint moan of pain issuing between his lips as he attempted to sit up. The stranger set his arm about him and gently raised him to his feet.

'Come now. Let's get you back to a less dangerous place. Are you much hurt?'

'I am recovering from heart surgery,' came the faint reply. 'I feel sick.' He suddenly vomited. The stranger held him as he swayed and handed him a handkerchief to wipe his face. 'I'm sorry,' muttered Peter, his face a mask of despair.

'Don't be. It's only reaction. Now lean on me, and be careful where you set your feet.' There was a bark and Peter became aware of the golden retrieve, Pasha watching him from anxious eyes. 'The dog led me to you,' said the lilting voice——'As did another, I think.' He set an arm about Peter, instructing him to lean on him. Peter did so, half closing his eyes, just trusting himself to that firm grasp. Each step caused pain to his wrenched muscles. At last they were on firmer ground. 'Put your arms about my neck.' He found himself lifted in strong arms and carried the quarter of a mile back to the road, where a battered grey Rover was parked in a lay-by.

'Now then——let's get you inside,' said the stranger, setting him down and opening the door. Peter slumped in the front seat, as the other man went round and got in beside him, as the dog scrambled onto the back seat.

'My name is Jack——Mary's husband,' he said. 'She said that you had gone walking——and that she was concerned for you—— so Pasha and I came seeking you!'

'Well you found me just in time——or maybe too soon,' came the weary reply. But Peter was looking up now and turning his dark gaze on Jack MacLeod from eyes red with weeping.

'Do you want to tell me about it,' asked the gentle voice? 'You say that you are recovering from a heart operation. Surely this is cause for relief——thanksgiving. So, it has to be something else.'

'There are reasons I cannot talk about it,' came the despondent reply.

'Will it help if I tell you I am a minister? Whatever you say to me, will never be revealed to a living soul——-Sir Peter.' The musician looked at him from shocked eyes. 'Yes—-I know you. I have the greatest admiration for your music. I was at the Albert Hall last year, to hear your Rose Concerto. It was the most wonderfully touching composition I have ever heard. I often sit into the night, when I have problems of my own to sort out—-and listen to the record I bought as soon as it was issued.'

'Does Mary know who I am?'

'She suspects. A man called Peter, who plays the violin like an angel—-who is recovering from heart surgery! There cannot be many such. Details of the near fatal attack made on you, was in all the newspapers.' He paused and looked sympathetically at Peter. 'I also read, that Rosamund, your lovely gifted young wife, had given birth to a son. So—-why then——are you seeking to take your own life?'

'I cannot tell you!' Peter's face was torn with anguish.

'Why? What can be so terrible that you will not share it with a friend?'

'Because you would shrink from me—-as all will when they find out! As Rosamund herself will—-and I can't let her find out. It will hurt her too much!' He started to rock back and forth, head clasped in his hands. Jack's arm went out about his shoulders, and gradually the quiet words of prayer penetrated the mind of the distraught man at his side. Then slowly Peter lifted his head and glanced at Jack from tortured eyes.

'You should have let me die——you see——-I have AIDS!' Jack's expression did not change. It was still one of deepest sympathy and tenderness. He took one of Peter's hands.

'Have you known this for long?'

'No! It happened only recently. The woman who tried to murder me—-she had AIDS. The police shot Lois——and she fell on me. We were both bleeding. The surgeon who saved my life, had the difficult job of telling me that I am now most certainly HIV positive.' Peter swallowed. 'You are one of the only people to know. For I have only told two of my musical colleagues Rodrigo Mendes and Ernst Morgenstern.'

'Why have you not told your wife? Don't you feel she has the right to know? Apart from the obvious risks to herself—-but then, I suppose you have decided not to expose her to those—-which is why you are here on Skye, instead of with that young son of yours and a wife who must be bewildered at your absence!' Peter nodded shamefacedly. Words started to burst from his lips as he poured his heart out to this quietly spoken highlander, whose eyes seemed to search out his soul.

'Why me———-,' he ended. 'Why did this have to happen to me? For years I grieved the death of my first wife. Then I married Rosamund. I tell you, Jack MacLeod, she is pure and lovely—-warm and passionate—-and shares my deep love for music. We have been so wonderfully happy this last year—-and now she has fulfilled all my dreams, by presenting me with a lovely little son, but a child I will never see grow to manhood, anymore than I will ever again be able to hold Rosamund in my arms!'

'Would you say that your wife lacks courage, Peter?'

'Why—-no! She has a deep inner courage—-and a peace about her.' Peter shook his head sadly. 'Why should she have to suffer the grief of knowing her husband has the scourge of this modern age—-a disease that carries a terrible stigma—-and causes the inevitable death of the sufferer and danger to those around him!' His voice was bitter.

'Does Rosamund believe in God, Peter?'

'Yes. She has a wonderful faith.'

'What about yourself, Peter?'

'I was just starting to believe in God———until this happened!'

'Do you think that God loves you any less now———because you have AIDS? Do you not think that He knows of your anguish—-longs for you to share your grief with Him, so that He can strengthen you? He loves you Peter, just as He loves all His children. You are blaming him, are you not—-saying to yourself that He should have prevented this happening to you. But Peter——-consider this! He Himself endured the anguish of seeing his own beloved son, Jesus, suffer death by torture on a cross of shame. Do you not think that such a God does not share your hurt—-is not longing for you to cry out to Him!'

'Then why has He not made Himself real to me? Why has He not helped?'

'Because God is a gentleman, Peter. He knocks on the door of our hearts, but will only come in if we open that door to him. But if we do so, oh the joy and peace beyond understanding!' The words that poured like healing balm onto Peter's soul came gently. Half remembered phrases from the Bible, once carelessly read, were brought to him now, in all their power and beauty by Jack MacLeod. At last a strangled cry burst from Peter's lips.

'I want to believe——I do believe! But, oh Jack—-how do I know that he will forgive a life of selfishness and pride! My mother devoted her whole life to caring for me, instead of living her own life—all that ever seemed to matter, was my music—my precious music! It overshadowed my duties as a landowner—and I even exposed my young wife to danger, by allowing her to continue to play at my side, late into her pregnancy, when I knew that her blood pressure was dangerously high. I shut my eyes to it, just so that I could have her playing the Rose Concerto at my side!'

'Peter. God has given you a wonderful gift—-that of music. You have devoted your life in producing melodies, which bring love and hope into the lives of many. Your 'Hope of the Nations' was the most inspiring work I have ever heard, the 'Rose Concerto', the most touching. Yes—-from what you say, perhaps you have been guilty of a little selfishness. So shall we just lay this before God now, as you confess your belief in his dear Son Jesus——and ask Jesus to come into your life and that His Holy Spirit may strengthen you in all that lies ahead.'

When Peter climbed stiffly from the car outside Tianavaig House, his face bore an expression of peace, despite the traces of weeping about his eyes. Jack opened the door and helped him in.

'Mary dear—-our guest is back. Will you run a hot bath for him? He is chilled from his walk—-not used to our climate yet!' Jack invited Peter to follow him upstairs. 'This is my study,' he said, opening a small oak panelled room, where a peat fire glowed. The room was lined with books, many of them religious in nature, but there were others aplenty on art, poetry and music. A further section bore titles in a language Peter did not recognise. Jack saw

his curious gaze. 'Those are in the Gaelic,' he said. He went to the
tray that bore a whisky decanter and glasses. 'Drink this——it's a
malt made on the island, Talisker! It's very good. It will warm
you.'

'Yes——it is good,' replied Peter sipping it appreciatively. 'But
will you not join me?'

'Oh——I rarely indulge. Keep this for guests, do you see.'
Then Jack hesitated and poured a glass for himself. 'But I think
this is perhaps one time, when I will take a glass.' He raised the
whisky, looking over its warm amber, to the sad face of the man
opposite.

'I drink to your next composition, Peter Bagshaw,' he said.
'May it be the most wonderful work of your whole career——and
with God's help, it will be.' He smiled. 'Mary spoke to me of
something you were playing last night. She was quite entranced
by it. Do I take it that you have started on a new work?'

'Why, yes. I was in fact working on my new concerto last night.
I found it coming to me in the States, before——before my last
performance there. I will of course have to fully score it later, but
I now have the shape of the first movement.' Peter's face showed
the firs sign of animation, since Jack had met him. 'Would you like
to hear it?'

'It would be an honour. Thank you——yes, I would like that
very much. But I hear Mary calling that your bath is run. Just you
find your way back here, when you are ready.'

Peter found the hot water soothing to his wrenched muscles.
The pain in his chest was quite bad and he began to wonder if he
had done serious harm to himself. Should he perhaps consult a
doctor? But that would mean questions. Yet as he dressed himself
afterwards, he realised that the pain was actually lessening and by
the time he knocked at Jack's study, it was easily bearable.

'Come in, Peter! How are you feeling now?' The intense blue
eyes searched his face. 'I was praying,' he said. 'Just laying all your
hurt before the Lord.'

'Why——that is strange,' said Peter slowly. 'I have been in pretty bad pain as a result of my foolishness——yet in the last ten minutes, it has been getting noticeably less. He hesitated and then said awkwardly——'Thank you, Jack.'

'No. Don't thank me——thank the one, who listens to our prayers and answers them.' He glanced at the violin Peter carried. 'Are you sure you feel well enough to play?' For answer, Peter drew the bow over the strings, wincing as he did so. Then the music started to soar and Jack MacLeod closed his eyes, as he listened enthralled to surely the most glorious and bewitchingly lovely theme he had ever heard. When Peter finally put down the violin, he found Jack had tears in is eyes.

'Thank you,' said Jack huskily. 'That was beautiful enough to be offered up at the gates of heaven itself. You must work on this, Peter——finish it soon, for it is a gift to mankind——and Peter, you must let Rosamund hear it.'

'I have been thinking, Jack would you be prepared to allow me to stay here at your house for a few weeks——until I have finished this last concerto? I mean——I know it's a lot to ask. Is it fair for instance, to ask you to house a man with HIV? Is it fair to your wife?' His eyes watched Jack's face, waiting rejection, but none came.

'You know my answer already,' said Jack quietly. 'Do you want to ask Mary though——ask her yourself?'

'But—that would mean telling her about my condition!' Peter's face was alarmed. 'You said you would tell no-one of my secret!'

'Nor will I. But Peter, sooner or later, you are going to have to take some people at least into your confidence. You will find, that strangely, the more people you tell, the easier it will be to do so and to come to terms with your fears————and the greatest of these I think, is that of rejection.' Jack packed his pipe and watched Peter shrewdly.

'You are right. Will you call Mary, please Jack.' Jack rose to do his bidding and within minutes, Mary MacLeod stood smiling I the doorway.

'Mary, my dear——our guest has something he wishes to share with you. So won't you please sit down.' As though she realised that what she was about to hear, was of great importance, Mary seated herself by the fire, tranquil hands folded in hr lap, as she smiled at Peter encouragingly.

'Yes, Peter?'

'Well——first of all, Mary I lied to you yesterday. I said my name was Lake, when in point of fact it is——'

'Bagshaw,' she interrupted softly?

'Why, yes. Lake is my wife's maiden name. I wanted to disguise my identity, and her name came to my tongue.

Mary——your husband just saved my life!' She looked across at Jack, startled, as he continued-'I was about to throw myself off the Aird, had in fact taken what should have been my last leap in this life! But Jack caught hold of me and dragged me from a deeper abyss than the one surging below the cliff. I owe my life and I think my sanity to him.'

'Praise the Lord,' said Mary softly. 'But what brought you to feel so unhappy, that you wanted to commit suicide?' She leaned forward, eyes soft with sympathy.

'I have the AIDS virus, Mary. Lois Challoner had developed full-blown AIDS before she attacked me in the States. When she fell on me, dying from a policeman's bullet, her blood was pouring out of her wound. I had an open wound, was bleeding from the stab wound to my heart, and so————!'

'Oh, I see! You poor man. What a cruel thing to happen. I'm so very sorry. What joy to you though, that you have a loving wife——and surely I heard, a bonny wee son? It was mentioned in the newspapers.'

'Yes——Tristam is indeed bonny. But I have not dared to take him in my arms, although I longed to do so.'

'Why ever not?'

'Because of the fear of infection for him! Do you think I would take any risk with my son?' He spread his fingers. 'I've been told that it can only spread through direct contact with body fluids. I believe we don't know all the facts about the disease yet? I have heard that kissing is safe—but how safe? A hundred per cent or only ninety nine per cent?' He looked at Mary hopelessly. 'The risk is too great. I have decided to keep away from them both—at least this seems to be the only correct thing to do.' He went on to tell them of how he had told Rosamund that he could no longer enjoy an intimate relationship with her, for fear of heart attack.

'Will you listen to me now, Peter. Maybe Jack hasn't mentioned to you that I am a nurse——have been one all my days, first as a theatre sister in Inverness, then when Jack and I married, returned to the island, turning to midwifery as well as general nursing. We are both officially retired now, yet both are called on in the community, to help in our own fields, which can sometimes overlap. Now——- as far as I know, we have no AIDS cases on Skye at this time. But certainly it is spreading, and so like everyone else in the medical profession, I have made it my job to find out as much as possible about HIV and AIDS, both in the treatment and the spreading of the virus. Indeed, Jack was visiting two young men in prison just a week ago, both of whom are HIV positive. As for myself, on my way back from Inverness, I called to see the daughter of a doctor friend. Both she and her husband are HIV positive—-and their little daughter was born with the virus. A difficult situation—for it is never easy dealing with any illness— and yet Peter, I found so much love in that small household.' She swallowed. 'Peter——you could live for many years. Are you going to deprive the woman you love of sharing those years with you? Is your little son to grow up never knowing a father's love? For you have much love in you Peter. It flows out through your music, which is full of tenderness and longing.'

'So——what is it that you are saying?' Peter leaned forward, staring at her intensely. She looked back at him from wise eyes, only slightly less blue than Jack's own.

'Put your trust in God, Peter. Go to that young wife of yours, for you must not deprive her of the opportunity of showing her love for you, and in doing so, to gain that special strength she is going to need, to guide young Tristam on his journey through life. Let him be able to speak in later years, of a father's love—-not merely that he is the son of a great composer. Let him have memories of a father tossing him up in his arms and playing ball with him——perhaps placing his first violin in his hands. There! I've finished! It's up to you now. Yes, there will be risks—-but they will be negligible with proper precautions.' She paused and looked at him. 'There is a telephone over there, Peter Bagshaw—-use it!'

Peter looked at the phone, then back at Mary. Then he glanced out of the window, where he could see the bay shimmering under the April sunshine.

'Mary—I know it is a lot to ask, and please just say no if it is not possible—-but could I ask Rosamund to bring Tristam up here to meet you both—-and to stay for a little while? Somehow I feel that I may be able to speak with her here in a way that would not be possible at Garnford.' A broad smile spread across Mary's face, and was echoed on Jack's features.

'Why—-bless you, Peter Bagshaw! Of course you can ask them here. It will be wonderful to have a little one under our roof again—-and as for you lovely wife, I long to meet her. Tell her to come and be very welcome!' Tears of gratitude glistened in Peter's eyes, as he rose to pick up the phone.

'Rosamund——Rosamund——-it's Peter! He's on the phone and he's asking for you!' Hermione rushed into the nursery, where Hermione was cradling Tristam in her arms. 'Oh darling——I'm sorry. Have I wakened him?'

'No——I've just fed him.' She handed the baby to Hermione and hurried to take the call in her bedroom.

'Is that you, Rosamund?'

'Yes, Peter. Where are you? Are you all right?'

'Yes. I'm all right darling! 'I'm on Skye—-the island you spoke about. It is the most beautiful place on earth, and I want you to bring Tristam up here to be with me.'

'But why did you go off like that? How could you treat me in such a way, Peter? Are you sure you really want me now?' Her voice was muffled with tears of relief shed now that she knew he was safe.

'I want you very much—-but Rosamund, when you come, there are certain matters which I will have to lay before you—-decisions that only you can make. So come—-and come quickly.'

'Shall I bring Hermione?'

'No. I think not. I have to speak to you on your own, Rosamund.'

'Very well. How do I get there? The night train from London——and change I suppose at Inverness?' She was forcing her mind to be practical, even though the fingers holding the phone were trembling.

'No——take a plane. Better still, a helicopter! Do you have the number of the pilot who took us up to Rannoch?'

'It will be in your big desk diary. I'll ring him now. What is your number, so that I can call you back?' He gave to her and then replaced the receiver.

'Jack—-where is the safest place for a helicopter to set down?'

'How about the field next to the house. The part near the fence is not in the least boggy.' The phone rang some ten minutes later and it was Peter Fenton the pilot. He wanted precise details and Jack spoke with him. He would leave tomorrow———be with them roughly at two in the afternoon.

Peter worked all through the night. Jack and Mary listened in their big, double bed, seeing the clouds float over the moon's face, as the mysterious throbbing chords, echoed through the house. At last they slept, as did Roberts in his room. But still Peter Bagshaw worked, until at five in the morning, he put both pen and violin aside and dropped fully dressed onto his bed.

It seemed no time at all, before Jack knocked at the musician's door with a cup of tea.

'It's nine thirty, Peter. I have to drive over to Heaste this morning. The minister who usually takes the service there, has a bad cold. Would you like to come with me? The service will be in Gaelic and so you won't understand the words—-but the singing is something I would like you to hear.'

'Of course—-I'd love to come. I will just wash and dress—-or should that be undress!' He looked down at himself guiltily, realising that he had not undressed the night before. 'Give me ten minutes, Jack.'

'Good morning, Peter. Here is your breakfast, Mr Roberts and Jack have had theirs.' Mary gave him a warm smile. 'Rosamund rang, just to confirm that she would be arriving between two and three. I didn't waken you, for I know you were working late last night.'

It was a long drive, amongst breath taking scenery.

The church turned out to be little more than a hut—-but as the people filed in with quiet smiles to Peter, he sensed the reverence to the great God they worshipped, as they sat with their heads bowed in silent prayer. Then Jack was standing in front of them, his intense blue gaze sweeping across the little congregation, as he opened the service. As Jack had said, Peter could not understand the service, which was entirely in Gaelic, but when the singing started, he listened in amazement. The unaccompanied voices of the Islanders were chanting in the Gaelic, in a sound that was as wild and lovely as the place itself. He felt himself stirred to the depths of his being, by the fervency of the worship. He found his own lips murmuring in prayer. When he looked up, it was to see Jack's eyes upon him.

As they drove back along the hilly, winding road, which Jack took rather fast in his battered Rover, Peter was deep in thought. The service had been totally different in form from that which he had attended in London, at Michael Howard's church——yet the same reverence had been there, the love and devotion, just differently expressed. He thought again about the extraordinary power of the singing. He had never heard anything like it before.

'Well Peter. How did you like it?' asked Jack, half turning his face. He still wore his dog collar under his waterproof jacket.

'I wish I had understood the words——but that singing! It was glorious, almost eerily beautiful. You know Jack, I think I will be able to draw from it in some way, for the second movement of my concerto.'

The hours seemed to drag once they were home. Then at last came the whirring sound of the helicopter. It circled overhead. Mary seized a tablecloth. She climbed through the wire fence, with the men at her heels and started to wave the cloth. Then Jack took one side with her, as they spread it on the turf, guiding the helicopter to a firm place to land. They waited until the rotary blades had ceased to spin——then Peter hurried forward. The door opened and the pilot climbed out, with a smile of recognition to Peter. Then he reached up and took the baby that Rosamund handed down to him——and then placed him firmly in Peter's arms, before he could protest. Then he helped Rosamund down.

She stood for a moment, looking very young and vulnerable in her soft, white leather suit, as her eyes sought out Peter——and the precious bundle he held. She walked over to him slowly and he handed the baby back to her with a troubled look. Then he saluted her gravely on the forehead, his lips barely brushing her skin.

'Rosamund——darling. He is far too delicate for my clumsy hands! Come——let me introduce you. This is Mary——and her husband, Jack MacLeod. He is a minister.' Rosamund's gaze swept over Jack's kindly face and then on to the sympathetic features of the silver haired woman at his side. She warmed to them at once. She held out her hand to Mary, only to be embraced by her. Then Jack slipped an arm around her shoulders.

'Come along, my dear. Let's get you and little Tristam indoors in the warm. Why——but he's a fine boy.' He turned his head to gesture to the pilot to join them Roberts was helping him to carry the cases to the house. Mary held the wire fence apart for them all to climb through, Jack taking the baby while Rosamund slipped through.

Mary served lunch. The salmon was fresh and quite delicious. The peat fire crackled in the hearth as they ate. But there was an uneasy tension between Rosamund and Peter, who still had not spoken privately yet. Rosamund had hastily fed and changed the baby before coming to the table. Now he slept in the padded carrycot, next to the double bed in the pretty pink bedroom that Mary had led her into. She immediately noticed that it contained none of Peter's things, but she made no comment. When she came downstairs, it was to find the others waiting for her around the dining room table. Jack said a grace and now they enjoyed their salmon, each locked into their own thoughts.

The pilot was saying goodbye to Peter, who paid him generously, asking that he keep their destination secret. The man gave his word and Peter knew he would keep it. Mary and Jack went out onto the lawn, to watch the helicopter take off and Roberts busied himself carrying the dishes from the dining room. Now Peter led Rosamund into the sitting room. He gestured that she should seat herself but she shook her head.

'Peter——I've been torturing myself with all sorts of depressive thoughts since you left me without even saying goodbye. Frankly, I just don't believe your story about a heart condition so serious, that we have to lead virtually separate lives. I have to know the truth——even if that means having to accept that you no longer love me.' She fixed apprehensive green eyes on his face, seeing the pain about his mouth and in the dark shadows under his eyes. Then she looked into those slate grey eyes and read the love there.

'Rosamund—dear heart. I love you now, more than I have ever done. I will always love you until my dying breath.'

'Then——.'

'No. Let me speak.' He reached out and took her hand and led her to the window. 'Look——isn't it just incredibly beautiful here! Darling, I have been working on my new concerto——and what I have to tell you is this. That it may be my last concerto.'

?But why, Peter?' for a moment he just looked at her, trying to get the strength to say the words that would change their life together for all time. Almost he lost courage, then——

'Rosamund. Tell me my dear, what do you know about a condition known as AIDS? You will remember that our friend Adrian Moulting died of it last year.'

She looked at him in surprise. What had Adrian to do with whatever troubled him. Then she saw the agony in his eyes—— and she knew.

'Peter——you don't mean——you can't mean. Oh, no! Don't tell me that you have AIDS?' Her frantic eyes scanned his face, begging him to deny it, but to her horror, her merely nodded his head sombrely, two tears rolling down his cheeks.

'Rosamund——I would rather do anything than have to tell you this——but yes, my darling heart——I do have AIDS. At least, I am what they call HIV positive. This is the condition that ultimately develops into AIDS.'

'But how, Peter——how? Surely it is a sexually transmitted disease, mostly associated with homosexuals.' Her lips were stiff as she forced the words out.

'Darling, it is true that it started out that way. But now unfortunately, it can be transmitted in a normal heterosexual relationship——also in tainted blood transfusions.'

She gasped! Blood transfusions. But of course——his operation in San Francisco! This must be where it had happened. But he was still talking and she tried to listen, although her breast was heaving so badly, her thoughts so disjointed, that she could hardly concentrate.

'When Lois stabbed me, she was shot by the police——do you

remember hearing about this, Rosamund?'

'Yes. Of course I remember. She fell on top of you and——?'

'Precisely. She had AIDS. Before she died, she made a cryptic comment to the effect that I would die, whatever the doctors should do for me——-that it would not be a clean death! It made no sense——until my surgeon, Charles Sylvester, told me that they had found Lois to be suffering from full blown AIDS. Her infected blood entered my body by the dagger wound she had directed towards my heart. Now do you see why I could not come to you at Garnford, as I was aching to do——-and why I can never sleep with you again. Oh, Rosamund——-Rosamund. It is the most cruel thing, for a man to have to reject the woman he loves for such a reason.' He turned away from her, walking to a corner of the room, not wanting her to see his tears——-not to have to face the rejection he feared.

'Oh, Peter. You poor, poor darling.' He heard the soft words and felt her hands pulling his face around. Before he could stop her, her lips found his and hung upon them. 'All right. We have a problem——a terrible problem. But we are going to face it together. Promise me——whatever you do, you will never go away from me again. Well——-do you promise me that, Peter Bagshaw? Answer me?' He looked down into her tear wet eyes, saw the resolution there, the love—and he gave her the promise she asked.

'I promise you Rosamund, that I will never leave you again——-not until it is beyond my control. You have my sacred word for that.' Then they were in each other's arms, hugging each other and crying all at once. And so it was that Jack and Mary found them, as they returned from waving farewell to the pilot. They hesitated in the doorway and would have stolen away again, only Peter saw them and beckoned them in.

'You were right, my dearest friends. Come and meet properly now, the wonderful girl I have for a wife.'

Then Jack and Mary hurried towards them, shaking their hands in delight. But Jack looked interrogatively at Rosamund. It must have been the most awful shock for the young girl. Was she really going to be able to cope? But as he looked into those green eyes, brimming over with love for her husband, Jack knew that she would indeed have the strength needed to support the man she loved. She clung onto Peter's arm now and he winced.

'What's wrong, Peter/'

'I hurt my shoulder——climbing yesterday. No. If I'm going to be honest with you in all things, then I have to tell you what really happened, was that I decided in a moment of despair, to end my life——to throw myself off a cliff. I almost succeeded, but Jack saw me——and dragged me back. He saved my life, Rosamund!'

'Peter! Oh how could you have contemplated doing something so awful to——us!' She looked at him in a mixture of shock and anger. 'That was a terrible and cowardly thing to do. But you are going to be strong now, Peter——you are going to live——and to compose——and make our son proud to call you father!' She looked at him firmly in the eyes and he nodded his agreement.

'I promise. I will never let you down again, Rosamund!'

CHAPTER FOURTEEN

'The post, my Lady.' Harrington bowed as he offered the silver tray to Hermione. She thanked him absently, and started to sort through the letters. She was sitting in the small rose drawing room alone, as she had been for the last eight weeks——for it was eight weeks since Rosamund's precipitate departure by helicopter, for an unknown destination on Skye. True, there had been several phone calls, from both Peter and Rosamund to reassure her that all was well and that her grandson was making spectacular progress. But so far, they had withheld their exact address, saying that there was something that they had to work out together, and asking her understanding for this.

She was trying not to allow the deep hurt she felt, to appear in her demeanour. It was the first time that her son had not taken her into his confidence, in his whole life and although she acknowledged his complete right to privacy in all things personal, at the same time, she was experiencing feelings of rejection. Now she gave an exclamation. It was a letter in Rosamund's handwriting——and the postmark was Skye!

She opened it with impatient fingers, her eyes skimming the first few lines, that asked if she were well——ah here it was, the information she had been longing for. They were staying in a little cottage, near the couple whose house they had shared for the first two weeks. She glanced at the address at the top of hr letter—'The White Cottage, Braes, Skye' and she gave a sigh of relief. At least she now had a tangible address at which she could contact them. Skye was wonderful, she read—-bluebells, primroses and violets—-magnificent mountains that played hide and seek in the mist, islands that glowed like pink jewels in the sunset and a people who were honest and kind.

She started to smile as she read. The letter was so full of joy.

Obviously everything must be all right, her fears about Peter's state of mind groundless. Peter was working on the last movement of his new concerto. The last movement! She gasped. He must have been working at a prodigious speed to have progressed at this rate, on an entirely new work. This of course, must explain why he did not even want his mother around when he was working so intensely. She heaved a sigh of relief. Then she read on. They wanted to stay on Skye for a further four weeks, so that Peter could complete the third movement—-but would she like to join them for the first week of July? Their friends Jack and Mary had a room for her—the cottage was very tiny, with only one bedroom and the MacLeod's house was only ten minutes walk away.

Hermione was relaxed and happy, as she wrote acceptance of their invitation and if she felt slightly hurt, at being deprived of watching her grandson's first few months of life, she pushed it to the back of her mind.

She completed her letter and rang the bell for her maid.

'Julie—-see that this is posted right away! Oh and Julie—-please bring me some fresh coffee!'

'Yes, my lady.' The maid, who was new, hurried to do her bidding. She was soon back with the coffee. Harrington came in behind her, bearing the daily papers. He watched as Julie poured the coffee. Hermione sat drinking it as the door closed behind them. What a pity, that according to what Rosamund had written, there was no phone at the cottage. She sighed, then turned to pick up the papers. Her face froze at what she saw on the front page of one of the tabloids, for it was a large photograph of Lois Challoner. She scanned the headlines in fascinated horror, then put her cup down, as she read the editorial below.

The huge block capitals attracting her attention stated NOTO - RIOUS SOCIALITE, WHO STABBED MUSICIAN, HAD AIDS!

But that was impossible. She read on, almost unbelievingly.

Reliable sources have revealed that beautiful socialite, Lois Challoner, who was fatally wounded by police, during her vicious attack on Sir Peter Bagshaw in San Francisco, four months ago, was infected by the AIDS virus! People everywhere were shocked at pictures of Lois lying across the body of the wonderful musician, whose music had enchanted millions. Lois was shot in the act of stabbing Sir Peter. The bullet that tore through her chest, inflicted a fatal wound. She died in hospital—the same hospital in which Sir Peter, following heart surgery, fought his way back to life. Many, who saw the TV news footage, were absolutely horrified, to Sir Peter lying on the stage amongst the offerings of dark red roses, offered in accolade for his beautiful Rose Concerto. The flowers matched in colour the pool of blood from both their bodies It is now thought that Lois mind had become unbalanced by the trauma of her inability to come to terms with AIDS, hence her insane attack on the maestro. Sir Peter himself has disappeared. This paper extends our sympathy to him in all he has suffered——-and our concern is for the health of this our most loved musician.'

The paper dropped from Hermione's fingers, as her mind flew back to those TV pictures, which she remembered having watched appalled. There had indeed been a dreadful amount of blood! Blood! Lois blood and Peter's making hideous stain across the stage, as the woman lay across her son! It was through blood——as well as through sexual activity——-that AIDS was transmitted! She read the paper again, her hands trembling. They were concerned for his health. Did that mean———No! It couldn't be!

Hermione rose to her feet and started to pace the room, thinking of all that had happened when Peter had returned home from the States last March. He had not wanted to embrace either Rosamund or herself——would not touch the baby———nor would he share a room with Rosamund! Add to that, the fact that he had left the house the next day, without giving his destination or saying goodbye to his loved ones. Could this be the reason for his erratic behaviour? Did Peter suspect that he had AIDS?

Then she relaxed. What a ridiculous idea! Peter had just been going through one of his broody stages, which inevitably happened when he was in the throes of composition. Just take that lovely, cheerful letter from Rosamund, which she had received this morning, seemingly charged with happiness, plus the fact that Peter was nearing completion of his new concerto——no, it was thing impossible, that Peter could have that awful disease. But deep down in her heart, knowledge was forming that such was indeed the case. She reached for the telephone and put a call through to Austria.

'Ernst? It's Hermione. Have you seen today's papers——about Lois Challoner? You haven't? Well——they say she had AIDS——draw attention to the fact that she and Peter were lying together bleeding. Oh, Ernst——I'm most terribly frightened, that Peter may have caught the virus from her!'

'Hermione——I will book the next flight——be with you later today. Where are you? In London or at Garnford?'

'At Garnford!' She said goodbye and replaced the receiver. Ernst had said that he would come——but had not shown surprise at her fears! Did he already know? Suddenly she remembered his words to Rosamund, when she as still in hospital after the baby's birth. He had something to the effect, that Peter, whom he had just visited in the States, might be suffering from depression. Depression because he had been told that he had contracted AIDS? If——Ernst had known all this time, why had he not warned them? How could a family friend treat them in such a way? But then——suppose he had made a promise to Peter. She knew she had struck against the truth.

It was 11 o'clock at night, when a car drew up at Garnford. Harrington directed a footman to take Maestro Morgenstern's bags, as the hired car was driven off into the darkness. Hermione was waiting in the rose drawing room.

'Ernst, my dear. It's so good of you to come like this. You didn't bring Svetlana with you?' She had half hoped that the very special woman, who had been of such supreme influence in developing Rosamund's musical talent, as well as bringing happiness into Ernst's life, would have come too. She had come to have a deep affection for Svetlana.

'Well no—-she is in fact in London——has been there for the last three weeks. I fear she has been missing the Fritz Klein Academy! She told me she didn't want to walk in my shadow all the while. I hope she will return to me—-but I love her too much, to put any constraints upon her.' His eyes were sad.

'Oh, Ernst. I'm so sorry. But she'll be back, you'll see. She loves you very much, that I know. Probably it was too great a change to take so suddenly——to leave all she had worked for over the years. She just has to come to terms with the fact, that what life is now offering her, is infinitely more precious and fulfilling, than teaching her students.'

'I fear it is partly my fault, Hermione. I've had a lot on my mind and I've simply done what I always have in life, in such circumstances——thrown myself into my music. She must have felt herself pushed into the background, which was far from the case.' Ernst looked very tired and despondent, but he forced a smile onto his face, as he took Hermione's hands.

'Dare I ask—-what has been the burden on your mind? It must indeed have been great, to have caused a rift between you and Svetlana.' She returned the strong pressure of his hands, as she said, 'Ernst—-was it the knowledge that Peter has AIDS, that so troubled you?'

'Hermione——only Peter himself can discuss such a matter with you. I——I cannot. Obviously you must have read more into what the papers said, than was perhaps meant—-but——.' He swallowed, not knowing how to continue.

'You promised him not to speak of this to me, didn't you—-when you went to see him in San Francisco?' Hermione looked him straight in the eyes. He put an arm round her shoulders.

'Hermione——-you said that, I didn't. But consider this, meine liebe hertz, if I had given a promise in any shape or form——-to anyone, then as a man of honour, I would have to keep that promise.' His earnest words, softly spoken, were all the corroboration she needed to confirm her worst fears.

'You don't have to say anymore, Ernst.' Tears started to roll down her cheeks and her shoulders started to shake with the emotion that had been suppressed all day. 'Oh, Ernst! That dreadful woman——-why did he ever have to meet her?'

'Don't cry, Hermione. I cannot bear to see you so unhappy. Whatever the future holds for——-all of us, you at least must be strong——-and very brave. Do you understand, Hermione.' He patted her back, as he held her close, comforting her as he would a child. Gradually her muffled sobs became less. 'Just think of this, my dearest friend——-Peter might have died in that dreadful incident. His little son might never have seen his father. But that hasn't happened! Peter has his little family close to him in Scotland, is happy and working on his Golden Concerto. I for one cannot wait to hear this work.'

'But how did you know he was in Scotland with Rosamund? He has been writing to you, hasn't he! He has trusted you, where he felt he couldn't confide in his own mother!' There was deep hurt in Hermione's voice. She stepped back, dabbing at her eyes with a minute scrap of lace. Ernst produced his own large handkerchief.

'He loves you very much, Hermione. Whatever problems Peter may have at this time, he probably feels he doesn't want to burden you before he has to. Do you understand?' She nodded her head slowly. 'Now promise me, Hermione, that you will not tell Peter your fears. It will be hard——-but anything that he has to tell you, let him choose the time and when he does, show that tremendous strength of yours, which has supported him against all hurt, his life long.' He fixed his eyes upon her with deep compassion, and as she looked up into the wise face of her old friend, who had been through so much in his own life, Hermione took a hold on herself. She knew that what he said was right. Instead of indulging in her own emotion, she should be thinking of Peter——and of Rosamund! She had almost forgotten the girl she loved so deeply, in concern for her son. Poor Rosamund! How was she coping with this situation, when her heart must be breaking? Then she thought of that lovely letter she had received—-was it only this morning? Already it seemed an age ago. There had been love and bright courage in that letter. Rosamund as well as Peter, was going to need all her help in the future—-and that dear little grandson of hers.

'Ernst——you must be starving.' She attempted to reach out to normality. 'What shall I have cook prepare for you?'

'I ate on the plane—-but perhaps a salami sandwich and a glass of wine!' She gave a glimmer of a smile at this. Dear Ernst, he never changed.

?Why——I declare I will join you in a sandwich, Ernst—-for I haven't touched anything since breakfast!'

It was Harrington who brought their light meal up to them. For once the unflappable Harrington had a slightly worried look on his face.

'Lady Hermione.'

'Yes, Harrington?'

'May I talk to you in private, later?'

'I have no secrets from Ernst. What is it, Harrington?' Hermione looked at him encouragingly.

'Well——there have been a number of telephone calls during the course of the day. People asking to speak with you—— concerning a rumour about the master's health. I told the callers that you were not available, for I had noticed that you looked—-a little tired my lady.'

'Was it in regard to a certain article in today's papers, Harrington?'

'Why, yes, my lady. I managed to discourage them today—but I have a feeling that we may have more callers tomorrow—-and perhaps eventually, the press.' His eyes were kind, his manner protective. Hermione thought quickly. Time enough for all this to come out, when it could no longer be kept secret. But for now, they had to ward off the inquisitive.

'If we have any callers tomorrow, asking similar questions—then please tell them that my son is in perfect health and having a much needed rest from work, in

Scotland——-as he has just completed a new concerto, which he has been working on in recent months, hence his absence from Garnford.'

'Why——but that is wonderful news, my lady,' exclaimed Harrington. Then he saw the sorrow in her eyes, and knew it for subterfuge—but that he had to appear to believe it and further to ensure that everybody else did. He gave her an understanding look. 'I will see that everyone is informed of Sir Peter's involvement with his new work.'

'He is going to call it the Golden Concerto, Harrington.' She gave him a tremulous smile. 'Lady Rosamund tells me that it is the most beautiful thing he has ever written——and that they hope to perform it at the Albert Hall in a few months time. So I expect we will be seeing a lot of Rodrigo Mendes again.'

There were indeed many who phoned Garnford over the next few days, but to all of them, Harrington gave the splendid news, that Sir Peter was in perfect health and had almost finished a wonderful new concerto, which they would all be able to hear later in the year. Almost reluctantly, the harpies of doom went away discomforted——-people from the county, friends who enjoyed the fabulous parties at Garnford, but were frightened at the threat to one of their number, now seemed to accept that all was well.

Rosamund lay in the grass under the warm June sunshine. The baby was in a little cradle at her side, covered with a muslin sheet, to keep away the midges, which were just beginning to appear.

Peter bent over and tickled her chin with a flower. It was one of the wild orchids that bloomed in shades of white, pink and purple, in the young grass. A crimson petal from a wild rose bush, drifted onto the baby's cradle. She stirred and raised herself on one arm.

'Oh, Peter——I must have fallen asleep.' She glanced up at him guiltily.

'You must have been overtired——and no wonder, for I kept you up to all hours last night, listening to my last movement.' Peter looked down at her triumphantly. 'Darling——I've done it——the final few bars! I was walking on the shore, just watching the waves, advancing and retreating, slowly receding——and it came to me. I have been putting the last touch to the manuscript. So tonight, darling heart, we will celebrate! Do you think Jack would have a bottle of wine we could buy from him? Perhaps you could cook something extra special tonight!' His slate grey eyes smiled down into hers, as he knelt beside her. She lifted her arms. Pulling him down, seeking his lips.

'You've finished? Oh, darling——darling! That is so wonderful,' she murmured between kisses. 'I cannot wait to hear it.' He started to return her embraces, his hand slipping over her breasts—and there, in the soft green grass, with the warm summer wind of Skye pouring over them, secluded by a bower of wild roses, Peter made love to Rosamund, in that way which they had devised, that offered tenderness and satisfaction to both. At last they reluctantly sat up and laughed, for little Tristam was giving an indignant howl, realising that it was way past his mealtime.

'I'll take him in and change——and feed him! He sounds quite cross, doesn't he, laughed Rosamund. 'His gums are getting bumpy and I'm beginning to wonder whether he is cutting a tooth!

That night, in the dining kitchen, white candles adorned the table, a small arrangement of wild flowers lifted their fragile heads from an old silver sugar bowl and Rosamund served a roast of ten-

der island lamb, cooked on the ancient stove that also provided
them with hot water. Jack bent his head and said a grace. Mary
helped Rosamund to dish up and the meal started.

'Later, as they retired to the little sitting room, with its battered
arm chairs and faded couch, Peter produced the bottle of champagne that Jack had amazingly provided. He dealt with the cork
and the champagne frothed down the sides of the bottle, as
Rosamund held out the kitchen glasses.

'To the Golden Concerto——-to my darling wife Rosamund
and lovely son——and to the most wonderful friends a man could
have——Jack and Mary!' He lifted his glass. They all drank with
him. Silence reigned——and Peter lifted his violin. Then they
heard the last movement. The sound of his music filled the night,
hauntingly beautiful, full of joy and hope——and the last lovely
chords receded, as wistfully, as the little waves that drew away
from the seashore, towards Ben Tianavaig.

'Peter. You have created something that will stir men's senses
for generations to come,' said Jack. His bright blue eyes looked
suspiciously damp. As for Mary, she was crying unashamedly.

'Oh dear,' said Peter awkwardly. 'I am terribly sorry if the music
has had such a depressing effect on you!' He put the violin aside
on the wide windowsill. For Rosamund also had tears streaming
down her cheeks.

'My dear Peter——God gave us emotions——and to some
favoured few, the power to move them. You have this gift to
excess. Whatever else happens in life, I will always remember this
evening, when in the peace of this little cottage, I have been privileged to hear music that has touched me to the very depths of my
soul. Thank you, Peter Bagshaw.' And Jack placed a gentle hand
on Peter's shoulder. Peter smiled. He knew intuitively, that this
new work, was indeed the best thing he had ever composed——
that his last concerto was indeed his finest.

Rosamund broke the spell. Tristam was giving a protesting cry
from the bedroom and she excused herself. Peter looked at Jack

regretfully, as she went out.

'Thank you both, for making this such a happy evening. I know that before very long, I am going to have to return to London, to work on the score with my friend Rodrigo Mendes. I don't want to go. I have been happier here on this enchanted island, than at any time in my life. I suppose that must seem to be an extraordinary statement to make—-when I am suffering from HIV—-and face an uncertain future. But the very real love I have experienced from my darling Rosamund—-and the help—-spiritual and in every other way from you both, well——-there aren't really any words to express how I feel. So I have let the music do it for me. Just, God bless you both!'

Two more weeks passed. Wonderful weeks in which Peter and Rosamund wandered up into the hills, clambering amongst the springy heather tussocks, being careful to avoid those places where the mosses gleamed bright golden green, masking boggy depths beneath. Dragonflies skimmed the air and larks sang their thin, ready song, high on the wing—and always there was the cry of the curlew and scream of the gulls. Once they stood spellbound, as a huge golden eagle soared overhead, making for his nest in a mountain fastness. Far below them the waters of the bay seemed to change from turquoise, to pearl, merging into softest amethyst.

On that Wednesday morning, they decided to walk along the seashore. Baby Tristam had been left with Mary, who delighted to care for the sturdy little baby, with his dark stare and sweet smile. She loved to tickle him and hear his funny little, chuckle, as his little arms and legs flailed in response. He was an adorable child, and Mary knew she would miss him very much when his parents moved away in a week's time. But first of all, Peter's mother was supposed to be coming on a visit. Mary had deliberately avoided taking any bookings for that week.

It was wet that morning and the weather suddenly colder. Clouds converged over the bay and it started to rain heavily. Peter and Rosamund were dressed in shorts and T shirts, the tide was coming in fast, the green waves crowned with white sweeps of foam.

'Quick—-let's shelter in here. This little cave is way above the water line,' cried Rosamund. Together they clambered up the sandy incline and crouched side by side in this refuge from the wind and sluicing rain. Rosamund was shivering and Peter put his arm about her, cursing himself for having insisted on their coming out, when the weather had looked so overcast. At least, he could have had sense enough to have brought anoraks with them. His throat, which had been burning when he got up that morning, felt worse—-as though someone had thrown pepper at it. He supposed he as starting a cold. The sky grew darker and a great flash of lightening sliced across the bay, followed by an ominous growl of thunder. Then indeed the heavens opened and it rained with unbelievable fury.

'Peter! Rosamund!' It was Jack's voice. They had been huddled together for an hour, the weather in no way abating—-and now suddenly, the comforting presence of Jack MacLeod filled the cave. 'I wondered if perhaps you had found this place. Mary was worried over you——and I have brought waterproofs!" He helped them to pull the clothing over their shivering limbs. 'Come along now—-Mary has a wonderful hot meal waiting for you at the house!'

That night Peter tossed in the small bedroom. His face was burning and his throat ached abominably—-also, he had strange pains in his groins. He felt sick. He tried to get up without waking Rosamund—-but as he put his feet to the carpet, he felt the floor coming up to meet him.

'How are you feeling, Peter?'

He looked about him in bewilderment, for gone were the white washed walls of the little cottage bedroom. These walls were indeed white, but obviously those of a hospital ward. He became aware of a thumping headache and a feeling of nausea. When he tried to talk, he found his voice came out in a surprising whisper.

'Where am I'

'In a private clinic in Edinburgh,' said a reassuring voice. 'My name is Walter Borthwick—and I'm a good friend of Jack MacLeod. I'm a doctor and I specialise in the virus that is causing your problem—-AIDS.'

'But how did I get here, doctor? I have no memory of arriving. The last thing I recall was of trying to get out of bed at the cottage.' He attempted to sit up and realised that he was very weak.

'Would it surprise you to know, that you are talking of Wednesday night. This is Friday morning! Rosamund went for Jack, when she found you had collapsed on the floor. At first she thought you had flu—-then began to realise that in all probability, you were suffering some early symptoms of HIV. She ran for Jack—-who rang me and we sent an ambulance for you. I myself travelled with it.' His smooth ruddy face softened to a warm smile and Peter thought the hazel eyes under shaggy brows looked kind. He judged him to be in his middle forties.

'Are you telling me, that you drove all the way from Edinburgh to Skye and back! Why then—-my heart felt thanks, Doctor Borthwick.'

'I would have come for any friend of Jack's—-but to be able to help you, Sir Peter. I count as a privilege.' He helped Peter to sit up higher on the pillows. 'It was just as well perhaps, that you didn't see the waves that crashed against the sides of the ferry boat—-but she is a strong vessel and it is very rare indeed that you cannot cross between Kyle and Kyleakin. Now—-do you feel hungry?'

'I don't think so,' said Peter with a grimace.

'I would still like you to eat something—-some toast—or a little cereal. You will feel better if you do.' As Peter nodded, the doctor called a nurse and asked her to attend to Peter. He sat in a chair and waited as Peter drank a cup of tea and managed some lightly poached egg and toast.

'Well—-how do you feel now?'

'Stronger! You were right.' Peter looked about him, taking in the ward with its flowered peach curtains and peach counterpane on the bed. There was a TV in the corner with headphones above the bed. 'So—-doctor. Does this mean that I have now developed full blown AIDS?' He tried to keep his voice calm as he asked the question. Doctor Borthwick shook his head.

'No, Peter. This is the reaction most people with HIV experience at the onset of the disease—-and it is in fact this, which often alerts them that something is wrong in the first place. In your particular case, because of the dramatic way in which you originally contracted the virus, you have been aware for some months that you were almost inevitably HIV positive. Your reaction over these last few days, has perhaps been more severe than might be expected. But then, you have only recently survived a stab wound to the heart and major surgery—-plus the fact that Rosamund tells me, that you have been pushing yourself terribly hard with your music—-not getting enough sleep! Well————-that cannot continue, you know!'

'Rosamund!' Peter's face bore a chastened expression. 'Where is she?'

'Here—-in Edinburgh. She may visit you later. I suggest that you remain here in the clinic for a few days though. There are a few tests I want to run. After that, Peter—well, you may just carry on with your normal life as usual. You will of course, continue to take those precautions for the sake of others, that will be a permanent necessity to maintain.'

'I understand. So this present illness will pass?'

'Oh, yes! A few days and you will have forgotten it.' He smiled and went out, but Peter lay there thinking. Forget it? That was hardly likely, for this was the first tangible sign that the nightmare had started! In that small Eden he had been living in, away from the pressures of the world, it had been almost possible to ignore the knowledge that had initially sapped his will to live. Now, secure in his growing faith in God, he no longer struggled against fate, but was resolved to take each day at a time, enjoying life to the full. But it was, nevertheless a blow, that the reality of his illness had become apparent.

'I have to think of them,' he murmured. 'Of Rosamund and little Tristam!' Then his thoughts flew to his mother. Surely this was the week she was supposed to be coming up to see them. He groaned. How was he going to tell her? How would she take it? Would she be able to accept his illness, in the same wonderful way as Rosamund?

He tried to distract his thoughts by turning on the television. One of those audience participation shows was in progress, where the charming compere, microphone in hand, wandered from one member of the noisy group, eager for attention, to another.

'My son has AIDS. He is sixteen and a haemophiliac. He had an infected blood transfusion, two years ago. Yes—-I know we may eventually get some kind of government compensation—-but how much is a life worth? My son was a music student—-studying the flute. I was told he had a brilliant future. Now all he will have, is a blighted past!' The woman's strong features were working with sorrow. The compere moved on to someone else. This time it was a young man, whose sallow features looked gaunt.

'I have AIDS,' he said. 'I'm gay—-and a drug addict, so perhaps some of you good folks will say—-serve him right! But have none of you ever taken a wrong path in your youth? And if so—-how would you have felt, to have death as your portion? Why can't the scientists come up with a cure? Why isn't more money spent on research? I bet you, if there was a major conflict in the world today, money in its billions would be spent in destroying life. So why then, can money not be found to save life—-to bring new hope to the hopeless.' He started to cough and those closest to him, drew back.

'Over here——,' cried a girl, holding a toddler. 'Yes—-here! I have AIDS and so has my baby. Laura was born with it. Her father died three days ago. He was supposed to be on this show——and so I have come in his place.' The compere's face was torn with sympathy.

'Do you know how you and your husband came to have AIDS,' he asked gently? The girl nodded he head.

'Yes——I know, because my husband John told me. He had sex with a girl in Blackpool. He had gone there with a group of rugby players—his friends. They all got drunk, and he ended up in bed with someone. Neither of us knew until it was too late, that John had contracted AIDS. His early symptoms were not recognised as HIV. I was already pregnant, before it was diagnosed. I have heard that in some cases, children can grow out of it——I mean, it just seems to disappear.' The toddler whimpered again. 'I can only hope that Little Laura will be one of the lucky ones,' she said in a choking voice——'And if she is, that someone kind will take care of her, because I will not be around to do it!'

'I too have AIDS,' came a cultured voice. 'I am a doctor! I neglected to take some basic precautions when attending a victim of a road crash!' The compere hurried from one person to another. A deeply tanned middle aged man was next.

'I do not have AIDS. But I am just back from Central Africa where it is rife. Thousands are dying of it. There are not enough doctors and nurses to cope——people are lying around sick and dying in the most awful conditions. It is enough to break your heart!' He shook his head in despair. 'There are innumerable young people dying of it in the States too,' he added. 'It is now one of the major killers in the U.S.A.!'

'Why does no-one care,' cried another young man. 'We need help! People treat you like a modern day leper. There is nowhere to go, where you can be accepted as just someone else with a medical problem If only there was somewhere that we could go to end our days with some dignity.' He put his head in his hands and broke down. His sobs were audible and shook his frame.

Peter closed his eyes. He started to pray. Then a strange thought came into his mind. He dismissed it——but it came back again, stronger and more insistent. He opened his eyes and fixed them once more on the screen. A little child was being interviewed.

'I have AIDS,' said the little one, clinging to an elderly woman. 'I wish it would go away. Mummy doesn't want me any more. I got it at the hospital in America——after an operation.'

'That does it,' cried Peter, climbing out of bed. He looked around for a robe and found one on a hook on the door. He wandered out into the passageway. Doctor Borthwick was passing and hurried to his patient's side.

'Doctor! Have you a telephone? Quick?'

'Yes, Peter. This way——in my office!'

Peter dialled. 'Is that the BBC? Right! This is Sir Peter Bagshaw. Yes, yes——the musician. Put me through at once to

your call in programme on AIDS! Why? Because I have it man. Now hurry!'

Doctor Borthwick looked at Peter's face in amazement. It was bright with animation. He obviously knew what he was doing——but why?

'Will you switch on your TV, doctor,' said Peter, as he waited. 'Tune it in to BBC5. He watched as the programme appeared. He saw someone approach the compere, who looked up in stupefaction.

'Folks——something quite unprecedented has happened. The world famous composer and violinist, Sir Peter Bagshaw is on the phone, asking to be heard on this programme. Now if we don't have any technical difficulties, you should all be able to hear Sir Peter within the next few minutes. ' People sat up in their seats, plainly puzzled.

'OK, Sir Peter——you're on,' said a voice on the phone. Peter took a deep breath.

'My name is Sir Peter Bagshaw——and like many of you in that studio, I am also suffering from AIDS——or to be more precise, I am HIV positive!' There was a gasp. 'I was infected during a concert tour of the States, in the course of an attack upon me, by a person suffering from it. Many of you may have read of the incident in the papers earlier this year—-or seen record of it on your TV screens.' Peter paused and plunged on. 'I am calling you from a clinic in Scotland and switched to this programme purely by chance. What I want to say now, is that as soon as is possible, I intend to turn Garnford, my large manor house in Hampshire——and its extensive grounds, into a combined centre for treating AIDS and a home where people may come and stay without cost to themselves. The only introduction you will need is to be HIV positive—-or to have AIDS. Thank you for listening to me. This decision will be implemented as soon as I can get the rooms altered and medical staff laid on. Good luck to you all.' He put the phone down.

'Peter!' It was Rosamund's voice. She was standing holding onto the door. He realised from her face, that she had overheard all that he had said. Her eyes went back to the screen. Smiles had broken out on some of the faces there. Other people just looked stunned. The compere for once seemed to have lost his usual aplomb.

'All I can say, from all of us here at the studio—-is thank you from the bottom of our hearts. And may I personally, salute a very brave man!'

'May I salute him too,' murmured Rosamund, her eyes shining with tears.

'Rosamund! I should have asked you first——it is your home as well!' He did not stop to consider that it was also his mother's.

'Dearest Peter. Now it will be home to those who desperately need one. I am very proud of you.' She ran into his arms. 'How are you feeling? Should you be out of bed?'

'No, he should not,' said doctor Borthwick firmly. 'Peter I must insist that you return to your ward. You must rest for at least a few days. After that, is you want any help and advice in setting up your planned AIDS centre then I will be only too glad, to assist you in any way!'

Hermione had been idly leafing through a fashion magazine. She had risen early and eaten a light breakfast. Now she was waiting for a phone call from Skye, to tell her when it was suitable for her to visit Peter and Rosamund, for she had received a letter from them only a few days ago, saying that they would phone from a friend's house on Friday morning!

She switched on the television. The fashion news no longer interested her and she pushed the magazine aside, as she became aware that the programme she had tuned into, was a chat show on AIDS. Immediately her complete attention was riveted on the screen. Her heart was moved to pity by all she heard from those suffering from the virus, as she shared their outrage that so little was apparently being done to help. She sighed deeply, thinking of Peter. Tears came into her eyes. Then she heard it—-the incredible announcement that Peter wanted to speak on the programme! But why? His message was short and to the point, admitting that he was HIV positive and further more, that he intended to turn Garnford into a treatment centre for AIDS sufferers. It came as a devastating shock to her. She felt numb. Their beautiful home to be filled with sick and maybe dying people? What would their neighbours think?

She paced the room, back and forth, hands pressed to her temples. Suddenly she stood still, a peace coming upon her, as she realised that what Peter had decided was right and good——-and she didn't care a hang what people thought! She had stood firmly behind her son all of his life—and she wasn't going to stop now! Of course there would be difficulties, and this she realised.

The first of those difficulties suddenly erupted. One of the young maids burst into the room. Her face was red and indignant.

'Excuse me, my lady!'

'Yes, Sarah?'

'Some of us were watching television in the kitchen. We heard what Sir Peter just said——about him having AIDS and wanting to turn this place into some sort of hospital! Well——we want to leave!' Her face expressed anger and fear.

'Sarah——if that is what you want, then you may do so of course—and I will see that you get a month's wages and excellent references. But won't you wait until Sir Peter returns? We are obviously still going to need kitchen staff and many others as well. I suppose there will be doctors and nurses to cater for, as well as patients. I know nothing about these matters, but I suppose every precaution will be taken to ensure that none of the staff are exposed to any risk. Nor is it an illness that you can catch easily——only through sexual intimacy and exposure to the blood of the infected person.'

'I don't care about any of that! I'm going——and so are most of the others!' As she shouted this, the cook suddenly stood in the doorway, her face grim.

'Oh, my lady——-I'm so desperately sorry about poor Sir Peter! As for this stupid girl and some of the others, well I'm ashamed of them.' Her plump rosy cheeks were redder than usual with emotion.

'Dear Mrs Honeyset——please don't upset yourself. It is of course understandable that the staff should feel concerned. What happened on that TV show just now, came as a bolt out of the blue to me also, you know,' she said unsteadily, fighting back tears of reaction.

'Well my lady, I just want you to know, that I can assure you all of the longer serving members of staff will wish to remain and to help in any way we can. Not only for you——-but young Lady Rosamund and Sir Peter are held in much affection by all of us. That's all I came up to say.' She nodded in a motherly way, then rounded on Sarah.

'Now as for you, my girl————you and the other three, can stay out of my kitchen until you go. I prefer to do everything on my own, rather than have any such feckless individuals around me!' She snorted and ushered the young girl out and it was noticeable that Sarah had lost countenance and hung her head. Hermione took a deep breath. There were obviously going to be many hurdles ahead. Just then the telephone rang and she ran to answer it. This must be Rosamund's call.

'Lady Hermione speaking.' She waited. 'Is that you, Rosamund?'

'No, Hermione————this is Helen Delaney–Smythe. First of all, I want to say how terribly sorry I am about Peter. It's just terrible——-but I suppose not unexpected, after his liaison with that American woman!'

'What do you mean,' gasped Hermione?

'That Lois Challoner! It stands to reason that he was messing around with her, doesn't it——-and that's why she tried to kill him! One wonders Hermione, whether in fact Lois caught AIDS from him——-and that's why she stabbed him!'

'How can you say such a thing————or even think it! You have been a friend of ours for years———a close friend and neighbour!'

'I hope I am still your friend, Hermione. But I am only saying to you directly, what others will say behind your back, so which is worse! Which brings me to the next thing I want to say. There is no way that Peter can turn Garnford into some sort of hospice for AIDS patients! Have you thought what it will do for property prices in the district? Apart from that, why should any of us have to endure the stigma of such a place in our area. It's just unthinkable. If Peter is feeling altruistic——-then let him donate money to set up an AIDS centre in somewhere like London or Glasgow, not here!' The angry voice ground to a halt, as Helen ran out of breath!

'I am sorry you feel as you do, very sorry. But Garnford is a private estate————and as such, Peter is entitled to take whatever

decisions he wishes as to how he uses the house or grounds.'
Hermione tried to keep her tones politely modulated, but it was
difficult.

'Oh—-we'll see about that, Hermione! You will have the county up in arms. There is bound to be some way in which we can
stop this thing legally—-and we will! Surely you cannot really
want your lovely home full of diseased people and drug pushers!'

'Helen—-I take it that you watched that programme on TV an
hour ago, just as I did?'

'Well, no———but Cynthia did—-and she rang me up and told
me about Peter's awful plans.' There was venom in Helen's voice.

'I did watch the programme, Helen. There was a young widow
and her little child———some young men—-and a doctor, who had
caught the virus whilst treating an accident case———and another
child rejected by his parents, because he had received infected
blood during an operation. Helen—-it could happen to any one
of us. Just try to understand that. It is in the interests of the whole
world, to try and find a cure—-and in the meanwhile, to show
compassion on our fellow men and women—-to say nothing of
those little innocents, the children! So as far as I am concerned, I
shall do everything within my power, to assist Peter!' She waited
for a response from Helen. Instead, the phone was slammed down
at the other end. She replaced the receiver with a sigh. Would
there be many who thought as Helen did? She supposed there
would. The phone rang again.

'Is that Lady Hermione? This is the 'Daily Search'. We would
like your comments on your son's plans to turn Garnford into an
AIDS research centre. Also—-of course this paper would like to
extend our deepest sympathy to Sir Peter. I know all my colleagues in Fleet Street will join me in this!'

'Thank you. You are very kind. I will only say at this time, that
my son has my fullest support in whatever plans he may have for
Garnford. Obviously I haven't had a chance to speak with him
yet—-but in my opinion, the idea of opening Garnford to receive

HIV and AIDS sufferers is excellent. The house is exceptionally large and the grounds beautiful—-and I am sure that anyone coming here, will feel happy in such peaceful surroundings.'

'That is a most wonderfully generous reaction, lady Hermione. Thank you.'

'Please could you ask the other papers not to ring for a day or two. I have a lot to do. But I promise to keep you abreast of all that takes place.' She put the receiver down and walked out of the room. She wandered aimlessly at first, visiting one room after another. At last, she entered the music room and stood staring up at the striking painting of Peter and Rosamund, that had been Sylvia's dying gift to them. It was indeed a wonderful picture, not only because it so faithfully portrayed the two violinists, fingers seeming to vibrate on their quivering strings, bows poised in quick movement. But it was also so full of warmth—and of the love shining out of their eyes and that even deeper love, with which it had been painted.

'Sylvia used her gift right up to the end—-despite her sickness,' whispered Hermione. 'I pray that my son may show similar courage in all that may lie ahead of him—-and Rosamund too!' She walked quietly out of the room and down the stairs to the great hall, staring as she did so, of the proud portraits of Garnford ancestors. What would they have said to see their heritage used in such a way? Would they have frowned at this Twentieth century son of their house, in throwing its doors open for such a purpose? Perhaps—-but then, what did the past matter, when the present and the future beckoned? Hermione shook the tattered garment of ancestral pride from her shoulders, never to take it up again.

'My lady.' It was Harrington. 'Cook has told me of the distressing affair with young Sarah—-her disloyalty and that of the others. If I had only known about it all in time to have dealt with it. I am so sorry——-and so deeply distressed about Sir Peter's illness.'

'Perhaps you may have had an inkling Peter had contracted that horrible virus—-after that newspaper article a few weeks ago, just as I had,' said Hermione softly. He bowed his head, without answering, but his eyes expressed that such was the case. 'Well, Harrington, we will just have to find out, how many of the staff will agree to remain, once Garnford is turned into the AIDS research and reception centre that Peter wants to create. Do I take it that you will wish to stand by him in this?'

'How can you ask such a thing, my lady. You know I will stay, as will many of the staff. Yes——-we will lose some—-and I suppose we must not judge them too harshly, but most will remain loyal and try to do all possible to help Sir Peter put his plans into effect.'

'Harrington——you're wonderful. I do not know what I would do without you and I mean that!' She put her hand on his arm and they walked slowly through the house, hearts full of sorrow mixed with determination to back Peter with all their strength.

In the meanwhile, Peter was busy phoning the States, putting in a call to Charles Sylvester.

'Is that you, Charles? This is Peter——Peter Bagshaw. I have something to ask you. Would you be prepared to bring your wife and children over to England and join me in a project at my mansion in Hampshire? I'm going to turn it in to an AIDS research centre. I need a medical team——advice on how best to convert the house into a retreat for sufferers from HIV and AIDS, where they can receive the most up to date treatment in privacy, amongst beautiful surroundings—-and where they can spend their last days amongst loving care. Well—-what do you say?'

'What can I say? Only——-yes! It's a magnificent idea. I'll have to ask the hospital to release me from my contract——and of course ask Sandra. Maybe I'm crazy to make up my mind on the spur of the moment like this—-but I'm your man, Peter!'

'Why, but that's splendid. I have another doctor here—— Doctor Borthwick from Edinburgh, who will help all he can—— but he has his own clinic to run as well.'

'Is that Walter Borthwick? I've heard of him. He has been doing a lot of research, which we are very interested in over here. But Peter—-the sort of thing you are considering, will take a great deal of money—-and I'm talking about hundreds of thousands—-more!'

'I know. I understand that it will cost about a thousand pounds a week for just one patient—-but then, money is no problem. Apart from inherited wealth, I have royalties on my music. I have also completed a new concerto, only have to score it——and given the anticipated publicity of my interesting condition, I imagine that recordings of it should bring in quite a bit too.'

'What? You have composed a new concerto since March? That's fantastic! Tell me, Peter——Rosamund——how did she take it?'

'She's been absolutely wonderful. We've been staying on a little island on the West Coast of Scotland, a dream place called Skye. It was there that I composed my last concerto, with my lovely young wife at my side.'

'You sound happy, Peter!'

'I am. When can you fly over here, Charles?'

'Hold on! I don't know yet. I'll call you back later today. What's your number?'

As he replaced the receiver, Peter's eyes were full of determination. He had found a new purpose in life—-and however long or short that life should be, he intended to bring that purpose to fruition!

CHAPTER FIFTEEN

The late October sun, stroked scarlet fingers through the bushes, as the last weary workman, downed tools and trudged down Garnford's gracious driveway, on the heels of his fellows. He glanced back at the dramatic picture the great manor house made, standing in relief against the burning sky, reflecting as he did so, that none standing in the front of the mansion, would guess at the frenzied building in progress in the grounds at the rear. No, nor of the long, one storey research building, already in use—and those four bedroom bungalows, which they were currently assembling from ready made, timber framed units. Then there was the thirty bed hospital wing, within the house itself.

Sir Peter had offered a substantial bonus should the work be completed by the beginning of November——and the men were determined to earn it. Considering that the project had been planned as short a while ago as last July, the progress made was nothing short of a miracle. The man gave a satisfied sigh, lit his pipe and walked on. He knew that other work was being effected within the house itself——this place of privilege that had housed the Bagshaw family for centuries and was soon to open its imposing doors to patients with this mysterious disease that was so rife in America. Yes——and was apparently now making noticeable inroads into the population of this country. Well, he at least, would be safely out of the way, before those AIDS people came up the driveway!

But if the workmen had left to seek the comforts of the 'Bull' and the 'Ploughman', others at Garnford were still busily involved in what Peter had named 'Operation Ebb-tide'. Charles Sylvester, Walter Borthwick and Peter Bagshaw sat facing an audience of local people, in the newly completed conference room. Not only were the village dignitaries present—the vicar, members of the local health practice, the grocer who was also a JP, two solicitors and Mrs Burde-Helmsley from Nutbourne Lodge. Many of the village folk were also sitting anxiously, faces taut with concern, while at the back of the room, sat some of the landed gentry from the surrounding countryside. A journalist representing the county newspaper held pencil poised over his notebook.

'What I want to know is, are these undesirables that you are bringing onto your estate, going to wander around the village— becoming a health hazard to local residents,' asked Mrs Burde-Helmsley?

'All of the men, women and children shortly to be arriving at Garnford as my guests, will find their needs catered for in every way here on the estate, where everything possible will be done to make them comfortable. As for those who are seriously ill, the dedicated doctors and nurses permanently resident, will provide the most devoted care.' Sir Peter paused, and treated Mrs Burde-Helmsley to a level stare. 'As for whether the future residents will take themselves into the village, well the answer to that is simply yes——in the same way that at present, they frequent the towns and villages where they are presently living.' He looked at the angry face of the solicitor sitting next to her.

'Yes, Mr Butterworth? You have a question?'

'I have indeed, Sir Peter! First of all though, I must say that like all others assembled here tonight, I have the deepest sympathy for you personally in the tragic way in which you contracted this illness. It was an appalling thing to have happened——that woman deserved her end! But whilst having compassion for you, nevertheless, we the community have to protest our rights. Our little village attracts many visitors in the summer months. How many do you think will come, when they hear that there is an AIDS centre close by?'

'I am sure that it will not adversely affect those tourists who pass through——not a few of whom perhaps, have come in the past because of the open days, that lady Hermione held at Garnford!'

'Well——,' came a jeering voice from the back. 'You certainly won't have any coming to visit the Big House anymore! Not if they know what's good for them!'

'Have you thought what is going to happen to property values, now you are importing drug addicts——and all the other dregs of society into the district,' cried a strident voice! Peter looked for its owner and saw Helen Delaney-Smythe, her furious face almost matching the magenta of her suit.

'How delightfully you phrase your concern, Helen! Again, I can only say that I believe your fears to be groundless. Garnford is fully three miles from the outskirts of the village. Anyone living within the village itself, who wishes to sell their house and has difficulties that are directly attributable to the proximity of 'Ebbtide' as we are calling the project here, can be in touch with my solicitors to discuss any help we may be able to give financially.'

There was a murmur of approval at this and Peter drew a quick breath of relief. He had known that tonight was going to have been difficult and indeed had a certain sympathy with the villagers, but none with those who had once been close friends, enjoying his hospitality in the past, for so many years. He felt a hand on his arm, as Charles Sylvester murmured to him-

'I told you that you would soon find out who your real friends were!' The American doctor turned to Walter Borthwick. 'I guess it might be an idea if you were to address them now,' he said. The Scotsman nodded and rose to his feet. The hubbub of voices quietened, as the people stared curiously at the stranger. Who was he? Did he have AIDS?

'My name is Walter Borthwick. I have a clinic in Edinburgh where we treat AIDS patients. I gave up a busy practice to do this, and have been called in by Sir Peter Bagshaw as a consultant on his own project. I have listened with sorrow, but not surprise, to the remarks you have been addressing to Sir Peter Bagshaw. If only you would really stop and think, you would see what a remarkably kind and generous response Sir Peter has shown to the desperate need HIV and AIDS patients present at this time. He is turning over his beautiful mansion and its grounds, as well as his considerable fortune, to help his less fortunate brothers and sisters suffering from a disease for which scientists the world over, are trying to discover a cure! Until then——we need the compassion of everyone in this country——in this village, as we try to do our own part in bringing help to the suffering and I don't just mean medical help, important though this is——but moral support!'

'Perhaps if some of these people had shown some morals—then you would not have a job, my friend,' shouted a distinguished looking man at the back. 'My name is Major Buckingham. I have no patience with layabouts and young people with loose morals, who play around with drugs, instead of doing an honest day's work! Most of them are gay too, by all accounts.'

'Well——I thank you for your views, Major! Would it interest you to know, that although a large percentage of AIDS victims was confined to drug users and homosexuals, in Africa the disease is now equally rife amongst heterosexuals and increasingly so in the States and indeed here in the UK. Many haemophiliacs are dying of AIDS as a result of infected blood transfusions——doctors have contracted the disease, when not taking full precautions when treating road accident cases, and then most tragic of all, are the little children being born HIV positive. Medicine does not discriminate on peoples relationships, or morals, Major——it treats disease——with humanity——with true caring——with true love of people, that draws doctors and nurses into their profession.' The doctor paused and wiped his spectacles. A man stood up to speak. It was the vicar.

'Doctor Borthwick——I just want to say, that I for one totally applaud what Sir Peter Bagshaw is making possible here at Garnford, for those poor people, giving all that he possesses to help AIDS sufferers. I would like to ask a question of those assembled here tonight——how many of you, would give of your substance to help your next door neighbour, let alone give away all you own to help him——never mind doing it for people you have never even met! If I can be of any help myself, then please let me know.' He sat down to a low hostile murmuring. Then someone else stood up. It was the head mistress of the local school, Mrs Parkhurst.

'I too am deeply touched by all that Sir Peter is doing to provide help for these unfortunates. I suggest they already have enough to bear, without it coming to their ears through the local press, that Sir Peter's neighbours are so blatantly lacking in Christian charity and common decency! ' And here she gave a long hard look at the busy reporter. 'I am available to help in any way too—you have only to ask!' She sat down and this time there was some muted clapping. Then Charles Sylvester rose to his feet.

'Walter——I think I will say a word or two now!

My name is Charles Sylvester. I am a surgeon from San Francisco. I met Sir Peter when he was brought to the State hospital where I was employed, when suffering from a stab wound to the heart. I was made aware of the fact, that the person who had stabbed him, was also being treated in the same hospital. It had been established through a routine blood test, that she was suffering from AIDS! As many of you will know, from the amount of publicity that the case attracted, she had fallen, bleeding profusely from a bullet wound, right across Sir Peter's body. He too was bleeding from the open wound, where in involuntary movement, she had withdrawn the dagger from his body. Immediately I was told this, I knew that short of a miracle, Sir Peter now carried the AIDS virus in his body.'

Now a moan of sympathy swept across the assembled people.

'Now it takes six months approximately, from the virus entering the body, before blood tests can establish that the person is indeed HIV positive. I had to tell Sir Peter that in my opinion he almost certainly had become vulnerable to HIV——and I told him for an

important reason. It was so that he could take all reasonable precautions not to pass the virus to others, in particular, to his wife
and baby son. Both he and Rosamund have found that the care
and deep love they feel for each other has strengthened Sir Peter
for the road ahead. Now I want to dismiss a few myths you may
be harbouring.' He turned. 'Rosamund?'

A slim figure detached herself from the side of the platform on
which the speakers addressed the crowd. It was Sir Peter's wife,
Lady Rosamund and a wave of curiosity consumed the villagers.
Poor girl, how terrible this must be for her. But the young woman
with her shining shoulder length blond hair, lovely features lightly enhanced by make up, showed no sign of stress, as she advanced
towards her husband, her stylish suit flame bright against the
brown velvet curtains backing the platform. All eyes were on her,
as she lifted up her face to Sir Peter, who bent his head and kissed
her tenderly.

A concerned whispering broke out. Charles Sylvester held out
his hand for silence, as Rosamund slipped her arm about Peter's
waist, to find the comfort of his arm about her shoulders. As they
stood facing the crowd, faces that had registered anger at the
beginning of the meeting now bore a softer expression.

'Ladies and gentlemen——there is a lot we do not yet know
about AIDS, but one or two points need stressing.' Doctor
Sylvester paused and glanced at the couple at his side.

?Sir Peter may quite safely kiss his wife without risk to her——she
can drink from a cup used by him, nor will she come to any harm
swimming in the same pool with him. If he coughs, or sneezes,
she cannot catch the virus from the air. As was said to you, at the
beginning of this meeting, HIV can only be transmitted sexually
or by taking infected blood into your own bloodstream, as for
instance by using contaminated syringes and needles. So there
you have it explained in the most straightforward terms—the
virus is only contained in infected blood, semen and body fluid.
Members of the same family can happily coexist without danger,

by taking sensible precautions.' He looked around the hall, trying to gage the effect his words had had. He thought he sensed a lessening of tension.

'Dad——can I see you for a moment?' He turned as a small, figure called to him from the side of the platform. He hesitated and then with a smile, beckoned his son to join him.

'Ladies and gentlemen——may I introduce my son, Richard! He is seven years of age——and HIV positive. When he was five, he fell off his bike onto some broken glass and severed an artery. At the hospital to which he was taken, they repaired the artery——and gave him a blood transfusion. That blood was infected with the AIDS virus.' He bent down and patted Richard on the head. ''Richard——-tell the folks what you have to do if you cut yourself.'

'Why——that's easy. You see, because I have these bad little bugs in my blood, I have to be careful that I don't bleed near anyone else. I have to call Mom or my teacher and they put on rubber gloves—and anything they use to clean me up with, has to be put into a plastic bag and burnt. It's a bore——but its just one of those things. My dad says, that one day the scientists will find a cure for AIDS——then children like me——and grown ups like Sir Peter——won't have to worry anymore. We didn't ask to get these little bugs you know——we would far rather be like all of you!' He gave the people a wistful smile as he said this, then turned to his father. 'Mandy wants you to come and say good-night, Dad!'

'Later, Richard——I promise. Now you go back to Mom.' The little boy gave a satisfied nod and ran off. There was absolute stillness in the hall. Then Helen Delaney-Smythe rose to her feet. When she spoke, her voice was husky. She gestured towards the disappearing figure of the little boy.

'I guess I just didn't think, before I spoke earlier——hadn't really got things into perspective. Peter——I'm terribly sorry, really I am. Will you forgive me? If I can help in any way, then count me in!' Her reward was a warm smile from Peter, and Rosamund held a hand out to her. Helen made her way awkwardly up onto the platform. She turned to the rest of the audience.

'I think that perhaps we should all think again, don't you? Little Richard could so easily be a child in one of our

families——and Peter one of our husbands, or sons. I only know that I was being unutterably selfish—and unfeeling. How about the rest of you?' Her gaze swept the hall

. She was well respected in the neighbourhood and gradually people responded. Mr Butterworth looked around him and then got to his feet.

'On behalf of my fellow citizens, I think that perhaps we should wish to extend our best wishes to 'Ebb-Tide'————-and that hopefully there will be mutual respect and understanding on both sides.' There was some subdued clapping and the people rose to their feet and started to file out. A room had been prepared with refreshments, but few went in to eat the smoked salmon sand-wiches. Most returned to their homes, their original anger drain-ing away, to be replaced by acceptance tempered by unease.

'Helen——that was a wonderful thing to do,' said Rosamund softly. She leaned towards her and placed a quick kiss on her cheek.

'Rosamund, I behaved like a selfish pig, thinking only of myself. But if I can help in some way, then I hope you'll let me.'

'We'll certainly take you up on that,' said Peter and held out his hand. She hesitated, but only fractionally and gave him a firm handclasp. 'Come and see my mother. She's with Ernst and Rodrigo in the music room. Charles——-Walter, will you come too?'

Hermione glanced at their faces anxiously, as they filed through into the music room, but it was to Peter that she spoke.

'How did it go, Peter? Harrington said there was a lot of angry talk in the village this afternoon.' Peter smiled at her reassuringly, seeing the strain on her usually serene features.

'Well—-things got off to a difficult start. People were worried—-understandably, until Walter and Charles spoke to them. But it was little Richard, coming onto the platform by sheer chance and then talking for a few minutes that really got though to them.

'He brought tears to my eyes,' said Helen bluntly. 'I was one of the worst characters at that meeting, Hermione. I said some pretty mean things and so did Major Buckingham. But little Richard just touched my heartstrings, as I think he did those of everyone else there.' Hermione took Helen's hands and squeezed them.

'Oh, Helen, I would probably have been just as worried and suspicious as the others, if I hadn't been directly involved as a relative—-and had everything explained to me so logically. Yes, there are certain risks with every major disease, but if people follow the rules, use a few wise precautions, then those risks are almost non existent. But come—-you haven't said hallo to Ernst or Rodrigo yet!' She indicated the two men who had been standing at the piano.

'Be greeted, Helen,' said Ernst, kissing her hand, while Rodrigo gave a slight bow. 'I am hoping that Peter will eventually be able to tear himself away from his plans for his future guests and give some time to the concerto that is to be performed at the Albert Hall in a few weeks time. After all—-I am playing in it myself, so have a vested interest in getting this dear friend of mine, to concentrate his efforts on his music!'

'Have no fears, Ernst! I promise you, that I am putting all that is in me, into the Golden Concerto. We start official rehearsals in a few weeks time. It will be my finest——if possibly my last concerto.'

'Peter——don't say that,' cried Rosamund. 'You will probably write many other, even more wonderful concertos!'

'You misunderstood my meaning, Rosamund. It is simply that I want to direct my energies in other ways, once this concerto is completed—-and the tour, which I hope to undertake, over. All of my life has so far been involved with music and its disciplines. Now I want to spend more time with my family—-perhaps visiting far off places I have never seen, with you dear love, possibly also revisiting countries where I have played my music, but never had a chance to explore as others do. There is so much waiting to be done, that is exciting!' He caught her to him and saw the worry disappear from her eyes. He would have to watch his tongue in future.

It was a cold, crisp November morning, some two weeks later. Harrington sat in his small sitting room, drinking tea with Mrs Honeyset, as they discussed the day ahead. The cook shook her head disapprovingly.

?That new girl is very slow to learn, Mr Harrington. She has been through Cookery College and thinks she knows it all. But some of the dishes which we have traditionally served at Garnford for years, seem to be beyond her! All I ever hear is—-well in college, we did it in such and such a way.'

'I am sure you will be able to guide and train her, Mrs Honeyset—-just as you have with so many others since I have known you. Let us not also forget, that she has come to us in the knowledge that she will be in contact with the sick people who will start arriving today.'

'Yes——that's true! I was very disappointed when we lost five of our staff a few months ago. Young Lisa will bring us up to strength though, taking into account, the four extra women you have found me recently. After all, we are already cooking for the staff in the research wing—-plus the doctors and nursing staff who arrived last week.' She drew breath. 'How many of those AIDS patients are supposed to be arriving today then?' She turned her rosy cheeked face towards him inquiringly.

'Well now——there is a young mother and her five year old daughter—-Joan Simpson and Bonny. Then there is a young man from Liverpool—Tommie Leydon. He is quite ill, and will be going straight into the hospital wing in the house.'

'I can't get used to our beautiful West wing being turned into a hospital unit,' said Mrs Honeyset with a sigh. 'It all looks so different! The false ceilings the workmen have put in——all that pastel coloured paint. But I suppose if it had to be altered, then I must admit they have done it very well. Lady Rosamund has chosen soft flowered curtains and bed covers that are far removed from what one usually gets in hospital——and those lovely paintings on the walls. They're the ones poor Mrs Lake painted, aren't they.'

'Yes, Mrs Honeyset. Lady Rosamund's mother had a rare talent for painting. I still remember her last visit here, when she was very ill—on day of the wedding. She was a very brave lady.' His voice was sad.

'She was——and her daughter is just as brave. Lady Rosamund never lets you see how terribly worried she must be about Sir Peter—always has a smile on her face and a word of encouragement for the staff. The workmen all adore her. Thank goodness they have all gone now though. All that banging and clatter!'

'But I suppose we must agree they made an excellent job! Those bungalows are wonderfully comfortable. Each one of the patients, will have their own bed-sitting room and individual bathroom——and can either use the well equipped kitchen in their own bungalow, or come up to the house, to the communal dining room. But at least you will not be involved in all that extra cookery for patient care. The dietician and her staff of three seem to have settled well into the new second kitchen next to the dining room.'

'I probably could have coped. But then again, to be honest, what with the family to cook for, as well as the doctors and nurses and research workers——well, it would have been difficult to have attended to the special meals needed to tempt the appetites of sick people.' She shook her head broodingly. She had served at Garnford for many years, right from Lady Hermione's marriage and early widowhood, watching Sir Peter growing from little boy, into earnest young musician——and later into world famous composer and musician. Never would she have thought in her wildest dreams, that the lovely old manor house, that had been home to them all for so long, would open its doors to doctors and nurses and research scientists——and patients with this strange new disease! She turned her practical face on Harrington.

'So then——there's a young mother and a little girl—the young man from Liverpool——and who else?'

'Derek Rogers. He is a man who has had AIDS for six years and according to Sir Peter, has been terribly treated by various people in the neighbourhood where he lived. His windows were bro-ken——graffiti sprayed on his front door——abuse hurled at him continuously.'

'Why——but that's terrible! Poor, poor man! Is he going into the hospital wing?'

'No. Into Heron bungalow.'

'All right. Now who else?'

'Two young men——who are close companions——Terry Smith and Tom Digby. Then there is a little boy called Norman. He is ten——and his parents have rejected him. Next there is a little girl called Samantha, whose mother died a week ago—!' The list went on, each case sympathetically discussed by these two, who had done so much through the years, to have kept Garnford the wonderfully welcoming place it had always been and would con-tinue to be.

Two hours later, the cars started to arrive, bringing the travel weary patients to the haven of Garnford. The bright November sunlight turned the falling oak leaves to a rich bronze, dappled with gold, and as the visitors were helped out of the cars, their eyes were met by the blaze of red, white and gold chrysanthe-mums in the flower beds bordering the manor house. The front door stood open, as Peter and Rosamund came forward to greet each new guest in turn. The scene was to be repeated time after time during that day, until eight o'clock that night, when the last patient arrived, accompanied by his wife.

'Is it really all right for me to stay here as well,' she asked Peter anxiously? 'Andrew has been quite ill——he is in a remission period just now, but————?' Her pretty face, framed by short, silky hair, was tense with worry.

'Of course you can stay——as long as you like! Molly——this is to be home for both you and Andrew. My name is Peter————and here is my wife Rosamund. Come this way——have something to eat first and then we will take you to your bungalow. You will be sharing it with a young mother and her baby daughter.' He shook hands with her and her husband, who rewarded him with a smile that was in his eyes as well as on his lips.

It was late that night, by the time Peter and Rosamund finally retired to their bedroom. Both were exhausted——but filled with a sort of exultation, that Peter's dream was coming to fruition. They realised that there might be problems and a few pitfalls, but were more than ready to cope with whatever would arise. The important thing was, that people who were suffering from a disease, unwittingly caught and who had received so little help and consideration from their neighbours, were now in a loving and caring environment, where they would receive the most up to date treatment. For those who were terminally ill, the right to end their days with dignity, surrounded by devoted men and women, each of whom had taken decision to come to Garnford, to cherish every patient who needed their special skills.

The following days were busy ones, as the patients became used to their new home——and they and the doctors fell into a smooth routine. Some needed but little treatment at this stage, just the security of being there with help at hand——and no condemnation. Gradually friendships were struck up, as people from many and varied backgrounds formed themselves into a community. They would walk in small groups, exploring the beautiful grounds——looking at the graceful swans on the lake——taking the

path of the fountains. The weather had turned unusually warm—
-an Indian summer. The children played on the swing, round-
abouts and slide that Rosamund had planned for little Tristam, a
few months before his birth. Now shouts of happy laughter came
from the playground, as a young nurse kept an eye on the children romping there.

But it was at the research building that people cast such earnest
glances. They had been told that scientists here were hard at
work, trying to come up with a cure——as others were the world
over. 'One day perhaps, God willing,' they would murmur. In the
meanwhile, there was a feeling of hope and tranquillity and in
most cases, their bitterness at a fate that seemed to have treated
them so cruelly, started to drain away.

At last the day came, when Peter told Rosamund that it was
time to return to London, to start rehearsals for the Golden
Concerto. He had taken advice from Charles Sylvester and the
three other doctors, that all was running smoothly and promise
was made to contact him, should there be any problems other
than medical ones. It was with relief, that Hermione heard the
news, for she alone had been feeling the new situation difficult to
cope with, though she would never have admitted this to them.
But as the Rolls drove smoothly along the drive and speeded
towards London, she heaved an inward sigh of relief. She was sitting in the back of the car with Rosamund, the baby firmly
strapped into his little padded seat, cooing loudly and chuckling
as Rosamund tickled his cheek.

Roberts was driving and Peter sat next to him silently, deep in
thought. He had pulled the sun screen down to shade his eyes
against the brilliant sunshine that dazzled, as the car sped free of
dense woodland now, and as he stared into it's mirrored surface,
he saw his mother's face reflected there. He realised that
Hermione had aged in the last few months. Fine lines were forming around eyes and across her forehead and her mouth in repose
had a slight downward droop. A deep pity for her was born in his

mind. So far all his thoughts had been directed on the effect his illness was to have on his own life and that of his darling Rosamund and little son—-but what of his mother? Had he really stopped to think what she also could be going through?

He remembered, how instead of her anticipated journey to meet with them on Skye, he had contacted her from the Edinburgh clinic, to inform her, that her visit to the Island of Mists was no longer necessary. He had gone straight into preparations for turning her beloved home of over forty years, into hospice for AIDS patients. Now at last, after all his feverish activity, he became aware of how his decisions had disturbed her life and that of her friends. He might if he were lucky, exist for a year or two longer—-maybe find his life prolonged over a much greater period, but subject to increasing illness. Certainly, unless the scientists made the much sought after breakthrough fairly soon, then certainly his years were numbered.

As he watched, he saw Hermione give a sigh—then smile slightly, as little Tristam made a grab for her sleeve. Poor mother—— what would happen to her once he was gone? True she had her bridge parties in London—-her coterie of music loving friends—-her interest in fashion. But Peter knew that he had always been the pivot around which her life revolved. Suddenly Hermione reached out a slender hand and gently stroked her little grandson's hair, then giving him her finger to hold. When he saw the look of tenderness on her face, Peter knew, as thought the future unfolded in front of him, what form his mother's life would take. She would transfer all her love and energy into helping Rosamund care for Tristam, perhaps even starting her grandson on that musical journey to which she had directed his feet. But was music the future he wanted for his son? He thought of his own hard life, with its triumphs and sorrows. Would he have changed it——substituted it for a life in the business world instead—perhaps the stock exchange—-or farming? No! A hundred times no! Music had been his all in all——would remain so until his last breath.

'He must choose for himself,' he said suddenly.

'Who must, darling?' Rosamund looked towards him, puzzled.

'Tristam. Neither of you must ever force him into music, unless he shows a natural talent——a need to play!' He turned his head, looking at both Rosamund and Hermione. His mother returned that look understandingly. But it was Rosamund who replied.

'I have the feeling, that this little one will have a mind of his own and a determination to match that of his father! He will take his own path.' As though to reinforce her words, the baby fixed his dark eyes, beneath their winged brows, on his father's face—- and staring back into his son's eyes, Peter felt his own filling with tears. He swung round to the front again, not wanting the others to see this show of emotion. There in the back of his car, was all he had longed for and dreamed of during the long years—a beautiful and loving wife, who shared his love of music, displaying a talent that blended so perfectly with his own. The gift of a fine, healthy son, the boy he had never thought he would father, as time bleakly passed, after his first wife's death. Now life had given him this immeasurable treasure, he was having to learn to relinquish it——and even with the strength he had found in his faith in God, the process of having to let go, was incredibly painful.

He must snap out of these negative thoughts! Whatever lay ahead of him, at least he wanted Rosamund to retain memories tinged with happiness. He knew she loved him very much. He studied her face in the mirror. How young she looked. Had he been terribly unfair in marrying a girl so much younger than himself? Yet how could that be when they loved each other so dearly. Yes, and this made it all the more frustrating, that he could not make love to her as fully as he would have wished, so that they were indeed one flesh. He thought back to the night of their coming together for the first time, on their honeymoon in Kinloch Rannoch. As he thought, a thin strand of music twisted through his head. What was it? He realised it was nothing he had ever heard before——and as he sat there, the slender theme expanded through his mind, until it completely absorbed him, releasing the anguish that had consumed him.

'Have you a pen and paper in your bag, Rosamund?'

'A pen—-yes. But only my telephone address book.'

'There is a theme I want to get down on paper.' Peter took the pen from her. She glanced around, and snatched the wrapping from Tristam's disposable nappies. She turned it inside out and handed it to him. Without comment on its suitability, Peter started to fill its crumpled surface with notes that flew from his pen at tremendous speed. Hermione and Rosamund exchanged delighted glances. There was a complete relaxation of tension as the rolls under Robert's sure hands, swept on towards London.

It was a week to Christmas. The London stores were thronged with busy shoppers and the magnificent street decorations in Regent Street attracting their usual slow moving traffic. Rosamund clutched her armful of parcels close to her, as she made her way out of the famous toyshop. She hailed a taxi and breathed a sigh of relief when eventually it set her down outside Hermione's flat in Hans Crescent. The uniformed porter opened the door for her, as she entered the building and stepped into the lift.

'Why, Michael——-Michael Howard! What a wonderful surprise!' She dropped the parcels on the carpet and reached out both hands to the young pastor, who had risen at her entrance, from his chair beside Hermione.

'Its good to see you again, Rosamund. How are you?' He searched her face, saw the shadows under her eyes, the air of defiant, slightly brittle happiness. 'I heard that you were back in London a while ago——-and wondered whether you would like to come and see Sue and myself in that lovely little flat, that Peter made it possible for us to live in. Your mother's garden has been carefully tended and I have been breaking the ice on the pool every morning, during this cold spell. I don't think we have lost any of the goldfish,' he said whimsically.

'I feel guilty. I should have come. I only said to Hermione last night, that we must attend your church for Christmas service—-didn't I,' she said, turning to Hermione who was stooping over the carrier bags full of toys.

'Yes, you did, darling. I have been telling Michael how involved we have been with Peter's rigid time schedule with rehearsals—-always out of the flat at eight thirty in the mornings and home late into the night! This is one of the few days, that we haven't slipped into the back of the hall, to listen to the concerto—-and watch Rodrigo shaping the orchestra towards the opening night, in two day's time.'

'It's good that you have such a dependable young nanny for Tristam. He certainly is a beautiful boy.'

'He crawls all over the place now,' smiled Rosamund. 'He is ten months you know—-and is starting to pull himself up and take a few wobbly steps.' She stopped talking and looked at him from serious green eyes. Her mask had dropped and Michael saw the pain which she hid from the world, now exposed, as she whispered between lips that trembled slightly—-'You know about Peter, of course—-that he is HIV positive?' he nodded gravely. 'Yes, everyone knows,' she continued. 'I wanted him to come and see you, when we first arrived back here in London—-but he said he was too busy with his concerto, but would try to find time after Christmas week, before his tour starts.'

'How has he taken things?' Michael's face was full of sympathy.

'First of all, he filled his life with all the tremendous energy it needed to set up 'Operation Ebb-Tide' at Garnford. Now he is blotting out with his new concerto.' She sighed and sat down on the couch. He seated himself beside her, as he asked-

'How is it, that he has not included you in this concerto? After the wonderful duet you played together in the 'Rose Concerto' I would have thought that he would have joyed in having you play at his side!'

'I asked him that, right back at the beginning. Indeed, I felt very hurt at first and for a long time he wouldn't discuss it. Then one night in bed, I asked him again—-and he told me.'

'What did he say?'

'That this would probably be his last major work. When he is no longer—-able to play the solo part, he wants me to take over—-in the future that is. Nor did he write a duet into the concerto, because he did not want me to play together with another violinist, when he is no longer at my side. Do you understand, Michael?'

'Yes—-I do. How is he keeping health wise at the moment?'Well—apart from a weeks long illness in late July, he has shown no symptoms at all. He admits to tiredness and to some tension—-but that could be reaction to the knowledge that he is HIV.' She paused as Hermione stood up, saying that she was going to see little Tristam. When she had gone, Rosamund looked gravely at Michael.

'When we were on Skye, Michael, he was helped by a wonderful retired minister, who actually prevented him at one point, from taking his own life.'

'What!'

'Peter was attempting to throw himself over a cliff into the sea, when Jack pulled him back—-dragged him to safety in more ways than one. Peter accepted Jesus as his Lord and Saviour on Skye—-and it was only after that, that he let me know where he was. He had left me you see, not wanting me to know that his surgeon had told him that almost inevitably, he was to suffer from AIDS!'

'Poor Peter——what he must have gone through. But it is most wonderful news to learn that he has been born again! This will help him so much. Oh, Rosamund, my dear——there are not words to tell you how sorry I am, that you should have to carry this burden. But always remember that Christ said—"Come to me all you who are weary and burdened, and I will give you rest!" His gentle arms are always open to comfort us, Rosamund—-and Peter will increasingly find this to be so.' As she heard Michael reciting Jesus own lovely words, Rosamund broke down. The months of holding her feelings in, had made her think her emotional citadel to be impregnable. Now, for the first time, she broke down and sobbed out all her hurts and fears to Michael. It was like a dam bursting. But the tears that shook her frame brought healing in their wake.

Michael released her hands, as he sensed she was becoming calmer.

'I'm so sorry, Michael. It's the first time that I have cried. I've always been aware that I must be brave for Peter's sake. Do you understand?'

'Yes, I do, Rosamund. But my dear———have you not thought, that perhaps in one way, it might help Peter himself, if he sees your sorrow—-because then he will be able to disclose his own to you, instead of having to hold onto it, as a lonely, secret thing! Never be scared of honest emotion. Have you not read, that Jesus himself wept, when his friend Lazarus died, sharing in the grief of his friends.'

Rosamund looked up. 'Yes—-I remember reading that. It was before he raised Lazarus from the tomb. Why did he cry, when so soon afterwards, he was to bring Lazarus out of that rock tomb?'

'Simply because he was consumed with sorrow and pity for the dead man's sisters in their grief———even as today, he joins with us in our sorrows and takes joy in our happy moments. He knows what you are going through, Rosamund—-and Peter. Do you think it was merely coincidence, that it was a minister who reached out a hand to pull Peter back from the abyss? No, Rosamund———he is watching over us all the time, only waiting for us to cry out to him. Always remember that, my dear.' She smiled in response. When Hermione came back into the room, with Tristam in her arms, it was to find Rosamund with tear stained eyes, but with a peace about her.

Rodrigo threw up his arms in exasperation.

'No! No————No! You have brought the tension to its

peak—-now you have to let it go, with its power gradually receding——going—-then gently surging back. Try again—now!' His baton rose. The orchestra attempted the passage again. This time Rodrigo threw his baton down and clasped his head in his hands. The musicians watched, waiting for another tirade. It didn't come. Instead, a quiet voice broke the stillness.

'When I wrote the finale, my friends, it was after walking along the seashore, watching the tide turning, the waves losing force, starting little by little, to pull back from the shore. Try to imagine this if you will—-moonlight flooding across the waters, golden——beautiful—and the waves slapping the shore, but gradually receding—-the phrase Rodrigo used, but now clothed in your minds with the wild loveliness of the night—-the sigh of the wind and the heart moan of the sea!' He lifted his violin and nodded to Rodrigo——-who raised his baton yet once again.

'That was perfection,' murmured Rodrigo to Ernst, as the musicians, tired but triumphant, filed out of the hall. 'Strange that I should have tried so many times, to make them understand—— and then Peter comes, and with a few words, brings that final enchantment out of their hands!'

'Perhaps not so strange. Who knows a child better, than the one who bore it,' reflected Ernst. 'Ah—there is Svetlana waving to me—and she looks cross. Menches kind——what is the time, Rodrigo? I promised her I would not be late tonight!' He did not stop for an answer, but hurried to the doorway, where his wife stood waiting. Peter approached Rodrigo as they watched the old pianist embrace his wife and walk out with her.

'What a relief that he is reconciled with Svetlana again. Did he tell you, that she is severing all practical connection with Fritz Klein, to devote herself to their marriage?'

'That is good——but I wonder how long she will be able to keep to it. Music in all its forms—-whether it is in composition, performance—or as important in its own way, the fostering of talent in others—-it is in our blood, Peter! But they love each other, and he is a lucky man!'

'He is—-and they have the rest of their lives to adapt to each other,' said Peter softly and sighed. Rodrigo looked at him, eyes dark with sympathy, for he guessed his thoughts. But his voice when he spoke was firm and practical.

'It is the final rehearsal tomorrow, Peter. Are you ready—-yourself I mean, for Friday? There will be many reporters there, after the performance and you may be sure that not all of their questions will be about the concerto!'

'I know that—-and I can handle it! After all, Rodrigo, I took time off two weeks ago, to conduct them around Garnford, when they made that special feature for TV. I find myself, that if you are completely honest with people, hold nothing back, that they respect you. Well my friend, I must get home to Rosamund—— goodnight——and my heart felt thanks, for all the amazing work you have put in on this last concerto.'

'You seem to make a point of referring to it like that——instead of calling it the 'Golden Concerto'!'

'Because in my heart, I know that it will be my last concerto. Posterity can name it what they will. Just that three month's tour and I'm through with performances. I shall devote the rest of my life to Rosamund and my son.' Rodrigo watched him go, and shook his head.

'You have incredible courage, Peter my friend,' he murmured.

Rosamund stood in front of the mirror, adjusting the skirt of her French gown, its champagne silk sculpted to breasts and waist, but falling in graceful folds to her dainty shoes. She wore a necklace of opals, so worked that they resembled a chain of rose tinted flowers, crusted in gold. Her blond hair gleamed like polished silk. She smiled and lowered her head as Hermione fastened the fragile spray of golden orchids, just above her right ear. Peter had sent it—-but the silk of her dress was too delicate for her to wear the flowers as a corsage, but nor did she want to reject her husband's gift, so Hermione had struck on the idea, of fastening them discretely against her hair.

'Darling—-you look absolutely lovely! What a brilliant idea, to wear pale gold for the 'Golden Concerto'! Why——I've never seen you look more radiant!' The compliment was absolutely sincere and Rosamund accepted it gratefully. This was Peter's big night. All that had been summoned up from the depths of his soul—-all that was vibrant with love and longing, was encapsulated in this work. It was as though he had gathered himself like a deer leaping a chasm, his talent flying through the music he had created with a soaring energy, that amazed even Rosamund herself, when she had listened to the final rehearsal yesterday.

'Hermione—-you look gorgeous too! Blue does wonderful things for your eyes.' She squeezed the older woman's hand. 'You know—it seems only yesterday, that you helped an awkward, gawky twelve year old, who bristled at you and behaved abominably. How did you ever manage to have patience with me!'

'I liked your spirit! Then——when your mother left you, I admired the courage you showed in what must have been a completely devastating situation for you. It didn't take very long, for me to love and accept you as though you had indeed been my own daughter——and see how good life has been to me. You really are my daughter now. Perhaps—-God gave us to each other, to provide the support and strength we both need at this time— and to be able to encourage Peter.' There was a glimmer of tears in their eyes as they embraced. Then they went downstairs, to where Roberts had the Rolls waiting.

Hundreds of eyes were directed towards their box, as they seated themselves. The evening started with Ernst Morgenstern seated before the gleaming keys of the magnificent concert grand. There was absolute stillness, as the old musician lifted those long, lean fingers that had charmed audiences the world over, with his virtuosity. The beautiful notes of Beethoven's Moonlight Sonata stole upon the air, to be followed by a dazzling rendering of the Waldstein. The clapping was rapturous. To have Ernst

Morgenstern and Peter Bagshaw on one programme was truly a musical feast.

Then——at last——what they had all been waiting for! The new work Sir Peter had named his 'Golden Concerto' was announced. Rodrigo bowed, waited as the last musician tuned his instrument—-then raised his baton. But it was not on the conductor that the hundreds in the Albert Hall fixed intent gaze—-but upon the master violinist and superb composer, standing so serenely before them, in his evening suit. Why, he showed no slightest sign of illness! The concerto commenced the music warm and tender, dreamily romantic. Then the mood changed. Peter lifted his bow——and the cascade of rippling chords, charged with passion and mystery, wrapped every person present in their own secret world of troubled desires.

The second movement was heralded by the clear, pure notes of a flute, to be cherished about by horns and strings, weaving a magic tapestry of sound, tapping into the depths of the spirit, questioning——-seeming to take one path—now another. Then Peter's violin broke startlingly through this maze of sweetly muted inquiry—-it's notes soaring majestically, in ravishingly beautiful curving theme, stirring all that was dormant in the human heart, with its throbbing intensity, where pain and passion vied, interwoven. The orchestra caught up the theme, in richly triumphant melody, that held the answer to life's hurt in its joyful challenge. Did any perhaps realise, that Peter's own inward battle, was so expressed in this musical gauntlet, thrown with such transparent honesty, to those who could pick it up?

The third movement borrowed some of the extreme passion of the second. Peter's violin poured upon the air, with such wildly, compelling energy, that the hall resounded to its tenderly pulsating song of love—-and always, Ernst's fingers caught vibration of the this wild emotion, as the movement rose to a peak of longing. Then Peter started a slow and beautiful theme, so tender that it hurt the breast. As the orchestra responded, each player remembered the picture of that moonlit seashore—-as the music released its power—-softly—-until the solo violin sobbed its last note—- and Peter lowered his bow.

Rosamund's eyes were full of tears as she looked down on him. She had heard Peter play so many times—and so wonderfully—- but never, oh never, like this! The audience after moment of complete silence rose to their feet, shouting their acclaim, waving their programmes, clapping until their hands hurt! The 'Rose Concerto' had been poignantly beautiful——but this new work was a masterpiece! Baskets of golden flowers of all varieties were carried onto the stage as the orchestra, Peter and Rodrigo took one bow after bow after another. Then the cry was for Rosamund. Startled she rose to her feet. She looked questioningly down on Peter, who beckoned to her.

It seemed to take an age to arrive there on the stage at his side. She raised her lips to his kiss. There was a moment's silence—-and then a great wave of applause, as they held hands together. At last it was finished, the audience making their way home by car, bus or train, the reporters rushing back to their offices to eulogise about Sir Peter's new concerto.

?The last concerto is the finest" ran one banner headline. "AIDS musician triumphs with startling new concerto" ran another. There was no doubting the music's success. Congratulations poured in from every side.

Peter was exhausted. He fell asleep as soon as his head touched the pillow. When he awoke the next day, it was to see Rosamund smiling at him, as she held out his breakfast tray. He sat up with an answering smile. Then it faded, as he realised that his head ached and his throat was hot and burning. He groaned inwardly. Not a cold——when he had to perform tonight!

'Rosamund——I don't really feel very hungry.' His voice came painfully. She looked at him, eyes wide with concern. He didn't look well. She put the tray down and reached out an exploring hand to feel his forehead—-which was hot and clammy.

'Peter—-how long have you felt unwell? Was there any sign of this last night?' She kept her voce calm, not allowing the apprehension that clutched her heart, to communicate itself in any way.

'I had never felt better last night.' He coughed. 'The exhilaration of being back on the platform again—-introducing a new work—was fantastic.' He sat up in bed, then clasped a hand to his throbbing head. 'Of all the times to get a cold!' Then as his eyes met hers, fear was born that this was no mere cold.

'Would you like me to ring your Harley Street doctor——-or is there anyone else I should call?' Her voice was quiet, as she stroked his hands. She had not mentioned Doctor Borthwick, but they both knew what she meant.

'Perhaps——-you should just get Walter to run the rule over me, Rosamund. Ring him, if you will—-but he is only to come if everything is running smoothly at Garnford.' She sighed in relief at his compliance and lifted the phone on the bedside table.

'Hallo——-is that you Walter? It's Rosamund. Peter has woken up this morning with a temperature, cough and severe headache. It is probably just a heavy cold coming on, or the flu——-but do you think you could spare the time to come up. Oh, thank you—thank you! You know the address?'

During the two weeks that followed, Peter was rushed into the South Bank Hospital, with pneumonia. Immediately upon arrival there, the staff placed him in intensive care——-in a unit that specialised in AIDS. They were delighted to liase with Doctor Borthwick, whose work in Edinburgh was well known to them. For Peter, it was a time of agonising pain in his chest, which dulled under medication. When eventually the illness had run its course, Walter said he wanted to remove him to Garnford, which until this point would have been dangerous to have done, for the virus that had invaded his body had been a virulent one. Moreover, that other virus which had weakened his body's natural defences to disease had, the doctor explained, now passed from its dormant state, into what was known as full blown AIDS!

CHAPTER SIXTEEN

Sir Peter did not return to Garnford in the Rolls, but in a special ambulance, with Rosamund sitting on the couch bed facing the one on which he lay. He had protested to Walter Borthwick that he was quite well enough to travel by car—-but Walter had been adamant. The attack of pneumonia had been very severe, with Peter spending the first forty-eight hours in hospital in an oxygen tent. X-rays still showed shadows at the base of both lungs and he was much weakened and accordingly, vulnerable to other infections.

'I feel so badly about the tour having to be cancelled,' muttered Peter, from a voice still hoarse. 'I was so looking forward to it——Bonn—Berlin—Paris—Vienna—-Rome! There was that invitation to Moscow as well!'

'Don't strain your voice, Peter. All right—-I know the cancellation is a disappointment darling——but just hold onto the fact, that the 'Golden Concerto' was the most marvellous success. When you are stronger, perhaps another tour can be arranged.' She reached out and stroked his hair and as he looked into the love shining out of her eyes, Peter felt ashamed that he had grumbled. From the time he had entered hospital, all his thoughts had been centred on himself—-the heaviness of spirit that had overcome him as realisation was born, that he was now suffering from AIDS proper—the prognosis far from rosy. He caught her hand and lifted it to his lips.

'Thank you, Rosamund.'

'What for, darling?'

'Just for being you——the most wonderful wife a man could have. Forgive my selfish words. After all, what does worldly renown matter really, when I already have the greatest treasure on this earth—you and little Tristam.'

'Plus your mother and friends——dear old Ernst, Rodrigo—
and the countless others who care for you so deeply.'

'Yes——I know. The hospital said they had never known such
a collection of get well cards and letters wishing me a speedy
recovery. Did you bring them with you, Rosamund—-for I want
to reply to each person individually.'

'Charles Sylvester and his assistant, young Doctor Sedgewick,
stood ready at the manor house door to receive him. Strong
hands supported him, as he entered Garnford. Harrington smiled
a greeting and so did Mrs Honeyset. A deep sense of relief flooded over him, as he realised that he was at home, amongst those
who were truly his friends. Of what real importance was it, that
he was not able to travel Europe, basking in the acclaim of the
thousands, who would one day hear his last concerto, even if he
were not able to play it for them. After all, someone else would.
Perhaps that someone would be Rosamund. He swallowed, as he
came to terms with reality.

Later that night, when Peter had retired early to bed, exhausted but at peace, Hermione sat with her arm round Rosamund's
shoulders, as the girl broke down and cried as though her heart
would break.

'I'm so sorry, Hermione. I was all right after the concert. Up
until then, I had been able to push Peter's illness to the back of
my mind, always hoping in my secret heart, that a miracle would
happen, to prevent Peter developing full AIDS. Now the shock-
ing, glaring truth—-that Peter is—-going to die—-in a few
months—-or a year or two at most, is hard to bear. I thought I
had come to terms with it, but that was only at surface level. Oh,
Hermione, how am I going to be strong enough to keep his spirits high, when I feel so miserable——so inadequate.' Rosamund
blew her nose on the handkerchief Hermione gave her and
dabbed at her eyes, where the tears were still welling.

'My darling—-don't be ashamed of your tears. You have been
wonderfully brave—and I know, will continue to be so. But there

will be times in the future, when we will all cry——-you——-and
I——-yes, and Peter. It is natural, Rosamund. Nature gives us this
safety valve to express grief. You mustn't try to disguise your feelings from Peter either.'

'Strangely that is what Michael Howard said—-to let Peter see
my hurt, so that he could uncover his own. He also spoke of
God's healing love. Oh, I wish Michael were here!' She screwed
the hanky into a tight ball.

'Rosamund——I want you to come with me. There is something that the workmen completed while we were away.'

Hermione paused outside a door that bore a notice—Chapel.
Obediently Rosamund followed her to the east wing. Hermione
pushed the door open gently. Rosamund gave a cry of surprise
and wonder. This room, which had once been used for holding
parties, had been completely altered. Now a stained glass window
replaced the original plain bay. On a raised dais an altar stood,
covered with a white cloth. Above it was suspended a dove caved
in wood. To the left of the altar was a pulpit——and to the right,
a painting hung. It was Sylvia's beautiful depiction of the Christ.
But how had it come to be here? Who had ordered this lovely
chapel to be constructed?

'How on earth did this come about,' asked Rosamund softly?
She kept her voice low, because she noticed the young man kneeling in the front row of seats, his head bowed in prayer. It was
Doctor Sedgewick——the young doctor who had caught AIDS
whilst helping the victim of a road crash. But quiet as Rosamund's
voice was, the man heard her and rose to his feet and turned
about.

'Why——Lady Rosamund——-Lady Hermione.' He came
towards them, a smile on his face. 'If you want to be alone here,
I'll go.'

'No Gordon, please don't do that! But perhaps you can tell me
something—-how did that painting come to be here?' Rosamund
pointed a finger towards it. Gordon Sedgewick looked at the

amazing painting.

'Yes——it's an extraordinary work, isn't it. A minister from London drove here two days ago and brought this with him. He told Charles, that he felt the lady who had painted it, would have wanted it to hang here.'

'It was my mother who painted that picture, doctor——when she was quite ill. She also painted the one hanging in the music room. She died of cancer only a few weeks afterwards. But she was so full of happiness always!'

'You can tell that——it pours out of her work! She was extraordinarily gifted. I imagine her paintings will give joy to hundreds in the years to come——in the same way, that your husband's music will live on after him, like that of all the great musicians. It must indeed be wonderful, to leave your stamp upon life in some way.' His voice was wistful.

'We all have different gifts, doctor,' said Hermione quietly. 'Yes, some people do leave their mark in the history books—— others though, place their touch upon our hearts, with their kindness and caring——and who is to say which is more important.' She smiled at him. 'I have heard how the patients love you, doctor—how you have been encouraging them and building up their spirits.'

'Oh——well——I guess you could say that for me it is therapeutic.' He looked down self-consciously. 'I must go.' And he hurried off.

'What a kind thing for Michael to have done. I know how he and his congregation treasured that painting,' said Rosamund. 'But I still want to know who gave the order for this chapel to be created. If it was Peter, why didn't he tell me?'

'Well——I suppose I must confess I personally instructed the builders to make a chapel——asked the local vicar if he would advise them. I have used my own money for it, as I wanted it to be my own gift to the patients. The vicar mentioned an old church that was to be demolished, because the structure was dangerous, but it had the most lovely stained glass window. It would be difficult to remove it—-a very delicate task—but it was undertaken by experts. The rest of the chapel was no problem. The room was redecorated, the dais built, the window reconstructed to take the glass. As for the pulpit and the dove—and of course, the altar, they came from the old church.' Hermione smiled at Rosamund's look of incredulity.

'Hermione—-you arranged all this, without saying a word to Peter or to me? What a lovely thing to have done—-the more especially as I know it has not been easy for you to accept all the changes at Garnford. In fact, I was quite worried about you, before Christmas, because you were unusually quiet—-perhaps depressed?'

'I was. Yes, you are right. I did find the changes here difficult to accept, and whilst feeling very sorry for the patients, felt deep in my heart, that their presence was an intrusion at a time when I was so terribly worried about Peter.' She looked down and sighed.

'But Hermione dear—-that was only a perfectly normal reaction. We all respond to grief in different ways. With Peter, it had been a mad rushing around, first establishing Ebb-Tide here, then hurrying off to London for rehearsals and the first performance of the Golden Concerto. It was his way of keeping anxiety at bay.'

'But what of you, Rosamund?' Hermione looked at the girl gently.

'I can only tell you, that I have tried to accept whatever is going to happen—not to blot out as I was trying to do on Skye. I am finding it very hard—-often finding myself on the verge of tears. But you see, at these times, I just pray—-and attempt to take just one day at a time.' As Hermione heard the quiet words, she took the girl in her arms and kissed her.

'You're so wise. It really is the only way, isn't it—-handing it over and just taking each day as it comes.' As they looked at each other, they smiled. This had helped, bringing the problems out into the open.

'Forgive me, ladies——but a visitor has arrived.' Harrington bowed. 'It is Mr Leopold Heine. I have shown him into the blue drawing room.'

'Leopold?' Rosamund looked startled. 'I didn't know he was in this country. Wasn't he supposed to be in Russia?' She turned to Hermione, who shook her head.

'He returned from Russia two days ago. I had a phone all from Svetlana. She and Ernst are living in Svetlana's flat in Kensington. As you know, Leopold stays there now, whenever he is in England. I completely forgot to tell you, that Svetlana mentioned that Leopold wanted to visit us. I said he could. You don't mind, do you Rosamund?'

'No——of course not. I haven't seen Leopold since that day he visited the hospital, shortly after Tristam's birth.' As they retraced their steps to the drawing room, Rosamund's thoughts drifted back to that cold December morning, just over a year ago, when the young pianist had declared his love for her. She remembered his ardent glance as he had declared that she was his 'Rose of Sharon'———and the sadness in his eyes, when she had gently rejected his surprising outburst. Had Leopold now found some-one who could return his love? She hoped so. Despite of her deep love for Peter, she knew herself to be deeply aware of Leopold's good looks and masculinity——of those passions smouldering just below the surface, which found dramatic expression in his music.

'Rosamund! Lady Hermione——forgive my having arrived so late in the evening——but when Ernst and Svetlana told me that Sir Peter was returning to Garnford today, with you both——I just wanted to visit, to——well——show my solidarity with you all. I only heard of Sir Peter's illness when I returned from my short visit to Russia.'

'Then you must be the only person in the music world, to have missed reading all the details in the press and on TV,' said Hermione!

'Possibly. But you see——I have been in Israel, in a little village on Lake Galilee. I decided a year ago, that I wanted to get away from music for a while. It was last April that I told Ernst where I was going. He didn't let you know then?' Leopold looked surprised.

'Perhaps that was because of his concern for Peter,' said Rosamund gently. 'His illness seemed to dwarf all normal interests over the last few months.'

'Of course. Rosamund——I do not know how to express my regret, that your husband is suffering from AIDS. Ernst told me of the wonderful project that Peter has set up here at Garnford. It must have taken immeasurable courage to have devoted himself to the needs of so many sick people, when he himself had to deal with his own situation. I do not think I could have behaved so!'

'He is a wonderful person,' said Rosamund softly. 'So——-you were not able to hear his last concerto—the Golden Concerto that is?'

'No. But I look forward to his next performance, once he is fit enough to return to the concert platform. How is he, Rosamund?'

'Recovering from pneumonia——-and full of fight!' She smiled proudly.

'Then may I ask you a question? Rosamund——what about your own health? Isn't there a risk to you and little Tristam in being in——-well in close contact, with an AIDS sufferer. Forgive that I am so blunt!' His dark eyes were fixed on her in genuine concern and Rosamund curbed the curt answer she almost gave him.

'How much do you know about AIDS, Leopold?'

'Next to nothing——except that the scientists are trying very hard to find a cure for it, so far unsuccessfully. Also, I have heard that it is the major cause of death in the USA amongst the young——-together with suicide. I do know however, that it is sexually transmitted—as well from acquiring the virus from infected blood.' He spread his long fingers out in front of him.

'Then—let me tell you all that I know about it.' She seated herself on the sofa and patted the cushion next to her. Then simply and naturally Rosamund explained matters pertaining to AIDS, to the young man who sat listening intently beside her. Hermione had gone quietly out of the room, to speak to Harrington about a room for Leopold. The Jewish boy's eyes were damp, as he placed one of his dark skinned hands over Rosamund's.

'Dearest Rosamund——even though Peter Bagshaw has this foul disease, I still think he is a lucky man, for a wife like you is a jewel beyond price.' The fingers he held, pressed his own——then were swiftly withdrawn. Rosamund rose to her feet, asking whether he would like to see Tristam, then together they made their way to the little yellow nursery, being quiet so as not to disturb Peter, who lay in the bedroom just beyond. As Leopold looked down on the little head on the pillow, long black lashes touching peach soft skin in sleep, the delicate face shaped so like Rosamund's own, and he felt deeply touched. He was about to speak, but Rosamund put a finger to her lips and led him out of the room again. They descended the stairs to find Hermione looking for them.

'Harrington is having a room prepared for you, Leopold——and we are about to have a late supper. So come along to the dining room.' Obediently he followed her, with his thoughts all centred on the lovely young woman at his side, whom he had gone to Israel to forget——but to no avail. He still loved he and always would, whatever the future held.

Peter was surprised to hear that Leopold was visiting, when he woke the following morning. Perhaps deep in his heart, he resented the presence of a man whom he knew cherished a tender feeling for his wife—but Leopold had never behaved in any but the most correct manner. After they had all taken breakfast together, Peter announced that he was going to visit his guests in their bungalows.

'Would you like to come with me, Leopold,' he challenged?

'Certainly,' replied the other, not allowing any apprehension to appear on his dark Semitic features, for he knew that Rosamund's eyes were on him. But for all that she had explained to him the previous night, that AIDS could only be caught in specific ways, he still experienced a certain unease. But the handshake he had exchanged with Peter that morning, had been firm, his dark eyes brimming with sympathy.

'Come along then,' said Peter.

'But Peter——should you be going out? It's freezing cold——a hoar frost. You can see the grass sparkling like silver in the sunlight.' Hermione's face was concerned. He just grinned at her. 'At least put on a warm coat. Don't forget, you are recovering from pneumonia Peter——not a cold!'

'Mother is inclined to be over protective,' said Peter, as their feet crunched over the grass. 'Rosamund on the other hand, has the intuitive good sense, to realise that I will never do anything to put myself unnecessarily at risk! She is a wonderful wife, Leopold.'

'You are a fortunate man——which is what I said to her last night!'

'What about yourself, Leopold? Have you found someone to share your life with yet?' Peter looked at him curiously.

'No. Perhaps one day——but until then, my music is completely fulfilling. Also Peter——I found a very special peace, when I was in Galilee.'

'Galilee? Surely that is one of the places spoken of in the bible.'

'You are right. I will tell you something Peter. Before Sylvia Lake died, I visited her studio and spoke with her. That amazing picture she painted of the Christ touched me in a strange way. I asked her many questions——and came away, with many more. One of the reasons I went to Israel, was to find the places where Jesus had walked, not only in Jerusalem——but in Nazareth, where he grew up, and Galilee, where he walked those green hills surrounding the lake. I knew that from there, he would have stared

at the snow covered peak of Mount Hermon, even as I did. A
strange feeling! I am a Jew, Peter——but Jesus became very real
to me. There was one day, when I stood looking at the ruins of
an old synagogue in Capernaum, when I almost sensed his presence.' He laughed a little self-consciously.

They walked on. Peter knocked at a door. Leopold had already
exclaimed in surprise, at the neat bungalows, set between trees—
-and the long building, which housed the research unit. Now he
looked at the young woman who opened the door to Peter. She
was very pale and tried to stifle a cough, as she smiled a greeting.
A baby girl, about Tristam's age, crawled across the room into
which she ushered them. The child had blond curls and dancing
blue eyes and Peter bent down and scooped her up in his arms,
tossing her up. Then he started to cough and sank down into a
chair. Julie looked at him in apprehension.

'You shouldn't really be out like this, should you sir! After
all——you only got out of hospital yesterday!' She walked into
her little kitchenette and returned with a glass of water. He sipped
it.

'Oh, I'm all right, Julie. How are you though? Oh——by the
way, this is a music friend——Leopold Heine.'

'Is he one of us,' asked Julie bluntly?

'No. He hasn't got AIDS——but perhaps when he returns to
his own friends, Leopold will be able to tell them of what he has
seen here——try to create more understanding amongst those
luckier than we——-!' He broke off, as there was a knock at the
door and in answer to Julie's cheery call to come in, a young
woman appeared, whom Peter recognised as Molly, whose husband Andrew had AIDS. They were sharing the bungalow with
Julie and baby Laura. Peter had a lot of sympathy with Molly, who
was supporting Andrew in the same marvellous way that
Rosamund was with him.

'Oh——I'm sorry. I'll come back later.'

'Please don't go on my account,' put in Peter smilingly. He

nodded to his companion. 'This is a friend of mine——Leopold Heine. He is a pianist and a good one. Perhaps we can persuade him to entertain us, before he returns to London.'

'How do you do, Leopold,' said the girl shyly. 'I suppose you are a classical musician? My Andrew is a keyboard player. He was with a group called 'Smokey Dreams'——I don't suppose you have heard of them,' she said wistfully. Leopold shook his head regretfully.

'No, Molly. But I am not often in this country and that is why. I would like to meet you husband. 'He smiled encouragingly at the girl, seeing the lines of strain around her eyes. But her gaze was already trained back on Peter.

'You asked how Andrew is—-well, he is in bed—-and I was about to call doctor Sedgewick. He is feverish. He has some odd purple looking blotches that were coming up yesterday, only today they are much more pronounced.'

'Let me see him.' said Peter. 'Julie——will you phone Charles Sylvester and Gordon Sedgewick please. Say that I would appreciate their coming here at once.' Peter took Molly's arm, for she was trembling. 'Come along. You mustn't worry. Andrew will be all right,' he said reassuringly. Leopold followed behind them. The man in one of the twin divans had tossed off the flowered duvet. His pyjamas jacket was open, revealing ugly looking raised purple blotches, just as Molly had described. His face looked a bad colour and clammy. Peter walked over to him and took his hand. The man forced a smile, as he saw who it was bending over him.

'How are you then, Andrew?'

'Feeling foul! I've terrible gripes in my lower abdomen and my head is aching badly—-feels muzzy.' He saw Leopold and attempted a nod of greeting. 'Are you a doctor?'

'No, my friend. My name is Leopold—-and like you I play a keyboard.'

'You do? Glad to meet you then. Take my advice though——

don't get hooked on drugs. That's how I got this lot——passing a syringe around!' He gasped out the words, as the pain he was experiencing caused him to grimace. Minutes later, Charles Sylvester and Gordon Sedgewick arrived and Peter left Andrew in their capable hands.

They went from one bungalow to another, greeting the patients who were delighted to see Peter back, but full of sympathy for the illness that had caused cancellation of his tour. Finally they knocked at the door of Derek Rogers. Leopold was shocked at the gaunt, almost skeletal appearance of the man's face, but he tried to keep his reaction from showing in his eyes.

'Peter——man, but it's good to see you!' Derek extended an ebony dark hand to Peter, who grasped it warmly. 'What happened to you then? I saw your concerto——heard it that is, on the TV. I had no idea that you were such a genius, I mean——there's a lot of fiddle scrapers——but you! You're something else again!' Peter grinned ruefully, as he accepted the compliment.

'I ended up with pneumonia, the night after the concert! Let me introduce my friend Leopold. He is what I think you might term——an ivory basher!' he watched as Leopold once again extended his hand and started to chat with this man who was one of the longest known AIDS survivors. Later, as they approached the hospital within Garnford's West wing, a camaraderie had sprung up between these two men, Leopold finding his heart going out to Peter, whom he had previously viewed as a spoiled member of the landed gentry. Now he glimpsed the stature of this man, who had reached out to others, even whilst attempting to spiritually encompass his own illness. It was not only Peter's personal courage but his humanity that so touched Leopold. He tried to imagine himself in Peter's place and had to admit that he would probably be filled with utmost despair. To have had the vision—the liberality, to have turned his house and fortune over to the project he had named Ebb-Tide was surely a most wonderful act.

They moved from bed to bed. These patients were the terminally ill, some of them too weak to sit up in greeting. But in all their eyes, was real gratitude to Peter Bagshaw. One man called to him in a quiet voice.

'Peter.'

'Yes, Tommie?'

'I don't think I have much longer. Can you arrange for me to see a minister fairly soon? I know the vicar calls———-and he is a great guy——-but———-?' He looked expressively at Peter, who stared at him, dark winged eyebrows caught together in thought.

'I know of a man whom I think would provide the comfort and strength you need. He lives in London——-but I believe he will come here, if I ask him to.' He stroked one of Tommie's hands. 'Are you in much pain, Tommie?'

'Well——-some. It's not that———-it's just an ache inside my soul, if you like. My life has been such a mess. Good, middle class home——-bored——-ran away at fifteen. Got caught up in club-land——-and you know what that means! When I realised why the men I first looked on as benefactors, had provided me with home and new clothes, I was sick———-furious. I felt degraded. But I decided to use the system——-get what I wanted out of life in that way.' He stopped talking and Peter thought he was going to sleep, but the young man with once good looking features, roused himself. 'I ended up with a burning hatred against society. I stole——-was caught. Borstal——-ran away. Back again———-twice, for I re-offended. Started drinking when I got out——-and———-well it all went from bad to worse—prison. I guess I must have been HIV positive before I even ended up in Brixton. I remember being ill there. It wasn't until I was out though, and started to get repeated illnesses, that AIDS was diagnosed.'

'Do you want me to get I touch with your family, Tommie?'

'Wouldn't do any good. They shut their door on me, when I first got in trouble. When the doctors told me I had AIDS, I was stunned——-even after the counselling you get. I felt very fright-

ened and alone. So I rang my Mum——told her. I was crying.'
He swallowed. Then he stared into Peter's dark eyes. 'She put the
phone down on me,' he said.

'I'm sorry——more sorry than I can say.' Leopold as well as
Peter had damp eyes at the anguish in the man's voice.' Look,
Michael Howard is a wonderful pastor, Tommie. I'm sure he will
be with you tomorrow. In the meanwhile, just remember you are
with friends. The doctors and nurses here are good. It's not just
a job with them. They especially wanted to come here. The scientists too are hard at work to find a cure. Maybe it won't come in
time for you or me, Tommie——but sooner or later, they will
come up with an answer to AIDS.'

'I know. I can only be more grateful than I can say, that you
looked in on that TV programme—-and acted as you did. Now at
the very least, all of here can exist—-and when the time comes—
-die, with some dignity. Not to have to feel a pariah anymore.'

'Don't exhaust yourself by talking more just now, Tommie.'

Before they left the hospital wing, Peter excused himself to
Leopold, while he went to telephone from the sister's office.
When he came back, he was smiling.

'I have just spoken with Michael. He's on his way. He also said
to look in the new chapel——said Hermione would show me
where it is!'

Later, at lunch, Peter chided his mother for not having told him
of her secret. She should have let him help her! But he admitted
to being delighted with the chapel, its simplicity——and the
beautiful window, showing Jesus parable of the Good Samaritan.

'But how did you get Michael Howard to part with your mother's painting of the Christ, that meant so much to him and the
congregation?'

'I promise you I didn't ask for it! Would never have dreamed of
such a thing! I certainly did tell him about the chapel though—-
and its purpose. The idea to have the painting hung in the chapel,
was entirely Michael's own.'

When evening fell, a battered Citroen drove up Garnford's broad driveway, and Michael Howard stepped out. He was not alone. His wife Sue and their two year old son Mark, and his baby brother Martin, all appeared on the threshold, as Harrington sent one of the maids for Peter.

'Peter! After we spoke on the phone, I prayed. Then I spoke with Sue, for the decision I had taken involved her co-operation. Peter, God has laid it on my heart, to come here and work with you. I have already asked my young American colleague, who was staying with us for a few days, to take over Horeb. I called an emergency meeting of the elders and asked them to pray with me over my decision—-its rightness. It was unanimously agreed that I should come here, and Pastor Jeremy Fry could take my place with them'

'Why, Michael—-that is more than I would have dared to hope for! You are so very welcome! I will have rooms prepared for you. All the bungalows are in use——but if you don't mind living in the West wing with the family? The little boys will be wonderful company for Tristam—-and Rosamund will be delighted to have you here, Sue! Ah——here she is!' He watched as his wife cried out in amazement, at the sight of the little family, as her arms went out to Sue.

'Rosamund——-your Mother's garden—-don't worry about it! Jeremy says that he likes gardening. We have let him have use of the flat, whilst we are here and I promise you he will look after everything.' She drew back from Rosamund, looking at her friend's face, to see whether she minded about the change of tenant in Sylvia's flat. But Rosamund didn't. What did such inconsequential things matter now! The important——indeed amazing thing was, that Michael and Sue were here, and wanted to stay and their support would mean so much.

Tommie Leydon died two days later. When he died, he was at peace——-a peace he hadn't found until now, in all his tragic young life. Peter never knew what had passed between Michael Howard and Tommie—-but when he last saw him alive, the young man had whispered through cracked lips, that all fear of death had left him. He knew that Christ had forgiven him.

Winter gave way to spring. The orchard was a froth of pink and white blossom, and the flowerbeds were bright with tulips and daffodils. Peter and Rosamund started to plan a trip to Europe. Then Peter's health gave way again. He had a severe throat infection, complicated by nausea and stomach pains.

When June came, he was feeling much better, but had lost a considerable amount of weight. Again he planned to get away with Rosamund and this time they found themselves on the plane for Austria. Ernst was waiting for them at the airport, with Svetlana. Many recognised the two famous musicians as they were clasped in each other arms and a small crowd formed. But Ernst soon had them all in his Mercedes and before long, they were in his quaint old house, its style and furnishings still reminiscent of the days, when Ernst's favourite musician, Mozart, had briefly stayed in it. Peter knew that one of the bones of contention between Ernst and Svetlana in the early days of their marriage had been that he refused to allow her to refurnish the house in a more modern style. But Ernst had been right. It might have ruined the very special atmosphere the house possessed.

Svetlana cooked for them herself and they realised that she had another accomplishment besides that of musician and teacher. But Peter did scant justice to the delicious smoked fish dish that she set before them and merely toyed with the sweet that Rosamund ate with such obvious enjoyment. Tristam looked at the grown-ups, from a face smothered in chocolate and cream.

'Kleiner Schingel ——-I think you liked this pudding,' laughed Ernst, as Rosamund started to mop her son's face with a napkin

'Rosamund—-would you allow me to look after Tristam, whilst the two of you enjoy exploring Vienna? What about getting away from the city for a few days. You could perhaps visit the ice caves at Werfen? No——that might be too energetic———but the countryside is so very beautiful at this time of the year!'

'Are you sure you could manage, Svetlana?' Rosamund looked at her doubtfully. 'He can be quite a handful, you know!' But she allowed the older woman to persuade her. Little Tristam she would always have with her——but Peter? She glanced at him, as they lay together in the bog double bed that night. Strangely the dim light from the rose shaded, bedside lamps, emphasised the dark hollows around his eyes, rather than softening them, throwing his eagle nose into relief against the structure of his high cheekbones. She realised that Peter had aged greatly in appearance from the vital figure she had married—was it only slightly less than two years ago? Her thoughts drifted back to their wedding night———as he had come into their bedroom in his short burgundy robe, which had soon fallen on the carpet in front of the fire, together with her filmy negligee. How amazing the heights of passion and tenderness of their first lovemaking, that wonderful night, in which Tristam was conceived. Now the little boy slept beside their bed, in a cot Svetlana had especially bought for him——and his father, exhausted after the journey, was already closing his eyes in sleep. She sighed. Only a year ago, much longer journeys would have troubled him not in the slightest!

They took Svetlana's advice and left Tristam with her, whilst they spent a few precious days in a tiny Alpine village, near St Johanne. The mountains soaring majestically heavenwards, would have dwarfed the mysterious peaks of Skye and the wild flowers, honey sweet, were fragrant beneath their feet. Yes, lovely as it all was——the sound of the soft wind soughing through the grasses, the clinking tinkle of cowbells about the necks of busily munching cows——the sheer extravagant beauty of the vista stretching out before them, of forest, mountains, rushing streams and lush valleys, nevertheless something was missing. That something was the matchless energy Peter had once enjoyed. Now, walking had to be at a sedate pace, so as not to tire him, any real climbing, right out of the question. But at least, they were alone together and this brought its own joy. But as it was, such happiness was tempered with the knowledge, only partially submerged in their minds, that soon, even quiet holidays like this, would, be a thing of the past.

'In a way, Rosamund was almost glad when they returned to Vienna. In the evening, when little Tristam was safely tucked in bed, Ernst played the piano—-Liszt, Chopin——and many of his own compositions. They had brought their violins with them, but Peter seemed content to listen to Ernst, or Rosamund and Svetlana playing together, rather than participating himself. One night, she started to play the slow movement from the Rose Concerto, when Peter had sworn softly and walked out of the room. Startled, she put her violin down on the sofa, to run after him.

'I'm sorry, Rosamund! I know it's crazy——but I cannot bear to listen to that concerto anymore. Please——just promise me—-that you won't attempt to play it again in my hearing!' His eyes were wild and hastily Rosamund whispered her compliance.

'Later that night, as they lay in bed together, she asked him a question.

'Peter——-have you really forgiven Lois Challoner? Do you still harbour anger towards her? Because if you do——then you have to let go of it, Peter, hard though that may be!'

'That woman robbed me of life—-of love——-of you! For its not the same now, is it? No——don't pretend Rosamund. You are tied to a sick man, who cannot make love to you properly—-who can't dance with you——and whom people look at with a sort of morbid pity!' He pushed his face into the pillow and to her dismay, Rosamund knew that he was weeping. Then firmly, tenderly, she pulled his shoulders around, making him face her. His cheeks were wet with tears and choking sobs shook his thin frame. Her lips sought his, clung to them, as their tears mingled.

'Darling——darling Peter,' she whispered, as he became

calmer. 'Of course your illness has brought changes—-but it has also deepened the love we bear each other, surely you realise that? Real love lies in the blending of two spirits, not merely the body's short lived rapture of passion's climax. Yes——the early days of our marriage were magic, and of course we miss certain things. It would be a lie to pretend otherwise! But the very real love we have for each other now, is immeasurably stronger, than the glitter of first romance.'

'But——I don't want to die—-to leave you, Rosamund! I love you—-so very, very much. And that little boy in the cot! I can't tell you what he means to me.' As though sensing his father's distress, Tristam stirred and gave a faint cry. Instantly Peter slipped out of bed and covered the little boy up, stroking his silky hair, until the soft breathing announced him sleeping again. As he returned to bed, Peter seemed more relaxed. His arms went out as he folded Rosamund to him.

'Rosamund——-I know what you said about Lois is true. I have been nurturing a hatred of her, deep in my soul all along. But it's wrong. Will you pray with me——that I may be able to let go of it—-to truly forgive.' She took his hands—-and that whispered prayer of theirs ascended to the throne of heaven itself.

The next day, Peter asked Rosamund to take Tristam out for a walk with Svetlana, as he wanted to talk alone with Ernst. He seemed much happier and satisfied that all was well, she set out to look at the shops with Svetlana. Both of them were wore flowered silk dresses, that fluttered in the warm breeze and Tristam in his push chair, looked adorable in a little sailor suit, with a white hat to protect his head from the hot sunshine. It was a marvellous morning. They made a few purchases and then sat and sipped their coffee at a pavement café, while they tucked in to one of the delicious pastries for which Vienna was so deservedly famous.

'Oh, Rosamund——what am I thinking of. I forgot to tell you, that I had a telephone call from Leopold this morning. He's in hospital.'

'What?' Rosamund almost let her cup slip and spilt coffee in her saucer.

'Oh——don't worry. He's not badly hurt. But it seems he got caught up in the unrest in Jerusalem. Some Palestinian lads were throwing stones. Things got nasty and many were injured. Leopold was concussed when a stone was thrown at him from the top of a wall. It caught him on the back of the head——and he was apparently trampled as he fell, in people's panic to get out of the way of the youngsters causing the trouble. He is being kept in for a couple of days——otherwise he had intended flying to Vienna to meet up with you and Peter. I told him you were leaving for England tomorrow and he said to give you both his love and best wishes, and a kiss for Tristam.' She watched Rosamund shrewdly, for the girl had paled at first. Now Rosamund seemed to have recovered her aplomb.

'Oh——poor Leopold! So long as he is not badly injured,' she said lightly. 'Is he finally going to settle in Israel, do you know?'

'He is not sure. He loves it there——but he loves his music too. He is ambitious and if he applies himself, probably has an exciting future in front of him. I must admit to being very fond of that young man.'

'I like him too. At first, I was put off by his brashness, but when you get past that, to the real person beneath, you realise that he has an amazing depth to his character.' They rose, paid the waiter, wiped Tristam's sticky face and made their way home.

That night, to Rosamund's surprise and delight, Peter picked up his violin and started to play.

'Rosamund——would you like to play the duet from the Rose Concerto with me,' he asked softly? Their eyes met and hers were damp as she nodded mutely. Then, for the first time since they had played it together in the States, the strings of their violins poured out Peter's beautifully moving theme. As the notes quivered on the air, they lifted up with them, the last of the anger that had been eating away at Peter's soul. That night, they expressed their love for each other and Rosamund found her body responding to his touch with throbbing passion. Long after she had cried out, and fallen happily asleep, Peter lay thinking. Then with a tired sigh, he fell asleep also.

In late August, they had a surprise visitor. It was Jack MacLeod. Peter, who was recovering from another bout of illness, got swiftly to his feet, as Harrington brought their guest in. If Jack was shocked at the change in Peter's appearance, he certainly allowed no sign of it to show in his expressive blue eyes, but went straight to the younger man and drew him close in a firm embrace.

'Peter——it's good to see you,' he said as he released him. 'I rang Rosamund last week and mentioned that I might be attending a minister's meeting in London——and she said to be sure to come and see you both. Where is she——and that bonny wee son of yours?'

'Oh, Jack——Jack! I can't believe you are really here! How long can you stay? Harrington——would you please send for Rosamund and Tristam! I think they are with Sue and her two rascals in the kiddies play area.' Harrington turned to go. But Peter changed his mind. 'No——wait, Harrington. What am I thinking of! We must offer Jack some coffee first, after his journey——and then I will walk to find Rosamund with him.'

Are you strong enough, sir,' asked Harrington in slight concern?

'Of course! Jack——we'll have that coffee——and lunch will be in less than an hour, unless you are starving, in which case——'

'Peter——I'm not hungry at the moment. I had a sandwich on the motorway, but coffee now——certainly that would be fine.' The minister's bright blue eyes examined Peter's face, seeing behind the ravages of his illness, to the man within.

?How is it with you then, Peter man?'

'Physically——I've been feeling foul! I've been experiencing one bout of illness after another. Walter Borthwick says the disease has progressed much faster in me than would be expected. He gives me another few months.' There was no bitterness in Peter's voice, as he said this, only a quiet acceptance.

'I'm deeply sorry to hear that,' said Jack sympathetically.

'Don't be, my friend—-for I am not. You see I would prefer to get it all over with, sooner rather than later, for Rosamund's sake. It's not easy for her you know, even though she is unbelievably brave—-the most tremendous support a man could have.' The maid brought coffee and as they drank it, Peter asked after Mary.

'She is well and sends all her love to you. You have no idea how often we speak of you and of Rosamund. Mary plays that recording you sent us of your Golden Concerto just about every day. It's a beautiful thing, Peter——and I feel very privileged to remember that it was in our house, that you composed most of it. Such a pity it was, that we couldn't get away last Christmas to hear you play it in person at the Albert Hall. But as I told you in my letter, Iain Forbes, the local young minister wanted to visit his folk on the Isle of Lewis——and so I took over his duties for him.'

Rosamund took one look at Jack and dropped Tristam gently to the ground in the sandpit, as she ran towards him, to be grasped in a bear hug.

'Jack! Jack MacLeod! Oh, how wonderful! Have you just arrived? I'm so glad you were able to come! Is Mary with you?' She plied him with one question after another, barely waiting for answers. Then she turned and called Sue Howard to her. The pastor's wife was pushing little Mark on the swing, whilst baby Martin squawked with laughter, as he bounced up and down on a large, inflatable red and yellow mattress. She lifted Mark down and came across to meet Rosamund's visitor, wondering at her friend's excitement.

'Sue——do you remember my telling you of our wonderful minister friend from Skye? Well——here he is——Jack MacLeod!'

Sue's pretty face broke into a smile, as she extended her hand.

'Jack——-Rosamund and Peter have told me so much about you——and my husband Michael has been longing to meet you. Oh look———-here he comes!' She beckoned to Michael, who was walking in the company of Derek Rogers. He excused himself to the tall, thin, black man, who waved a greeting to Peter and Rosamund and walked on, as Michael came over to the little group in the playground.

'Why Peter——-you're out! Are you feeling better then?'

'Bit weak——-but otherwise not so bad! Michael———this is Jack MacLeod from Skye!' Peter indicated the silver haired Scotsman. Michael's eyes brightened in interest. He had heard so much about Jack and his wife Mary, experiencing a deep curiosity about the man, who had saved Peter's life, as well as leading him into commitment for Christ. As he looked into the older minister's eyes, Michael immediately sensed the warmth and love that flowed from the heart of this quiet man of God. There was instant sympathy between the two men. Peter and Rosamund looked at each other in comic dismay, as their visitor disappeared with Michael, who called that he wanted Jack to visit one of the new patients with him.

?Well——there goes our visitor,' laughed Peter, leaning against the swing frame for support, for he felt very fatigued, yet was extremely happy.

'Where's mother? I want her to meet Jack! She never did get to visit Skye, did she, Rosamund.' But Rosamund shook her head.

'Don't you remember, Peter——I told you that she had driven to London, to visit her hairdresser and to do some shopping. She will probably be back tomorrow, so Jack can meet her then. I know they will like each other.' She slipped an arm around Peter's waist. One of his arms rested lightly on her shoulders, as they walked slowly back to the house.

'I was speaking with Glen Summers this morning. He tells me, that he feels his research team are getting near to a breakthrough——although, mind you, he said something similar last month,' shrugged Peter, as he stopped for breath.

'Dearest Peter—-it has to come eventually. Let's pray that it's———' Her voice trailed off uncertainly, for she had been going to add, in time for Peter. But he understood her unspoken words and squeezed her hand encouragingly. Then he glanced back, to where Tristam was playing with Martin in the sandpit, under the watchful eyes of Sue and the nursery nurse. Rosamund knew that his longing eyes were seeking out the years ahead, wistfully trying to envisage his son as a schoolboy——-a teenager——-a man.

'Sir Peter——-a Mr Christopher Wade has arrived and is asking to speak with you. He's in the blue drawing room.' Harrington bowed. With an exclamation of surprise, Peter excused himself to Rosamund and mounted the stairs, his face deeply curious.

'Chris——Chris Wade?' Peter looked at the young man standing before him in dismay. He would not have recognised the cellist, had Harrington not given him his visitor's name. It was to Chris Wade that he owed his release from Lois Challoner's earlier attempts to ensnare him into a disastrous marriage. He remembered now, as he looked at Chris, how the man had admitted to spending a night in Lois arms——and as he looked, Peter realised in dismay, why the sad faced musician looked so gaunt and thin.

'Yes—-it's me. I wondered———if perhaps——-you might find room for one more guest at Ebb-Tide?' He looked down at the suitcase at his feet, 'I remembered that you once said, that if you could ever help me——-.'

His voice faltered miserably.

'Lois?'

'Yes, Peter——-Lois!' He attempted a smile.

Peter's arms enfolded him then, as anger against the dead woman almost erupted in his heart again. But he reminded himself that he had forgiven her, and after a difficult moment was able to resume that forgiveness and pity for the woman who had cost him so dear. Now, as he looked at the man he had just released from his embrace, that pity extended to him also.

'I'm more sorry than I can say, Chris. Yes——come and welcome. I will sort out accommodation for you.' The tired smile on his new guest's face smote him with its tale of tragedy. This young American was a fine cellist——should have had a brilliant career ahead of him. He saw Chris examining his own appearance, his eyes betraying how shocked he was at Peter's own changed looks.

'If only our paths had never crossed that of Lois Challoner,' exclaimed Peter in frustration.

'I know Peter,' said Chris gently. 'But don't lets forget—— someone else gave it to her. I think it is only charitable to assume that she had no idea of her condition, when she tried to trap you into marriage and slept with me. Of course——she obviously did know, by the time she attacked you. Perhaps it was the knowledge that she would lose the beauty of which she was so proud, that deranged her mind. I don't like to think that she was completely evil——just sick——frightened, and angry at fate.'

'She was also heavily involved in the occult, according to police reports,' said Peter. 'But holding a grudge against her, can do no good to either of us, can it Chris. I must admit that for a time, I harboured a terrible anger against her in my heart. Then I prayed——just laid it before Jesus——and it completely drained away.'

'You are lucky that you have a faith to sustain you,' said Chris Wade. 'I have none! I'm not angry at Lois though——just very scared.'

'Don't be. Come——I want you to meet my wife Rosamund. And then, I also want to introduce you to two very special men who are at Garnford just now.' He led him to his wife and asked Harrington to let Jack MacLeod and Michael Howard know that they were wanted, when they were free

In the meanwhile, another life was being touched, by the comfort and caring, loving protection offered at Garnford.

CHAPTER SEVENTEEN

The French hairdresser applied the tint to Hermione's hair, his deft movements hardly noticed by her, as her racing thoughts returned again and again to Peter. Why had this horror come into all their lives, just when at last they were so wonderfully happy! Pictures stole into her mind, of Peter and Rosamund on their wedding day—-her son kissing his lovely bride. Then she remembered that first performance of the Rose Concerto, when flushed with triumph, he had accepted the plaudits of the audience, with the girl he loved so dearly, at his side. The hairdresser held a mirror for her to admire his work, and startled, she realised that two hours had passed.

Hermione stepped out of the salon, secure in the knowledge, that as far as her external appearance went, she was looking her elegant best. As her dainty high heeled shoes tapped their way along the Knightsbridge pavement, the skirts of her finely pleated pink and grey silk suit swirling in the breeze, she gave the appearance of any other wealthy, still youthful looking matron, enjoying a leisurely saunter around Brompton road's exclusive shops. But had you looked beyond the perfection of beautifully styled golden hair and discretely applied make-up enhancing her features—-you would have seen shadows barely concealed around the deep blue eyes and a hint of sadness about the softly curved lips.

She paused outside her favourite jewellers, yet—-as her gaze swept over the glittering gemstones, her thoughts were far away. A voice broke her reverie.

'Hermione———but this is incredible!' Startled, she looked at the figure coming towards her from the shop's doorway, bowed out by the uniformed doorman. It couldn't be——but it was—— Rodrigo Mendes!

'Rodrigo. What a lovely surprise! I didn't know that you were over here. When did you arrive?' She held out her hand as she spoke and he clasped it warmly.

'Why——only this morning——and believe it or not, my visit was expressly to see you, Hermione.' He released her hand and offered his arm, his dark Spanish eyes shining with pleasure. Several passers by turned their heads, as they recognised the famous conductor, escorting his charming companion.

'Well——what was so urgent that you had to come to London, seeking me?' She turned her blue eyes on him questioningly. 'If its to ask if Peter is now fit enough to undertake the tour which was cancelled——then alas, the answer is no. Indeed I fear that it may never take place now. He is far from well, Rodrigo.' Her voice trembled slightly as she spoke and his arm pressed hers in sympathy.

'I am deeply sorry to hear this, Hermione. But although of course, wanting to see Peter and to inquire into the state of his health——this was not the main reason for my coming to Britain this time.'

'Then——what,' she demanded, perplexed?

'That I prefer to tell you in a more private place,' he said exasperatingly. Hermione decided to invite him to her apartment, still convinced that his advent was in some way connected with Peter's music and determined that he should put no pressure on her son to resume his career, when his strength seemed to be failing day by day.

'Can I offer you coffee——something to eat? I have chicken in the fridge and ham. We could have a salad?' He shook his head.

'Later, Hermione, I will take you out to lunch. I certainly wouldn't mind a brandy though.' She went to the cocktail cabinet and poured him one and a sherry for herself. He set his lips to the glass and put it aside, as he seated himself next to her on the sofa.

'Hermione——I know how sick Peter is, because I ring dear old Harrington almost daily and also talk with Charles Sylvester.

I first met Charles in San Francisco you know, at Peter's hospital there. Indeed I was probably the first person to learn that in all probability, my dearest friend had been infected with the AIDS virus.'

'But――-you never said anything!' She looked at him in shocked surprise.

'I gave my word to Charles――and also to Peter. By the time you heard the distressing news, it had been made public knowledge by Peter himself. Do not be angry with me, querissima.' The endearment slipped out softly and she barely noticed it.

'Well, its water under the bridge now, Rodrigo. Ernst behaved in exactly the same way――and I honour you both as loyal friends to Peter. So then――what is it that has brought you here to London?'

'This,' he said simply and withdrew a small packet from his jacket pocket. He handed it to her. She undid the wrapping and found that it contained a ring box. Surprised, she opened it――and found herself staring at a magnificent sapphire. The stone was beautifully mounted and surrounded by diamonds. She gasped.

'This is for me, Rodrigo――but, why? What have I done to deserve such a gift?' She made to try it on the forth finger of her right hand――but Rodrigo stretched out his hand and gently took it from her. He took her left hand in his.

'No――Hermione, mi querida――on this hand!' Before she could stop him, he had slipped it on her engagement finger, which still bore her late husband's wedding ring. 'Hermione, what I am going to say now, was meant to have been said two years ago, but I always lacked the courage. My dear, I have loved you for many years――but never, never found the words to tell you this. Then two years back, when Peter married Rosamund, I knew you would be able to relax as a mother, because he had embarked on a new marriage and such a happy one. You have given your whole life over to Peter, haven't you? Shut out any thought of a personal life for yourself, beyond the superficial round of social engagements.'

'But——I've been happy,' she murmured defensively. 'Oh——Rodrigo——you honour me with this proposal——but its quite out of the question. I am older than you, for one thing——and certainly much too old to think of getting remarried. I'm in my fifties.'

'I know exactly how old you are, Hermione and yes, I am five years younger. But at our age, what do a few years matter one way or the other!' He looked at her, registering one fact——she had not said that she did not love him. Suddenly he pulled her gently into his arms and his lips moved over hers. At first she resisted almost violently——then, she seemed to relax——and Hermione found herself returning his kisses, with a passion she had not known herself capable of. Breathlessly she pulled away.

'This is ridiculous. Apart from anything else, Rodrigo——how can we possibly consider marriage, when my son is so desperately ill.' She looked at him with eyes that were shimmering with tears. 'Walter Borthwick says that Peter only has a few more months. Every time he succumbs to a new bout of illness, he becomes immeasurably weaker. All my thoughts are of him——do you understand?' He drew her close again.

'Yes, my darling——I understand so much better than you realise. I know what you have been going through——the terrible strain——the hurt to the heart——and yes, I know what the outcome must be, short of a miracle. But it is because of it, that I want you to have my support as a husband. More than this too——I want Peter, to know that his mother will be loved and cared for in a very special way, by someone whom he himself names dear friend. Surely you see, Hermione, that it will give Peter much pleasure to know that we have pledged ourselves together.'

She sat looking at him. Yes, she had admired this man for many years. He was extremely good looking and most wonderfully talented. But it was more than this. Between them, unacknowledged until now, had been that very special chemistry between one particular man and woman that leaps every boundary.

'Say that you will marry me,' he whispered authoritatively.

'But——Rosamund and little Tristam, are going to need me—
-so very much, and perhaps soon!'

'You will always be ready to stand by them, whenever they
need you—and so will I! Eventually we will make our home in
Spain, Hermione. I have a villa in the shadow of that beautiful
mountain outside Marbella—La Concha! Around you there will
be fountains playing——gardens ablaze with flowers——and less
than a mile away, the Mediterranean glitters bright blue. An old
goatherd goes past every morning with his flock, and——"!' She
placed a hand over his lips.

'Rodrigo! How can I ever leave England——or Garnford? I
know—-have made myself face the fact——that Peter may not be
with us for much longer. But someone will have to look after
Garnford——and I don't know if it is right to expect Rosamund
to do this. Because of all the sick people living there, she will
never be able to let go of——-oh——-you know what I am trying to say!'

'I do, Hermione. Garnford will always be there if you want to
return to see it—-but quite honestly querida, I think it would be
the best thing in the world, for both you and Rosamund, eventually to walk in the sunshine again.'

'I must think about it, Rodrigo.'

'No, Hermione——actions not thoughts are what are needed
now. I ask that you honour me by wearing my ring as pledge.
Agreed?' For answer, her hands stole up, and slipped around his
neck, one hand stroking his dark waving hair.

'Agreed—-Rodrigo.'

For a minute, Rosamund and Peter were speechless, as
Hermione displayed the beautiful sapphire, sparkling on her finger. Their eyes expressed bewilderment until Rodrigo spoke.

'My dearest, young friends——soon indeed to be my children,
try to understand, for without your love and understanding, our
plans will be meaningless. In this world of ours, there is always a

mixture of joy and sorrow——and perhaps sometimes, when there is an imbalance, we can no longer see one for the other. Peter—- my dearest, dearest friend——and Rosamund, you whom I have fondly watched grow from shy little girl into delightful young woman! Please believe me when I say that the two of you mean more to me, than anyone else in the whole world——apart that is, from the wonderful woman standing at my side, who has given of herself unstintingly, all of her adult life. Does she now not deserve your utmost love, when only at my strong insistence, has she agreed to become engaged to me.' His words faltered to a stop, his dark eyes pleading for acceptance. It was Peter who spoke first. His eyes softened and he walked mutely up to his mother and drew her gently into his arms.

'My darling,' he said huskily——-'All my life, you have loved and cared for me——helped me as a youngster, to embark on my career as a musician, always guiding and encouraging. When Natasha died, it was you who helped me to keep my sense of per- spective, when I so nearly lot it. Then——just look at the way you took Rosamund into your heart. She was your daughter, long before we were married. Yes, and now——since I have been ill, you have given your strength to ease our aching hearts.' He paused and pulled Rodrigo close to them. 'So mother, all I can say is——that it is the most wonderful news, that you and this dear friend are to get married——and I know Rosamund agrees with me!' He looked over his shoulder to Rosamund appealingly. She ran forward with a soft cry, and threw her arms around Hermione.

''I only ask one thing,' said Peter suddenly. 'I want to see you married——while I am still here to give the bride away!'

'Excuse me,' asked a well known lilting voice——'But do I gath- er that congratulations are in order?' It was Jack MacLeod. Everyone started to talk at once, trying to explain to him. That night Garnford resounded to music. The news sped around the estate and soon doctors, nurses, research workers and patients joined with the staff in offering congratulations to Hermione, whose graciousness and patient kindness had won all their hearts.

So it was, that in late September, a wedding was performed in the little chapel at Garnford. Michael Howard conducted the touchingly simple little ceremony.

Hermione wore a gorgeous pale pink dress, with soft, floating panels. Her hat was trimmed with tiny roses and seed pearls, whilst about her neck she wore Peter and Rosamund's gift, a necklace of gleaming pearls, with intricate clasp. Rodrigo's face was working with emotion, as he proudly slipped the heavy gold ring on his bride's finger, as Michael pronounced them as man and wife. The party that followed in the great hall, was attended by all who were fit enough to be present——and guests of honour were Ernst and Svetlana. A telegram was read from Leopold, still in Israel. Jack and Mary had flown down from Skye for the occasion and were taking Rodrigo and Hermione back with them, to spend their honeymoon at Braes. This had been Rodrigo's idea. He had long wanted to see the place where Peter had composed his haunting Golden Concerto and although Jack warned them about the midges, they were determined to go adventuring on Peter's magical island.

That night, after Hermione and Rodrigo had departed, Rosamund suddenly felt terribly alone. For a while, there had been all the excitement of planning the wedding, to occupy her. Now, as she saw Peter sink listlessly into a chair, reality caught up with her again.

'How are you feeling, Peter?'

'Very content——wasn't it a wonderful wedding, darling!' He smiled, but the tiredness in his eyes, tore at her heart. 'Mother looked radiant, didn't she——and Rodrigo, well, very debonair! Do you know, it's the first time, I have ever seen Rodrigo less than in command of the situation.' He gave a faint chuckle. 'Come here, Rosamund——sit on the arm of my chair, I want to speak with you.'

'Yes, darling?' She seated herself obediently. Once, he would have pulled her into his lap, she reflected.

''Rosamund—-there are some few months until Christmas. We both know that it may be my last one————-no————don't get upset, but listen. Last Christmas, I played the Golden Concerto at the Albert Hall, while you listened to me. This year, I very much want to have you play my part, whilst I listen for a change. But so as not to let you have everything your way wife——I would like, if I am fit enough, to play the Rose Concerto with you, on the same bill! Well——what do you say? When Rodrigo's feet touch the ground again after his honeymoon, would you be prepared to start working towards such a concert?' His eyes were shining in anticipation and in spite of her apprehension of the strain that such a concert would put upon his health, Rosamund found herself agreeing. It was as though a flame had been rekindled.

'Do you feel like coming into the music room now——to try one of the solo movements of the Last Concerto?'

'Oh, Peter—-I wish you wouldn't call it that!'

'Why not? After all——I have always felt that the Golden Concerto sounded a trifle flamboyant as a title.' Then his face saddened as he said softly. 'You know, Rosamund——it will probably end up being called the Last Concerto! But after all, its whether a work can really move people that matters—-not what its called.'

But two days later, Peter Bagshaw lay in the hospital wing, in high fever. He had strange aches in his abdomen and groin——and his neck was stiff and swollen and every so often, he retched painfully. Charles Sylvester assured Rosamund that this illness would run its course as the others had, but that Peter might be considerably weakened by it.

'Michael——Peter's worse. Will you come?' Rosamund tapped at Michael and Sue's bedroom door and when they opened and saw her white face, both of them pulled their dressing gowns on and followed her. Peter had screens around his bed and Walter

Borthwick bent over him.

'How is he, Walter,' asked Michael?'

'Very weak———but he's holding on,' Walter replied. 'He is asking for you. Perhaps you would like to speak with him alone?' The doctor gently took Rosamund's arm. She was weeping. Sue slipped her arms about her, as they led her aside.

'Can you hear me, Peter?'

'Michael?'

Yes, my friend. Have you much pain?'

'Not really———but I keep feeling as though my life is on a sort of thread———and as though that thread is stretched and may snap.' He was quiet for a moment, then———'Michael—-I want you to pray with me.'

'Of course, Peter.'

'No, listen———there is something special, I want you to pray about. Before the thread finally snaps———-I want one more thing out of life, for Rosamund's sake. I want it very badly.' The whispered voice came between cracked lips. 'Will you pray———that I may regain enough strength, to play in one final concert at Christmas———with my wife?' His slate grey eyes stared from the dark sockets in his face, with a strange longing.

'Why———Peter. Of course I will pray with you for this. We will call it a prayer of faith. Just lay it before our gentle Saviour.' Michael knelt beside the bed, clasping one of Peter's hands between his. The words he spoke, as he laid Peter Bagshaw's petition before Jesus, were some of the loveliest, yet the simplest he had ever uttered.

'Lord———-You of your bounty gave wondrous gift of music, to your servant Peter. Please Lord, let him use that gift, to Your glory at Christmas, before his strings sweeten the choirs of heaven!' Other words he softly spoke. When he rose to his feet, Peter was sleeping———but with a look of utmost peace on his face. Michael pulled the screens aside and beckoned the others.

'Peter will be playing at that Christmas concert,' he stated with

quiet confidence. Walter looked at him. Did the pastor have so little understanding of the seriousness of Peter's condition? Then he
turned to his patient——looked down at him in surprise. The
laboured breathing was now soft and even. He rested a gentle
hand on Peter's forehead——it was cool. He gave an exclamation
of amazement.

'Why——the fever's left him! I do not understand it. I have
never seen such an amazing recovery!'

When the honeymoon couple returned, it was to hear that
Peter had been ill, but was now tremendously improved. Rodrigo
smiled his wonder at Hermione, that Peter wanted to work on a
Christmas concert. But Hermione looked troubled. She feared
the consequences the strain might have on him. But he looked so
happy, as did Rosamund.

The next weeks passed. October's golden leaves were shredded
bronze by November. Still the research team worked round the
clock, liasing with other similar work groups around the world.
Always they seemed on the verge of success, but a feeling of sadness spread across the little community, as the news leaked out,
that Joan had died. Little Bonny who was less than a year old and
HIV positive was now motherless. But not for long! Michael and
Sue Howard took a very serious decision. They were to adopt the
baby girl. They knew the future difficulties——but more important than these, was the fact that the little fair-haired child needed love and parents. Sue spoke with the officials and social workers, filling in forms and accepting that there would be a fairly long
period before Bonny would eventually become one of their family legally, there was no doubt in anyone's mind, that everything
would go through smoothly. In the meanwhile, they were to be
classified as the child's foster parents.

Andrew seemed to be much improved, after his own severe illness, to the extent that he wanted to go to Ireland for a few days,
with his wife. As for Derek the amiable black man kept everyone's
spirits up with his cheerful good humour, even though he too

sometimes had his difficult days. He had made friends with a new patient, Abdul Achmed, trying to break down the suspicious attitude of the new arrival, who eventually warmed to Derek's overtures. Similarly, all other patients, although respecting each other's privacy, nevertheless were totally supportive of each other and the deeply caring response to each other's needs made the work of the medical staff considerably easier.

Bu December, Peter and Rosamund were back in London. Peter had experienced one set back———-sickness and fever that had lasted for two days, but without leaving him with the usual severe weakness, that had attended other bouts. Now, as he worked with the orchestra again, Peter seemed almost his old self. True he was painfully thin———-but he seemed possessed of boundless energy. Rodrigo expressed himself absolutely amazed, as he listened to Rosamund and Peter, practising the slow movement of the Rose Concerto together. It was just like the old days———-except now, there seemed to be an added tenderness in the rendering that was touching in the extreme.

Rosamund had practised the Golden Concerto time and time again, under Peter's watchful eyes. He was a much sterner taskmaster than Rodrigo. But as she listened to him reminding her, of the golden moonlight playing on the midnight waters of Skye, she captured the magic he sought———-and her playing reflected the power and poignancy of his own.

Hermione was wearing a white silk gown, sewn with hundreds of golden sequins and wore Peter's pearl necklace. She looked regal and serene. Rosamund also wore white, a plain, simple dress, such as she had worn on the first occasion when she had performed at the Albert Hall. At her neck hung Peter's first gift——- the jade tear pendant. Her fair hair gleamed like silk in the footlights, as she stepped onto the stage at Peter's side. The hall was packed———-every seat taken and many standing, but just relieved to be there for what promised to be a most memorable concert.

All eyes were on the stage. Those who knew Sir Peter Bagshaw were shocked at his changed appearance. Rodrigo raised his baton——and the first beautiful movement of the Rose Concerto stole upon the air. Now it was not the emaciated countenance of the vital man, whose violin soared to such rising crescendo that mattered, nor the loveliness of the young girl at his side——but the sheer, throbbing, beauty of the music they created. Peter was playing as never before. People sat absolutely still in their seats, enchanted by the passion and heart tearing emotion of the work. Then again——in the third movement, came that extraordinarily beautiful duet, as together, Peter and Rosamund's fingers flew over the strings, as their bows moved faster than the eye cold follow, producing wildly lilting, soul searching chords. The rich texture of the work, the purity of expression held the audience spellbound——until its wild anguish gave way to the incandescent joy of the finale!

Peter lowered his violin and stared at Rosamund. The triumph in his eyes was such as she had seen there many times in the past——but only the two of them, knew how great this particular triumph had been——and at what great cost. Then——as the audience exploded into applause, Peter drew his wife gently into his arms and kissed her, while a sea of red roses flooded onto the stage.

'How are you feeling, Peter?' Rosamund looked at him with utmost tenderness, as he sat in the box, next to Hermione. The interval was almost over and she had to leave to make her own solo performance in the Golden Concerto. He was looking very pale, but his slate grey eyes glowed with a deep happiness.

'Darling, Rosamund——I'm fine. Thank you for tonight. Now——off you go! Play well, my heart's darling!' She bent and kissed him and smiled at Hermione, whose own eyes were damp with the tears she had shed, watching and listening to them playing together. Now it was time for Rosamund to go on alone.

Rodrigo lifted his baton——and the Golden Concerto commenced. Again the audience sat entranced, marvelling at the mastery of the young girl in the white dress, whose violin sobbed in muted inquiry, during the first movement. She glanced upwards at the box where Peter sat and smiled, before the second movement started. The orchestra under Rodrigo's powerful leading, poured such deeply moving melody upon the air, that even the hardest heart there softened. Then Rosamund's violin soared above all, tenderly imploring, now throbbing with mysterious power. As the second movement came to an end, Rosamund looked up to the box again. Had he been pleased with her? She thought it had gone well——? Where was Peter——Hermione? A cold hand of fear clutched her breast———for suddenly she knew, why Peter no longer smiled down at her. She felt frozen——wanted to scream——to run. Then Rodrigo lifted his baton, and discipline took over. She started to play almost automatically.

Then——it seemed to Rosamund—that another hand was placed over hers as she played, for never in her life before, had she managed to produce such exquisite tenderness——and as the finale brought its own gentle ebb tide——Rosamund and that other——played the last sobbing chord of Peter's **Last Concerto**.

The applause was deafening. Rosamund bowed and attempted to smile. Then someone approached Rodrigo, who gasped in dismay and came to set an arm about Rosamund.

'Rosamund——I have some bad news——!'

'I know it already,' she said simply——'Have know it for the whole of the last movement. Rodrigo——he helped me to play it!'

'Ladies and gentlemen,' said the official gravely, as the audience, suddenly aware that something was wrong, subsided into troubled silence. 'Ladies and gentlemen——I have some tragic news for you. During his last beautiful concerto, Maestro Peter Bagshaw passed away. Music has lost one of its finest sons. May we now salute a very brave man——and his even braver young wife.'

She stood in front of them, in her simple white dress, the jade tear clasped in her fingers, as there was a waive of subdued applause——and people started to leave, with the feeling of awkwardness the reality of death always brings. Rodrigo assisted Rosamund from the stage. Hermione came from the wings, face swollen with weeping and folded the girl in her arms.

'Rosamund——darling, it happened very quickly. His breathing became laboured, then he just murmured, very softly—-"Tell Rosamund I love her and always will." And then he said——"I'm ready, Lord—-thank you!" He sighed and seemed to fall asleep.' Hermione's eyes were full of compassion, as she held the girl to her.

'Oh, Hermione. His last wish was granted, wasn't it. He was on the stage there with me just now, helping me.' She broke down and Rodrigo lifted her up in his arms, and carried her out of the hall.

They brought him back to Garnford. Later, there was another short journey. Rosamund sat in the little crematorium, frozen faced. At her request only family and close friends were present——but every window niche was ablaze with red roses, every inch of the polished dark wood casket, that held all that was mortal of Peter Bagshaw, was covered with fragrant blossoms. Michael Howard walked to the front of the chapel, as Ernst, who was seated at the organ, started to play one of Peter's favourite hymns. Michael started to talk, telling all present of Peter's recent prayer of faith——that he should recover sufficiently to be able to play at a last concert, with his beloved wife at Christmas——and how that prayer had been so wonderfully answered! As she listened, the tears she had been holding back started to prick Rosamund's eyes. She only partially heard Michael's lovingly worded farewell to Peter. Then the casket disappeared from view, as Michael said——-

'My friends—— even now, Peter will be sharing his music with all the angels of heaven. Let us give thanks to God, who is the giver of all good gifts, that his servant Peter has left such a legacy of magnificent music, not only for us, but for future generations to enjoy!' As he spoke, a recording of the finale from Peter's Last Concerto throbbed hauntingly through the chapel. For a moment, as she closed her eyes, Rosamund seemed to feel the warmth of Peter's cheek against hers—-and heard a whisper——- 'Be strong, my heart's darling.'

Outside, in the crisp December air, Rosamund still had memory of his presence. Yes——there was this indescribable pain of parting——but she knew, one day this would heal——that life must go on——and that at home, a little boy, who looked so much like Peter, was waiting for her. Would he remember his father? He was after all, not quite two years old!

She bent to get into the car, when someone touched her arm lightly. She looked up from tear stained eyes and saw the handsome face of Leopold Heine. His own eyes were damp, as he took one of her hands.

'Rosamund—-my dear—there are no words I can say to help you in your loss, except that I grieve with you. Peter was the most wonderful man I have ever met—-and I feel privileged to have been able to call him friend.' He spoke humbly, his eyes sad.

'Thank you, Leopold. Peter is at peace now—-and happy, that I know for an absolute certainty. His music will live on—-and so also, will the work that has started at Garnford. I know that sooner or later, a cure will be found—-and that one day, people like Peter, will no longer have to face death from AIDS.'

Back at Garnford that night, as she walked about the bedroom she had shared with Peter for two and a half years. The loneliness—the emptiness of that room without him, seared her heart. She touched the pillow where his head had lain—-the little icon he had given her, which was on the table next to the bed. Also on that table, was the beautiful music box that Ernst had once given her. She opened it, absently. The music tinkled softly in the stillness of the room. She was about to close the lid again—-when she noticed the small leather bound book Ernst had placed in its recessed compartment. She lifted it out. She had thought that the words would be in German—-but they weren't. She began to read. All night long, Rosamund read those words, their tenderness and wisdom, bringing healing to her broken heart. To her amazement, she realised Ernst had spent the war years in a concentration camp. The record of his sufferings, and the nobility of spirit that had allowed him to forgive, shone through the finely written pages. She read—————————'When pain reaches black fingers, into the labyrinth of our minds, only God's lamp of love, can dispel the darkness.'

'Oh, Ernst——dear Uncle Ernst,' she whispered. 'Your words contain life's greatest truth.' Then she slipped into bed—-and slept.

Rosamund didn't want to leave Garnford, but Hermione and Rodrigo were mildly insistent. Harrington smiled at her reassuringly, as her luggage was lifted into the boot of the car.

'Don't worry about Garnford, my lady. When you return, you will find it running as smoothly as ever. One day—and of this I am sure—-Garnford will no longer be needed as a hospice, but return to being a home again, for you and little Sir Tristam——— and then, God willing, for his children.'

Rosamund hugged her little son in her arms, as she carried him into the plane. Spain was waiting—-a new life. Hermione and Rodrigo helped her to settle Tristam in his seat, his mother's arm protectively around him. Minutes later, the aircraft taxied down the runway for take off. As it lifted up into the sky, a man stood watching, as it disappeared into the clouds.

'One day————sweet Rosamund, you will take another journey,' murmured Leopold. 'When your grieving is over, you and I will take it together.' The plane disappeared from view, bearing Rosamund into the sunshine.

CONCLUSION

There in what had been Peter Bagshaw's study and after all these years, still seemed to bear lingering trace of his presence, the eyes of all were slightly damp at the conclusion of the story, as events had been related, first by one, then another of those involved. The extraordinary tale was absorbed with amazement and awed respect by both of the young men, who for the first time had heard it in its entirety. 'Mother——thank you for giving us the truth behind Garnford,' said Tristam softly. 'From now onwards, I will do all in my power, to help with the work being carried out here.

I will try to raise money through my music and——.'

'We will both raise what we can through concerts and the sale of CDs,' put in Uri. He glanced across at his brother. 'Trist! Perhaps we could arrange a series of concerts——jointly playing the 'Last Concerto'. Let it be known that the proceeds would all go to medical research, to help all those at Garnford——and for AIDS sufferers across the world!'

Tristam reached over and caught his brother's hand.

'A wonderful idea, Uri! What do you think, mother?'

'I think that the dedicated and courageous musician, who spent the last years of his life, setting up 'Ebb-tide' here at Garnford, would be very proud——touched indeed, that the two of you, should engage in such a project.' Rosamund brushed away a tear as she spoke, but there was a smile about her lips.

Later that night, after the passion of their love making, Leopold held Rosamund close against his heart in the old fashioned, four-poster bed, as he kissed her tenderly, stroking her hair back from her forehead. He raised his head and looked down at her.

'You know, Rosamund darling——it was only tonight, that I completely understood all that you had been through——and the measure of Peter's courage. I do not think that I could have behaved with such altruism—-such true humanity—-had I had to face the fate that was his.'

He sighed and sank down, rolling over beside her. 'I never really knew the stature of the man,' he said quietly. Perhaps he just hadn't wanted to recognise it,' he thought, as he lay there in the dark.

'Peter was twenty years your senior——a man and a seasoned musician, when you first met,' she said. Her fingers reached out and touched his cheek. 'And you know, you never stopped to realise, that I had loved him since my childhood———-the immense depths of our emotion.'

'I only do know that I have always considered myself to be second best with you,' said Leopold with the slightest trace of bitterness.

'How can you say that! My love for you is just as deep, just as strong———but different! I could not imagine life without you Leopold——my dearest husband!' She drew his head close to hers on the pillow. They kissed——a long, satisfying kiss and in that embrace, Leopold's slight envy and resentment towards Peter Bagshaw was finally laid to rest.

'Rosamund. What would you say, if after I have finished the film score——that you and I, together with Uri and Tristam were to arrange a grand concert tour, playing the Rose Concerto and the Golden Concerto!'

'Do you mean it, Leopold?' Rosamund went tense with excitement.

'I do.'

'Then I thank you, from the bottom of my heart——and if far away in God's heaven, Peter should be aware of what you are planning, then he too would be overjoyed!'

The next day, the little party toured the estate, calling at each of the bungalows in turn, meeting those who had come either to stay, or for some respite care. Thanks to modern drugs, symptoms of AIDS could be helped considerably, in a way that sufferers in third world countries were as yet unable to benefit from. The major drug companies charged exorbitant amounts of money for their medication.

'It's true, isn't it, that millions just cannot afford the tablets that would prolong their lives,' Rosamund asked and the doctor who was accompanying them nodded sombrely. Then a slight smile softened his lips.

' A growing pressure for change is starting to be exerted on the drug companies, by ordinary people from all around the world. Change is beginning to happen——slowly——far too slowly. But it is coming, Lady Rosamund! Poverty——AIDS——the many diseases that afflict countless millions of our fellow citizens in distant lands——the reality of all this is at last filtering into people's consciousness, with knowledge acquired through TV images——the net——newspaper reporting. Change is coming!'

'So you truly believe——?

'Yes. I do! One day, God willing, we will find a cure for the scourge that is AIDS. In the meanwhile we work and hope.'

'My late husband, Peter Bagshaw was passionate in his belief that a cure would be found for AIDS——offered the last years of his life to help in his own way——through his music!'

Tears glittered in her eyes but she blinked them away.

'His music——and his gift of Garnford,' said the doctor softly.

'His music will continue to bless the world,' said a deep voice and Rosamund looked up at her husband's face. Leopold bent and kissed her. 'We will all see to that!'